New York Times bestse— creates "A PITCH-PE— AND HISTORY" (*The Denver Post*), "POWERFUL AND COMPELLING" (*The Washington Post*) thrillers

Critical acclaim for Robbins and his heart-stopping historical novels

"A historical thriller with the punch of a full metal jacket."
—*The Denver Post*

"Breakneck-fast and laced with real-life vignettes."
—*USA Today*

"The action is exciting and the pace furious."
—*Baltimore Sun*

"Gripping . . . breathtaking."
—*New York Post*

"Robbins has an uncanny ability to provide just the right amount of historical detail without overwhelming the plot."
—*Publishers Weekly*

"Brilliant storytelling."
—*Kirkus Reviews*

"A first-rate tale of war. . . . Thoughtful, gritty, and compulsively readable."
—*Library Journal*

"The best WWII Pacific campaign novel in a long time. This is a terrific story of the triumph of the human spirit, loaded with suspense, historical accuracy and fast-paced action."
—*Publishers Weekly*

Broken Jewel is also available as an eBook

More praise for *BROKEN JEWEL*

"Another blend of fact and fiction from master alchemist Robbins. A remarkable story, brilliantly told."

—*Kirkus Reviews* (starred review)

"Riveting. . . . The story of incredible courage, compassion, patriotism, and just plain stubbornness in the face of extreme adversity. . . . Robbins's magnificent story . . . will inspire readers to learn more."

—*Library Journal* (starred review)

"Somehow the war in the Pacific has never had the extensive coverage devoted to the war in Europe. David L. Robbins memorably redresses this situation . . . meticulously researched."

—*Richmond Times-Dispatch*

"A tightly constructed wartime thriller."

—The A.V. Club

"David L. Robbins has a knack for airdropping into historical situations that are tightly sprung with pathos and controversy. With the little-known but epically scaled raid on Los Baños, he has found the perfect subject to ignite his many talents. Here is a white-knuckled thriller that is also sensitively enfolded in rich layers of historical resonance."

—Hampton Sides, *New York Times* bestselling author of *Blood and Thunder*

"An enormous accomplishment, a richly detailed page-turner and history conjured through vivid prose. Robbins brings to life the humanity of men valiantly fighting to keep it for themselves. If you wanted to know what your grandfather, uncle, or father went through in the war, what they felt, saw, and did, read *Broken Jewel*. It touches on the mythic."

—Doug Stanton, *New York Times* bestselling author of *Horse Soldiers*

"Set in a WWII prison camp in the Philippines, *Broken Jewel* is both a touching love story and a thriller of a read."

—James Bradley, *New York Times* bestselling author of *The Imperial Cruise*

"A tour de force, a must-read for all who need to be reminded of the transcendent power of the human spirit."

—William S. Cohen, former U.S. Secretary of Defense

"David L. Robbins has long been acknowledged as a master of historical fiction. In his latest page-turner, *Broken Jewel*, he has crafted another deeply moving epic of love and heroism. Unforgettable male and female characters, heart-pounding excitement, beautifully crafted prose. By far his best yet."

—Alex Kershaw, *New York Times* bestselling author of *Escape from the Deep*

"A masterpiece—a monumental, stirring, brilliantly written book about a story that needed to be told. This is how history was meant to be written. Nobody does it better than David Robbins."

—Brian Haig, *New York Times* bestselling author of *The Hunted*

"Focuses on the unbreakable spirit of two comfort women, both unforgettable characters. Robbins takes us on a profoundly moving journey of human possibilities through the saga of these wounded women."

—Dai Sil Kim-Gibson, filmmaker, *Silence Broken: Korean Comfort Women*

ALSO BY DAVID L. ROBBINS

DAVID L. ROBBINS

BROKEN JEWEL

POCKET BOOKS

NEW YORK LONDON TORONTO SYDNEY

Pocket Books
A Division of Simon & Schuster, Inc.
1230 Avenue of the Americas
New York, NY 10020

First Pocket Books paperback edition September 2010

POCKET and colophon are registered trademarks of Simon & Schuster, Inc.

For information about special discounts for bulk purchases, please contact Simon & Schuster Special Sales at 1-866-506-1949 or business@simonandschuster.com.

The Simon & Schuster Speakers Bureau can bring authors to your live event. For more information or to book an event, contact the Simon & Schuster Speakers Bureau at 1-866-248-3049 or visit our website at www.simonspeakers.com.

Cover design by Jae Song

Manufactured in the United States of America

10 9 8 7 6 5 4 3 2 1

ISBN 978-1-4165-9061-3
ISBN 978-1-4165-9381-2 (ebook)

For Captain Michael John Beach.
In the heart and mind, and on the
high seas, I have no better friend.

Preface

ON FEBRUARY 23, 1945, the U.S. Marines hoisted the Stars and Stripes on the peak of Mount Suribachi, above the bloody island of Iwo Jima. The photograph of this event became one of the iconic images of World War II.

Elsewhere that morning, another powerful and important episode in the Pacific War was playing out: the raid by the 11th Airborne Division on the Japanese internment camp in Los Baños, on the Philippine island of Luzon.

Were it not for that famous picture on Iwo Jima, the world's memory of that day would be of the liberation of 2,100 starving and endangered civilians. General MacArthur remarked, "Nothing could be more satisfying to a soldier's heart than this rescue." Colin Powell has called the mission "a textbook operation for all ages and all nations." The mission forms the basis of this novel.

Broken Jewel, like all my historical works, is grounded in closely researched actual events, places, and people. Some of these events are sources of controversy.

One of *Broken Jewel*'s principal characters, Carmen, is a Filipina "comfort woman." The subject of these women continues to be a flashpoint for vigorous disagreement in Japan and those Asian nations conquered by the Japanese during World War II. The debate extends across the full spectrum, from outright denial by many Japanese to fierce recrimination by the surviving women and their descendants.

The girls were typically virgins aged fourteen to nineteen at the time they were kidnapped or tricked into sexual slavery by the Imperial Japanese Army. They were then sent to battlegrounds across the Pacific. The number of comfort women is indeterminate; estimates hover between 200,000 and 300,000. As many as 80 percent came from Korea, but every nation that fell to the Japanese saw its young women taken by the thousands.

This novel does not aim to present the issue in a contemporary light but as a fictionalized yet authentic rendering of what such an atrocity might have looked like from day to day in a dangerous time and setting. Several excellent nonfiction works exist to highlight the current status of these women and their fight for recognition, as well as to relate the terrible testimonies of many. Still, the experience of the comfort women remains one of the most compelling, sad, and least-chronicled chapters of the war.

Carmen is a fictional amalgam, as are the novel's other principal characters—Remy Tuck, his son Talbot, and the American paratrooper Bolick. While composites, each is based on the adventures and fates of actual internees and soldiers.

At the back of the book you will find a series of annotations to help you understand and appreciate the true events depicted on these pages, plus the identities of the real people whose actions, sacrifices, courage, willpower, and even hatred form the remarkable basis for this story.

DAVID L. ROBBINS
RICHMOND, VA

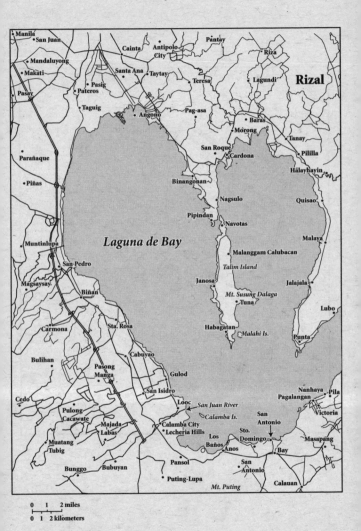

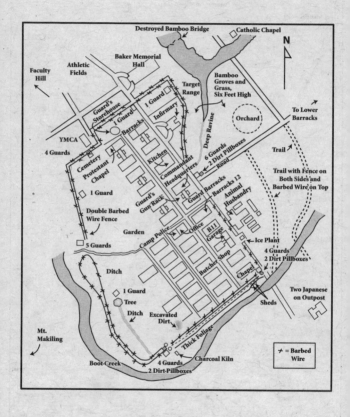

gyokusai—broken jewel

From the sixth-century Chinese history
Chronicles of Northern Ch'i, stating that
a man of moral superiority should die
as a shattered jewel rather than live as
an intact tile. He should choose to die
heroically in battle rather than surrender;
death over dishonor.

Atrocities follow war as the jackal follows a
wounded beast.

—JOHN W. DOWER, *WAR WITHOUT MERCY*

the hooligan, the gambler,
and the comfort woman

Chapter One

REMY TUCK had not seen his own reflection in three weeks. He'd lost his shaving mirror in a poker game to a man with jaundice. Remy hadn't tried to win the mirror back. Lately, he played only for food.

He sat under a giant dao tree near the barbed wire, rolling dice on a plank. The faces of the internees around him told him enough of what he must look like. Scooped-eyed and hollow-cheeked, three of them bet with Remy for the prize of an egg, while the rest read or dozed. One of the gamblers, a former mechanic for Pan Am, tipped his sharp chin up away from their game. Remy stopped rattling the dice to gaze through the dao's branches into the dispersing mist of a warm December morning. The far-off hum of an American plane—the Japanese had no presence anymore in the Philippine sky—added its burr to the calls of birds and insects in the scrub and bamboo inside the camp, the jungle outside it. Remy put down the dice. The whine of the airplane shifted to a higher tone. Something dived their way.

Remy rose first. He stepped out of the shade of the great dao. The tree provided him a favorite, cool place to sit, read, or run a quiet game of craps away from the guards and the Catholics.

He pulled down the brim of his old fedora to better search the lush horizon for the plane. At age forty-five, his eyes remained sharp, though fading sight was common inside the wire, where vegetables had grown scarce. Remy squinted to squeeze more distance into his vision. By the engine's winding he expected it to come in low. This would be a fighter, not one of the big bombers that hammered the Japanese garrison in Manila every few days. Remy scanned west, beyond the fence. Three miles off, slips of fog clung to the forested slopes of Mount Makiling. To the north on terraced hillsides, bent Filipino farmers trod behind carts hauled by scrawny carabao, water buffaloes. Everything's starving, Remy thought, except the fat dao tree.

Others moved out of the shade with Remy to find the plane. One of the dice players, the old piano player, black McElway, spotted it first. He said with a chuckle, "Hot diggity dog, look at 'im."

The twin-tailed fighter appeared out of the northwest, above the bay, a green sliver returning to Mindoro from a dawn raid over Manila.

"Everybody," Remy announced, "inside."

The fifteen men and women under the tree got to their feet. Some had to reach down to help the ones slowed by the blue ankles of wet beriberi.

Remy hurried beneath the dao to the plank. He snared his dice and the egg he'd been about to win. He returned the egg to McElway, who offered a broad, rickety mitt for a grateful shake. Remy gripped the man's elbow to hustle him and the rest along before any of the two hundred Japanese guards came to do it for them.

Everywhere in the camp, internees scurried for the two dozen sawali-and-nipa barracks. Guards on the dirt paths clapped, beating a rhythm of urgency. They shouted at anyone they observed meandering, *"Bakayaro!"* Idiot. Some brandished bayonets, jabbing them in the air as if they would skewer any malingerer.

Nearing his own barracks, Remy lagged for one more glance at the fighter coming hot and steady. The plane traced the earth so closely it blew through the smoke from a chimney in the village. McElway climbed the few bamboo steps into the barracks. The old man tugged Remy behind him.

"Come on, man. You don't want that trouble."

Remy made a beeline for the cubicle he shared with McElway and four other bachelors. Throughout the barracks, the ninety-plus men already inside shambled for their own bunks, grumbling at being forced under cover by a hotrodding pilot. Before Remy could poke his head out the window, the fighter screeched past, shaking the sawali walls and bamboo timbers.

Remy hopped up to his top bunk. He stuck his hat on a nail. The snarl of the fighter faded quickly southward. Remy smelled exhaust. Dangling his legs, he pictured the view from the cockpit, of speed and freedom, turning this way or that, no bayonets or wire fences. He imagined a horizon, the soft curve of the world.

"He's coming back!"

All the men crowded into the hall to rush to the south-facing windows. Alone, Remy hurtled to the back doorway. Here he had a view across the southern grounds of the Los Baños camp, between the guards' office and one of the married barracks. Four guards there watched the fighter bank wide above the jungle. Mount Makiling caught the plane's engine noise and threw it back across the camp in echo. None of the men in Remy's barracks cheered. The Japanese would not stand for that loss of face.

The plane leveled its wings. Other fighters had buzzed the camp, but those pilots had stayed on course after their joyride and disappeared. None had done this, come back.

The four Japanese outside their office sensed something different, too. They ducked behind their bamboo porch. Elsewhere in the camp, other guards scurried and shouted.

The fighter bore in, menacing behind its slow, swelling roar.

In the barracks, someone hollered, "What the hell's he doing?" From Boot Creek, cuckoos and bush doves flitted out of the tangle of palms and acacias; an indigo egret flapped away, spooked. The fighter dropped below the level of the foliage along the ravine. Remy lost sight of it.

No guards stood in the open hoping for a one-in-a-million rifle shot. The hidden plane closed in, trembling the floorboards under Remy's sandals.

Outside the southern fence, a storm of wind and knives mowed through the treetops above Boot Creek. The stones of the ravine drummed and split. The bedlam halted as fast as it started, to begin again in the next moment farther along the ravine. This second burst stopped quickly; a third barrage did the same. Then a long rip of bullets pelted the remaining length of the creek.

The next instant, the fighter followed its guns. Only fifty feet above the camp, it blasted by at a speed that beggared any machine Remy had seen in his life. The men in the barracks leaped across the hall for the opposite set of windows to see the American go. Remy in the doorway watched this amazing thing; when the war and internment started, no one in the camp had ever seen a single wing plane, only the bi-winged versions. Now this modern wonder climbed, acrobatic and straight up, with a howl of everything American that Remy needed it to be, swift, unyielding, harshly potent. When the pilot turned the twin-tailed fighter onto its back in a snappy barrel roll, Remy shook a fist beside his hip to keep the gesture out of sight of the guards.

McElway sidled next to him. "You got the best view."

Remy raised his nose, reluctant even to point. "Nah. He's got the best view. His gets to change."

The old man showed moon-pale teeth. "What do you

reckon that fella was doin' shootin' up the creek like that? Three short ones. Then that long one."

"Showing off. Telling the Japs to go screw themselves. I don't know."

The piano player raised a fingernail yellow as his teeth. "That there, I think. That was Beethoven's Fifth." He dotted the air with his finger. "Dun dun dun *daaah*."

Remy considered the old man's lean face. Mac kept himself shaved, a rarity in the camp. He'd cozened a whole year out of a single razor blade. McElway was one of the few Allied negroes living in Manila when the Japanese captured it in January '42. They'd asked him to sign a statement supporting Nippon's efforts to free all races in Asia, including his own. If he would sign, they'd leave him alone. Mac patted his piano, said *"Paalam"* to the Filipinas in the whorehouse, and got on the truck with the other Americans.

Remy hadn't considered the musical quality of the strafing run. The pilot banked one more time, then flattened his wings for another sortie.

"This flyboy looks harebrained," Remy said to Mac, "so maybe you're right, Maybe it was Beethoven."

Topsy Willets, once a stout fellow who'd lost all but his double chin, shouldered his way between Mac and Remy. He stuck his head out the door to see the fighter returning. In Manila, Topsy had been manager of Heacock's Department Store and a regular at the University Club. He'd been a clever merchant, a transparent poker player.

"Right about what?" Willets asked.

Mac told him his guess about Beethoven's Fifth.

Willets shook his head. "I like Clem's idea better."

Clem, a carrot-topped Scots merchant seaman, had missed getting out of Manila by two days before the city fell. He got drunk and was late for his ship. Last week, he went to see one of the internee doctors, who told him he had dysentery. Clem's room was next to Remy's. He'd taken to moaning at night.

The week before, that same doctor had killed a family's dog to add it to that day's stew rather than see food meant for the internees go to keeping a pet alive. A son from the family beat him up over it. The doctor swore he'd do the same again and did not understand such selfishness.

Willets said, "Clem figures it's Morse code."

Mac recast the musical notes: "Dot dot dot *dash*."

"That's V," Willets said, raising two fingers. "For victory."

Clem's right, Remy thought.

He stepped out the door, onto the topmost bamboo tread.

Last month, sixty-year-old Scheyer was punished for standing outside while American planes were overhead. Scheyer had been manager of the Wack Wack Golf Course. Before the air raid, he'd eaten some flowering bulbs that turned out to be indigestible. Twenty minutes later, with the planes coursing past, he walked a few paces from his married barracks to throw up in private. Sentries nabbed him and took him to the front gate. They forced him to stand in the sun on a narrow concrete block for ten hours. If Scheyer wobbled or stepped off, they struck his legs with cane rods. The guards watched from lawn chairs. Scheyer left the camp hospital a week later with the backs of his legs still raw from a lack of iron in his blood.

The fighter pilot's engine wailed in approach. Remy said to him, "Attaboy." He took another stride down the bamboo steps.

Twenty yards off, one of the guards kneeling beside the office spotted him. The guard waved madly for Remy to retreat. He shook a small fist.

The fighter barreled closer, a mile off now. At that speed the Yank would blow by the camp in seconds. Would there be another machine gun melody? Was the pilot intending to chew up more jungle, maybe some of the camp this time? The huddling guard had seen enough of Remy. He got to his feet, unshouldered his rifle. He was not going to allow an American prisoner to gloat.

Remy split apart two fingers on his right hand. All he had to do now was raise the arm.

Brown hands lapped over his shoulders. Remy was tugged backward up the steps. Inside the barracks, Mac released him. The guard raised an angry finger at Remy, then resumed his squat behind the office steps.

Mac whispered in Remy's ear. "What you thinkin'?"

Remy kept his voice low for only his friend to hear. "Whyn't you grab me sooner? Jesus Christ. I almost did that."

"I figure you a grown man. Had some sense."

Remy rattled his head at himself. A gambler did not get carried away, ever.

Everyone in the barracks riveted their attention on the fighter. This time, the pilot didn't line up on the ravine outside the camp but aimed his nose inside the wire, straight for the great dao tree. He cut his airspeed.

The plane came in low and slow. Again, none of the guards tried to potshot it, though this time they might have had a chance. When the plane closed to within a hundred yards of the camp, its canopy slid open. The pilot faced the twenty-four bamboo-and-grass barracks, the weedy yards and worn paths, the two thousand Allied prisoners, and jackknifed his hand into a salute.

Remy, Mac, and Topsy Willets ignored the consequences and returned the salute. Behind them, the barracks rustled. Remy pivoted. In the windows, all the men had their hands flattened across their brows.

From the opened cockpit, a small package tumbled to

land in the trampled grass of what had been the camp garden. Coursing the length of the camp, the pilot held his salute until he slid shut his canopy and gunned the motor. He dipped the fighter's wings, climbed into the last purls of mist above the jungle, and disappeared south.

No one in the camp moved. Slowly, to the departing growl of the fighter, the guards came out from the pillboxes, shadows, and various crevices they'd dived for when the plane first loosed its guns on the creek. The small package lay untouched in the open. None of the Japanese came near it.

Clem stirred first. "Maybe they think it's a bomb."

Mac said, "I hope it's a couple chocolate bars." The old man bared his teeth at the long-absent taste. His gums had faded to a milky pink.

Remy couldn't guess what had fluttered to earth; from seventy yards away it looked like an olive green ball.

"We'll find out," he said, "soon as Toshiwara crawls out from under his desk."

Every barracks waited for the commandant to sound the all-clear bell. Once the signal was rung, Remy could return his attention to winning McElway's egg. The last drones of the plane ebbed below the creaks of the rafters and the chirps of birds returning to the thrashed ravine.

Most of the men spread themselves on cots. A dozen queued in the doorway, to return to their assigned chores interrupted by the air raid. Firewood detail, cooking, tutoring, maintenance, sewing, administration; the men, women, and children in the camp handled hundreds of tasks, like in any small town.

The silence in the wake of the plane deepened. The collective breath of the internees was held. Guards ran pell-mell toward the field.

From the barracks beside Remy's, a tall boy strode with hands in pockets. He wore his black hair over his ears. His long-legged gait, in sneakers and patched shorts, was swift enough to carry him to the packet before the Japanese could beat him to it.

Once more, Mac lapped a hand over Remy's shoulder. Mac pressed to hold him in place, though he needn't have. Remy had no intention of going out there. He'd already had one brush with hotheadedness this morning. Besides, the boy had an independent streak. That's why the Japanese had taken him out of Remy's barracks and housed him next door, in No. 11 with the other troublemakers.

The boy, who'd grown gangly in his nineteen years, closed in on the packet, outpacing the guards. He bent his long frame to pluck it from the grass, then unraveled it into two parts. The first was just something to weigh the package down; he cast this off. The second item the boy held aloft, to show the camp a green box of cigarettes.

Willets snorted. "That's gonna be bad."

A tall man, Janeway, crowded beside Remy in the doorway. He'd been a bridge builder on Bataan, with a reputation for graft that stuck with him into the camp. Remy would not bet with him, he was known to welch.

"That's gonna get him more than a *binta.*" Janeway patted Remy's arm. "Sorry, old man."

Janeway was right. The Japanese were not going to let the boy off with a slap. Far from it. Remy winced, quelling the impulse to pop Janeway in the jaw. Not because Janeway deserved it for his statement, but Remy wanted to lash out at something and Janeway had deserved it other times.

Close by, for Remy's ears only, Mac clucked his tongue. Perhaps it was the old man's brothel years that had taught him to speak softly.

"What is the matter," he whispered, "with the men in your family?"

Out in the field, the Japanese neared the boy, who maintained a purposeful, theatrical unawareness of them closing around him.

Remy answered, "I don't know."

Again he wanted to raise his arm and flash the V sign, this time so his son could see it. The gesture would serve no purpose. The boy was not facing him, nor was anyone.

From the commandant's office in the center of the camp, the brass gong tolled the all clear.

"But look at him," Remy said to Mac above the ringing. "He's goddam terrific, ain't he?"

Chapter Two

TWO JAPANESE wrapped Hua in her bedsheet. Carmen stood aside and closed her own short *haori* robe across her bare belly. The soldiers hoisted Hua off the thin tatami mattress, to lug the corpse out of the small room down the two flights of stairs. Carmen in her black sneakers followed.

Outside the building, the guards set down the body. They were replaced by two more who took up the ends of the blemished sheet. Hua had soiled herself as she died and was being carted to her grave with it gathered around her. Carmen kept at a distance, to be allowed to attend. If she drew attention to herself, she might be sent back inside.

The grave had been dug thirty paces from the rear of the academic building. The new guards struggled with Hua for the short walk to the hole, sometimes skidding her swathed body through the dirt. They were not large men, the Japanese.

One other guard waited beside the shallow grave. Corporal Kenji watched the approach of the body with hands folded, respectful and quiet, a contrast to the complaining pallbearers dragging the body as much as they carried it.

The two soldiers set the body beside the hole. They put hands on hips and arched their sore backs. Kenji, lean and taller than any of the other Japanese, beckoned with a long finger for Carmen to come closer. She approached, keeping her robe shut, but remained on the opposite side of the grave from Kenji.

Hua was not allowed to be buried in her bedsheet. The

two soldiers gripped it by the corners and spilled her into the hole. She landed oddly on her side. She seemed caught in the middle of a seductive gesture or dance, both hands above her shoulders, wrists cocked. Like Carmen, Hua was naked beneath her yellow *haori*.

One of the guards balled up the sheet. He tossed it across the grave to Carmen.

"*Sekken o shite.*"

Kenji interpreted. "He wants you to wash it."

The pair of soldiers stalked off. They clapped their hands to be rid of the job.

Carmen rolled the sheet tighter to bundle away the odor. She laid the balled linen at her feet, nodded to Kenji.

"How did she do it?" he asked in English.

"Why?"

"If I am to pray for her, I should know."

Last night, after the final visitors, Hua entered Carmen's room with hands cupped as if bearing something fragile. She squatted like the peasant girl she was. Carmen's small room had no chair, only a tatami, a table for a lamp, and a basin for the disinfectant water. Nothing covered the window, which faced south above the barbed wire.

Hua opened her hands to show Carmen a dozen pills. She mimicked lapping them up.

Hua said in English, "I kill."

Carmen corrected her. "I die."

Kenji's gaze fell into the hole with Hua. "Where did she get the pills?"

"From soldiers. Where else?"

Carmen hardly knew the girl. Hua spoke only Chinese; the few words of English last night were the only ones that passed between them in the three months Hua had been assigned to the *shuho* at Los Baños. Before her arrival, Carmen had been here alone for six months.

Hua quickly contracted gonorrhea. The doctor gave her a 606 shot. The medicine made her bleed too much. Hua was taken to the infirmary. The doctor scraped her uterus. She could not have babies afterward. The doctor told Carmen these things as a way of reminding her to make all the soldiers wear condoms.

Hua had been short and round-faced. Her skin bore the yellow pallor of the Chinese. She was not popular with enough of the soldiers and did little to ease Carmen's burden. As Hua grew more ill, she faded to pasty white. The soldiers preferred taller, thinner Carmen, her angular Spanish face, flesh the color of wet sand. Because Carmen was Filipina, she had the tinge of the exotic for the guards and the battle groups on their way to Manila.

The *shuho* served twenty to forty soldiers every day. While Hua was in the hospital, Carmen serviced them all, as she did before Hua came to Los Baños. When the Chinese girl returned, the demand for Carmen lessened only among the soldiers passing through Los Baños, not among the frequenting guards of the camp.

The Japanese would not wear the *saku* if they did not want to. If they were refused sex, they sometimes became violent. Carmen had been beaten, cut by the sword of an officer, and—with the war turning bad for Japan—offered suicide pacts by sad and mortified boys who clouted her when she refused to accompany them into the afterworld.

In Japanese, Kenji prayed over Hua. Finishing, he glanced across the grave to Carmen.

"Can you pray some more?" she asked.

"Why?"

"I'm enjoying the sunshine."

"We are finished."

From her robe, Carmen pulled a wooden tag. This belonged to Hua. It had hung on a peg next to Carmen's tag, on a board on the third-floor landing. Across the top of the board was inked a banner reading 従軍慰安婦, *jugun ianfu*, for "military comfort women." This was not how the soldiers referred to the girls; they called Hua and Carmen *pii*—a vulgar Chinese word for vagina. The *shuho* was on the third floor of what had been the school for animal husbandry at Los Baños Agricultural College. The comfort station opened six months after the Japanese brought their internment camp here. The animal husbandry building stood vacant alongside the crowded camp, the *shuho* the only activity inside.

Hua's tag had been inscribed with 花, the kanji character for "flower," the meaning of the girl's name in Chinese. The soldiers visiting the *shuho* who wanted the Chinese girl saw the tag and asked for "Hana." Carmen's tag was inscribed with the character 歌, for "song." The soldiers called her "Songu." Kenji did not. He let Carmen keep the token of her real name.

Carmen dropped Hua's tag into the grave. She pointed at a shovel stabbed into the clay mound beside the hole.

"When will they cover her up?"

Kenji did not answer. His attention had floated upward into the morning, south beyond the barbed wire. The American planes most often came from the south.

"Do you hear that?"

Carmen did not want to go to her room. The sun and breeze across her skin were precious.

"May I stay out a little longer?"

"Go inside."

She knelt for Hua's bundled sheet. This brought her closer to the girl in the grave. Carmen mined herself for some sense of Hua's release and tragedy. Instead, she muttered *"Salamat,"* in brief gratitude for the soldiers Hua had occupied away from Carmen. She appreciated, too, that Hua's suicide meant her own tag on the board upstairs had been turned over for these few minutes to say Songu was unavailable, allowing Carmen to stand under the open sky.

The sound of the plane swelled. Kenji followed her to the door of the animal husbandry building before jogging off.

She hurried up the steps with Hua's sheet. At the top of the stairs, the old Filipina woman who with her husband ran the *shuho* for the Japanese barked at her, "Move, girl!" Carmen did not know the names of either of the collaborators. She'd been instructed to call them Mama and Papa.

The old woman raised a hand as if to swat her. Carmen paid no mind. Grumbling, Mama turned over Songu's tag on the board. Carmen went to Hua's room in the south wing. She stuffed the reeking sheet beneath Hua's table to wash the linen tonight with her own and the day's used condoms. She crossed the foyer to her room and stood on her tatami to see the American plane from her window above the camp.

The internees all moved indoors, as they must. Carmen looked for Kenji, so easy to spot, tall in his soldier's cap. She found him between barracks, pointing the way for the internees to get out of the open. The internees walked with little urgency despite the shouts to hurry, *"Hayaku!"* The exceptions were the two hundred nuns and priests who hustled into their twin barracks near the southern fence that the internees called Vatican City. In the camp, the Catholics had a reputation for following orders, according to Kenji, who talked to Carmen of his job, the internees, the war. He smuggled her extra rations. Often, she listened and ate during her allotted time with him instead of having sex.

Thirty minutes with a comfort woman cost a regular Japanese soldier 1.50 yen. Kenji claimed his monthly pay was only 15 yen. Privates and corporals were permitted to visit before noon. Noncommissioned officers paid 2 yen, until 2 p.m. Junior officers paid 2.50 and senior officers 3 yen. Only senior officers were allowed to sleep with Carmen overnight. The old *makipili* couple collected the money and handed the soldiers chits. Papa knocked on the doorframe outside her curtain when time was called. Mama handed Carmen none of the cash, claiming it went to pay for Carmen's food, clothing, and expensive medicines. Carmen should not ask for money, Mama had scolded. Japan fought for her liberation and for the whole Pacific. Carmen must give all and ask for nothing. Mama believed in this bargain. Carmen did not have such consolation. Money or no money, this was not liberation.

From her perch, she watched the American plane bore in on the camp, skirting thickets and bamboo groves. The fighter came alone, with no plain intent. The guards looked frightened, and well they should be. Carmen knew the Americans, knew they could be crazy and act without design. These traits were unfamiliar to the Japanese.

The fighter flew past the camp only meters above the barracks. The propeller's wake peeled thatch from roofs. The camp shuddered and the engine drowned out everything. Carmen cheered from her window, aware that the old *makipili* woman might hear her.

The American fighter zoomed kilometers past the camp before wheeling around. The twin-tailed plane was sleek, green as the jungle. American bombers and fighters had appeared above Los Baños for the first time last month. Rarely in the mornings was Carmen able to observe; she could hardly rise from her mattress with a soldier pressing her down. Never would Carmen smile for America when a soldier was between her legs, she did not care to be struck. But this morning, she could watch from her window and thanked little Hua once more for making it so.

Again, the pilot lined up to fly past the camp. He came in low like his first pass. This time he machine-gunned the ravine in several bursts. The violence seemed an amusement for the flier. The Japanese remained stunned and behind cover. Carmen thumped the flat of her palms against the wall, adding her own pounding to what the fighter gave the ravine. The pilot shot past, then banked above the bay for another pass. Approaching this time, he slowed, opened his cockpit, and dropped something small inside the barbed wire. He saluted his countrymen and allies and flew away. Carmen watched him go for a long time, until sight and sound of the plane vanished.

The camp remained rigid. No internees spilled from their barracks, no guards resumed their stations. The commandant's gong did not ring. The small package in the grass seemed to send the camp out of kilter, as if one more American thing inside the wire, even so tiny, was one thing too much.

The instant the boy appeared, the quiet ended. From fifty meters away, she knew it was him. His long amble into the field sent the same ripples through the camp as the fighter plane. He wore his dark hair long, almost longer than Carmen's. From her window, she heard people scattering to other windows to see, then cautious calls between barracks, the ones blocked from a view of the field asking what was happening. She heard his name, not for the first time, but always the same. This was how Carmen had named him in her heart. That Tuck boy.

He was the only American outside his barracks. The boy did not hurry across the field but walked with a grace and length that outdistanced the Japanese.

Carmen's chest tightened. She whispered, "Go back, boy."

He reached the packet first, bent for it. He unwrapped his prize and thrust it high for the camp to see. He held a small box, no larger than his hand, and faced Carmen in her high window.

The guards closed in. With movements as calm as his strides had been, the boy lowered his arm, tapped the box once, and popped a cigarette to his mouth. He reached into his pocket for a lighter. He blew one cloud of smoke before the guards reached him and knocked him down.

In the camp, the gong sounded. Internees poured from their barracks, making their way to the field to see for themselves what that Tuck boy had done, and what he would reap.

Mama rapped knuckles on the doorframe. She entered, pushing aside the curtain. The old woman, creased and brown, carried a plate of rice balls and a steaming bowl. The soup held salted water with a strip of boiled fish.

"Get away from that window. I'll have it boarded up."

Carmen turned from the boy. He became lost in the field beneath a tangle of soldiers, in front of a growing semicircle of gawkers. Carmen imagined the cigarette still on his lips under the pile of Japanese.

"And if I could," she asked the old woman, "what would I do to you?"

Mama set the food on the floor beside the tatami. Behind her, the curtain parted again. The entering Japanese held it aside for the old woman to leave.

Carmen lay back while the soldier set his ticket on the table. She opened her scarlet robe and spread her knees, keeping her feet flat on the mattress. The guard fumbled with his pantaloon buttons and with slipping the *saku* over his erection. He knelt on the edge of the mattress. Carmen tilted her chin to the ceiling, gazing backward out the window. Unnamed and unwatched, the soldier lowered his breath to her neck. Carmen put a rice ball in her mouth.

Chapter Three

◆

THE JAPANESE were going to see an American pick up whatever had been dropped into the camp. They weren't going to make him rush or break into a run. He'd stroll as if they didn't exist.

Once he stood over the package, Tal measured the seconds before the guards arrived. He needed to hurry.

He knelt on the grass. The pilot had wrapped a pair of goggles around a small olive box. Cigarettes. Tal uncoiled the goggles, cast them aside. Printed on the box was the brand, Lucky Strike, and the words "I shall return. Gen. Douglas MacArthur."

Tal faced the two dozen barracks. Every head crammed into a window or opening was riveted on him. Seventy yards off, motionless in the doorway of his own barracks, stood his father. Old McElway held Remy back.

The charging guards shouted, closing fast. From his doorway, Remy shook a fist. Good enough, Tal thought. This was for Remy and the rest, and especially for her, because he could do it and it had to be done. Tal drew a deep breath to steel himself.

He thrust the cigarette pack high over his head, where she could see it. She was in her window in her red robe. Tal wanted to run through the camp, stop beneath her sill and toss the smokes up to her like roses, just to give her something because no matter what little he had, she surely had less. In six months, they'd seen each other every day. Always she seemed worn, but was never less than beautiful and that made her heroic. She perked up whenever she saw him. They made little waves to each other, lifted chins. He'd winked but had never gotten near enough to see if she'd returned it. They'd never spoken. This morning, if he could run right up to the barbed wire below her window and shout "Hello" and "What's your name?" what more could the guards do? He was already in dutch.

Six Japanese galloped his way. Two had rifle stocks poised to crack him. Tal had only moments left. No sense wasting good smokes after all the trouble MacArthur had gone through to deliver them.

Tal tore quickly at the pack and shook one out on his lips. He flipped open his silver Zippo to flick for a flame. He'd stolen this lighter two years ago from a Japanese who'd left it on a tabletop close to an open window. Tal hoped for a light on the first try. The guards were only yards away and not slowing. The Zippo scratched and fired. Tal lit up the smoke. He blew as big a cloud as he could into the faces of the guards, and made them run through it to tackle him.

Flanked by four armed guards, Tal entered Major Toshiwara's office, leaving outside the silent crowd that had followed from the field. Remy walked at the front of the gathering beside Mr. Lucas, the youngest member of the Internee Committee.

The commandant's office was sparse save for a desk with no papers, a lamp, a tiny bonsai in a clay pot, and a porcelain rice bowl branded with the rising sun. The commandant's fan oscillated, looking for him in the empty chair.

Tal still throbbed from the thumping these small guards had given him on the grass. He'd balled up and taken it. Nothing was broken—they hadn't pounded him with real enthusiasm—but his ribs ached from a rifle butt and his ears rang. Though none of the guards smiled now, neither did they seem particularly interested in continuing hostilities. All four were much older than Tal.

A quiet rap sounded on the office door. Mr. Lucas stepped inside. The man, lanky and balding with a sharp face, shook a censorious nose at Tal while moving to a corner. The room had grown warm and close. The whirring fan did not alleviate this.

After minutes, Tal had not sweated but the guards perspired, browning their khaki tunics at the pits and collars. These four had run, yelled, and clouted while Tal hadn't exerted himself beyond a quick stroll into the field, then covering up while they whaled on him until Mr. Lucas and his father begged them to get off.

Toshiwara entered. The little commandant stared straight ahead at his waiting chair, avoiding eye contact until he was seated. At his rear came Lieutenant Nagata, second in command of the camp. Stocky and seething, Nagata planted himself in front of Tal. He dropped his right shoulder, badly telegraphing the *binta*. Tal braced and withstood the slap with a straight spine. Nagata cocked his hand for another wallop. He bellowed, *"Rei!"*

Tal dipped the burn in his cheek toward the floor, bowing at the waist ninety degrees, hands at his sides. Behind him, Mr. Lucas took the same posture.

The commandant spoke in a weary voice. *"Jubun."* Nagata, called off, took a backward step.

Tal straightened, fixing his eyes well over the head of Nagata. The short guard spun away, taking his place behind Toshiwara.

Another guard entered. This one stood as tall as Tal. Toshiwara waited in and out of the fan's swinging breeze. He fingered his bonsai, releasing a long breath through his nose.

"Fuson."

Behind the commandant, the tall guard translated.

"Insolence."

The commandant laid his hands on the desk. He looked onto the backs of them while he spoke. Tal listened to the translation, gazing at the top of Toshiwara's gray head.

"What can be done? I am called from my garden to discuss insolence."

The commandant tapped his chin. After moments, he pointed at Tal.

"You believe yourself to be a young samurai. I can see this. You are a warrior in your heart. I respect this. In return, I will give you a lesson today."

"Commandant . . ." At the rear of the room, Mr. Lucas took a step. Nagata heaved up an open palm to warn him from making another move. The committee man stilled. The commandant never averted his eyes from Tal. Behind him, the tall soldier continued to interpret.

"A samurai has courage, yes. But he uses this only in the name of his master. He does not flout authority. You are a prisoner in Japanese-held territory. We are the masters in this land. Yet you feel no embarrassment in this. You walk into the field to smoke a cigarette dropped by an American plane, to embarrass us instead. A samurai may never accept his defeat, or his disgrace, but he will take his proper place. He plots revenge, yes, but shrewdly. He does not do it with such crudeness, so openly."

On all sides of Tal, the guards, even the interpreter, nodded. Only Nagata stood inert as a gargoyle, hands locked behind his back. Tal's cheek sizzled from the *binta*.

The commandant continued. "You wish to earn respect. From the people in the camp. From your father. But I know you to be a thief. Lucas has told me this, others as well. A samurai does no such dishonorable thing as thievery. Honor is above everything, even life. Loyalty to a principle. This is Bushido."

The commandant was done speaking directly to Tal. He cast his eyes again on the petite perfection of his bonsai tree. He stroked the tiny branches, spoke to the simple clay pot.

"You think you understand suffering, young Tuck. You believe much is warranted in its name. This is true. The samurai builds force of will from misery, it strengthens his belly, knocks away the rust of the body. Once you are at peace with suffering, you will find honor."

The commandant smoothed his hand across the emerald of the tree as if over the crown of a child. The fan cooled him as best it could. Like Tal, the commandant did not sweat. This was worrisome.

Lucas spoke. "Commandant."

Toshiwara did not look up from his plant to respond. *"Nan desu ka?"*

"The boy will be punished by the Internee Committee. Let us handle our own. His actions will get him an adequate sentence. You have my word."

The interpreter turned Lucas's words into a monotone, devoid of the committee man's attempt at authority. The commandant awaited the translation. Then the interpreter spoke for him:

"Adequate, perhaps, but the insult was directed at Japan. So Japan will decide what is adequate in this instance. And what is instructional."

Lucas was undeterred. "Commandant, with respect, that's a violation of a long-standing agreement we have had with other commandants and with you. The Japanese handle matters of security. The Internee Committee is in charge of administration. The boy did nothing to breach the security of the camp. That makes this a *civilian* matter for the internees to deal with. We will punish the boy."

The commandant rose in the middle of the interpreter's words. "Nagata?"

The stumpy lieutenant grunted, *"Hai."*

Without another word or glance, the commandant walked out of the room. The click of the closing door set Nagata in motion. He gestured to be followed outside.

Mr. Lucas said, "I protest." The interpreter did not translate this.

Tal pivoted amid the four guards around him. They marched him from the office. The waiting crowd remained in the hundreds. Shadows slanted in the warm early sun. Remy in his battered hat had not moved.

The guards rushed Tal past his father. Nagata strode in front with a military cadence. Lucas stayed behind on the commandant's steps to address the crowd. Only a few dozen hung back to listen. The rest trailed Tal, led by Remy.

The guards escorted Tal to the pillars of the main gate. Outside the wire, six more Japanese manned a pair of dirt pillboxes. The men were dank and dusty from standing beside the road, faded by the sun, lean and hungry. They showed no measure of eagerness for the boy being marched toward them for a reprimand. They seemed abused in their own way. With the first barked order from Nagata, all the guards snapped to stiff attention. Tal's legs weakened to see the gate was not being swung open.

Wasn't he going to be forced to stand outside the wire on a cement block for ten hours, like Mr. Scheyer? Tal had made himself the promise before he'd stepped out of No. 11 that he was ready to do twelve hours, fifteen. The camp would see, and so would she. This was how he would tell her to keep hanging on, by showing that he would endure also, and that they would do so separately and together.

The tall interpreter moved beside him. "Yours will be a different penalty."

Tal's father and the crowd had been stopped from following. They stood back in a quiet, hardened picket.

"Walk here," the interpreter said. He led Tal to one of the concrete posts framing the gate. "Raise your hands." The interpreter's manner stayed emotionless.

Tal hoisted his arms. The interpreter laid a palm against his back to make him step forward, put his arms around the post. Nagata spat another command. One guard outside the wire removed his leather belt. He wrapped this around Tal's wrists, securing him to the pillar.

Tal focused on his breathing to fend off panic. His bladder stung with urine suddenly pressing to be relieved. He tightened his gut against it, refusing to add that humiliation. He filled his lungs and held, to stop from panting. He balled fists on either side of the post and squeezed.

Nagata moved close. He spoke in Japanese, words the interpreter did not bother to reveal. Tal assumed it was a pronouncement of punishment.

Nagata tugged out his own leather belt. He held it up for Tal to examine. He stepped to Tal's rear, out of sight.

Tal had only moments. Once the beating started, he'd be unable to gird his body more. This had all gotten out of hand. He found his father at the head of the gathering, held at bay by the guards.

Remy spread empty hands in front of him, implying, This is a waste, boy, what are you doing?

The first lash from Nagata struck between his shoulder blades. Tal's threadbare shirt did nothing to cushion the strap. With little flesh on his frame, the belt beat against his bones. He felt the shock in his teeth and in his heels.

Tal turned his head behind him, into the camp, to her building. He glared at Remy. In distress, his father ran both hands through his hair. Remy looked down the wire fence, for the red robe in the third-floor window.

He shook his head. No.

With the second flail of the belt, tears welled in Tal's eyes.

He fleered his lips and grit his teeth. He buried his head beneath one raised arm, stuck his nose in his armpit, and kept it there while Nagata beat him, first across the back, then on the buttocks and against his bare calves. With every blow Tal growled into his own shoulder, made the noises of an angry, whipped dog, and made himself remember it.

Nagata thrashed him a long time. When Tal's hands were finally untied and lowered, he could not form a sentence or a coherent thought. He could only summon willpower to keep his knees from buckling. The Japanese left him by the gate pillar. Blurry, Tal watched them walk off without understanding that he was no longer being beaten. The pain from neck to ankles had not quit. Tal swayed forward. He did not know where he might go or why but sensed only that a stride was required of him.

His forearms were lifted and supported, as if he were in an easy chair. The buzz of his pulse and the hurt searing his awareness masked many sounds. One voice cut through.

"Easy, boy. Easy."

Tal freed his hold on himself. Remy did not let him fall.

Tal woke facedown on a white linen pillow. His head felt weighted as if by chain mail. Both arms lay heavy along his sides.

He raised his head to see where he was. The sensation of crackling, a breaking shell, preceded a burst of agony across his shoulders. Tal collapsed into the pillow, mouth open.

When the ache passed and he could focus, he rolled one eye above the pillow. Tal lay on a cot in a row of four, all of them made with white linens. Shelves of bottles and cardboard boxes filled the wall at the end of the room. An old man lay nearby, gaunt Mr. Goldstein, with rattling breaths. Mr. Goldstein had been an accountant in Manila, with offices above the Exchange Café. A doughboy in World War

I, he'd been a lifelong fight fan, had managed a few middle-weight pugs, and just last month asked Tal if he might like to train to be a professional boxer when the war was done. He said Tal had the broad shoulders for it. Though he'd left America, Mr. Goldstein was always optimistic and patriotic to a fault. Tal had not known he was in the infirmary.

Tal tried to reach to the cot on the other side of him, to jostle Remy. His father snored. Moving the arm almost cost Tal his consciousness.

"Hey."

Remy did not move.

"Remy."

His father snored, squeaking the bedsprings. He removed the fedora balanced over his face. "What?"

"Wake up."

Remy set the old hat aside and swung his legs to the floor. He did not stand but put elbows to knees. He wore sandals, cut-off shorts that were unhemmed and unraveling, and a brown vest buttoned over a white T-shirt. Remy kept the distance between them. Tal was relieved, so tender was his back that the heat of anyone standing close might agitate him.

Remy pressed his palms under his chin, touching his index fingers to his lips. This was one of his few tells as a gambler. It meant he was sure of his cards.

"You're a vexatious boy."

Tal nodded against the pillow.

"How bad does it hurt?"

Tal closed his eyes for a moment, intending to take stock. "I can't really describe it."

"They give you anything for the pain?"

"They got nothing to give."

Remy grabbed a drinking glass off the table between the cots.

"I figured. I brought a little something."

From beneath his mattress, Remy pulled a bottle filled with a strawberry-colored liquid. He emptied the bottle into the glass then brought the concoction under Tal's nose. The sniff of fermented guava curled Tal's nostrils.

Remy whispered, "Bomber lotion."

"Where'd you get that?"

Remy grinned. "Don't ask your old man questions, boy. Like I don't ask you. No sense us being disappointed in each other."

"Got a straw?"

"After a fashion." From another pocket Remy withdrew a thin reed of hollow bamboo. He placed one green end in the liquor, the other into Tal's mouth.

"Suck it all down. That's right. It'll take the edge off."

The red mash tasted bitter and had a syrupy texture.

Tal finished the glass. Remy rinsed it out and drank the remains. He did the same with the bottle. Bootleg alcohol was strictly prohibited. A year ago, homebrew had been readily available on the camp's black market. The past few months, it had grown scarce with every other form of nutrition.

Tal asked, "What time is it?"

"Just past dinner. You been out around ten hours."

Tal licked his lips, looking for his hunger. He figured it must be there but was hidden in his body. He didn't worry, it would return.

Remy settled again on the neighboring mattress. "That was some shellacking you took."

"How bad's it look?"

"Nagata wore you out pretty good. You got a few cuts, mostly around your neck and shoulders. The nurses didn't have any gauze, so they made some strips out of sheets. You're already scabbing up. Down your sides you're red as raw steak. Back of your legs'll heal all right. Your ass came out the best. You're a Tuck, so that's gonna be your strong suit."

Tal bit his lip. "Don't. Nothing funny."

His father held up a hand in apology. He produced a second bottle from under his mattress. "Got you some *sabila*. Had to play a Dutchman for two hours to win it off him, or I would've been here sooner. You were out like a light anyway."

Remy stepped beside the bed. Tal's back prickled with alarm when Remy reached down to him.

"Remy, don't."

"It's all right. I gotta take off these bandages to get this cream on you. The Dutchie says it's native aloe, good smuggled stuff. It'll help you heal right."

"Can't you get a doctor to do that?"

"The docs find out I got this stuff, they'll want me to share. And that ain't gonna happen. Now get a hold."

Tal rotated his face into the pillow. If he were going to grimace, Remy would not see.

His father picked at the edge of a cloth strip, then gently tugged. The bandage did not lift away. Scabs had woven themselves into the fabric.

"Hold your breath, son."

Tal cursed into the pillow, and sucked in.

Remy plucked at both edges of the bandage, not in a rip but a steady peel. The clots broke free with the lifting cloth, snapping the crust. Tal seized on the cot, gnashing his teeth into the pillow. The hurt rivaled the worst of Nagata's belt.

His father stroked the back of his head.

"One more."

The second strip, lower on his back, came away with equal anguish. Blood trickled down the corduroy of his ribs. Remy mopped it with the bandage.

Tal did not unclench his teeth until Remy said, "All clear. Come on out."

Remy poured lotion into his hands. He rubbed his slicked palms first across Tal's neck, then over his shoulders. Tal flinched at the touch. Immediately the aloe relieved the gashes and flay marks. Tal breathed easier under the fragrance of the *sabila*. He noted, too, the first soothing wash of the guava liquor.

Remy spread the rest of the aloe over Tal's back, then pocketed the bottle. When he was done, Tal found enough painful flexibility to roll onto one side, facing his father.

"I'll get some more of that stuff," Remy grinned. "The Dutchie tugs his earlobe when he's got good cards."

"You touch your lips."

"Do I now? Anything else?"

"Why should I tell you?"

"Good boy. Don't."

"How long have I got to stay here?"

"Doc Lockett said a couple days. You'll be moving a mite sore for a while. He says to let those cuts breathe, then we'll put some fresh strips on 'em. You go ahead and rest. I'll keep the flies off your back."

Tal closed his eyes. The aloe and bomber lotion lulled him toward sleep. He gazed up at Remy, who had not moved from his cot.

"Thanks."

"No worries."

His father strode behind Tal to wave away a fly. The air whipped by his hand made a breeze against the *sabila*.

"What were you thinking, boy?"

"I dunno. Maybe I wasn't."

"You definitely looked like someone who was thinking." Remy swiped again at the fly.

Tal asked, "Why do you gamble?"

"The way I figure it, there's two worlds. The one we see and the one we don't. It's like fishing. We know what's on top of the water, but not what's underneath. Could be fish, could be rocks, or just nothing. Gambling's like dropping a hook into a pond. If I win, I know I'm in the right place, doin' the right things. When I lose, I suppose I need to be doin' something different. It's sort of the way God and I have worked out how to talk to each other. I play, and He lets me know what's on His mind."

Remy leaned closer to Tal's injuries. When he spoke, Tal felt his father's breath.

"I reckon you overplayed your hand a little out there today."

"She didn't even see me."

"She's a whore, boy."

"Come around here," he said.

Remy made no move. "She ain't worth you being laid up like this." Remy sucked his teeth. "Goddamit."

Remy returned to his seat on the adjacent cot.

Tal said, "Don't call her that again. She's not a whore."

"What is she, then? She screws Japs, that's all I need to know."

Tal flexed his jaw as he had under Nagata's lash. She stood in her window on the third floor, Tal saw her there and never anywhere else. She wore only a red kimono, holding it shut across her naked belly and small breasts. From a hundred feet away or a thousand, she appeared sad and afraid, disgraced and innocent. He watched her because she was beautiful. He loved her because she endured.

His father scooted backward on the mattress, lifting his sandals off the floor. "I'm sorry I said that."

"I don't know what she is. I'm gonna find out."

"Okay, kiddo." Remy nodded. "What the hell, we're all stuck here. She probably is, too."

Remy popped to his feet. He yanked the white sheet away from a neighboring cot. The bare tick mattress showed rusty stains. Remy bit into the linen to start a rip, then tore away a long strip.

Mr. Goldstein, a hand quaking on his frail chest, asked, "What're you doing, Tuck?"

"Watchin' out for my boy, Mr. G."

"Good," the old man urged from his laboring throat. "Good. Keep him strong. He'll do something one of these days."

"Sure as shootin', Mr. G."

Tuck tore another strip. The rest of the linen he respread over the mattress, doing his best to tuck away and conceal the missing portions.

"Listen."

"What."

"I talked to Lucas. He says you can move back in to number twelve. Till you're up on your feet."

Tal rolled back onto his stomach. Exhaustion and the guava mash were catching up with him.

"No."

"You're gonna be healin' for a while. I can take care of you better if you're with me."

Tal shut his eyes for sleep, and against the sight of Mr. Goldstein wasting away.

"Remy?"

"Yeah?"

"Why do you think I got myself thrown out of your barracks in the first place?"

Tal let slumber approach. Above his dulling back, his father's hand chased off another fly, cooling the aloe.

Chapter Four

S HE SAT up to her elbows to watch the young soldier.
He laid his ticket on the table beside the door. The
thin chit lay on a pile of ten, fifteen, she did not know; never
did she count, Mama simply swept the vouchers away at the
end of the day. The Japanese greeted her with a quick nod.
"Songu."

He set both hands to work undoing his pantaloons, then
stopped to remove his cap. He held it by the brim, searching
for a place to hang it or set it down. He put it back on his
head, sheepish and uncertain. She watched him between her
brown knees.

Carmen did not recognize him, he was not one of the
camp guards. Early this morning, a long convoy had rattled
past the camp. This boy was likely on his way to Manila.
Someone in his unit brought him, perhaps on a dare, to the
shuho of Los Baños.

The boy's khakis dropped in folds around his boots and
leggings. He wore a loincloth which he pushed down his
thighs. At the edge of her tatami, he stood naked only at the
hips. He had small tufts of hair above his penis. He looked
down at himself, raw in this room smelling of Mama's bleach
mop. Behind Carmen's head, through the open window, a
bird cawed. This drew the boy's attention. He looked up,
biting his bottom lip. He seemed to want to be out there
instead, in the air, flying off. Carmen saw that this was his
first time with a woman.

She pointed at his penis, not meeting his eyes.

"*Saku.*"

Surprised—did he expect a corpse with no voice?—the soldier made a perfunctory bow. With both hands, he hauled up the accordion of his pantaloons to rummage in a pocket. He found the paper envelope. Without lowering his pants, he tore the packet open, then had to push down his breeches again to let his penis stand between the tails of his tunic. He held the rubber condom ring with fingertips. He halted, with no notion of how to put it on. Carmen wanted to send him away, push him out the window to give him his chance to fly. She remained motionless except to gaze down at her own bare hips, the black tuft that was hers, and considered that if she had a penis there, she would not be on this mattress. That was the difference, but it seemed not enough to explain things.

The soldier held up the ring to her, asking for help. Carmen stared back deadpan. He drew his lips over his protruding teeth, determined to figure this out.

The Japanese boy did the wrong thing. He poked a finger into the rubber ring, pushing the condom out to its full, flaccid length. He lowered the sack to his penis and tried to tug it on like a sock instead of rolling it back. The condom slid on partially, leaving half its length dangling. His breathing became irregular with his frustration.

The boy's glance rose from his own chaos to her vagina. With a grunt, he determined to get rid of the condom, pinching it at the tip to yank it off. The thing snapped when it jerked free.

Before the boy could bend his knees to the tatami, or Carmen could raise a hand to stop him, the soldier ejaculated. His stream landed in milky beads across Carmen's stomach and inner thigh, onto her open robe. She looked down at the trail and thought nothing of the boy's warm semen on her skin. She knew what would come next, the necessary trade for being done with him quickly. Averting her eyes, she sat up straight to make her face easy for him to reach.

The boy's hand clapped against her temple, sweeping her off balance. She tumbled to her side, not catching herself but acting out the receipt of a great blow. She lifted a hand to her cheek and whimpered, to assuage his loss of pride. The boy stood over her, dripping.

The Japanese raised a finger to his bulging lips, making the signal for silence. Say nothing. Carmen nodded, aping fear.

He flung the condom to the floor and pulled up his loincloth and pantaloons. Carmen did not take her hand from her cheek, to show the sting was mighty. The soldier buttoned and buckled himself into place, glaring at her to drive home their compact, that he would not strike her again if she told no one. Carmen lowered her eyes, the final act of her role.

The soldier drew himself up, almost to attention, to leave her room and the *shuho* looking satisfied and commanding. Carmen supposed he was a year younger than she, perhaps two. He gazed down his nose and nodded approval, beginning the deception that would last the rest of his life. He spun on his heels and swept beyond the curtain. Carmen lowered her hand, bothering only to hope that his life would be short.

Papa dropped an empty straw basket inside the curtain. In Tagalog, he said, *"Labanderiya."* The old man surveyed the little room, Carmen on the mattress, on her knees at the open window. Continuing in their native tongue, he said, "Why don't you jump? It might kill you."

Carmen turned. She released her red *haori,* to let it hang

loose and expose her belly, thighs, and waist, to taunt Papa and tell him he meant so little to her.

She asked, "Why don't you jump with me?"

He rattled his head before glancing once behind him, down the hall to where his wife sat as hostess and guard.

"It might not kill me. Come. Laundry."

Carmen stood from the tatami. She had not seen that boy Tuck in four days. She did not consider that he might be dead. She hadn't seen his punishment, but knew that, whatever it had been, he'd chosen it. The boy was strong and measured himself against what the Japanese could dish out. She would see him again soon, striding about the camp, making himself visible. That was why she wore a red robe, to be easily spotted by him. But he was in hiding, and her robe needed washing.

She shed the robe into the basket. Naked in front of Papa, she took from a pile of clothes, neatly folded in a corner, a pair of discarded khakis and an undershirt. She stripped the yellow-stained sheet.

Papa led the way down the hall, approaching Mama at her station on the landing. The old woman flipped over Songu's wooden tag.

On the board hung another tag, bearing the symbol 弓. Carmen halted, basket in her arms. "What is that?"

"Another girl. *Chosenjin*."

Mama used the Japanese word for a Korean.

"Where is she?"

"Talk less, Songu. Wash more." Mama jerked her head at Papa for him to lead Carmen down to the laundry room.

A sudden commotion erupted in the south wing, across the foyer. The drape over the doorway of Hua's former room billowed outward. A tin water bowl clattered into the hall. A girl's screech followed, then a soldier backpedaled through the curtain to collect the bowl. The young man's tunic was darkened with the thrown water and his dropped trousers coiled around his ankles. His penis was big enough to see beneath his shirttails, pink with no *saku*. He stumbled once, almost tripping, then lifted a hand to check his cheek for blood.

He bellowed, *"Konoyaro koroshite yarou ka?"* Carmen had heard the phrase often enough. Shall I kill you, bitch?

The soldier hobbled back into the room. Again the girl screamed. The metal bowl clanged again, like a gong. Someone had been struck with it.

"Chosenjin," Mama repeated.

"Come." Papa motioned Carmen to the stairs.

Carmen reached into the basin, sinking her arms to the elbows. She agitated the water, kneading the mass of socks and loincloths the camp's guards had piled for her to launder.

She'd reused the gray wash water four times. Soap had become a rare thing, rationed beyond food. Papa sat at the top of the stairs to the basement laundry room, humming to himself. Every so often he clambered partway down the steps to make sure she was working and that her own sheets and crimson robe were placed aside, to be cleaned last.

She rinsed and wrung socks, a hundred pairs, it seemed, with pruney fingers, then tossed them into the straw basket. She recalled the times she and Hua had worked side by side, always without speaking. When did Hua decide to kill herself? Was it during any of the hours they were together scrubbing or doing laundry? At rare shared meals? Carmen wondered if she might have seen this change come over Hua, like the shadow of a crow, a sign of death. This troubled her, that she had not been aware of Hua's decision to take her own life. Carmen could miss it in herself; the shadow might cross her and she would not know it.

A Korean. Carmen knew nothing of Korean. Again she would be sentenced to silence alongside another woman sharing the same miseries. Did that help push Hua to suicide? If the girls could have spoken, would Hua be alive? Could Carmen have stopped such a momentum as death?

She finished wringing the last sock, then tossed her sheets and robe into the tub's feeble suds. She sat aside to let her things soak. She'd stay confined in the basement until Papa grew bored and ordered her out. Then she would dawdle outside in the sunshine to hang the socks on the clothesline that ran beside Hua's grave.

On the cool concrete, Carmen folded her legs. She sat on her heels, a prayerful pose, breathing in the must of the basement and the fading tang of the wash water. She imagined herself in Manila, in her Quiapo barrio. Her mother washed clothes with water from the fountain outside the Catholic church, with great clouds of suds boiling over. Carmen grilled *cucuruchos* on hot coals to sell to American soldiers who gave her tips. Her father and uncles tended the ponies that pulled their *karomatas*, hauling passengers and cargo, whoever paid. The smells of her barrio, sweat in the crowded boulevards, starch in the habits of American nuns, pork and peanuts on her grill, dung from the ponies, a flower in her mother's hair, oil on her father's hands—all were absent. She stared at the wan surface of the wash water and found no magic in the basin, no images of Quiapo for her there, only the scarlet shoulder of her floating robe. Carmen sensed nothing except a procession of Japanese, the two old collaborators who handed them tickets, and that she'd had a home, a family, and a time that were not here.

And that boy Tuck. He was near, but on the other side of the barbed wire.

At the thought of the boy, Carmen scooped her *haori*

out of the tub. She wrung it over the basin. Some of the cloth's red dye dripped out. The robe was her beacon, drawing the boy's eye to her window. What if the robe kept draining itself, all the way to white, and he could not see her? She feared she would not get another red robe.

The boy's disappearance for four days did not worry her. Carmen knew he would come back to her. She grew frightened that she might vanish from him. She was not the boy, did not have his strength. She could not be certain she would always return. Hua would not.

Carmen tossed the robe into the straw basket with the soldiers' socks. She swirled her soaking sheet and pillowcase in the basin, hoping to capture some of the robe's lost red dye in her linens, to color them even the slightest shade of pretty pink.

At the top of the stairwell, the door opened. Carmen drew the sheet out, to wring it fast before Papa could make her carry it upstairs sopping wet.

The old man did not come down the steps. He held the door open for a small girl clutching her own armload of sheets.

The girl tottered down barefoot. Beneath a green silken *haori,* she was naked.

Quickly, Carmen reeled her pillowcase out of the basin, to make room for the girl's washing. She squeezed cascades back into the tub, pulled her wet things away, and gestured for the girl to use what little soapy water remained.

With short strides the Korean girl approached into the glow of the electric bulb. Blue bruises circled her ankles. She'd been in manacles. One side of her jaw appeared swollen. She stood a full head shorter than Carmen, no more than a child.

Carmen backed off from the basin, holding her damp linens. She pushed away, too, the laden straw basket. The girl came to the washtub with slow, careful movements. Carmen stood in the recesses of light, motionless.

The girl set to her washing without hurry or glancing around. She dunked her sheet, not letting it soak, and ground her knuckles into the fabric. She laundered like a farm girl. Her hair was jet like Carmen's and boxed short below the ears.

Carmen asked, "Do you speak English?"

The girl made no response. Carmen repeated, "English?"

Pounding her laundry, the Korean shook her head.

Carmen stepped into the ring of light. At the top of the staircase, Papa shouted, "Songu!"

Carmen halted. The little girl did not interrupt her scrubbing. Carmen stared at the Korean's back. She wanted to tell her, Do not wash your bright green robe unless you must. Do not fade.

Carmen dropped her linen on top of the straw basket and gathered it up. She headed to the stairwell.

The girl turned, expressionless. She said, "Songu."

Carmen halted. "Yes."

The girl released a hint of a smile, a guarded thing. She said only, "Yumi."

Carmen nodded, as if to seal a secret. She climbed the steps to Papa.

The sun fell beside Mount Makiling. Carmen knelt in her window eating a rice ball, fish gruel, boiled weeds, and a cup of carabao milk. She wore her robe, dried and fresh from the afternoon's sun and jungle breeze. The dusk deepened to indigo behind the mountain, vermilion clouds in the west like a fire in heaven. Carmen imagined herself in her crimson *haori* a part of the sunset, dropping from sight and gone.

Beyond the barbed fence, curfew hushed the camp with the settling twilight. The Japanese restricted the Americans and Europeans to candlelight or coconut-oil lanterns. Few internees had these luxuries. The barracks dimmed into starlight and the glow of a rising moon. Even the guards' barracks and offices stood dark. Red dots bobbed along the boundaries, where soldiers smoked and patrolled the wire. From the Protestant chapel at the northern end of the camp, hymns floated over the nipa roofs, beneath the bolstering constellations. To the south, closer to her perch, stood the hut built by the Catholics for their worship. The Catholic songs, familiar to Carmen, seemed stodgy compared to the Protestants' praise. Over the past year, though she had lost God, Carmen found herself preferring the Protestant service.

Through the rest of the afternoon, she'd heard nothing from the girl Yumi. After dark, Carmen could not sneak across to the south wing and sit with her; either Mama or Papa was always on guard; they slept on mats on the landing. Carmen, a Filipina, was being held captive by her own countrymen. When the Americans returned, and they promised they would, there would be a reckoning, not only for the Japanese but the *makipilis*. Carmen mulled over vengeance while listening to the hymns. She'd grown up Catholic, and the faith held that revenge belonged to God alone. She assumed the Protestants believed the same. Carmen accepted this without concern because it had no relevance for her. She'd abandoned the God who'd abandoned her. Perhaps the two of them could make peace after the war. Carmen suspected they would not. Just the same, she hoped He would avenge her.

A bustle sounded outside her curtain. Mama pushed the drape aside. The old woman fluttered to her. Carmen faced her with the same stoniness she mounted for the soldiers.

"Girl, come here. Let me see you. You're a mess. Why anyone would touch you I can't understand." Mama pinched both of Carmen's cheeks. "I've told you to wash your face with tea, you'll look younger."

Mama untied the sash holding shut the red robe, to expose Carmen's front. Carmen gazed down at her own jutting pelvis and ribs. She noticed that even Mama was losing her fat.

The old woman said, "Officers are here. Chew this."

Mama rolled blades of sweet grass between her palms into a pulpy ball. Carmen parted her lips to take the mint taste on her tongue.

"Give me more." She held out her hand. Mama dug a few green bits from a pocket. Carmen stuffed them into her nostrils to ease the stink of the man waiting outside her door. The officer was likely passing through Los Baños on his way to Manila with the rest of the troops she'd serviced that day. But unlike regular soldiers who dropped only their pants, officers stripped bare to lie with her on the tatami, sometimes until dawn. The smell of their feet and boots, unwashed chests and armpits, their nocturnal gases . . . Carmen would lie awake until he left.

Mama gathered up the plate, soup bowl, and cup from Carmen's supper. At the curtain, the woman spoke into the hall. "*Irasshaimase*." Please come in.

The *makipili* woman held back the drape for the approaching officer. His boots marched down the hall in a quickened pace. Carmen drew a breath through her nose to test the grass blades.

Nagata stepped past the curtain. Mama bowed low and left, pulling shut the drape.

Carmen stepped off the mattress. She copied Mama's deep bow, using the moments facing the floor to compose herself.

Why had she been given this devil? The brute Nagata. Watching over the camp, she'd seen him swagger and bellow, slap prisoners, even his own soldiers. Every sunup he stood at the head of roll call, sweat-stained, croaking orders, more like a frog than a human. Nagata had gone to Hua, but had never come to Songu's room. The commandant himself had visited twice, a fragrant, tired old man who slept quietly like the flowers in his garden. But Nagata? Why was he here? She stared at his boots until he grunted that she was permitted to straighten.

He strode close, shorter than her. He pulled down his cap, spun it into a corner. Without a word, standing at arm's length, he stripped away his uniform. Button by clasp, Nagata did not pull his eyes from Carmen, measuring her. His glare made clear his disgust. Carmen could not guess what rankled him, her brown flesh or his own need of it?

He kicked away his boots, adding to the pile in the corner. He peeled down his leggings and pantaloons until he stood only in a frayed loincloth. Nagata had a glutton's gut in a camp of starving people. His cheeks and shoulders were soft. Carmen checked her own features, keeping mute when Nagata pushed the robe off her shoulders. She did not kick the robe away but let it pool at her feet. He pressed down on his loincloth, tugging out to avoid the head of his risen penis.

Nagata moved close. He breathed as if sniffing her. His hand circled her wrist to raise it between them. He pincered her skin between his fingers.

"Speak Eng-rish?" he asked.

Carmen nodded.

Nagata pursed his lips. He pinched harder. Carmen swallowed a squeak.

"Spanish," he muttered, gauging the skin between his fingers. *"Shita no ningen."* Nagata made a dry spit. "West. No good." He thumped his own sternum. *"Yamato minzoku."*

He let loose her wrist. Carmen did not rub the spot he'd pinched but dropped the arm to stand nude and erect.

"*Saku,*" she said.

Nagata rubbed hands over the globe of his belly. He shook his head. Carmen shook hers in return.

Nagata muttered, "*Pii.*"

He grasped her shoulders, spun her to face away from him. He shoved her, pushed until she feared he might drive her out the open window. She braced against the sill. From behind, Nagata lowered his grip from her shoulders to her waist. He kicked at one ankle to spread her legs.

She felt his belly first against her buttocks, then the shaft of his penis searching for her vagina. Nagata had trouble entering her, his girth, his short stature, her dryness. He growled at his failures, dribbled saliva into his palm and rubbed between her legs. He would not turn her or throw her onto the mattress. Carmen held tight to the sill. The hymns from the Protestant church reached her. She shut them out.

His penis entered. She buttressed her arms against the sill, fixing her focus again on the Tuck boy's sleepy barracks. Where was he? She needed the boy outside her window to see this degradation, lock eyes and share this, divide it and carry half for her. The boy was not there. He surely was not watching, or he would have run to the wire below her window, risked anything. She feared she might crumble before Nagata's slamming belly, his grunts, and the stench, even filtered by the sweet grass in her nose. She was rammed into place, framed in the window. This was what Nagata intended. The show of domination was not for her but for the entire camp to watch.

Don't run, boy, she thought. Stay inside, stay safe. I will do this.

She stiffened her legs, whitened her knuckles. When Nagata's satisfaction arrived he endured it silently, as though in a display of discipline. He separated from Carmen. Her legs failed. She buckled to the mattress below the sill, out of sight.

Nagata replaced her in the open window. He spraddled his legs and stood above her, testicles drawn up tight. She crawled from beneath him. Beside the tatami, she squatted over the basin of manganic acid and water to splash between her legs. The disinfectant stung. She welcomed it to rout Nagata out of her.

Swelling his naked chest, he put fists to his waist. Nagata pouted, gazing over his camp. She dried herself and slipped her robe on. Outside, the Christian hymns were done.

Nagata raised an arm at the night. He passed his hand across the camp, a broad arc from the ravine on the left to the bamboo grove on the right.

"Aw-rr," he said. He meant *all* of them.

Nagata reeled the hand in. He turned to Carmen to finish the sentence.

"Aw-rr die."

With that, he lay facedown on the tatami. His stomach squashed beneath him. Nagata waggled a finger at the electric lamp on the small table, for Carmen to extinguish it. She pulled the chain. In the dark, she stood beside the mattress.

All die. Was Nagata going to murder everyone in the camp? How could he do that? Why do it? The internees weren't soldiers, just famished civilians, women and children. The boy Tuck, would he die?

She knelt to the tatami. Gulping down fear and revulsion, she lay beside him.

Nagata snorted, awake with the first dribbles of light in Carmen's window. She pretended sleep. With one eye, she watched him don his uniform. Nagata sat roughly on the tatami to slide on his boots. This made it difficult for Carmen to continue her deception. He stood and kicked the mattress.

"Okinasai."

Carmen stifled a fake yawn and rubbed her eyes. She got to her feet in the dim room. Outside, jungle birds twittered at the rising dawn.

He said, *"Rei."*

She bowed. He put on his cap.

He waited at the curtain for her to pull it aside. She did not. He grunted and did it for himself. Carmen followed.

Mama was puffy-faced on the landing. She bowed to Nagata.

The three waited. Outside in the camp, the morning gong rang.

Nagata faced the south wing, hands behind his back. The curtain across Yumi's room slid aside. Commandant Toshiwara emerged, hat in hand.

Nagata watched his superior advance. Little Yumi padded on bare feet in the old man's wake, her robe belted and verdant even in the drab light. When the commandant reached the landing, Nagata snapped into a bow, Mama, too. Carmen caught Yumi's eye and both bowed low.

They held until Nagata straightened. Toshiwara put on his cap, inclined his head in a shallow nod to Mama. To Yumi, the commandant gave a deeper nod.

"Sayonara, Yumi-chan."

The girl curtsied on bare legs. *"Sayonara, mata irashitte kudasai, onjin-sama."*

Toshiwara headed down the stairs. Nagata strutted after him.

When the pair of officers was out of sight, Mama sloughed back to her mattress in a corner of the landing. A half-drunk bottle of rice wine waited on the floor.

"Go back to your rooms. Don't make me chase you off."

Carmen retreated toward her wing, Yumi to hers. Carmen tapped her forefinger and thumb together, to mimic a speaking mouth. She pointed down the stairs after the officers.

"Nippon?" she asked, aiming a finger now at Yumi. Did the girl speak Japanese?

"Go," Mama muttered.

Backing away, little Yumi answered. *"Hai."*

Chapter Five

TINSLEY, a tobacco buyer before the war, elbowed Remy.

"Look at the little bastard go."

"Shut up, Tinsley."

Old McElway, also crowded into Tinsley's dark cubicle, added, "Shut up, both of you."

The tobacco man answered with a licentious cackle. He stepped away from the window facing the animal husbandry building to lie on his bunk.

McElway whispered at Remy's shoulder, "This is hard to watch." The piano man coughed into his palm, then looked into his open hand with disgust and wiped it on his pants. He left the window, muttering, "I ain't had none in three years. I got to watch this shit? I don't think so." Mac pushed aside the sawali mat covering the door to head down the hall.

Seeing Nagata, the most loathed man in Los Baños, having sex was difficult enough. Nagata did it openly, lit up in the third-floor window, taunting the camp. Seeing him screw the girl his son had somehow idealized made Remy's mouth go dry.

Remy wanted to join Mac and mope back to his own cubicle. He hadn't had a woman in a long time, either. Two American prostitutes were in the camp; Remy had known them both in Manila. In Los Baños their trade was banned by the Japanese and the Internee Committee. Privacy existed nowhere in the camp, even if a man could find the money and the energy. Both whores had become irritants to the Internee Committee, with little taste for manual labor and few valuable skills on their feet. Remy avoided them.

He stayed fixed in the window. Remy kept private that he was absorbing this insult in his son's name.

He ignored Nagata writhing behind the girl. Even from three stories below he could see the man's expression was a gloat. Remy focused on the Filipina, braced hard against the windowsill. She kept her face turned from Nagata, a cold, absent expression. Remy did not see in the girl what his boy did, neither nobility nor beauty. He did see that she suffered.

A dozen barracks had a view of this, many of them bachelor quarters. Likely, a couple hundred men were scuffling for window space to see this, maybe a few priests in Vatican City. The girl stared straight ahead. Where was she looking?

Remy strode out of the room. Tinsley sent him along with a hoot. "Gotta go take care of business, Tuck?"

Remy made his way through the building as quietly as he could. Many of the men had left their bunks when Tinsley rumbled through the building hissing that there was something to see. Monitors in every barracks were assigned to maintain curfew and lights-out hours. Remy tiptoed to the back door. He ducked, waiting for the guard to stroll out of sight.

Darting across the open path, he shot up the bamboo steps of Tal's building.

Barracks No. 11 was where the Japanese put those internees they believed required the most vigilance. All young men, these were the camp bravos, with defiant attitudes, troubled pasts, and recurrent infractions of camp rules, petty thieves like Talbot. The residents of No. 11 bore their lodgment here like a badge; their misbehavior was resistance. The Internee Committee branded them hooligans, claiming their pranks and misdemeanors did nothing but increase tension with the guards and risk retaliation. Remy's sympathies, as a gambler living on the fringes of the rules, were often with the boys.

He crept down the hall, shushing the voices who greeted him, and made his way to Tal's room.

Remy pushed aside the woven mat covering the doorway. Tal lay shirtless, facedown on his lower bunk behind mosquito netting. He hadn't moved in five days except to sit up and eat the meals Remy brought him, take a leak in a bucket, or sit on the floor for a sponge bath. The stripes on his back appeared mottled and gruesome, but healing. All five of his roommates were absent.

Remy knelt beside the bunk. He lifted the net.

"Boy."

His son snorted and shifted. "Hmm."

"Wake up."

Tal blinked into the pillow and raised his head. He grimaced in the pale light. The lava of scabs wrinkled along the boy's upper back. Remy could not guess how painful such a small motion must be.

Tal cleared his throat. "What is it?"

"Let me help you sit up. Come on."

"Why? What time is it?"

Remy took the boy's arm. Tal gritted his teeth, swinging his feet to the bamboo floor. He glanced at the empty bunks in his cubicle.

"Where's everybody? What's going on?"

"It's all jake, just listen. There's something going on. Everybody's gonna be talking about it in the next hour or so. I wanted you to hear about it first from me."

Tal rubbed his chin to wake himself. Remy watched the small flickers of the boy's eyes as the knitting wounds across his back pricked at him.

"What is it? Is it me?"

"No, you ain't in any more trouble, not for the moment anyways. I'm here to make sure that sticks. You got a temper, we both know that. My goal here is to make certain that when it hits, I'm standin' next to you. Can't see any way around it."

"Remy?"

"Yeah, boy."

"You're making it worse. Just tell me."

"Nagata. He's doing your girl. In the window of her building. I reckon a lot of folks are watching."

Remy had both hands ready when Tal tried to stand from his bunk. He didn't push down on the boy's wrecked shoulders but on his thighs, holding Tal in a sitting position.

"There's nothing you can do. Let it roll on by."

"Is he doing it right now?"

"Far as I know."

"Is that where everybody is?"

"That's my guess, yes."

"Show me."

Remy rattled his head. "You got no need to see this. It's just gonna make you madder."

Tal leaned close. His thinned lips showed the price of the movement.

"Exactly. Show me."

The boy started to stand, heaving past Remy's hindering hands. Remy relented, giving the boy his own shoulder to prop him. They moved into the corridor toward the buzzing of young men at the far end of the barracks.

Remy brought his mouth to Tal's ear. "Anyone else know about you and the girl?"

"No."

"Keep it that way."

Remy sensed the strain of every step for his son. Since

Tal's beating, this was the first time he'd left his room. The boy walked hunched. Remy nodded as Tal set one bare foot in front of the other, proud of the gumption and at the same time fearful of the boy's rashness.

They approached a clot of boys in the corridor. "Comin' through," Remy said. A path was made for Tal walking gingerly on Remy's arm. Remy strode in first, Tal followed, and every boy, even the few adults who lived in the barracks, made way. They gazed at Tal and his wounds with quiet awe.

Tal took his arm from Remy's grip. He strode to the window. Remy stayed at his side should he need to clap a hand over his son's mouth.

Darkness prevailed save for stars, a wedge of new moon, and the light from the girl's room. She stood in the window, enduring Nagata behind her. The girl's features remained graven, fixed straight at No. 11, where Tal stared back, invisible to her.

Tal clenched his jaw. Remy raised a quiet hand behind the boy's back to calm him. Tal made no move or sound; the others in the room followed suit for no good reason other than the boy's presence.

Tal stood with hands open at his sides. His face dropped all trace of anger and took on the same distant look as the girl. The two could not see each other but they seemed to lock eyes. The boy appeared struck by her misery, glaring as if the whole rotten spectacle was just for him.

No one spoke or left the room. When Nagata finished, the girl did not step back from the window but plummeted out of sight. Tal set his hands on the bamboo sill as though to leap out of the barracks.

"Time to go," Remy said, turning his son from the window. Those in the room made way. Someone wished him well, saying, "You're looking better, buddy." Tal did not seek support on Remy's arm to leave.

Once in the hall, the boy put a hand around Remy's waist. They made their way back to Tal's room. Remy lifted the mosquito netting. Tal eased into his bunk.

Tal screwed up his face and, for the first time in days, lay on his back. Remy dropped the netting, then sat with his own back against the bunk. The other boys had not returned to the room.

Remy listened to Tal breathe. He'd done this thousands of times, simply taking in the sound of his son's living. The boy coughed, a young man's throaty voice, but Remy heard the soft hack of an infant.

He closed his eyes, to better see the grave beside the bush hut where the boy's mother lay. The rough cross he'd nailed together from wooden slats never lasted more than a season; he'd made Sarah a new marker every spring for four years. There was not a chance that now, eight years after leaving her behind, any trace was left of her or their home. The last vestige of the woman and that place rested in Talbot. Remy envisioned the hut in the outback the way it must stand today, a windblown wreck, the grave mound a rocky pile if the sands hadn't shifted over it. Quickly, Remy abandoned the dismal image for a better one, before the hut or grave even existed, just a flat parcel of crown land near a creek, sheltered by trees, beside the road.

He'd met Sarah in 1924, two months after leaving Louisiana. He'd booked passage on an Australia steamer. Others were trying to escape the poverty in the Delta by heading west, bootlegging, trapping, alligator farming, or joining the army. Remy, at twenty-five, had worked as a mechanic, a blacksmith and farrier, and part-time for the local sheriff delivering warrants. One day, while shoeing a plow horse for an old coon-ass, the man chewed a weed and talked about gold, how he was going to pack up and head Down Under, where the water flushed the wrong way, they ate kangaroos, and all the folks were criminals hiding out. But dang him, he said, if they hadn't struck gold down there. He figured a hardworking American from the bayou could do better than any of those backward folk. Remy knew the man would never go, told him so, and received a cuff upside the head. The old skinner dared him to go if it was so easy a thing. Remy, with no better prospects than an adventure, agreed that maybe the man was right about how well a Yank could do. He packed a trunk, kissed his mother, and lit out for New Orleans.

The ocean crossing ran long, smooth, and blue. It was a sea journey like the one his father took to France in 1917, a voyage from which he did not return. Remy saw the Panama Canal, switched ships in San Francisco and again in Hawaii. He spent no time in Sydney after landing there. Remy knew little of cities and had no confidence that his fortune waited in one. He stayed only long enough to learn where the gold-fields were. The original strike back in 1851 had been in Bathurst, two hundred miles northwest of Sydney. Seventy-five years later, prospectors had chased the color all the way to the coast, and the new goldfields lay around the towns of Woolgoolga and Coffs Harbour. Remy caught the first train north, arriving in Coffs Harbour the next morning. Near the station, he inquired in a Chinese-run hardware store about accommodations. The white girl at the cash register told him of a room to rent upstairs. He took it for two days, figuring he needed one to get himself a parcel of land and another to court the tall, raven-haired Aussie girl.

Remy was mistaken. Securing rights to fifty hectares, roughly a hundred and a quarter acres, took a single day at the courthouse, where he filed a Miner's Right of Claim and agreed to pay five shillings a year, equal to fifty cents back home. The girl required a week.

Sarah Elias Pendergrass hailed from a large family of

ranchers west of Coffs Harbour. She was one of twelve siblings, ten of them girls. Her parents had no particular use for her on the cattle property and let her go off with the American who talked of wealth. Remy married Sarah at the hardware store. Mr. Yung, the owner, was also a man of the cloth, though it was Buddhism, and performed the ceremony.

That afternoon, Sarah saw the property for the first time. Out of nothing, she conjured the house they would live in, walking the land to find the ideal spot, designing the limits of the building with a foot dragged in the dirt. This ability to see what did not exist became what Remy loved in her most. He grew convinced it was what allowed her to love him.

Remy set up a bush camp under the shade of wild grapevines, gum trees, and she-oaks. The tent became both parlor and bedroom; washing and cooking was done over a fire pit beneath a tin lean-to. Locals began to drop by with the odd tool and helping hand. None left without a meal of Sarah's fried fish or 'roo steaks, boiled crayfish from the stream, dumplings, and buttered biscuits. At night, the fire warmed men playing squeezeboxes and mouth organs, women swaying with babies on their hips. Remy believed he'd found his adventure, his woman. Next was to build his home. Then find the gold.

The hut's construction took six months. Remy excavated for the floor, then poured a mixture of termite clay, dried cow manure, and chopped hay. Trees on the property provided rafters and framework. An iron roof was laid with much help from the growing rank of able-backed friends. Sarah kept the men hammering and hoisting all day with billycans of strong tea and plates of johnnycakes slathered with honey. After the iron chimney and hearth were fashioned and installed, Sarah told Remy she was pregnant.

He did not take a day from his labors to celebrate the

news; Sarah did not ask him to. They bore down harder and swifter to raise their home from the bush. When the news of Sarah's condition spread, their circle of friends intensified their efforts as well. Eastern Australia was in the clutch of an outbreak of dengue fever. Remy and Sarah wanted their baby born inside the house, protected from the mosquitoes.

Neighboring banana farmers contributed dozens of hessian fertilizer sacks. Sarah stonewashed these in the river, slit them down the seams, and sewed them into bolts. Remy nailed the bags across the studs. Sarah followed, troweling the bags with an ocher slurry of termite clay in thick layers, to make fine adobe walls. Stores in Coffs Harbour provided empty packing crates. Remy used the pine boards to make slats, shelves, even furniture.

The outside of the hut took its final shape. Remy had purchased little, only the roofing iron, twine, nails, and creosote. All other materials had been harvested out of the bush or donated by neighbors and friends. Remy and Sarah, tanned and strong, admired their home hand in hand. Her belly had begun to show. Remy wanted to move her out of the tent and into the hut. She demurred until one more chore was completed.

Over the six months of their marriage and work, she'd been collecting newspapers, magazines, calendars, and posters. With a paste of flour and water, she coated the mud walls with a hard shell of newsprint, to smooth and insulate them. Next, Mr. Yung arrived with long sheets of brown wrapping paper that Sarah glued in place. Finally, she created her own wallpaper, festooning every room with cutouts from the colorful prints she kept dry in Remy's trunk. The kitchen glowed with a frieze of apricots, apples, plums, peaches, oranges, and watermelons carved from the labels of jam tins. Remy could not afford glass for the windows, but the push-out shutters he'd made were adorned with travel posters, outdoor scenes, and landscapes. When the shutters were closed against the night or weather, Remy and Sarah and the coming child would not be isolated from the world but surrounded by the Eiffel Tower, a sunset, an ocean, a pasture. In the baby's room Sarah crafted a fresco of ships, stars, animals in the jungle, the Egyptian pyramids. She told Remy she would have a son, but if she were wrong, she had a cache of flowers and rainbows stashed in his trunk.

Just as she'd said, Talbot Mark Tuck was born in August, one year after Remy's arrival in Australia. The boy was laid in a crib made from oak that Remy cut from his own land. The parents covered the infant in a kangaroo skin and sat up nights by kerosene lamplight, listening to a windup gramophone that Remy bought for his wife the week after the birth.

The boy came into the world healthy and stayed that way. Sarah tended him, joining the community of women around them with youngsters to mind. Remy turned his attention to his fortune.

He'd long ago dropped any intention to mine for gold. Remy had watched men, many of them friends, endure hardship, poverty, disease, just to get a glimpse of the color in the ground. Every day of their lives was a lottery and an addiction. Of the thousands who lived in tents or the holes they dug, a few hit on a nugget or shook dust in their pans. Most found enough to make themselves a wage and no more. Remy took a long look at the prospector's life and decided that while it might suit him, it would not do for Sarah and Talbot.

He decided instead to rely on the skills he'd brought from the bayou. Many miners had a horse or donkey needing shoes. Every one of them had a pickaxe, a shovel, chisels, iron tools that broke against the hard clay and granite reef.

On the part of his parcel nearest the road, Remy opened a blacksmith's shop.

For five years, he serviced the goldfields as farrier and smithy. Most of the miners he worked for were foreigners to Australia, they were Chinese, Irish, English, Italian, Afrikaans, men who'd chased gold around the globe. From each he learned something new about the world, the vast range of humanity, language, culture, appearance, history. More important, Remy saw what all men share in the base of their hearts. Any man will risk anything, for luck.

To keep the miner's claim to his property, Remy and friends sank a twenty-foot shaft not far from the house. He expected to find nothing below the ground. The boy, only six, hauled up buckets of dirt, Sarah lowered the workers lunch and tea. When the hole came up empty, it was not without benefit: the Tuck family was rewarded with a new long-drop privy.

Remy never knew where the mosquito came from. Maybe it was the privy, though he threw lime into it once a week. Maybe the stream, which ran low sometimes in drought and pooled. Sarah's death from dengue was the result of her strength. She refused to be laid up by the fever and shivers, she did not let chores go undone from hurting joints and a terrible ache behind her eyes. Remy protested that he should fetch the doctor, but she insisted she was fine. Her symptoms subsided after three days. A day later the pains returned, just as Remy's radio reported a second, small outbreak of dengue in New South Wales. He lit out for Woolgoolga and the mines to find the physician. Remy took two days to bring the man back, almost by the coat collar, but the medicine the physician left behind did little to stem Sarah's fever. In the goldfields, a hundred had died. Within the week, Sarah was swept out of her body. Remy fashioned a new pick and shovel in his shop, used them to bury his wife, then smashed them on the rocks in the stream.

That winter, Remy closed his business. He'd lost the heart to strain over a bellows, travel into the goldfields to repair and deliver tools, go to the farms where the shoeing work was done. Hard work was what he'd shared with Sarah. Without her the sweat lost its sweetness.

A year before her illness, Remy had played his first card game in the canvas city of the goldfields. On that single evening, he made more by the turn of a card than he could with a week of pounding iron. Remy found himself a cool hand at the table, with a clear mind and a bland face regardless of the cards or the money in the pot. He'd grown up on the bayou reading horses, mules, and the vagaries of hot metal. He'd tricked and chased down deadbeats to serve them the sheriff's warrants. A drunken, gambling miner in Australia posed much less of a challenge for Remy to judge.

He hired an old teacher to nanny the boy while he rode off to the camps. Often, Remy would be gone for several days. He discovered there was more money in the miners than in the mines. He took to arming himself with a pistol, to protect the rolls of cash he carried.

For four years, Remy played poker. He won many times over what he might have earned as a smithy. He never cheated, and was never deemed a sharp. The boy grew taller, brighter; he walked a mile each way to the schoolhouse. Remy taught him cards, ironwork, what he'd learned at the mines about mankind, and about the boy's mother. Talbot cried sometimes for her loss, though his recollections of Sarah were dimming. Remy told him there was nothing they could have done to save her, she was chosen by God and taken. God was the only one they couldn't outwit or bluff.

The Aussie gold rush petered out. The camps dwindled. The new color was being mined elsewhere; the latest hot spot was the Philippines, especially after the United States raised its price for gold. In 1935, Remy sold his land, home, and all his furnishings. He laid a wreath of vine and oak on his wife's grave, added a new cross and more stones. With his nine-year-old son and a grubstake of fifteen thousand Australian dollars, he boarded a liner for Manila.

Upon arrival, Remy changed his mind about a city as a place to find his fortune. He let go of his plans to head for the gold mines of northern Luzon, and took a house in the San Nicolas district of Manila. With little effort, he found a community of ten thousand Yanks, half military, the rest diplomats, businessmen, and their families. The gents were eager to sit at a friendly game of cards over gimlets and cigars to escape the tropical heat. Many Manila watering holes catered to them: the Army Navy Club, Bay View Hotel, Polo Club, Dixie Kitchen, Elks Club, the opulent Manila Hotel. Under layers of smoke, around dewy highballs and skidding cards, the expatriates talked of the Depression in the states, Roosevelt's economic policies, Japan's plans for Manchuria and her growing designs on all Asia. Remy kept them chatting, distracted and drinking while the games were played. He made himself welcome with tales from Down Under, a quick wit, and a ready billfold. He never won too much in one game, and would not fleece any player to the point where the man would refuse to play with him again or spread an ill word. Remy Tuck became known as a professional gambler, an honest and pleasant one. Players at every skill level liked to tilt against him.

In time he became a poker partner of Doug MacArthur. The general lived in a wing of the Manila Hotel. When President Quezon commissioned MacArthur to build the Philippine Army, the general insisted his quarters be every bit the match for Malacañan, the presidential palace. MacArthur's penthouse suite was constructed with seven bedrooms, the same as the palace, featuring a surrounding promenade for him to walk, ponder decisions, and put himself on display above the city.

Remy found MacArthur to be a congenial player. The general could not tolerate a conversation he did not command, but no one challenged him in this regard. He could nurse a scotch and water for hours. At home, the general didn't smoke his famous corncob, his "battle pipe," but constantly had at hand an old briarwood. In the study, surrounded by the man's ten-thousand-volume library of military history, Remy was careful to make his own bankroll on the other guests. He did not hesitate to toss a few bets to the general every session.

MacArthur recommended to Remy an amah for young Talbot. The general explained that a Chinese nanny was better admired in the expatriate community than a Filipina *yaya*. The boy should also be enrolled in the American Catholic school in Intramuros. Though Remy would not take the general's money, he did accept his advice.

Talbot grew tall and lean like his mother. He wore his black hair longer than the fashion. Slowly, Manila began to drain the boy of his good nature. He became a poor fit for polo, golf, sculling, even baseball at Rizal Park, and the other recreations of his station and race. Talbot preferred more solitary pursuits: reading, walking the old city, sketching. He became an able student and a handsome lad, but friendless outside the home, detached and surly in it. Remy's gambling pursuits held no interest for the boy. Tal's ennui threw up a barrier that Remy did not know how to cross. He recalled the bush hut he'd built out of termite clay and manure, iron, and wood, for this boy. He resented his son's distance, and asked behind the boy's back for the return of the cherished part of him that was Sarah. He believed that Sarah would love him through the boy, but somehow Talbot prevented this, cheating Remy. Just as Talbot did not warm to his father's voice, the boy did not hear his mother within him.

Remy, popular away from home, found reasons to stay

away. The amah cared well for the boy; he was eating and handling his studies. Remy lived and played in the company of the professional class of Manila. He had money, liquor, games, women brown and white, to keep him out nights. He saw his son less.

In late 1941, few believed the Japanese would, or could, invade the Philippines. Why anger such a power as America? Hadn't MacArthur spent years preparing the islands to repel exactly such an attack? When Pearl Harbor was bombed, followed hours later by the destruction of the naval and air stations around Manila, the American community was shocked but confident the general would defend them. In the week before Christmas, the Japanese army landed forces on Luzon at Lingayen Gulf and south of Manila at Legaspi Bay. Japan expended little effort in overwhelming MacArthur's numerically superior but poorly equipped and undertrained Filipino force. On Christmas Eve, when the general abandoned Manila for Bataan and Corregidor, most foreigners realized the time had passed for them to make their own escape. Manila was a besieged and cut-off city. On December 29, MacArthur came on the radio:

> Do not follow the army to Bataan. Get together in
> groups rather than be taken as individual families.
> Destroy any papers showing a connection with the
> U.S. Military Reserves. Pour all intoxicating beverages
> down the sink. May God be with you. I shall return.

Remy, like all the Americans, had known few Japanese in Manila. There'd been the rare Rotarian businessman, polite and unoffending, or quiet employees in restaurants and private homes. No one could fully comprehend the tales of berserk Japanese soldiers raiding and pillaging across China, fueled on violence and alcohol. On New Year's Eve, in the last hours before the Japanese rolled into Manila, Remy and the entire foreign community drank every bit of scotch, bourbon, rum, and gin they could tolerate. The rest they denied the enemy by smashing the bottles in the streets beneath the gleams of exploding fuel dumps at Cavite Naval Base. Tal, at fifteen, drank his first liquor and broke the bottle before passing out.

Remy and Tal were interned at Santo Tomas, a university in central Manila. The Japanese corralled seven thousand westerners on the campus, a space suited for half that. Remy continued to gamble, staying below the notice of camp administrators who'd banned the practice. He used his winnings to buy extra food from the camp bodega for himself and his son; the rest of the cash he gave to a ring of women smuggling money through the wire to the "battling bastards," those captured American soldiers who survived the death march from Bataan and were caged in Cabanatuan.

In captivity, Tal flourished. He'd been freed from the constraints of school, though several academics in the camp had set up classes as high as university level. Tal's quiet nature hid a steely willpower and icy nerve. The boy had grown into a young man with a poker face. Tal got involved with the folks smuggling food into Santo Tomas and messages out. He worked as a courier, slipping notes to the Filipino guerrillas who masqueraded in the camp as servants or suppliers to the Japanese. Tal learned the clever ways of chicanery and thievery. He snipped the corners of transported bags of rice so they would leak grains for him and his comrades to sweep up. He lured the commandant's chickens over the coop wire. He tossed wet bamboo shoots into a cook fire deep in the night to make them crump, waking the guards with fears of gunshots. Tal lifted anything from the Japanese that wasn't nailed down and ate it or sold it, adding the money to Remy's stash headed to Cabanatuan. He became the one returning late to his cot in the administration building. Remy didn't ask where the boy had been, avoiding the smooth lie his son would have told. Remy heard of Tal's exploits mainly from the admiration, or scoldings, of others over dice and cards who called him brave and crazy.

Remy discovered that Tal had inherited his cool and Sarah's single-mindedness. Though he'd never set foot in the States, the job at hand for all Americans was resistance against the Japanese. Tal, almost of a soldier's age, fought in the only way he could behind barbed wire. He stole, he mocked, he refused their hold on him.

In May 1943, after sixteen months at Santo Tomas, the Japanese asked for eight hundred volunteers to transfer to a second, smaller internment camp seventy kilometers southeast of Manila, on an athletic field at the University of Los Baños, near the shore of Laguna de Bay. Unmarried men of good health were required to build the new camp to relieve the crowded conditions at Santo Tomas. Internees who inspected the new site declared it unfit for habitation, with impure and insufficient water, a malarial mosquito problem, inadequate medical facilities, and a lack of food resources in the area. The Japanese ignored these protests. Only 280 volunteered to go, Talbot among them. Remy added his name to stay with his son. The rest of the contingent was selected by lottery. Twelve nurses captured on Corregidor, the only military personnel in the camp, were sent also.

Los Baños emerged quickly. Thirty sawali-and-nipa barracks went up, three for use by the Japanese for garrison and staff offices, the rest for barracks, kitchen, garage, and a pair of chapels. The men boiled water until they could complete a deep well, suffered through an E. coli breakout, and burned more calories than the Japanese supplied them. By the end of the year, 1,400 more internees were transferred from Santo Tomas. Tal had worked as a carpenter, Remy in the blacksmith shop.

By the beginning of this year, 1944, the tide of war on the Pacific had turned against the Japanese. With every American victory, the guards enacted increasingly punitive measures. Midway, Guadalcanal, New Guinea, the Solomons, each ignited a new round of harassment, extra roll calls, tightening freedoms, cutbacks on food. Talbot, whippet lean, responded by studying every inch of Los Baños. He knew the vulnerable places in the wire, blind spots among the guard towers, the location of every bullet, bed, gun, vehicle, and morsel of Japanese food inside the camp. He continued his smuggling efforts and his thefts.

In March, two Filipinas started up a commissary at the camp's south gate, selling fruit and vegetables to the internees. They also were part of an intelligence network set up by the guerrillas to bring in mail and communications from the resistance. Tal became their most frequent courier.

Also in March, the red-robed Filipina appeared in her window above the camp. She gave sex to the guards and any soldier passing through the village. Tal saw this with everyone else. Somehow he fell for her.

In July, Lieutenant Nagata arrived from Santo Tomas as the new Los Baños supply officer. His first act was to reduce the rations in the camp by 20 percent. His second was to restrict any commerce with the locals for the fruit that fell from the trees outside the wire. Nagata shut the two women down immediately, knowing nothing of the smuggling. Tal redirected his efforts to thieving from the Japanese.

In November, a typhoon swept across the camp. Tal snuck out in the night, dodging nipa fronds from the roofs flying in the hundred-mile-per-hour wind. The guards caught him in the commandant's garden digging up vegetables. The Internee Committee stepped in to punish Tal, dodging tougher justice from the Japanese. The committee clapped him in the camp brig for ten days. While Tal was in the lockup, the final Sunday concert was played. The internee musicians announced they no longer had the energy to rehearse, despite the boost in camp morale their performances gave. In a final tweak at the Japanese, and a nod to Tal, the orchestra played "Prelude to the Thief of Baghdad," "Orpheus in the Underworld," "The Prisoner's Song," and "I Want to Go Back to My Little Grass Shack." On his release, Tal was removed from No. 12, Remy's building, and inserted into No. 11, branded by the guards as one of the troublesome boys.

Then five days ago, in the second week of December, the American fighter flew over the camp and dropped the cigarettes. Tal would not let them lie in the grass unclaimed. That was a courageous act, and hardheaded. That was, Remy was convinced, Sarah.

Remy shifted on the hard floor, taking in his circumstances. He measured the distance from where he sat to where he thought he'd be when he left the bayou twenty years ago. Remy was a prisoner in a foreign land, a gambler with a badly beaten son, a dead wife, no money nor home to return to, skeletal ribs under a shabby T-shirt, and sandals. He thought of his father buried in France, his wife under the rocks in Australia. Maybe his own mother had passed on in Louisiana; he didn't know. Would he add to the family legacy, depositing his bones in the Philippines? Would Tal join him here, or would the boy die in yet another country?

Remy swatted at a mosquito. The action rattled the bunk at his back. Tal stirred. The boys would soon be coming back to their racks. They would certainly have things to say about the Filipina.

He whispered, "Boy?"

"Yeah." Even in a hushed tone, Remy was struck by the man's voice. The little boy had joined Sarah, both were gone.

"Remember. Close to the vest."

"Okay."

"How you feelin'?"

"I'm all right. Remy?"

"Yup."

"I'm gonna kill him."

Remy shook his head, forcefully enough for the boy to feel it in the bed frame. He turned to face his son. Tal stared straight up, into the bottom of the top bunk.

"Look at me," Remy said. The boy did not. "You're not killing anybody. What you're going to do is survive. You and me both. We'll leave Nagata and the rest for MacArthur and his boys. They'll see to it, I guaran-damn-tee you."

Tal seemed concrete. Remy had to hurry before his roommates pushed aside the sawali mat over the door.

"You don't have to defend her honor, kiddo. That's over, that's gone. What she needs to do is exactly what we're gonna do, and that's still be alive when this place gets put to the torch. She'll get it back one day, but not now and not here. You understand me?"

Slowly, still hardened, Tal brought his eyes to his father.

"Tell me we'll save her, too. Tell me that."

There was Sarah looking right at Remy, maybe not so gone at all. A job to do. Her two cool-handed men to do it.

Remy rested his back against the bunk. He'd sleep here beside his sore, bedridden, hard-assed son, so that neither of them got too lonely.

"Sure, boy. We'll save her."

Chapter Six

◆

TAL AWOKE from a dream of fire.

He had not been aflame in the dream, but others he did not know burned. None of the charred people ran, they stood in place like torches. Tal ran among them.

He sat up quickly. He did not think to worry if his scabs might stick to the mattress. When he realized he was upright in his bunk and had not torn his back open, he exhaled in relief.

Tal lifted the mosquito netting. Remy had gone, slipped out before sunup. The others snored in their racks.

Early dawn tinged the camp in gray half-light. The last hoots of an owl echoed in Boot Creek. Cool air drifted in the window across his bare back. Tal rose. After five hobbled days, he stood on his own.

He looked at his ankles, swollen from lying still so long, mottled with red bites. Bedbugs. The mites used the mosquito nets to travel from bunk to bunk.

He slid on his sneakers and, shirtless, walked away from his rack.

Others were awake in the predawn camp. Vatican City stirred early for morning prayer. Some folks got a jump on the rising sun to do what physical activity they could manage. Fifty men lined up at the gate for the day's firewood detail in the Makiling forest. Cooks ambled to the kitchen to stoke fires, peel *kamotes,* hull rice, make ersatz coffee. Women worked in Toshiwara's private garden; Nagata had shut down the internees' plot in October. Two men strolled to tend the Brahman bull the commandant kept to haul the firewood sled in from the jungle. Every ounce of food that went down the big bull's gullet was eyed covetously. A month ago, the internees killed their last dozen pigs. The animals had contracted anthrax. All the camp's visions of butchered meat, chops, sausage, and scrapple went up in smoke. The internees, dashed and hungry, salvaged a few buckets of boiled blood for their evening *lugao*, rice porridge. Nagata refused to let the internees spend their own money or trade their jewels to replace the pigs.

The older men Tal passed winked to see him on his feet. They acknowledged the brown mantle across his shoulders as hard won. Each of them had some outer mark, the protruding bones of malnutrition, red lesions from pellagra, the indigo patches of beriberi. Tal drew himself upright at their nods, undoing the last of the cringe that had crept into his posture.

The best time to visit the latrine was always before breakfast. Tal's insides had been twisted and tight since his beating. This walk had unraveled the blockage. Many pairs of barracks were connected by a six-hole outhouse. Tal entered to find four internees already in place. He dropped his pants, sat, and concentrated.

When finished, Tal stood outside the latrine, reacquainting himself with fresh air and the rising sun. Old McElway approached. The man limped a circle around Tal, whistling at the boy's crusted shoulders.

"Sonny, you ain't never gon' get laid."

"Why not?"

"Come on, no woman wants to climb in bed with a fella lookin' all whupped up like that. That's like sleepin' with a lizard or somethin'. You got to be smooth and pretty, like me."

"You played piano in a whorehouse. You had an advantage."

"Still smooth and pretty."

McElway was neither. He was fading from starvation. His eye sockets had deepened, taking on the dark of a well. Veins stood out in his neck, forearms, and forehead. Because he could not eat enough, something slow and hungry was devouring him instead.

Tal played along with the old negro's patter. "I'm pretty."

Mac twirled a long finger around Tal's head. "Yeah, with your hair all down your neck. You pretty like a gal. But brother, you ain't smooth." McElway laid a hand on Tal's arm. "Your daddy, you know. He talks about you like you Superman."

"Remy's okay."

McElway nodded his agreement. "You Superman, Talbot?"

"What're you getting at?"

The piano player cast furtive looks left and right. "I got something I need done. It's mighty important."

"Important to who?"

"The whole camp."

"Then why are you the one asking me?"

"'Cause the camp don't know. Come on, walk."

McElway led, ambling away from the latrine to the worn path between barracks. Tal waited until they were clear of people before speaking.

"What do you need me to do?"

"How well you know the camp?"

"Every inch."

"You been outside it? Under the wire?"

"Not since we put it up. No."

McElway walked, looking at his own feet. They dragged.

"Think you could get outside?"

"I reckon."

"I'd do this myself, boy. You know that. But I ain't up to it."

"What do you need?"

Mac ran a rheumy eye across Tal's shoulders, measuring him to determine if he could do this thing.

"Two weeks ago, I put word out to the local guerrillas. I needed somethin'. I heard yesterday they got it. I'm supposed to meet somebody outside the camp to pick it up."

"When?"

"Tonight."

"What is it?"

McElway spit. "Can't tell you that. Can't nobody in the camp know but me."

"Why not?"

"In case the Japs catch you on the way out. 'Course, they probably gon' shoot you, if they do."

"And if they catch me on the way back?"

"You throw it away. It's small. Then they shoot you. Or bayonet you."

"And if they don't catch me?"

"You bring it to me tomorrow morning here at the latrine. Then you go 'bout your business."

Tal stopped walking. Mac quit more slowly, taking a few extra steps. He came back to Tal.

"Tell me what it is," Tal said. "I'm not risking my ass for something I don't know what it is."

"Sonny, you just got to trust me on this one."

Tal waited while a missionary couple walked by on the path.

"I trust you, Mac. It's you don't trust me."

The old man dug a leathery hand into a pants pocket. He pulled out an egg.

"You take this. Eat the shell, too. Get you some calcium."

"Keep it."

The old man shook his noggin. He folded Tal's young hand over the egg.

"You got to heal."

With a fingertip, Tal broke a hole in the egg. He sucked out the yolk, swallowed, then shoved the shell whole in his mouth and crunched down.

McElway put up his pink palms. "You think about it some more. Get back to me. And don't tell nobody."

The camp loudspeaker announced a roll call.

No one could determine the reason; roll calls were infrequent, only when the commandant had a punitive purpose or the guards suspected someone might have escaped.

At seven o'clock, all 2,100 internees lined up in front of their barracks. Outside the infirmary, those who could stand from their beds arranged themselves in shaky queues.

Tal remained shirtless, waiting with everyone else for Toshiwara to emerge from his hut. With Christmas a week away, the Philippine sun kept enough of its strength to make standing in the open morning uncomfortable. The plaints of children drifted from the several married barracks.

After half an hour, the internees stiffened with the appearance of Nagata. He strolled from the commandant's headquarters.

The boys of No. 11 muttered: Why was Nagata conducting the roll call, not the commandant?

Tal lost sight of Nagata among the buildings. He heard the first barracks count off. When they were done, the residents would remain in place until the entire camp had been counted. This would take over an hour, with no sitting, water, or shade. The sun began to bake on the raw swaths of Tal's rib cage. Next door, Remy raised his fedora in a morning greeting.

Another half hour passed before Nagata, his tall interpreter, and two more guards tromped in front of No. 11. The purpose for the roll call remained hidden. Nagata, drenched in the rising heat, swaggered like a bantam rooster, hands on hips.

The monitor of No. 11, a good-looking Australian kid named Donnelly, had worked in the San Miguel brewery before the war. He called the boys to attention. *"Kiatska!"* Tal figured that Donnelly had brewed the bomber lotion Remy'd brought to the infirmary.

Tal came to attention with the others. Nagata's lip curled in distaste. He said, *"Komatta yatsura."*

The tall guard interpreted. "Naughty children."

Nagata pointed behind him, across the camp and beyond the wire, to the window in the third floor of the animal husbandry building.

"You rike? Huh?"

Somebody in the lines mimicked a farting noise. Quickly, Donnelly belted out the order to bow. *"Rei!"*

So that was why this roll call was being conducted by Nagata. He was on a victory tour after last night.

Tal looked to the girl's window. No trace of her red robe had appeared in the window all morning.

Everyone stood bent at the waist, face to the earth. Tal bowed last.

"Ahhh," Nagata purred, noticing him. "Tuck-san."

Tal kept his head down. Nagata's boots halted in the dirt in front of him.

Fingers ran across Tal's scabs. Nagata tapped lightly, testing them for hardness. Tal winced at the ground. He preferred the feel of Nagata's belt.

He readied himself for more of Nagata's viciousness, likely a smack across the back to break open the knitting wounds.

The guard's hand withdrew along with his boots. Strolling to the front of the formation, Nagata said, *"Wakatte kita ne,* Tuck-san."

The interpreter's voice followed. "I think you have learned, Mr. Tuck."

Tal held the bow, hands balled at his sides, until Donnelly released No. 11 with the shout, *"Yosume!"*

When Tal came erect, his eyes rested on the girl in her red robe standing in her third-floor window. Both arms went over her chest, crossing to her own shoulders. She stood like this, wrapped in herself, touching Tal's wounded places on her own flesh, while Nagata watched the ninety-six young men count out, calling their number in line and *"Ai!"* for "present."

When they were done, Nagata and the guards strutted to No. 12, where Remy waited. Tal caught his father's eye. Remy gave him the okay sign. When he looked back to her perch, the girl was gone.

A half hour later, with the roll call completed, the internees moved into their barracks for the morning meal. Tal took his ticket and waited in line. He received a plate of mush made from three-quarters corn meal, the rest rice; many of the boys in the barracks, even the thinnest ones, had developed a protruding rice belly. Every scoop of gruel was eyed jealously by the next in line to see that equal portions were meted out. Tal ate alone. Many of his barracks mates dropped by to tell him they were glad to see him up and around.

Staring out a window, Tal licked his finger to scoop up the last grains. The camp was sunlit and half dead. Much had changed in the past six months. Things that had helped keep drudgery at bay had been canceled by the guards or quit for lack of energy. No more softball games, Sunday concerts, theater shows, debates in Baker Hall. Nagata had confiscated all Red Cross relief packets and turned away every effort of the local Filipinos to help feed the internees. The few camp doctors estimated they were down to less than a thousand calories a day, not enough to sustain normal activity.

Fresh out of his bunk, Tal wouldn't have to resume his chores in the repair department until tomorrow. He could sit in the shade with everyone else. He could watch himself dying.

He turned from the window and left the barracks. Next door, Tal entered the dining room of No. 12. McElway sat finishing his own puny breakfast. The man shook his head, for Tal to speak with him outside.

In the open yard, McElway sauntered up slowly, a sore hitch in his step.

"All right," Tal said. "I don't give a damn. I'll do it."

"What you angry about?"

"Don't worry about it. I'll go."

McElway rubbed the back of his neck. "Naw, that ain't gonna do."

"What do you mean?"

"I don't want you to go if you don't give a damn. You got to care, 'cause you got to get back safe."

"I will."

"Now you see, that's just young and dumb talkin' right there. No, I don't need no hero tryin' to prove somethin'. I need what's waitin' for me in that ravine. A man who wants to live is the man gon' bring me that back." McElway scuffed the dirt with his toe. "I want to live. You bet." He seemed sad, resigned to something.

"I'm all right, Mac. I can do it. I'll be safe."

The old piano player dug a finger into Tal's chest above his heart.

"Let me tell you somethin'. I done a few things in my life I regret. Yeah, I played in a bordello, and I drank some. And I done some other things I ain't sayin', 'cause they over with. Now you look at me straight and tell me sendin' you under that wire ain't gonna be one more thing I feel bad about."

"It won't be."

"It best not. My conscience has got all it can handle."

The old man grinned, his cheerless mood disappeared as quickly as it had come on him.

"All right. After midnight. In the ravine behind the infirmary. Someone from Terry's Hunters will be waitin'. You get it, you hide it, and you bring it to me outside the shithouse tomorrow morning, same time as we met today."

"All right."

"And you gon' like the password."

"What is it?"

McElway raised both long, dark arms and waved them, as if flying.

"Superman."

Tal had nothing to trade for a cigarette. He spent the first half of his day trying to steal one. He came up empty, so went to Remy in the shade of the dao tree to have him win one.

His father asked, "Just one?"

"That's all I need."

"What for?"

"Settle my nerves."

"You ain't the nervous type."

"Let me know when you get it. I'll owe you."

"You don't owe me. I'll handle it."

In the afternoon, Remy found Tal in his bunk. He handed over a wrinkled Lucky Strike and sat on the bunk next to Tal's.

"I hope you enjoy this. It cost me most of a coconut to get it."

"Thanks."

"You're in the rack a little early today. You all right?"

"Just resting up. Staying out of the sun."

"Restin' for what?"

"Nothing."

Remy poked out his lower lip. "All right. Hey, what were you and Mac talkin' about this morning?"

"Women."

Remy laughed. "That's good. He's got me beat in that department. Maybe after he tells you what he knows, you'll let me in on some of the good stuff."

"Sure."

His father curled his nose, sniffing. "I can win you some soap next."

"Soon as these scabs let me shower, I'll use it."

Remy patted him on the arm, then stood. "That'll make us even for the cigarette. I'll see you."

Tal tucked the Lucky Strike under his pillow. He stayed in the bunk until late in the day, dozing to be alert that night. At 4:30, he emerged for supper, the only other meal of the day.

In line, he accepted a half-pint bowl of stewed green papayas, *kamote* tops, garlic, onions, and a dash of salt. Meat was available only two days a week; tonight was not one of them. Onto his plate, the server plopped a dipper of *lugao* and another of slimy *talinum* greens. Again, Tal tried to eat his meal alone, but was joined by Donnelly and five other boys from No. 11.

"Tuck," the Australian said, sitting, "no worries, but could you put on a shirt for meals? You're hard enough to look at without those." Donnelly rotated a finger over Tal's shoulders.

One of Tal's roommates, Santana, a rangy Filipino-American whose father was a prisoner on Bataan, piped up. "Did you hear that fart noise I made at roll call?"

Everyone at the table snickered. Donnelly said, "I thought you'd shit yourself." Tal added, "So did Nagata."

After supper, he walked the perimeter of the camp, as close to the wire as the guards would allow. He passed the dao tree, and the overgrown plot where the internees had kept their garden until the Japanese made them stop. The Protestant chapel stood empty. He stopped at the infirmary to have a nurse examine his shoulders. While he waited, he wandered to the rear of the one-story building, to glance out a window at the spot where he would cross tonight. A back corner of the infirmary hid the fence from one guard tower; six-foot-high cogon grass masked it from the other. Outside the fence, a bamboo grove ran all the way to the deep ravine. Tal turned away when the nurse called for him.

She admired the progress of his scabs. The weeping had almost stopped, and they were thickening despite the poor nutrition in the camp. Tal figured this was Remy's doing, the odd bits of food his father snookered from others and brought him.

Leaving the infirmary, he counted the number of Japanese patrolling the fence tonight. He measured the distance between them, their level of attentiveness. He'd have thirty seconds between guards, no more. At ten o'clock, the camp would go into blackout. His enemies after midnight would be the clear night sky, a quarter moon, a careless footstep.

Before returning to his bunk, Tal strolled on the asphalt strip directly beneath the girl's window, next to the wire. He'd never dared this before, walking the same path as the guards. Set against what he intended to do that night, this act seemed tame. A guard saw him and threatened with his rifle. Tal cast a wish up to her empty window, that she might find it when she returned. He veered off the tarmac, back into the camp.

He passed the garage, ice plant, and butcher shop. Strolling into the Vatican, he found the Catholic chapel quiet. Sundown services hadn't started. The ladies nodded and smiled, the men inclined their heads. Though the missionaries, nuns, and priests were as spindly as anyone in Los Baños, they seemed to have something extra in their systems, as if they could eat God. Tal considered returning for the evening mass before heading under the wire hours later, just to sit outside the chapel and listen.

Walking out of the Vatican, he decided he would just lay in his bunk and wait. Like his father the gambler, Tal would try fate in his own way.

With the sun long down, Tal took the Lucky Strike from under his pillow. He stuck the cigarette between his fingers and walked out of the barracks as if in search of a light. He ignored a call from a boy who had a match.

Tal made his way between buildings to the kitchen. Amid the married quarters, he heard through windows mothers putting children down, fathers making up bedtime stories, elder couples coughing. One old husband insisted his wife eat the last of some beans. "I'll be fine," he said. "They're for you."

The camp loudspeaker announced the approaching curfew and lights out by playing "Chasing Shadows" by the Dorsey Brothers. Tal looked to the stars to ask if this was an omen.

The kitchen was the largest of all the structures Tal and the eight hundred had built at Los Baños. Chopping tables, shelves, and cool storage filled more than half the interior space; the rest was given over to a half dozen fire pits built of cinderblock. Above each hung a metal pipe for a vent; Remy in the blacksmith's shop had forged these. Cauldrons and griddles dangled on chains from iron rods driven into the earth.

In each pit, coals smoldered. The fires would not be allowed to go out overnight, for the breakfast cooks arrived before dawn. Tomorrow's cordwood was stacked in a corner. The fire tender, Mr. Kolko, stood from his seat on the firewood. He'd been a rubber engineer in Manila. Three years ago, with the Japanese closing in on Manila, Mr. Kolko held a ticket on the SS *Corregidor* departing the city. The boat, scheduled to leave at midnight, sailed two hours early because the captain was afraid of the nightly air raids. Kolko didn't arrive in time to take his berth. The ship wove without escort through the minefields of Manila Bay. An hour out from the quay, she struck a mine. Split in two, she went down in minutes with a thousand passengers and crew. Because of this reprieve, Mr. Kolko, of all the internees in Los Baños, was an affable man.

"Master Tuck," he said, "you know that no one's allowed in here at night."

Tal held up the cigarette. "Yes, sir. But it's kind of impossible to find a light anymore. You mind?"

"Oh, sure. Go ahead. Your shoulders are looking a darn sight better, I'd say. Still smarting?"

"Like the dickens. I'm managing."

"Good for you."

Tal reached into one of the pits. He selected a long, well-charred stake. He brought the glowing tip of it to the cigarette on his lips.

"I might apply for this job." Tal ambled along the row of hanging pots.

"It's quiet. Calls for a lot of discipline. Staying awake, I mean."

What Kolko meant to say was that being alone in the kitchen at night took discipline not to steal. Tal overlooked the slight, in light of his own reputation as a thief, though he'd never filch a thing from any internee.

Tal carried the smoking stake with him. He used it to bang each hanging cauldron. Good-natured and laughing,

Kolko chased him out of the kitchen still holding the burnt stick.

Outside, Tal finished the cigarette. The loudspeaker announced the 10:00 p.m. blackout. He rolled the hot stake in the dirt to put out the last embers. Dodging attention, he hurried to the latrine beside No. 11. Beneath the toilets, in a dark recess, he stowed the blackened stick. He rummaged in a nearby garbage can for an empty tin. He washed this in the shower room, filled the container with water, and left it under the latrine next to the stake. Tal joined the last stragglers into the barracks.

From his trunk, he donned khaki shorts and set out an olive undershirt. He lay awake while his roommates clambered into their racks one at a time. Donnelly, the barracks monitor, was the last in the building to settle after checking every cubicle. When the barracks had sunk into a hushed chorus of snores and mutters, Tal rolled from his bunk.

Grabbing his sneakers and shirt, he crept outside to squat in the shadows at the foot of the latrine. The camp in blackout burned electric lights only in scattered buildings, the chapels, the infirmary, kitchen, and soldiers' quarters. An early moon hung low over the jungle; stars winked. Fifty yards away, directly in front of Tal, a guard patrolled the fence, rifle strapped to his back. The next soldier would be eighty strides ahead, another the same distance behind. Tal waited in the shadow of the latrine, breath held, slotting himself into the rhythms and motions of the nocturnal camp. He cooled his nerves to surrender himself to the task, relaxing his hands. He had to piss, the same sudden need that had welled up when Nagata bound his hands before his beating. Again he forced the urge aside, thinking this a signal of fear. Tal could not see the girl's third-floor window from where he hid. He imagined her resting, and resolved not to wake her tonight. He pulled on the drab shirt, then scooped up the stake from beneath the latrine.

With fast hands, he broke off bits of charcoal, ground them between his palms. He rubbed the black dust up and down his bare arms and legs, across his face and ears, the back of his neck. When he was finished, he tested his newly ebon skin in the shadows. Tal was pleased. He'd become night.

He drew a deep breath and hunched close to the earth, ready to go, gripping the black stake. The guard walked farther along the fence, off into the darkness. Tal counted to fifteen to mark the moment when he could move halfway between the patrolling guards.

Carrying the stick, he left the cover of the latrine. Months ago, the grounds between barracks had been well maintained, weeds cropped close. With the waning strength of the internees, the trails and grasses grew neglected. Tal moved off the path to slide through the careless brush.

Leapfrogging shadows, ducking and patient, he wound through the married barracks, past the commandant's office. At the kitchen, he peered in a window to see Mr. Kolko snoozing on his firewood stack. A chin of moon had risen in the east. Sweat trickled down Tal's brow. Worried that his cinder mask might be washing off, he smeared his face again with char. For the first time since leaving his bunk, Tal sprinted.

He reached the barbed wire behind the infirmary without noise. Setting one sneaker on the bottom strand, he pressed down with his full weight to gather as much slack as possible. The rusty wire stretched and sagged. Tal propped up the wire with the stake, then, flat on his back, shimmied under the barbs, scraping his scabs. He cleared the strand by less than an inch. On his knees on the other side, he yanked loose the stake. Five steps later, he used the same technique to slide under the second wire barrier.

Tal stood, free in the world for the first time in three years.

He tasted the air and found it heavy with scent and invitation. The earth ran farther than he could endure.

He could disappear, join the resistance. He could find food.

He was on her side of the wire.

Tal stowed all this away, because he had given Mac his word. He would have these possibilities again. He headed into the bamboo grove and tall grass.

Moving with cautious moonlit steps, Tal considered how easily he'd made it out of the camp. Los Baños wasn't built as a prison for soldiers but was designed as a holding pen for civilians. Where would the internees go if they got loose? The Japanese controlled the entire island. No westerner could blend in with the Filipinos. Any escapee found outside the camp would be shot on sight. The only safety, uncertain as it was, existed inside the wire.

Tal crept through the tall grass until he found the edge of the deep ravine. Palm trees growing out of the steep bank leaned their fronds over the creek bed. Rounded stones lined the bottom; stars shimmered in still pools between the rocks. Tal picked his way down the slope, clinging to scrub to keep from slipping.

He selected a boulder to crouch behind. Tuning his ears up and down the channel, he keyed his ears for footfalls on the pebbles, or a splash in a puddle. He bored his eyes into the dark and stayed hidden. No longer afraid, he urinated quietly into the bank.

Tal became aware of the creatures prowling the ravine. Bats fluttered low, hunting the bugs that pestered him behind his boulder. The old owl the camp listened to every night switched trees many times and hooted from different branches. Something—a village dog, a big rat, a porcupine—scrambled across the creek bed. A fruit bat with a wingspan longer than Tal's arms swooped through the trees.

"Password."

The voice made Tal jump. It came almost from beside his ear. He saw no one.

"Superman," he whispered.

A brown Filipino, thick as a wrestler, leaned out of the bank, almost on the spot where Tal had relieved himself. The guerrilla seemed to have merged with the plants and rocks, then shed them for his own form.

He put forth a hand, Tal shook it. The guerrilla wore no camouflage or face paint, just a shirt, shorts, boots. Standing right in front of Tal, he was hard to see.

"Emilio," he said. "Terry's Hunters."

"Tal." He hesitated, wanting some unit to put with his name, too. "Barracks Eleven."

"Where's old McElway?"

"He couldn't come. Not feeling well."

"I like him. He has good *pagkatao,* spirit. Tell him Emilio said to feel better. Give him this."

The guerrilla handed over a folded envelope, taped shut. Tal rolled it between his fingers to feel the contents. Small, a cylinder, probably glass.

The guerilla said, "Put it away."

Tal slid the envelope into his pocket.

Emilio said, "Good luck." He turned to go, donning blackness in his first step away.

"That's it?"

Emilio halted. This was the first Filipino that Tal had spoken with in months. He wanted news of the war, perhaps to send a message to the girl, to say or hear something intrepid to take back inside the barbed wire. The guerrilla gazed back with silent eyes as if out of a cave. Tal took Emilio's cue and turned away. He heard only his own passage across the ravine's stones.

Reaching the outer fence, Tal paused in the grass until the next guard strolled past. Again, he used the stake to hoist the barbed wire, shimmying on his back inches below it. Scabs opened inside his shirt. He grunted, coming to his feet between the fences. Tal jammed the stake under the final wire, with only twenty seconds left until the next guard rounded the corner of the infirmary. To spare his shoulders, Tal lay on his belly squirming back into the camp.

He hurried, without the same caution he'd used leaving the camp. He kicked his foot behind him in the dirt to crawl the last distance under the wire. His sneaker nicked the stake, jarring it loose. The strand snapped down, rattling against the concrete pillars. A hissing twang shot in both directions.

Voices rose from the main gate forty yards to his left, *"Asoko da!"* and the guard tower beside the infirmary, thirty yards to his right, *"Nan daro?"*

The clatter of weapons and boots hastened his way.

Tal jumped from the dirt, ignoring the stick. He didn't know where to run. He could dash into the infirmary. But the place was well lit and he was covered in charcoal. What if a guard saw him? He had to make it back to his barracks.

Shouts swelled around him. Tal had to move, somewhere. He hurtled away from the fence toward the nearest barracks. Maybe he could slip inside, find someone to hide him until he could clean up. Then if he were caught out after curfew, at least he could deny going anywhere near the fence and the charred log that would betray him. Tal reached the shadows of the building and caught his breath, got his bearings. He crept toward the doorway.

Voices rose from behind the infirmary. The Japanese had seen the stick between the two fences, and they now knew someone had snuck under the wire. Would they figure out that someone had crawled *back in*? That might buy him a few minutes.

Easing beneath a window, a child cried out over his head. Tal cursed himself. He'd gone under the wire to even the score with Nagata, prove he wasn't broken by the bastard's belt. He couldn't ask the folks inside to join him in that. Anyone caught concealing him would risk the same punishment, and it would be severe. Tal searched, fighting a mounting dread. The Protestant chapel, the commandant's office, the kitchen, all had lights glowing. The rest of the camp remained dark.

He took Mac's envelope from his pocket should he have to get rid of it on the run.

No general alarm had been sounded yet. Tal tamped down his breathing to hear himself think. He had to come up with the next move. The guards were spreading around the camp, alerted out of their normal patrol routes. Some hunted outside the wire behind the infirmary while others scanned the grounds inside. With them wandering all over like this, there wasn't a clear path back to No. 11. Tal crouched, undetected but stymied.

Someone leaped down the back steps of the kitchen. The figure scampered to a neighboring barracks, where it skidded to hunker in the shadows like Tal. What was going on? Why was someone else out in the night? Had McElway sent two? This made no sense. Tal felt caught up in something larger than he'd bargained for, and this frightened him more. He tried to recognize the silhouette.

A crash, like gunfire, erupted inside the kitchen. Then another, and a series of loud cracks sent the other runner bolting into the dark.

Who was this? Did he cause the explosions? Tal had no time to unravel it, and no choice. The guards ran toward the clanging kitchen, rifles ready. Inside, Kolko careened back and forth, confused by the bangs popping on all sides of him. Tal shot to his feet, clutching the envelope. Relying on the sharp bursts for cover, with the guards flocking to the kitchen and dazed Kolko, Tal raced for No. 11.

He darted past buildings with sleepy faces in the windows, roused by the commotion. Tal hoped that his charcoal disguise and speed would keep him anonymous in the dark to those who saw him. No one spoke. Many of the heads disappeared, with the internees' instinct to avoid trouble. Behind him, the cracks from the kitchen stopped. Tal barreled the last distance. Huffing, he dived into the shadows of the latrine attached to his barracks.

He rolled to his back, ignoring the pain across his shoulders, amazed at his luck, good and bad. Someone had saved him. Those detonations out of the kitchen had been set, *timed*, to distract the guards. Who'd done it? Not McElway. The runner was too spry. Mac had sent him, no question. Tal intended to take it up with the old man in the morning. It was going to be hard to complain that Mac hadn't trusted Tal to pull it off. He almost blew it. Still, it stung having to be bailed out of trouble that his own clumsiness got him into.

Tal could not lie here and savor being alive. A standing rule had cropped up in Los Baños: whenever something in the camp was amiss, the guards headed to No. 11.

He scooted under the latrine for the water can he'd left there. Tugging off his dirty shirt, he scrubbed the charcoal from his skin, then rolled the tin far beneath the latrine. The shirt doubled as a towel.

Bare-chested, Tal crept up the steps into the barracks. Donnelly met him in the doorway. "Out for a stroll?"

"I wanted to see what all the noise was."

"Yeah," Donnelly smiled. "A bloody lot of banging around this time of night. Any ideas?"

"Nope."

Tal dodged around Donnelly to head for his bunk.

"Hey, Tuck?"

"What."

"Why do you smell like a campfire?"

Tal froze without an answer, only for a moment.

"I stopped by the kitchen tonight. Helped Mr. Kolko stoke the pits."

"Yeah, that must be it."

"Donnelly?"

"Yeah."

"Why've you got grass stains on your knees?"

The Australian grinned, without looking down at himself. "Praying, mate. Praying for all of us. G'night."

Donnelly walked off to his rack, Tal to his. He tossed the shirt under his bunk and lay down his head.

His roommates made no sound. They were obviously awake.

In the bunk over his head, Santana whispered, "Hey, Jesse Owens is back."

His roommates tried to stifle their giggles. Tal listened, incredulous and scared at how little could be kept secret inside Los Baños.

Five guards arrived with kerosene lanterns and bamboo sticks to roust the boys. They made only a cursory search, not sure what they were looking for. They found nothing, and heard only more fart noises.

After the guards withdrew, Tal's adrenaline ebbed. He lay awake for hours with jungle caws and hoots floating to his window. He built vivid images in his head, of great gliding wings, snuffling creatures, and Emilio.

Once he closed his eyes, the clamp on his fear came off. Tal had not been as frightened running through the camp as he was now safe in his bed, reliving what might have happened. When he slept, it was fitful.

He awoke in the early morning tired but with lifted

spirits. In the half-light, he considered that he had, in fact, come through all right. The boys around him knew that he'd gone under the wire, certainly Donnelly had told them. They could be trusted. They'd know he'd pulled off some dangerous thing. Tal would not talk about it, and that would fan the story even more.

He pushed aside the mosquito netting to go meet Mac. He tapped his pocket, checking for the envelope. Again he was tempted to probe it, but resisted as Mac had told him to.

Outside, the old man waited by the latrine. Beside him stood Remy.

Tal stopped. Mac waved him over. Only a few were up and about, all of them paying attention elsewhere.

When Tal came close, Mac waggled a finger. "Before you jump down my throat, your daddy knows."

"Knows what?"

"What's in your pocket."

Remy kept quiet, hands behind his back.

Tal said, "How come he can know and I can't? I'm the one who went outside to get it."

Mac jerked a thumb at Remy. "And he's the one who saw to it your ass got back in. You best thank him."

Tal asked Remy, "What did you do?"

His father shrugged. "I asked Donnelly to watch out for you. He got your roommates to keep an eye on you, too. Donnelly followed you through the camp last night. When he saw the guards headed your way, he snuck into the kitchen and tossed some bamboo bombs into the fires."

Mac chuckled, cavalier, white of tooth and gums. "Everybody knows ol' Kolko don't stay awake. Anyways . . ." The old man held out a hand. "You made it and here you are. Thank you. Now, let's have it."

Tal cupped the envelope in his palm. He felt ambushed and cheated that Remy was involved and knew what was in the envelope. Remy had doubted that Tal could do the job on his own. He'd arranged Donnelly to be backup. Remy had saved the day.

Tal passed the envelope over. Remy put out a hand, too.

"You did a good job. Put 'er there."

Tal did not take his father's mitt.

McElway wagged his head. "You got no call to be that way to him. He done nothin' wrong. It was me. I asked your daddy if I could send you."

"You what? You asked *him* for permission?"

"Yes I did. What you expect a man to do? I ain't gon' risk a man's son without his say-so."

"What's in the envelope, Mac?"

"You lookin' at the only two people in this camp know what it is. It's gon' stay that way. For your own protection."

"You weren't too worried about my protection last night."

Remy spoke. "All right. You're done."

Tal walked off. Again, he had no inkling which way to go inside the bounds of the wire, only that he could not go far enough.

yasegaman—"emaciated endurance," referring to spiritual and physical purity; a core virtue of the samurai

the holidays, shovels, and
Camp Freedom

Chapter Seven

C HRISTMAS MORNING, Carmen accepted her small bowl of rice. She set it on the bedside table and stood in front of it, so Mama could not take it back.

"I won't do it," she said.

"Yes, you will. The little *chosenjin* will, too. You'll both go."

Mama was right. Choice·in Carmen's life had become rare, like food.

"Get out before I slap you."

The old *makipili* considered Carmen. "Will you, now?"

"Stay and find out."

"You lack trouble in your life, Songu? Hmm?"

Carmen held her ground.

"Well, I do not," Mama said. "Be ready in five minutes."

Carmen ate her rice sitting on the mattress, avoiding the window. She did not want to be seen by the boy this day.

She had little preparation. She dressed in her cast-off soldier's uniform, the only clothing she possessed beyond her *haori*, and laced her black sneakers.

Buttoning the tunic, Carmen no longer sensed the un-named soldier who'd worn this uniform. Her first days in the *shuho*, she'd wondered if he'd been killed. When Papa had tossed her the outfit, she checked it for holes or blood, finding none. For months she loathed the absent solider as much as any of those present who used her. His ghost touch was as close as theirs. She tried to launder him away. Then days ago, without expecting it, the soldier in the khaki was gone. This happened the morning after Nagata disgraced Carmen in front of the window. Not just the soldier in the cloth but all the Japanese and the *makipilis* were gone to her. Her quiet hatred seemed to have withdrawn, as if it were not enough. It cooled into something harder, nothingness. She'd begun to act in temperamental and fearless ways, like the threat just now to give Mama a *binta*. This had happened to Hua, Carmen understood. The Chinese girl had lost her fear of death and she'd acted, against herself.

Carmen slid aside the curtain to wait in the hall outside her door. She stroked the black drape. The curtain was her captor, too, for it hid what happened in this room. She bunched the fabric and yanked, to pull it down. The drape and rod resisted. Carmen readied to pull again, just to break something. Corporal Kenji arrived at the top of the stairs.

Kenji, already thin and pale, seemed a scarecrow when he looked down the hall at her. He went first to the opposite wing to collect the Korean girl. Carmen let the curtain unfurl from her hand, accepting the uselessness of pulling it down.

Kenji returned to the landing with Yumi. The girl also wore sneakers and a tossed-off khaki uniform too large for her. In the three days since the girl had come to the *shuho,* Carmen and she had little time together. During the day they were allowed outside at different times, and at night one or both lay with officers. Twice, Carmen had watched Commandant Toshiwara come to Yumi after nightfall.

The two girls followed Kenji past Mama. The old woman turned over the wooden tags for Songu and Yumi, 歌 and 弓.

Carmen walked down the stairs beside Yumi. The Korean girl stood no higher than Carmen's chin, but there was little delicate or timid about her. At the bottom of the stairs, leaving the building's rear door, the girl swung her arms in her gait, mocking the uniform she wore, and bounced in her sneakers. She seemed merry, on an excursion. Carmen marveled at how unfazed Yumi was; the girl could not have understood what was happening. Even so, Yumi's mood infected Carmen. She joined the girl in an exaggerated march behind Kenji.

The soldier turned on them. "Stop it," he said to Carmen. "Others will see." At Yumi, he barked, *"Yamate!"*

Kenji led them to the main gate. Carmen made a point of looking into the eyes of every guard she passed, so they could view her on her feet and not her back.

A car and driver waited. She climbed in the rear beside Yumi and rode away from the camp. Carmen left the place and the Tuck boy behind. He could not come today, he would not see. She would do this without him.

Little Yumi took her hand.

"Kenji-sama?" Carmen asked.

The soldier turned from the front seat. His spare face and drawn lips expressed his shame.

"Do not ask me to stop this. I can't. The order came from Toshiwara. Even he was given an order."

"I want to ask you something."

"Yes."

"What does the symbol on her name tag mean?"

"It is an archery bow."

"Will you ask her a question for me?"

"Yes. One."

"What is her real name?"

He spoke to her in Japanese. Yumi replied, her glance flitting between Kenji and Carmen.

Kenji said, "Her birth name is Yun Soo Min. She says it means cleverness and excellence."

The Korean girl reeled off more fluent Japanese. Kenji's face curdled. The driver grunted over his shoulder. Yumi finished and smiled.

Kenji said, "She says the bastards who conquered her land made her take the Japanese name Yumi. It means 'helpful beauty.' She says this is not likely."

Kenji muttered something on his own to Yumi. When he finished, he turned to face forward.

Carmen asked at his back, "What did you say?"

Kenji answered. "I told her I was sorry, there was nothing I could do. And to mind her tongue."

The car headed east toward the sun. Yumi kept Carmen's hand in her lap. The road wove through villages and towns Carmen had never seen. She'd not been farther than the outskirts of Manila before she was taken to Los Baños, and during her time in the *shuho* had not once left the camp. The road ran through uncut forests, alongside paddies dried up or weeded over, past farmlands barely worked. Carmen could see plainly that the Japanese had brought much of the hunger on themselves. Only a few carabaos and mules plowed the fields, no cattle grazed. The Japanese must have taken the animals from the farms for their own labor or tables. Only a smattering of peasants worked the soil. Carmen assumed the rest had been jailed or killed, or driven into the resistance. Not one young girl walked free in the villages.

Twenty kilometers from Los Baños, the driver pulled to the shoulder at a sign for the village ahead, Rizal.

Carmen took her hand from Yumi. She reached around the girl's shoulders to hug her. Yumi laid her head against Carmen's breast and Carmen kissed the back of her dark hair.

The driver gestured into the backseat, sweeping his hand across the girls.

"*Ike!*"

Yumi got out, Carmen followed. Kenji spoke to the driver. The men argued while Carmen and Yumi waited beside the road. After heated words, Kenji joined the girls outside the car. The driver reversed his course and motored away.

"I will stay with you," Kenji said.

The three stood on the shoulder, staring into the village. Carmen became thirsty. Yumi kicked stones into the ditch.

Carmen touched Kenji's arm. "Thank you."

He would not look at her.

"Will you ask her another question for me?"

"No." The tall corporal raised a hand. "Listen."

From the village a hundred yards away came a sound of crunching. In seconds the noise grew louder, a horde coming their way, the din of boots on the tarmac.

"It's time," said Kenji.

The Korean girl moved first. She peeled the khaki tunic over her head, then dropped her overlarge pants. She was bare in seconds, standing only in sneakers. Yumi rolled her clothes together and handed them to Kenji. She thrust her small breasts, her short muscular thighs, up the road to face the soldiers, like the archery bow of her symbol. Above the grind of the soldiers' approach, catcalls fluttered.

Yumi spoke to Kenji, then gestured to Carmen.

He interpreted. "She says it's too hot for a long walk in clothes. Come, sister."

Kenji turned his back to allow Carmen to strip. She thought this a naïve and wasted kindness.

Hesitating, Carmen undid the buttons of her tunic. She glanced down at her brown bosom. In the confines of the *shuho*, day after day, her body had been pummeled beneath the squalid and sour weight of the Japanese. She lived naked under her thinning red *haori* for weeks at a time. But this, in the sunshine, being forced to walk stripped in front of a thousand troops to draw them onward, she had built no calluses against this. She was Filipina. This road was her country. The villagers who would gawk were her people.

Naked, Yumi stepped in front of her. The girl lowered Carmen's motionless hands, replacing them with her own on the buttons. Gently, she disrobed Carmen, attending her emergence, folding the clothes. She gave them to Kenji. Carmen, like Yumi, remained in her sneakers.

The column of soldiers arrived, swarming all three of them on the road. Passing, they whistled, made guttural noises, some touched the girls.

"Walk," Kenji said. "Please."

All the soldiers were filthy and haggard, and some looked exhausted. Many appeared no older than Carmen, teenagers. This unit must have just landed on the coast. They were marching west across Luzon toward Los Baños, then probably on to Manila. Someone assumed they'd go more eagerly if they were shown that comfort women waited for them ahead.

Carmen faced into their current. The soldiers flowed past with hands sliding across her stomach and buttocks. One cupped her breast, shouting to his mates, *"Kurisumasu desu!"* It's Christmas.

Kenji gripped the girls' clothes. He repeated, "Please."

Again, Yumi took Carmen's hand.

Carmen and Yumi led the tired column. The men marched with no banners, cadence, or pomp, just scuffling soles. The girls walked quickly to stay out front, away from the soldiers' dirty hands. Kenji lagged one step behind them as a buffer. He, too, was an object of whistles and vulgarity, some of which Yumi found amusing and asked Kenji to translate for Carmen.

After the first two kilometers, they entered the village of San Lorenzo. The street remained empty; the citizens and their children peered from huts or the pitiful fields. Lined faces and silvered heads brought to mind Carmen's parents and her grandfather. They would not comprehend this if they saw. She could not run out of the procession to tell the watching people, I am not a whore, I am not disgraced. She drew her spine erect to explain herself, that she was a slave like them and humiliated like them, but she was not beaten. Beside her, Yumi, who had walked like this from the outset, nodded.

Word spread ahead of the column. In the next village, San Buenaventura, the road was lined with folk. Villagers held out cups of water to the girls. An old woman stepped into the road to spread a quilt across Carmen's bare shoulders. Carmen thanked her and handed the blanket back. Filipino men balled fists, called to her in Tagalog to stay strong, *"Lakasan mo ang loob mo,"* and we'll get even, don't worry, *"Makakaganti rin tayo, huwag kang mag-alala."* A few younger ones shouted, *"Hukbalahap,"* the name of a Communist guerrilla group.

Beyond San Buenaventura, into the eighth kilometer of the walk, the soldiers' fervor waned. The procession entered a long stretch of trees close by the road, killing the breeze. The tarmac grew warm, the march became a trudge forward. The girls' nakedness at the head of the column turned absurd. Carmen grew numb to the soldiers behind her and they, by their scraping boots and complaints, paid little attention in return. She shared the last of a bottle of water from the village with Yumi. The girl spared a swallow for Kenji. On Carmen's brown skin, the sun made no dent. She worried about Yumi's pallid complexion.

"Kenji."

"Yes."

"Lay her shirt across her shoulders. She's burning."

"I cannot."

Carmen stopped walking, the first time in an hour. She wheeled on Kenji to pull from him the girl's tunic. He did not resist. She covered Yumi's shoulders, then resumed the walk.

No one in the shuffling ranks behind them objected. Carmen left herself fully naked. Those with the stamina left to do so could gape at her alone.

"Carmen?"

She did not look at Kenji.

"What?"

"I want you to know. I am a good man. I am educated."

A bead of sweat dribbled between her breasts. The blue marks of chains around Yumi's ankles had not faded. Kenji's statement made no sense. Carmen did not judge him. He was Japanese. Nothing could alter that.

He continued. "When the war is over, I will save you."

You can only keep me alive, she thought. The Tuck boy can save me.

She asked, "Will you do me a favor?"

"If I can."

"I want you to translate to Yumi for me. I want to talk to her."

"About what?"

"I want to know where she's from. How she got to the *shuho*. And I want to tell her about me."

"But . . . do you have an answer for what I just said? That I will save you?"

"Why would you save a *pii*?"

"I've never called you that."

"No. You haven't." She touched his arm. "Will you talk to her for me?"

He looked back at the thousand soldiers. "Now?"

Carmen gestured at the blank road stretching on-ward. "I've got nothing on my hands at the moment." She laughed alone at the pun. "Yes, Kenji-sama. Now, if you please."

Yun Soo Min kept her name for her first five years. At age six, she told her mother she wanted to go to the school in their village of Kon Ham in North Cholla province. The mother agreed, but the father said that women who study become foxes. He did not know a letter of the alphabet or a single written symbol but he could thresh rice, drive an ox, and raise a family. The mother won out. When the child returned from the village on her first day of school, she told her father the Japanese teacher had ordered her to go by the name Yumi. The father slapped her and the mother.

Carmen asked if the girl had brothers. Yes, two older boys. Both were taken to Japan to work in war factories. She did not miss them, they were as ignorant and harsh as her father.

Would she rather be called Yumi or Soo Min?

Yumi was fine. One name was given by her father, the other by the Japanese. Neither was preferable.

How did she come to Los Baños?

Yumi corrected the way Kenji asked the question. He used the term *jugun ianfu,* for "comfort woman," a phrase Yumi would not accept. She said, "I am *gunyo sei dorei.* A military sex slave." Carmen, walking naked, was struck at how Kenji could translate these words without expression.

Yumi said that, for years, recruiters of young women roamed Korea. They claimed to be seeking volunteers, girls to travel to Japan for work in munitions factories, first for the war in Manchukuo, later for the fight against the Americans. Large advances of money were offered to families who sent their daughters to join the *jungshindae,* "voluntary female war workers." The girls would work off the payment and earn enough to live on their own.

Yumi wanted no part of this corps. She had no wish to see Japan as a laborer like her brothers, and even less desire to help her father gain a sum of cash he would likely squander. She wanted just to learn and one day teach others. Her father insisted she join; she was useless on the farm, too small and light to walk on the rice plants to separate the stalks from the grain. Even carrying her books from the Kon Ham school she did not weigh enough, he said. So she should go with the Japanese and help her family that way.

The *jungshindae* were shadowy, Yumi knew this. The recruiters searched for virgins, to be gifts to the emperor. Why should a virgin work better in a factory? Yumi had not even started her menstrual bleeding. To avoid the recruiters, she wore her hair in the style of a married woman, gathered at the back and secured with a long *pinyo,* hairpin. Without telling her parents, she accepted a marriage proposal from a very old man, figuring he would be her last resort.

One evening in the autumn, at the beginning of the school term, her father called her into the rice field. He put her in the ox cart and drove past the village to an inn with the smells of wood smoke and bitter kimchi swirling in the day's ending light. The inn was lit by electricity. Soldiers came and went. Yumi's father left her behind, saying he would return in two hours. She was to work for the innkeeper and bring home her pay.

The innkeeper put her in a tub of steaming water. The man's wife scrubbed Yumi, then gave her cotton underwear and a silk kimono. Yumi was left barefoot. The innkeeper ordered her into a room upstairs.

Inside sat a Japanese officer, dining alone on sake and dried squid. He patted the floor cushion beside him for Yumi to join him at the table.

Come, he said. We'll enjoy ourselves.

Yumi told him she did not know him, so how could she enjoy herself?

I am a Japanese soldier, and I have no one to talk with.

Then you should talk with Japanese people. I am Korean.

The man stood in front of Yumi.

Sit with me. It is an order.

I am not in the army.

He laid his hands on her shoulders.

But you are, he said.

The soldier was a fighter, he knew how to sweep Yumi's legs from beneath her in one move. He landed on top. He brought his face close as if to kiss. Yumi had never been kissed on the lips by a boy or a man, but she understood what was happening.

She did not waste effort screaming, the innkeeper and his wife would not help. She turned her face from his mouth. She kicked and flailed at him. He struck her across the face. Yumi had been hit her whole life by her father, so this did not slow her. She slapped the soldier flush across his own cheek. He took a fist to her.

Yumi could not stop him from spreading the kimono and dragging off her underpants. He climbed on top and stuck his *thing*—this was the English word Kenji used, though Carmen thought it needlessly delicate—into her. Yumi felt torn in half. The pain roused her enough to bite the officer's shoulder. He did nothing but pound himself into her harder.

The Japanese would not stop. Yumi decided that fighting him would only bring more pain. She chose stillness, flopping her arms and legs flat to the floor like a doll. The Japanese humped, grunting to his finish. Finally he pulled out and Yumi's body was her own again. It felt foreign to her, so different and ugly from what it had been only minutes before. He stood. Blood slicked his groin and smeared her thighs. He buckled his uniform in place. He drew back his boot as though to kick her, then left the room.

The innkeeper's wife brought a cup of tea.

Here you are, little one.

I want my father.

He will be back tomorrow. You stay here tonight.

Did the soldier pay you?

Yes. For the meal.

In the morning, Yumi was given back her clothes and taken to the village train station. She stood in a line with two dozen girls, all taller than her, most a few years older. The line moved toward the train. Black tar paper covered the windows. Yumi watched for her father to arrive to take her out of the line. A soldier at the head of the queue eyed the girls before choosing which darkened car they would climb into.

Manchukuo, he'd say to one. This girl went left and the soldier made a notation on his clipboard. Philippines, he'd say next, and that girl turned right.

Yumi reached the head of the line, heart leaping to her throat. My father, she said to the soldier with the clipboard.

Philippines, he said.

Surrounded by soldiers on the platform, Yumi could not run or fight. The old man she'd engaged herself to could not help, he didn't know she was here. In her panic she could not even recall his name. Yumi stepped aboard the train. She peeled back an edge of the black paper that sealed the window.

Her father appeared on the platform. He spoke to a soldier who handed him a rice-paper scroll, then he walked away. Yumi cursed her father like she had her body the night before; neither belonged to her now.

Traveling into the night, the train carried Yumi and ten girls west to the sea. Every one of them was from a poor village. They'd all been virgins, told they would be sent to Japan for factory work to repay a large loan made to their families. Each had been raped, some more than once, yesterday. After trading stories, they slept in one another's arms as if dissolved together by tears. In the morning, they boarded a cargo ship bound for Manila.

"Then," Carmen said to conclude Yumi's tale for her, "you came to Los Baños."

Yumi listened to Kenji's translation. She answered for herself in English.

"No."

Kenji's expression changed to surprise as he translated Carmen's inquiry. Where have you been? He shook his head with the girl's answer. "At the Round Pearl."

This was the biggest *shuho* in Manila. Carmen's father had spoken of it, of brisk morning coffee sales from his cart. The Round Pearl held more than a hundred girls, from every nation Japan had conquered plus trained prostitutes from Japan's Amakusa Islands.

How long was Yumi there?

A year. She celebrated her fourteenth birthday at the Round Pearl.

Carmen asked, "Why do you have bruises on your ankles?"

Yumi had tried to escape from the truck that brought her to Los Baños four days ago. She jumped from the back. Soldiers ran her down and hobbled her with ropes. But she was glad to be in Los Baños now. She had an *otosan,* a father figure, in Toshiwara. He promised he would look after Yumi. And a sister in Carmen.

The road to Los Baños entered a stretch of forest. The girls, Kenji, and the thousand soldiers walked in the shade. Yumi pulled down the tunic that had covered her while she told her tale. Instead of returning the shirt to Kenji, she spread it in a cape over Carmen's shoulders, tapping Carmen on her bare sternum to show that it was her turn to speak. Only the one listening would walk naked for the soldiers.

Carmen spoke. Kenji reversed his translation, turning her English words into Japanese for Yumi.

Carmen had not been tricked like Yumi by the Japanese. No money changed hands. She was Filipina, a citizen of a battleground country. Because the Japanese had fought for this land, they felt no need for petty deceptions. They simply kidnapped the young girls here. Carmen was seized from a street corner in Manila standing with her father at his *carinderia*. Her father resisted the soldiers and was beaten. Carmen begged them to take her and leave the old man alone. They did. The one who raped her that night at the police station was a member of the Kempeitai, the Japanese military police. He told Carmen that if she tried to escape, the Kempeitai would not look for her, they would come for her family, who were very easy to find.

Listening, Yumi's features fell in more sadness than when she'd told her own tale. Carmen's father had fought and suffered blows to protect his daughter. Yumi's father had sold his child away.

Carmen swept the tunic off her shoulders. She handed it to Kenji. Both girls walked naked again. Carmen took Yumi by the hand.

In the town of Calauan, the soldiers fell out for rest and water. Kenji handed the girls their rolled-up clothes. He walked off to find the commanding officer of the troops. Carmen and Yumi dressed.

The sun rode high in a clear noon sky. The little town had been decorated for Christmas. Evergreen wreaths hung on many doors, candles burned in windows. A life-size crèche had been built in the center of town. Soldiers went to it and threw Mary and Jesus in his crib from the shade of the stable. Soldiers took their places on the cool straw.

Kenji returned. "It's enough," he said. "We can go. We'll flag down a truck on the road."

The three walked toward the edge of town. Tired soldiers called rude farewells. Carmen told Kenji she would ask at a hut for some food and water.

"No."

"Why, Kenji-sama?"

"You're not allowed to have contact with locals. You know this."

"What I know is that Yumi and I are thirsty and you have no water to give us."

Carmen chose a house. She left Kenji and Yumi to knock on the door beside humble sprigs of holiday pine. An old woman answered. She cocked an eye past Carmen to Kenji standing in the road with the Korean girl.

"Paano ako makakatulong sayo," the woman asked warily. How can I help you?

Carmen answered in Tagalog. "May we have something to eat? And some water. We have been walking for four hours."

"Are you whores?"

"No. We are captives at the Los Baños camp."

The old woman crossed herself. "I've heard of this." She turned to shout into the hut. "Benito!"

A scrawny teen boy poked out his head. The woman waved a hand at him, to make him hurry. *"Magsalok ka ng tubig at longganisa."* Fetch water and sausages.

Carmen said, "Thank you."

"Nothing. At the camp, you give the soldiers sex?"

"We don't give, old woman. They take."

"Forgive me."

In moments, Benito hustled around the corner with a jug of water and three brown links on wax paper. The smell of pork set Carmen's mouth watering; the rarity of the gift ignited a regret for her sharp tone with the woman.

"You are kind," Carmen said.

The old Filipina handed over the jug and sausages. "What is your name?"

"Carmen."

"Carmen, do you talk with the soldiers?"

"No."

The woman smiled. Behind her, little Benito grinned, too. Before the old woman shut the door, she said, *"Ulitin mo."* Start.

Chapter Eight

REMY SHEATHED his bolo. He squatted on the mossy earth to pour his canteen over his head. Two others quit work when he did and sat with him in the shade on the soft ferns. The guard Ito turned his attention to the forty-five men in the firewood detail who were not taking a break.

Keppinger, on one side of Remy, panted heavily. He'd run a dairy business on Bataan before the war.

"Son of a bitch," he lamented. "I can't draw a full breath."

The other fellow, the journalist Owen, agreed, shaking his head. "I'll tell you. Next they'll be sending a hundred of us out here. I'm weaker'n a kitten."

The talk referred to a decree two months ago by the Internee Committee doubling the number of workers on all heavy details, like logging. The poor nutrition and failing health of the camp were responsible. Because the men often sacrificed food for their wives and children, they suffered more. Last week the doctors issued a report declaring that every internee of Los Baños had intestinal worms. The men of the camp could not work like men, another blow to their pride and willpower. As Remy saw it, the struggle was not just to stay alive but to stave off becoming submissive, as the Japanese wanted to make them.

Remy took a few swallows, then capped his canteen. Ito limped across the jungle floor, which was littered with brush and branches shaved from the logs. The cart groaned, almost full. In the traces, Toshiwara's bull complained with every switch on the rump to drag the sled onward.

Remy watched Ito. The guard was one of the many Japanese in Los Baños to have seen combat, a veteran of the Chinese campaign and Burma. He'd been known to show off his scars from bullets lodged in his hip and shoulder, or the one that had creased his chin. On all sides of Ito, internees sawed at trees, split them into cordwood, tossed the logs into the cart. The guard took down his cap to run a sleeve across his brow.

Remy rose from his haunches and backed away. Owen hissed, "What're you doing?"

Remy raised a finger to hush him. Keppinger waved Remy back to the ground, whispering, "You're gonna get us all *binta*-ed. And you're gonna get shot. Damn it, sit down."

Ignoring them, Remy slipped away from the detail. His gambler's instinct told him this was a play he could make. Ito was a proud soldier, pawned off to Los Baños as broken goods with his limp. He might turn a blind eye to disobedience so long as the infraction was not done in his face. Still, Remy could only risk being gone for a minute. Keppinger and Owen slid closer together, to close the gap where Remy had been.

Staying low, he ducked into the thick brush. Pulling out his bolo, Remy hacked through the overgrowth to a spot he'd kept his eye on all morning, waiting to get near enough to sneak off. The forests around the campus brimmed with fruits and berries; before the war, the university had been one of the Philippines' experimental agricultural stations. In the first two years of the camp, the Japanese let the internees feed themselves from the coconuts, mangoes, cassavas, and bananas, the bounty growing wild within easy reach of the camp. This stopped when Nagata arrived.

Remy folded to his knees, finding his object. He filled his pockets with tiny wild tomatoes, red and wasted out here in the woods. He told himself to quit picking once his pockets began to bulge, but couldn't stop. He crammed many into his mouth.

When he'd stashed as many tomatoes as possible in his pants and tunic, even filling his fedora before screwing it back on his head, he spun behind him for the other prize he'd spotted. With the bolo, he dug beneath several green stalks topped with yellow flowers. He ripped them out of the earth, then cut away the gingerroots. Remy ate several more tomatoes to make room for them.

Crouching, he scampered back to the logging site. He crept up behind Owen and Keppinger. The two slid aside to let him sit between them again.

"I miss anything?"

Keppinger laughed. "Just me shitting myself. I swear, Remy, you got ice in your veins."

Owen nodded. "I will not play cards with you. Ever."

"Don't know about ice," Remy said, "but I do have these."

He dug out a handful of the tiny tomatoes. Ito stayed busy watching the last logs fill the cart.

Remy let them stuff their mouths. In the sun, Ito turned just as Owen gulped the last tomato.

The guard gazed at the men, tapping a palm against the rifle stock hanging at his side. "Go now!" the Japanese shouted to the detail. The bull seemed to understand and bellowed its concurrence.

The men shouldered their axes and saws, many drank the last of their canteens in the line forming around the cart. Ito took his station, limping at the front.

The path down the mountain to the camp took thirty minutes. Remy kept near the back of the line, to avoid Ito's scrutiny. Others near him raised eyebrows at his stretching pockets. Remy considered handing out more tomatoes, even popping a few into his mouth to ease the lumps, but he knew the power of starvation. If the men saw him eating one tomato, if he gave one more away, he'd have to give it all. He couldn't do that.

The detail eased down the last of the slope, emerging from the jungle. The west gate of the camp lay two hundred yards ahead. Ito stood to the side of the path, letting the men and the ox cart shamble past him. Remy's gut wrenched. What was Ito doing? Remy had no time to figure out the guard's intent. He moved a step off the path toward the last of the trees, as if to take a leak. He would dump all the tomatoes out of his pants and shirt.

"You!" Ito called, pointing. "Tuck-san!"

Remy froze beside the path. The remaining men slid past, clucking their tongues. Young Donnelly the Aussie patted him on the shoulder. "The brig's not so bad, mate."

The internees at the head of the line approached the gate. The bull bellowed, knowing its day's work was near an end. Remy shuffled toward Ito, the two of them alone on the path.

He stopped in front of the soldier. Their eyes met. Remy bowed.

Ito motioned for Remy to straighten.

He poked one of Remy's bulging pockets. Then, with a disapproving look, he tapped a finger to his own temple.

"Atama ga warui da ne."

Ito was telling Remy: You're not being smart.

He gestured for Remy to empty his pockets and hand over everything. Remy had no choice and did as he was instructed. He kept secret the stash of tomatoes in his hat.

Ito tasted one of the tomatoes and found it agreeable. The rest he pushed into his own pockets with the wild gingerroots, until they bulged as much as Remy's had. The guard nodded. He swept the back of his hand down the path for Remy to move to the camp. Approaching the wire, Remy bit his tongue. He'd been shaken down by Ito.

At the gate, two guards waved Remy past a pair of dirt pill-boxes. Machine-gun barrels bristled in the firing slots. Three other guards lounged on chairs, paying no mind. Far ahead, the bull was led to the kitchen to have his sled unloaded.

Ito followed Remy into the camp. He stopped for a quiet word with the guards on their feet. He sprinkled some of Remy's tomatoes into their waiting hands.

Remy headed for his barracks, steaming.

"Tuck-san."

Ito jogged beside him. He gestured for Remy to follow.

When they were away from the gate, Ito burrowed into his pockets. He poured the tomatoes and roots into Remy's cupped hands. Ito motioned for him to put them away quickly. When Ito had returned the stash, he plucked one more tomato to pop into his mouth. He pointed back at the gate, wagging his head, no. You could not have gotten back into the camp with these.

Remy stowed the foraged food. He bowed again to Ito.

"Domo arigato."

Ito inclined his own head. *"Kurisumasu."* Christmas.

Remy stood straight and turned to go. Ito stopped him with a hand across his wrist.

"Tuck-san."

"Yes."

"Nippon. War." Ito jabbed a thumb downward at the earth. The war was going badly for Japan.

"Yes, it is."

Ito put the thumb into Remy's chest. "You," he said. He hooked the thumb at himself. "Ito."

When it's over, you remember Ito.

Remy handed the soldier another tomato.

Lazlo was a hoarder, the most despised white man in the camp. In the early years of Los Baños, he and his wife had collected food and supplies, speculating on the shortages they bet lay ahead. Now they sold and bartered at exorbitant rates. They lent money for usurious terms. Lazlo and his wife were the only folks in Los Baños to keep a pet alive, an obese Siamese cat. Remy wanted the Elgin watch on Lazlo's thick wrist. He played carefully, meticulously. He'd lost three hands in a row to Lazlo. He worked on losing a fourth.

Remy tossed six more tomatoes on the grass between them, adding to the pile of Philippine pesos, a toothbrush, and a small cup of cornmeal. Lazlo pitched in two more pesos. The other three players in the poker game had already folded, the stakes had outrun them. Remy bid them out, to keep the game between him and Lazlo.

"Call," said Lazlo.

Remy set down his cards. Others outside the circle kept alert for guards and the clergy wandering over to the shade of the dao tree. Remy showed a pair of tens. He figured Lazlo would have two pairs.

The man laid down his cards, threes and fives. His turkey neck bulged, savoring the pot. He swept his winnings through the grass. Remy admired the Elgin. Time to take it.

"You know," Lazlo chortled to Remy, "luck ain't the only word your name rhymes with."

Remy aped a good-natured manner. "Never heard that one before. Good one. Deal."

Remy waited two more hands until he had the right combination of cards and Lazlo flush with confidence. Lazlo rubbed his cards between forefinger and thumb, trying to feel the gold in them, betraying them to Remy.

Again, Remy bet everyone but Lazlo out of the hand, letting his stake get pared down to a handful of tomatoes. The rest of Remy's stash sat in front of Lazlo, who'd been nibbling at them without sharing.

"I don't think you got the muscle, Remy, ol' boy."

Remy scratched his chin. "Sure do like this hand, though. Hmmm. What to do."

Lazlo went for the kill. He unfurled an American ten-dollar bill and laid it in the pot. Remy enjoyed the sensation, like a fish striking his lure.

"Can you cover, Remy?"

"I don't want your money."

Lazlo rotated a gold ring on his finger. Few in the camp had any jewelry left; most valuables had been traded to the guards for food, medicine, soap, milk for children, cigarettes. Lazlo wore his ill-gotten prosperity on his hands and wrists, in his jowls.

"Don't want your ring either."

"I'm listening."

"That Elgin."

The man grinned. It didn't matter to him which item broke Remy's bank. He slid off the watch and plopped it on the grass. He plucked away his ten-dollar bill and devoured two more of the tomatoes he'd won.

"Now," Lazlo said, "you."

Remy lowered his head as if bowing to Lazlo. With both hands on the brim, he lifted off his fedora, careful not to spill the three dozen tiny tomatoes inside.

With a flourish, he set the hat in the pot.

"Call."

"Well, I'll be." Lazlo gestured to the other players in the circle. "He's slick, ain't he?" Lazlo spread his cards across the tomatoes in Remy's hat. "Slick that, mister."

Three nines.

Remy picked the Elgin out of the pot. He held it to his ear to make sure it ticked properly, examined the crystal for scratches.

"Oh," he said, as if absentminded. He flicked his cards to the grass. They landed in a perfect fan. Three jacks.

✳

From the Protestant and Catholic chapels at opposite ends of the camp, Christmas hymns spread over the grounds in the lowering sun. The internees had done their best to decorate, stringing shiny tins like tinsel around the taller bushes, tying bows out of colorful cloth. Little of excess existed in the camp, almost everything was used or devoured. The Christmas spirit, like the internees, was starved but not extinguished.

Remy waited near the back door of the kitchen, where he could keep an eye on the infirmary. Smoke from the day's final meal billowed out of the iron chimneys Remy had fashioned a year and a half ago. Six cooks filed out the back door, chores done for the day. Remy waved, knowing the story of each, trapped here with them and two thousand others for so long. The departing four men and two women were as gaunt as any internees, though they worked with the camp's food. This credential, more than anything, testified that they were honest.

With daylight almost gone and the mosquitoes ramping up, the guard Ishikawa left the infirmary. He lit a cigarette strolling across the road toward Remy. The little soldier glanced in all directions, clumsily furtive, plainly nervous. He was not armed.

Remy did not stroll out to meet him but retreated closer to the wall of the kitchen, under the overhanging eaves. Ishikawa dropped his cigarette. Remy was sorry to see him do that; he would have asked to smoke the remainder.

Remy held up the Elgin by the band. In the dying light the watch glistened like an ornament. Ishikawa reached. Remy raised it away, Ishikawa was so short.

Remy snapped his fingers. "*Ya. Dame.*"

Ishikawa produced two vials of clear liquid topped by rubber seals. From another pocket he drew a syringe with a capped needle.

"Okay?" Remy asked. "The real thing?"

The guard may not have understood but nodded enthu-
siastically. "Okay."

Remy swapped the Elgin for the morphine.

Ishikawa disappeared with his lucre. Remy palmed the
drug and syringe and headed for the barracks.

He found McElway sitting on the edge of his bunk,
playing checkers with Father Corrigan by lantern light. The
squares of the board had been drawn with charcoal on a
plank; bottle caps were checkers. The two sat alone in the
cubicle.

Remy greeted the priest. "Padre."

"Remy."

Father Corrigan was among the oldest men in the camp.
For twenty years he'd served in the mountains of Luzon in
the wildest of regions, even among headhunters. He'd been
scrawny the day the Japanese brought him in and had not
lost or gained a pound since.

Though the residents of Vatican City tended to keep to
themselves, Corrigan was a garrulous sort and well liked
among the lay internees. For old McElway's three years of
imprisonment, he had little truck with the missionaries and
Catholics, being for much of that time unrepentant. But he
recently told Remy that Corrigan would likely outlive him
and he would need someone of God's folk to speak well of
him beside his grave. That was why McElway played checkers with the priest now.

Remy eased onto his bunk to watch the game. By instinct he looked for stakes; what were the two playing for?
Nothing. That wasn't like Mac, who always angled for an
edge or an egg. The man's darkly veined hand shook lifting
a bottle cap. He seemed more frail than when Remy had
seen him at dinner picking at tonight's *lugao*. The meal had
been particularly awful. Bits of grub and worm had gotten

cooked into the mush; Nagata supplied the internees with the lowest possible grade of rice. They groaned and ate the bugs for the protein they added, except for Mac, who gave half his bowl away.

Mac hadn't shaved, an undeniable sign that he was running low.

Father Corrigan won the game. Remy thought he should have let Mac win, but the outcome seemed not to matter. Corrigan put the board away. Mac needed the priest's help to lift his legs into his bunk to lie down. His head, swollen as a jack-o'-lantern, hit the pillow with a groan of pain and disgust.

Corrigan knelt beside the bunk. Mac's long, piano hand filled both of the priest's. Remy bowed his head while Corrigan prayed. Mac did not close his lids but stared into the bottom of the bunk close above him. Both eyes glistened and he seemed afraid, as if his way to heaven, too, might be blocked.

The priest finished the prayer. He placed McElway's limp hand on the mattress.

"I'll stop by tomorrow, lad."

After Corrigan left, Remy took the man's spot beside the bunk. The veins in McElway's arm stood out like railways.

"I got you a Christmas present."

"Is it a woman?"

"Nope. That's for New Year's Eve. This is for the pain." Remy held up the vials and syringe.

Mac lifted his head from the pillow to cough, stifling it into a balled hand. The knuckles showed the scars of his history, smoothed-over wounds from a lifetime of struggle. His father had been born a slave in America. Mac had known little comfort in his life, even after coming to the Pacific. Women and music had been respites from jails and trouble. Once the camp doctors gave him the word three weeks ago that he had lung cancer, starvation and all of its spawn—beriberi, colitis, parasites—robbed him of his reserves, hastening the certain. Remy was determined that his friend's passage from this world would at least be eased.

McElway dropped his hand. Blood had spattered the back of it.

From his vest pocket, Remy unfolded a paper packet. He'd sliced the wild gingerroot as finely as he could.

"Open up."

McElway lowered his jaw. The tumors in his rotting lungs rattled in the well of his throat. Remy laid a portion of ginger on the man's tongue, ghostly white from anemia. Mac chewed.

"It's ginger. I found some today. It'll help with the nausea. Maybe get your appetite back."

Mac patted Remy's knee. "Gimme the jelly roll."

"I've never done this before. You know how, right?"

"Yeah, I done a few needles. It ain't hard."

McElway talked Remy through the injection. Remy pierced the point through the rubber cap of the first vial, which contained 10 cc of morphine. Mac told him to draw only one cc into the syringe, and be sure not to suck in any air.

"Small dose," Mac said, "we ain't got much. Go ahead. Find a good vein." Mac balled a fist to help his vessels protrude. "Now, stick the tip in, come in at an angle."

Mac's skin resisted the needle. He seemed covered in leather. Remy pushed harder to pierce the vein. The skin gave way, the needle punched through.

"Don't shove the plunger yet. Pull in some blood."

Remy drew back on the plunger. A scarlet swirl entered the syringe, clouding the liquid. Remy pushed in the morphine. Mac released his fist when the needle was withdrawn.

The opened vein in Mac's arm wept a bead of blood.

Remy tore a piece of cloth from his own bedsheet to tie over the leak.

"Why don't you just go to the infirmary like a regular person?"

"I ain't regular."

"I knew that before I asked."

"I'm gonna stay right here. Got a job to do."

Mac coughed again, violently. The clatter in his chest reminded Remy of rolling, snake-eyed dice. The old black man raised his chin, the morphine kicking in. His eyelids fluttered, he sank into the pillow and mattress. He raised a shrunken, blind finger at Remy.

"And you gon' do it when I'm done."

Chapter Nine

THE U.S. NAVY provided the fireworks for New Year's Eve.

At sundown a hundred planes attacked the rails and roads running west from Los Baños. The boys of No. 11 cheered on the air raid from every window. They imitated the whistles of falling bombs, punched the fellows around them in the shoulders with the thumps of explosions. After full darkness fell and fires flickered beyond the trees lining the ravine, the boys gathered in the dark mess hall to yammer about liberation. The word in the camp was that the Yanks had already landed on Mindoro and would invade Luzon next. Manila would fall soon. Tonight's air raid had been meant to soften up the Japanese.

After the raid, no one went to his bunk. The night was a holiday, and the excitement of the bombs did not ebb. At ten o'clock, Donnelly, the camp bootlegger, produced three jugs of home brew.

"Mango madness," he proclaimed. The boys stood in awe that Donnelly could have done this.

Tal drank with the others. The moonshine had to last until midnight. He sipped whenever one of the jugs passed his way, but managed little drunkenness. A few selfish boys guzzled, one of them a lout named Peavey who on his best days Tal found difficult to tolerate. In Manila, Peavey had been a self-styled adventurer, a rich man's son, a layabout. He'd convinced his father he'd gone to the Philippines to study tribal sociologies. The old man sent him a monthly stipend. What money Peavey did not carouse away, Remy and others took from him at poker tables. Annoying and worthless as Tal considered Peavey to be, he did have something Tal noticed and, with the prodding of the moonshine in his system, suddenly wanted. A pocket watch.

Peavey slumped in a corner, hit hard by the mango liquor. Tal had little trouble detaching the fob and sliding the watch out of the man's pocket. He palmed the timepiece and got in line for one more slug of moonshine. Lifting a kerosene lamp from a hook, Tal slipped out of the mess hall. He headed for the north end of the barracks.

This was Donnelly's room and would surely stay empty past midnight. He set the kerosene lamp on the windowsill. He lit it, breaking curfew. The other buildings in the camp remained wrapped in moonless black, with the only light coming from electric poles along the wire.

He set the watch on the sill. He'd return it tomorrow, just hand it to Peavey and walk off.

Five minutes remained.

He gazed up at her dark window just forty yards away and three stories up. He did not know if she stood looking down at him. He did not need the girl to be in her window for him to be here. Remy had talked many times of faith, in God or cards, how it required no answer. Even Toshiwara had said it; loyalty to an ideal.

By lantern light Tal kept an eye on the sweeping second hand of the pocket watch. He counted down the final moments of 1944. "Ten . . . nine . . ." At zero, he whispered, "Happy New Year."

In the ravine outside the barbed wire, frogs croaked, a monkey screeched, insects chirped like the ticks of the watch. Somewhere in the camp, a man's voice rose in "Auld Lang Syne." A few scattered others picked up the tune, but not enough to drown out the life in the surrounding jungle.

The girl's building remained lightless. Tal painted her inside the frame of her dark window, scarlet and brown. He doused the lantern and sat with her in his share of the dark.

Tal sat on the back steps of No. 12, pushing a fork into a dollop of stewed *talinum* greens and *kamotes*. A mug of ersatz coffee cooled beside him. He ate the paltry breakfast on the steps of his father's barracks because it had a good view of what was once the camp garden, where the Japanese did jumping jacks in nothing but loincloths.

Nagata paced in front of the hundred guards, half the camp garrison. He waved his arms, shouting, *"Ichi, ni, san, shi!"* Buttocks and pubic hair flashed with every jumping jack. The guards couldn't get into unison. Nagata halted the exercise and made them start over, together, only to encounter the same poor result.

The half-Filipino Santana joined Tal on the steps.

"You gonna finish that?" He indicated Tal's partially eaten breakfast.

"Yeah. Shut up."

Santana chuckled at the Japanese. "Man, they look as bad as we do."

The guards appeared tiny and listless in the morning sun, except for thick Nagata. Along with their joggling private parts on display, every one showed the stripes of ribs.

Tal said, "I reckon Toshiwara figured his men could use some shaping up."

"They could use blowin' up."

Tal scooped a forkful of boiled greens into his mouth. He thought of his short time outside the wire two weeks ago. He could still join the guerrillas. They ate better than this.

"The Yanks are comin' for us," Santana said, "right?"

"You saw that air raid last night. They're coming."

"You think they'll get here in time?"

"In time for what?"

The boy pointed at the guards now trying push-ups, with Nagata kicking at them.

"I dunno. But what do you think they're exercising for?"

The question was unnerving. Before Tal could devise an answer, Father Corrigan strode around the corner.

"Good morning, Talbot." To Santana, the priest said, *"Mabuhay."*

"Father."

The priest said to Tal, "Your father needs to speak with you. He's in the garage."

"What's he doing in there?"

Father Corrigan held out an arm inviting Tal off the step and on his way. "He'll tell you."

Tal scraped up the last of his breakfast and handed the empty plate to Santana. He made his way through the warren of barracks, thinking over what Santana had hinted at. Was Toshiwara actually trying to turn the guards, most of them skinny, lame, and old, into fighters? To fight who? The Americans? No, the camp guards, even the ones who'd seen combat before, would never again make frontline soldiers.

To fight us? he wondered.

Tal entered the garage door, determined to ask Remy his opinion. He found his father shirtless, crafting a casket out of green bamboo.

Remy spoke without interrupting his work. "Mac's dead."

Tal approached into the cool of the garage.

"When?"

"Last night sometime."

"Where's he now?"

"Still in bed. I only told Lucas. The others in our room are keeping it quiet 'til I get this done. Lucas asked Nagata if I could have some lumber. Bastard said no, of course."

The casket Remy made was ingenious, bamboo poles tied with ropes like a raft, notched and fitted into the shape of a six-sided coffin. Remy fashioned it with no tool but a bolo.

Tal said, "I'm real sorry."

"I know."

Tal sat on a bale of straw to watch his father finish. Remy's muscles flexed, stringy without body fat, the skeleton beneath knobby and easy to see.

Tal said, "I'll help you haul him up to the graveyard later on."

"That'll be good. We'll get a few fellas. Maybe find some piano music for the loudspeaker. Say so long. I guess Corrigan'll want to talk. Maybe we'll get them two prostitutes to say something. Balance it out."

Remy laughed at some recollection of Mac. He chopped at more bamboo rods. With a craftsman's hands he roped them to form the casket's lid. He carved two short pieces into a cross and affixed it to the lid.

Remy smiled. "You know, I took his meal ticket this morning so I could go through the chow line twice. I lied and said I was taking the plate back to him. I didn't want to run out of steam while I was doing this. But I got to tell you . . ." Remy folded to the dirt floor, mopping his brow, ". . . two times nothin' is still nothin'. I'm beat."

Remy looked over the green burial box he'd built for Mac. Tal rose from his hay bale. With Remy's bolo he cut six lengths of rope, and tied handles to each of the walls of the coffin.

"Good thinkin', boy. Come on."

Remy hauled himself off the ground. Together they carried the casket out of the garage, through the camp. Internees on the paths and in the windows stopped when Tal and Remy passed with the coffin. Men removed their hats. The news of Mac's death spread this way.

They entered Remy's barracks. Outside the room, Remy said, "Set 'er down."

He rested an arm on Tal's shoulder.

"Look. This ain't pretty."

Tal tried to envision what lay behind the sawali. Even surrounded by war, he'd not yet seen a dead man. He lived every day among the dying and figured that was enough.

"I'm all right."

Remy squeezed Tal's shoulder. "Good. There's somethin' else. Mac asked me to bring you here. Not just to cart him off."

"What'd he want?"

"I'm gonna show you. But first things first. Here we go."

Remy set aside the lid of the coffin. He pushed back the mat to enter the room. Tal, close behind, was struck by the dark stick figure on the lower bunk. Mac lay sucked dry like an unwrapped mummy. His head had swollen and his hands, always large, seemed the hands of a colossus against his shrunken body. Tal's gut quivered, a shudder of revulsion just as Remy had warned. Tal stood rooted, staring. Though he knew cancer had done this, he chalked Mac's death up to the Japanese. Again he considered Remy's thinning frame, his own slender wrists, and Santana's question: *You think they'll get here in time?*

Remy moved, startling Tal into motion. Gathering the corners of Mac's bedsheet, they hefted him through the doorway. The old piano player fit well into the casket Remy had made for him. Remy crossed his friend's arms, adding to the image of a mummy, then folded the sheet around him. Remy fit the top of the coffin in place. Mac disappeared beneath it. Tal said goodbye to the man he suspected had been the least educated in the camp and among the wisest.

Remy gestured Tal back inside the room. He let the

sawali drop, then stepped close. He lowered his voice to a whisper.

"I need you to move back in here with me now."

"No. I like Eleven."

"Son, it's not a question of what you like. It ain't that simple. Things are bad, and it's my guess they're likely to get worse. I think you believe the same."

"Yeah. I reckon."

"Keep your voice down. This is what Mac wanted. I agreed. Now, I'm gonna show you something. Afterward, if you decide to move back into Twelve with me, we'll both go talk to Lucas. You tell him you want to take Mac's bunk, and you're gonna stay out of trouble. Lucas'll make it square with the Japs."

Remy checked the hall outside the sawali. Mac rested in his green coffin alone; the building remained quiet.

"Gimme a hand here."

Remy set his grip under the frame of the bunk bed. Tal helped him lift it to the center of the room. On the uncovered space of the bamboo floor, Remy knelt to dislodge a slat. He reached into a cavity beneath the floor, to pull up a glass bottle secured to a wooden base. The bottle had been wrapped in copper wire; alligator clips and an earpiece from a military radio hung off it. Remy pointed at a miniature electronic tube between the clips.

"This is what you brought back through the fence."

"What is it?"

"A germanium diode."

"No." Tal pointed. "I mean the whole thing. What is it?"

"Turns out ol' Mac had a hobby other than gals. He built crystal radios."

Remy connected an alligator clip to a loop in the wire encircling the bottle. He held the earpiece to his ear, then reset the clip to a different loop.

"Come here. Take a listen."

Tal knelt and took the earpiece. The sound came through faintly, but clear and without static.

"*This is KROJ. The Voice of Freedom.*"

Tal pressed the earpiece hard into his head. "Where's that coming from?"

"California."

Remy reached for the earpiece. Tal was slow to let loose.

Remy returned the radio to silence. He set it in the hole below the floor. The two of them replaced the bunk.

Remy sat on the edge of his mattress. Tal stood, still gaping.

"How long?"

"Two years. We started back in Santo Tomas. You know all them rumors in the camp? The Americans take New Guinea? Guadalcanal? Leyte?"

"Yeah."

"Me and Mac started 'em. And now it's gonna be you and me."

Tal glanced at the bare mattress where Mac had died. "I want the top bunk."

"You got it."

Chapter Ten

O NE SOLDIER cried when he ejaculated. He ran from the room before he'd fully pulled up his pants.

The one after him had his *saku* break. Carmen cleaned herself in the manganic acid. The sting raked her insides.

Another knocked away her rice ball and slapped her for eating while he was on top of her.

One more cried with his climax. He turned his back to sit on the mattress. Sullen, the soldier tugged on his pantaloons. For two weeks Carmen had been careful whom she selected. She lay behind him, propped on one elbow, and chose this one. He wore glasses with round black frames and seemed bookish, shy, raw.

She asked him why he cried.

He made no answer. Carmen gentled a hand on his arm. "English?"

He nodded.

"Talk?" she asked.

She waited until his boots were laced. The weeping young soldiers gained better control over themselves when restored to their uniforms. She tried again.

"Why do you cry?"

He hesitated, staring at his boots. In broken phrases and accented English, he said he was frightened. His division was bivouacked seven miles south of Los Baños, around San Pablo. Carmen and Yumi had walked through that town.

She prodded him with touches and innocent queries.

He was part of the 8th, the Tiger Division. Their task was to block any American invasion force out of the east from reaching Manila.

"Are they strong, your Tigers?"

He described a division heavily armored with artillery and a tank unit.

"How many men?"

Ten thousand.

"Why are you afraid? That is so many."

They are *beiki.* He searched for the English. American devils.

The soldier stood. He dug thumbs into his sockets to dry his eyes. He said he could see that Songu had little comfort for herself. If he could come again, he would bring food.

"Yes," she said. *"Domo arigato."*

The boy straightened his tunic, hardening his bearing before leaving her room. He could spill tears in front of a *pii,* nowhere else.

"Chukun aikoku," he grunted. He would die for the emperor. He said this as if to make Carmen proud of him.

He left. Carmen washed him away, stinging again. When she was finished, she dumped the basin out the open window into the camp. She set the emptied bowl in the hall, turned it upside down. This was the signal for Benito, the new mop boy in the *shuho* and a guerrilla with Terry's Hunters, to come to her room.

In the late day, Carmen ran with Yumi across long shadows. They chased butterflies in the yard, rested in the shade of the animal husbandry building. Kenji observed from nearby.

The girls wore their green and red robes, unconcerned with being naked beneath. Carmen relished the grass under her toes and buttocks. They held hands, as they often did when together. They spoke in their four tongues, Carmen choosing Tagalog instead of English when she did not want Kenji to understand. They also tried to communicate with inflection and pantomime. Carmen told Yumi about the Tuck boy, unsure if the girl understood. They taught each other numbers; Carmen counted to ten in Korean. They traded words. The one Carmen tried most to remember was *han,* Korean for "grudge."

Kenji left the girls outside for an hour, the longest they'd been together since Christmas. When four American fighter planes coursed low over the camp, he approached and said, "Inside." Yumi got to her feet quickly. She spoke sharply in Japanese. Kenji registered nothing at her rebuke. Yumi stomped to the rear door of the building, leaving Kenji and Carmen behind.

He reached down to help Carmen off the ground.

"I can do nothing with her," he said. "She's a pet of Toshi-wara."

Carmen did not let go of Kenji's hand. "Kenji-sama. Come inside. Have sex with me."

The tall Japanese drew back his head in surprise.

She said, "It's been weeks since the last time."

"I haven't had money. Our pay has been slow. And . . . I thought you might be angry with me."

"Over the walk? That wasn't your fault. Besides, you stayed with us. I'm not mad. This one is free. If Mama says something I'll spit in her eye."

"Why?"

"If you don't want to, forget it."

"I want to. I have tried to be kind. Like today. Outside for an hour."

"Yes. So come, Kenji-sama."

She let him follow her closely up the steps, knowing her robe only partially covered her bottom. On the third-floor landing, Mama turned Songu's wooden tag over to mark that she was available. Carmen leaned past the Filipina woman to snatch the tag from its hook. She took it with her down the hall, towing Kenji by the hand. She dared Mama with a look. The old *makipili* glared daggers.

Carmen let Kenji enter first, then lowered the curtain behind him. She shrugged off her robe to stand in its red folds. Kenji removed his cap, then undressed meticulously. Most soldiers did no more than drop their pants, but Kenji, almost tenderly with himself, unclasped his many snaps and buckles to bare his entire body. He stood naked with her in front of the tatami. Carmen was struck by how underfed Kenji had become. His belly had sunk behind his rib cage, his hip bones protruded like a woman's. She ran a hand up the indentations of his ribs.

Kenji had no condom with him. From a drawer, she handed him a newly cleaned one. She lay on the mattress, watching him try to tug the *saku* over his erect penis. The *saku* had no lubricant after washing. Carmen took it from him, spat into it, and spat into her palm to rub saliva over his erection. Kenji stretched the sheath into place. The low sun pouring through her window turned his yellow skin to gold.

Kenji knelt between her spread knees. She spat once more into her hand to moisten her vagina. This was pleasurable for Kenji; his coated penis bobbed once. She said, "Now."

Kenji lay forward. She braced for his weight and found him light and little burden. She reached down to guide him inside. He gasped, nestling his head beside her ear. Carmen wrapped him in her arms and let him hear her breathe. She watched the rectangle of sunlight on her wall, wondering if she might see it move as the sun set.

Because the sex was free and at Carmen's invitation, Kenji conducted himself as if it were significant. He propped himself on his hands to look down on her searchingly. He thrust as if to please her, but ended by rounding his lips in climax. He smiled, then rolled next to her to lie on his back. The shadow of a bird flew through the square of light on the wall. Carmen lowered her knees.

Surely Mama sat in the foyer fuming that Songu had taken down her wooden tag. Carmen would only have a little more time before the old *makipili* banged on the door-frame. Carmen lay on her back, to speak without facing Kenji. Her breasts, never large, drained by hunger, flattened to shallow dollops.

"I want you to speak with Yumi."

In her periphery, Kenji turned his eyes to her. "I do speak with her for you."

"I have a different reason, Kenji-sama. She lies with Toshiwara. I want to know what he tells her."

A lull separated them. Kenji gazed a long time at the side of her head.

"Why?"

"Because I've begun to work for the guerrillas."

Kenji sat up. "Don't do this. Carmen, the war is going to end soon. I swear, when it's over, I'll take you home to Japan. I'll marry you. Everything will be all right."

Carmen did not pull her eyes from the ceiling, finally touched by the rising box of light.

She said, "When this is over, so many will be dead. Maybe you or me. It's hard to tell. Let's wait. Will you talk to Yumi for me?"

"Who is your contact in the guerrillas?"

"I will never tell you that, Kenji-sama."

"I could involve the Kempeitai. They would ask you."

"I would tell them. Two or three more people will die, that's all. I don't think it would affect the outcome. And I could not marry you in Japan."

Kenji rose to his knees on the tatami, a beseeching pose. "Don't do this. It's not safe."

"Safe?" Carmen sat up to laugh loud enough for Mama to hear, perhaps Yumi in the faraway hall. She gestured to her small room. "Do you think this is worth keeping safe?"

Carmen left the mattress. She collected her spilled robe off the floor, informing Kenji by donning it that he should dress, too.

He had much to put on, from socks and boots to cap. When he was belted and buttoned inside his khaki uniform, he drew himself up, to leave like any crying boy, with a flimsy show of dignity.

"Is that why you brought me up here, for free? To persuade me?"

"Yes."

"I won't do it."

She asked, "Will you turn me in?"

Kenji shoved aside the drape to leave.

"No."

Chapter Eleven

R EMY SAT in the bottom of the grave. The hole needed
another twelve inches. He wanted Mac to have all the
depth that was rightly his, all six feet.

Clem, Topsy, and a half dozen others from No. 12 stared
down from around the lip of the hole.

"Climb out, man," Clem called. "I'll finish up."

"I need a minute. I'm all right."

"Christ," Clem groused.

Remy rested. He questioned himself for insisting on
finishing the last measure of Mac's grave alone. These others had volunteered to help, they respected and mourned
Mac, too. Remy supposed his need for a last gesture, some
repayment for Mac's friendship and bravery, was greater
than theirs. He couldn't tell the men starving and looking
down at him about the times the old negro had shared his
trouble, or kept Remy out of it. The two had developed a
trust that would have cost both their lives if breached. Before the war in Manila, Remy had snubbed the old piano
player the times they'd crossed paths. These things created
a debt that Remy struggled to settle up now, even as he
realized he could not.

While he rested, Mac's body stiffened in the bamboo
coffin inside the ice house. Remy gazed up out of the grave,
saddened by the view. He left the shovel in the pit and
climbed the ladder to sit on the edge, dangling his feet.
Clem clambered to the bottom and with a reddish fury dug
away more inches of earth. Remy's hands ached and his

chin fell to his chest. He was filthy and wished he were a stronger man.

Remy sat for tired minutes while Clem flung dirt clods. The others said nothing over the scrape of the shovel. The grave neared a proper depth. Clem slowed, then stabbed the blade into the bottom to mop his brow. Before the Scotsman could lift the spade again, the shout of an approaching guard turned the heads of the men around the hole.

The guard, pint-sized in ragged shorts and gartered socks, hustled up. Without a word, he set his boots on the rungs of the ladder. The soldier descended enough to grab the handle of the shovel. Clem, with newfound energy, latched on and tugged back.

"No, no, no, pal. I need this. Grave. See? Digging grave. Got to finish."

The Japanese dropped off the ladder. Landing, he unshouldered his rifle to make his point. Clem released the handle. Remy and the others cast down shadow from the low-slung sun.

The little soldier climbed out with the shovel and hastened off. Puzzled, Clem could dig no more without a tool.

"What the hell?" he asked, ascending the ladder.

With the sun touching Makiling, Remy went in search of another shovel and an answer. Clem waited for Remy's return, the others drained away.

Remy made his way toward his barracks, to find Tal. His son would have an idea of what was happening in the camp. Along the way Remy walked past a dozen guards, all with picks and shovels. At the commandant's office, five Japanese—one of them Nagata—burned papers in trash cans.

Remy found Tal on the steps of No. 11, smoking a rolled cigarette. The boy sat with a bunch of others and one teenage girl watching the Japanese scurry around the camp. Remy reached for a drag on the cigarette. His tongue picked

up the tang of dried eggplant leaves used to stretch the tobacco in the camp.

The girl, one of the missionaries' daughters, was sweet
on Tal's roommate Santana. Her preacher father disap-
proved, as Santana was half Filipino. She slid aside on the
steps to make room for Remy.

"You done?" Tal asked. "You look done."

"There's about six inches left. Clem was finishing the
hole, but one of the guards snagged the shovel. Anyone
know what that's about?"

Santana answered. "An hour ago the Japs went through
the whole camp grabbing every pick and shovel they could
find."

"All of 'em?"

"Far as I know."

Remy told the boys he'd seen Nagata burning documents.

Bascom, a young Irish trumpet player at the Army
Navy Club before the war, piped up. "MacArthur must have
landed. The Jappos are getting ready for a brawl."

"No," Tal said. "MacArthur's not on Luzon yet."

"How d'you know?"

Tal said cryptically, "That's just the word."

Remy grinned at his boy. He made up his mind. Mac
would just have to accept a hole close to six feet deep. He
likely would; Mac wasn't fancy.

"Bascom?"

"Yeah?"

"Go to the cemetery. Tell Clem all the shovels are gone
and there's nothin' we can do about it. Then fetch Father
Corrigan there."

"This for old Mac?"

"It is, son. Thank you."

The boy lit out for the cemetery.

Remy stood from the steps to address the five remaining. He knew each of them to be strong-willed and clever. He was proud that young men and girls like these were his son's friends. What a loss, he thought, if even one of them did not survive. The Japanese were lucky these kids were locked up behind barbed wire. If they were on the outside in army uniforms, they'd be hell. The Japanese better dig deep with those shovels and picks, Remy thought, because other American boys were not far off.

"You all knew Mac. He was one of a kind. He thought highly of each of you, as I do. I can't think of better folks to help me carry him to his reward. You game?"

All agreed.

Soon, Mac's green casket was carted through the camp. Remy asked Lucas to play over the loudspeaker two of the records he'd found in Mac's trunk, Fats Waller's "Keepin' Out of Mischief Now" and Art Tatum playing "Over the Rainbow." Two hundred internees followed the green casket to the cemetery. Remy figured there would have been more if they'd known what the quiet old man had been doing for them with his homemade radio, and if the camp wasn't buzzing over the Japanese trenches and flurrying about. Those folks who did come out to say so long spoke well of Mac, and that was enough. They circled the grave with heads bowed while Father Corrigan talked about redemption. Remy wondered if that was what Mac was looking for on the other side, or if he still had a hankering for a woman.

When Corrigan wrapped it up, the boys from No. 11, without shovels, pushed dirt over the coffin with their hands. Remy did not stay to watch. He lurched back to his barracks, dog tired.

"Tuck."

Someone jostled his shoulder. Remy popped open his eyes.

"What?"

"It's Marcus. Wake up."

Blurry, Remy set his bare feet on the bamboo floor. He made out the silhouette of Marcus Lazenby, an easygoing Luzon banker, North Carolina bred. Marcus served on the executive committee.

"What time is it?"

"A little after one. Come outside with me."

"What for?"

Lazenby spread his hands, affable even in an agitated state. "Come outside first."

Remy slid into his sandals. He grabbed his fedora off its nail and left his son and the others snoring behind, or at least pretending so they wouldn't be disturbed. He followed Lazenby, shaking off sleep. On the bottom step of the barracks, under the stars, he asked what was the big deal.

The banker clapped, excited but muffled.

"The Japs are leaving."

"What?"

Lazenby shushed him. "Keep it down. We can't spread the word just yet. But the Japs are heading out, sure as shooting."

"How d'you know this?"

"Toshiwara sent for some of the committeemen. Told 'em they had to gather up the rest of the shovels in the camp, 'cause the guards been ordered to go dig trenches down south. The Japs are afraid MacArthur's gonna land any day now."

"I've gotta wake up Tal."

Lazenby extended a hand. "Lucas says to let folks sleep. It ain't a good idea to have two thousand folks cheering while the Japs pull out. Let 'em go quiet. We'll holler in the morning after they're gone."

Remy held his ground. "Then why'd you wake me up?"

"We need help bringin' in the shovels. We've got to go through the whole camp. And when folks ask you what's up, just say you don't know. One word, Remy, and it could get out of control."

Remy joined ten executive committee members and a handful of volunteers to visit every barracks. They roused sleeping bachelors, married couples, and children to inquire for their shovels and picks. Each reclaimed tool was stacked at the guards' barracks. In an hour, another four dozen shovels were located. Every internee Remy awakened, from Vatican City north, asked what was going on. Remy only shrugged and said, "We'll find out soon enough."

When the chore was completed, Remy did not return to his barracks. He made his way to the main gate, where what looked to be the entire Japanese garrison, all two hundred guards, milled around a dozen trucks. Toshiwara's 1939 Oldsmobile stood in front of his office with the trunk open.

Remy joined two dozen committee members, volunteers, and a few men who couldn't sleep, gathered outside the commandant's office.

Lucas emerged from Toshiwara's door. He came down the porch steps to speak to the small, edgy crowd of internees.

He reported, "Nagata's in there. The man's wearing a towel wrapped around his head. He's got a half-empty bottle of Johnnie Walker in front of him and he's counting Jap pesos."

Lazenby asked, "What'd he say?"

"Get out."

The internees waited outside Toshiwara's office while guards loaded all the picks and shovels into the trucks, then climbed onto the truck beds after them. The entire camp was ablaze with more electricity than Remy had seen in the place.

Once the guards and tools were loaded up, the commandant arrived to climb onto the porch with his tall interpreter. Nagata weaved out of the office. He'd doffed the towel and looked bleary. Toshiwara addressed the internees. The interpreter spoke:

"We are leaving. We have been called to join the defense of Luzon. Your Internee Committee is now in charge of the camp. We leave you two months of rations."

Hearing it from Toshiwara himself, Remy wanted to grab Lazenby and dance a jig. He kept his poker face.

Toshiwara continued to speak through the translator. "You will see soldiers from another unit guarding the gates. It is your responsibility to feed them. Understand, you must exercise your own discipline. The soldiers will not be many, and they are here only to protect you. I recommend you stay inside the camp. We cannot guarantee your safety if anyone goes outside the fence."

Lucas raised a hand to ask a question but Nagata stepped in front of the commandant. He waved the men away. "Finish! Go!" Toshiwara disappeared into his office. Nagata stayed behind to glower until the internees moved off.

Lucas led the men to gather beside the kitchen.

"Look," he said. "Let 'em go. Let's keep everybody in their barracks for another few hours. This is great news but we're not out of the woods. We're still in Jap territory and we're still defenseless. But . . ."

Lucas paused, flummoxed for how to describe the event. Remy couldn't contain himself. "But holy shit."

"Perfect. Thank you, Tuck. All right, committee members, we've got work to do. The rest of you, lay low, stay mum. We'll see how this all shakes out at sunup."

Remy went to sit on the steps of No. 12. The electric lights knocked out the stars; even the birds and animals in the ravine and jungle kept still at the activity inside the wire. Remy ached to go inside to wake Tal with the news. The boy would find it hard to contain himself. The smartest play right now was just like Lucas said, sit still and let the camp wake up to the guards gone.

Remy gazed through the waning dark to the dao tree, ancient and impassive. He studied it, tried to emulate it, and, to no surprise, found he could not do so. His curiosity lifted him from the steps, to walk beside his long barracks to the side facing the fence.

Reaching the path there, he looked to the girl's third-floor window. An electric bulb blazed inside. She, too, was awake and waiting.

Chapter Twelve

TAL LANDED like a cat on all fours on the bamboo floor. He checked Remy's bunk, but his father was already gone. Tal jumped into his ragged shorts, crammed his feet into his sneakers, and beat it out the door behind Donnelly, who'd come to No. 12 to wake him. The others in their bunks stirred, but the two were away before they could ask what was going on.

Outside in the dawn, the camp was turned upside down. People ran in every direction with no destination. Tal took his own first steps in this new world Donnelly had wakened him to, without guards patrolling the wire or manning the pillboxes and towers. The notion of freedom, fresh with having just tumbled out of bed, left Tal frenetic and speechless.

He jogged behind Donnelly, dodging people bustling out of barracks, clogging the paths. He slowed at his first sight of the girl's window. She did not appear in her crimson robe. Where was she? Wasn't this her liberation, too? Had she come down, finally? Was she in the camp looking for him? With a clutch in his gut, he wondered: What if she had gone? What if the Japanese took her with them?

"Come on, mate!" Donnelly halted to wait for him.

Tal waved Donnelly on; he'd catch up later.

The Aussie disappeared into the waking and jubilant internees. Tal walked to the road and fence below her window. He didn't know her name, what could he call out? Others ran past, telling him to come along. Tal stayed in place, fingers hooked between the barbs.

The camp's excitement swirled around him. People headed for the open grass in front of the commandant's office. Tal felt a pull to join them, a leap in his heart at today's long-awaited freedom. His legs would not turn from the fence and the high, silent wall on the other side.

"That's why I didn't wake you."

Remy crossed onto the tarmac.

Tal asked, "You think she's gone?"

His father took off his fedora to rub his graying pate. "I got no idea. But I do know the Japs are. Let's go find out what the deal is. After that, I'll walk outside the gate with you. We'll have a look, see if the lady's in."

"I want to go now."

"I said we'll go together, boy."

With a hand on Tal's shoulder, Remy turned him from the fence. They followed the crowd to Toshiwara's abandoned office.

The whole camp population, even wobbly ones from the infirmary, pressed together on the weedy lawn. Lucas stood on the commandant's porch with the Internee Committee, raising hands for quiet. A microphone and amplifier had been set up. The elated mob hushed with great effort.

Lucas nodded to Bascom, who raised his trumpet and blew reveille. Families held hands. Remy linked his arm through Tal's.

When the last note sailed into the brightening morning, Lucas stepped to the microphone.

"My friends. By now you all know, the Japanese have gone."

The crowd erupted into a riotous cheer. Remy tossed his hat in the air, the thing spun high and fell into someone else's hands. They threw it, and another, before the fedora was handed back. Lucas called for attention.

"There's much of importance to cover this morning. But first, I want to ask Father Corrigan to offer up a prayer."

The old priest moved to the microphone. He began, simply, "Our Father, who art in Heaven . . ." Every voice in the camp joined him. When the invocation was done, Corrigan offered short prayers for those who had died in the war, and of thanksgiving for the freedom of Los Baños.

The priest stepped back from the microphone. A scratchy rendition of Bing Crosby's "Star-Spangled Banner" issued from the camp loudspeakers, followed by a raspy recording of "God Save the King." With the day's first rays glowing inside the wire, an old U.S. flag, wrinkled and discolored from years at the bottom of someone's trunk, went up the bamboo flagpole. Beside it waved an equally tarnished and proud Union Jack.

"By agreement of the executive committee," Lucas announced beneath the flapping of the banners, "this site is now renamed Camp Freedom!"

Cheers burst again. Remy and Tal hugged everyone on all sides and each other long and well. They stayed with an arm around each other's waist while Lucas continued his announcements. High overhead, three American planes headed south.

The camp, he made clear, was not out of danger. They remained deep in a war zone, surrounded by hostile Japanese forces and *makipili* sympathizers. Despite rumors, there had been no confirmed reports that U.S. forces had landed on Luzon. And the fact that the Japanese had left the camp did not mean they were not still a threat. A dozen guards from a new unit had arrived in the early hours and stationed themselves outside all the gates. Lucas knew nothing about the new guards except that the camp had to feed them.

He explained that for the camp's safety, everyone must continue to conduct themselves as they had before. That meant staying inside the camp boundaries. No one should go to the village seeking food or supplies. The Japanese had left enough food for eight weeks . . .

". . . but that figure was calculated by the rations the camp suffered under while the Japanese were in charge. We'll try to work with the locals to buy more. I think we can do better than Nagata." This drew wide laughter and applause.

The committee felt the 10:00 p.m. curfew needed to stay in effect, with lights out an hour later. A curfew roll call would be put in place to assure that no one was outside the wire.

"Of course, there'll be no need to bow during roll call."

The flags came down. Lucas advised all to preserve their discipline, the trait that had kept them alive to this point. He released the crowd to another tune over the camp loudspeaker. Bing Crosby crooned again, "Don't Fence Me In."

The looting began immediately.

With Lucas and the committee hardly off the porch, internees entered the commandant's office to root for food and souvenirs. Others raided the guards' barracks, another group made a beeline for the paddock to claim Toshiwara's bull. Tal and Remy joined seven men headed for the Japanese storehouse, off limits until now. The locks were beaten off the bamboo doors with rocks. Inside the men found stacks of corn, beans, rice and grain sacks, hoarded by the Japanese.

One man did not wait. He shoved forward to heft a fifty-pound sack across his shoulders. Remy put a hand on the man's chest when he turned to walk off with his prize.

"Clem," Remy said, "leave it."

The Scottish sailor shifted his eyes to the others itching to make a grab for the food.

"No way," the man said, hunched under the sack. "This food is ours. We bloody well earned it, all of us did. I'm taking mine. You leave yours, if you want."

Another man, Molina, who'd worked for General Motors, pushed to the front. He, too, lifted a sack of beans onto his back. Tal moved beside his father, blocking the man's route away.

Remy spoke. "You just said it, Clem. This belongs to all of us. There's folks that ain't here loadin' up. It's their food, too. The kids. And the sick ones in the infirmary who can't carry as much as you. It's theirs as much as it is yours. So set it down and we'll all share."

"I'm hungry," Molina said.

"We're all hungry," said several at Tal's back.

Remy turned on them. "And you'll all eat. But you'll eat the same."

Tal reached for the bulky sack across Molina's shoulder. The man resisted. Tal said to him, gently, "We're not Japs, Mr. Molina. We don't starve folks." Tal pulled the bag down and lugged it back onto the pile inside the storeroom. He returned to his place beside his father. Molina stomped away, perhaps to find easier pickings elsewhere in the camp.

Clem dropped his bean sack at Remy's feet. The others retreated, following Molina.

"Then why'd you come over here, man?" Clem asked. "If you didn't want to grab something afore the others."

"I reckon I had a change of heart."

Clem rattled his head walking off. Remy slid down the face of the storeroom door to sit in the dirt.

"We'll wait 'til someone from the committee shows up. They can fix the lock and post a guard."

Tal gazed down at his father, unable to see his face under the brim of the fedora.

Remy said, "That wasn't their fault. Starvation'll make anyone crazy."

"Why aren't you crazy, then?"

Remy crossed his ankles and his arms, as if to take a nap.

"Soon as I saw all that food, I thought of Mac. All the things he had on his soul. I reckon he's facing up to them right now. Then I saw you next to me, and I asked, what kind of father steals from folks outright in front of his boy? I figured if a man can do one thing less he'll have to answer for, it might be the right move. Considerin' our circumstances."

Circumstances? The Japanese were gone. Plenty of food had been found in the camp, and Lucas said the committee would deal with the villagers for more. MacArthur was right around the corner.

"What's wrong with our circumstances?"

"We're still a long way inside Jap territory. There's plenty of blood gonna run before this is over. Trust me. One thing I know from listenin' to that radio. Japs don't surrender. And they don't like people who do. That's us."

Remy tipped back his hat's brim to eye Tal.

"How 'bout you? You have a change of heart?"

Tal pulled on the handle to the storeroom door, jostling Remy leaning against it.

"Nope."

He closed the door behind him. On his knees, by the light between bamboo slats, Tal flicked his Zippo to burn a corner of a burlap rice sack. He clapped hands to smother the flame when the hole was big enough. He filled all his pockets. From outside, his father said, "Hurry up, boy."

Tal slipped through the door. Remy stood, looked down at Tal's bulging pockets. He laid a hand on Tal's shoulder.

"I guess a fella can't make a courtin' call without a present. Wait for me at the gate."

Three Japanese guards nodded when Tal and Remy walked past. They were of the same mold as the men and boys who'd patrolled the camp before this morning: short, not fit or well fed, with little military bearing. They looked like children playing at soldiers. Their guns were real.

"Keep walking," Remy muttered. Ten strides outside the main gate, he asked, "They following us?"

Tal glanced over his shoulder. "No."

His father's face lit up. "Ain't that somethin'?"

Tal and Remy were the first internees outside the gate. Others saw them from behind the wire and pointed, shouting, "Hey!" There were the two Tucks, father and son, breaking a rule not ten minutes after it was set.

The animal husbandry building loomed fifty yards from the front gate. Tal's palms tingled with every closing step. He had no idea what to say to the girl, no way to express what he'd been feeling these past months. He might blurt something stupid. And what *did* he feel? He knew nothing about her except that she'd borne abuse day after day and stood in her window wrapped in red, unexplainably lovely, as if untouched. He'd ask her name right off and introduce himself. But that would be awkward; they seemed beyond that sort of formality, exchanging names like strangers. This was complex. Entering the shadow of the building, his lack of a plan fluttered with the butterflies in his chest. He glanced down at his bulging pockets. He looked clownish.

His father stopped him. Remy cleared his throat.

"Look here," he said, hiding again behind the fedora's brim. Remy scraped the grass with the toe of his sandal. "I suppose this is a dollar short and a day late, but you . . . uh . . . What I'm askin' is, you done this sort of thing before?"

"Calling on a girl?"

"Well, yeah. That's part of what I'm gettin' at. I mean, there's a few girls in the camp."

Tal glanced through the barbed wire. The camp seemed even smaller from the outside. He'd never noticed the handful of girls interned with him beyond their shared predicament. He doubted if they'd ever noticed him. He was always in trouble or chasing it. He'd turned nineteen in prison, and along with losing his freedom he'd arrived near the end of his teen years a virgin. He wished for his mother, Sarah, to be with him now, not Remy. He thought cheaply of his father on the subject of women and did not want his advice.

"You're talking about sex."

Remy shuffled more on the weedy lawn. "Yeah."

"So what are you saying about her?"

"I'm not sayin' anything."

"Yeah, you are. You're saying because of what she's had to do with the Japs, that it's the first thing she's going to do with me. Well, maybe not, Remy. You think of that? Maybe we'll really like each other for better reasons. And maybe this isn't your business."

Remy held up both palms. "All right, all right. Fair enough. I just wanted to say I was sorry if I'd let you down. As your father and all. I just want it to turn out right for you. For you both. That's all."

"Okay."

Tal headed for the rear door of the building. Next to him, Remy kept pace. Inside, Tal stopped his father at the foot of the steps.

"I can do this alone."

"No. We got no idea who's still in here. Might be a Jap guard got left behind. I'll hang with you 'til you see the girl. Then I'm gone. This ain't negotiable, son."

Remy led the way up the stairwell. Turning the corner onto the landing for the second flight of steps, an old Filipina bounded down at them from above, gripping a broom by the handle.

"Go back inside the camp!" she snarled. "You can't be here!"

On the stairs, she swung the broom once to ward them away.

Remy asked, "Lady, who the hell are you?"

"Guards are still here. You better get inside the fence."

Remy answered again. "We're here to see someone."

Tal put a hand in his father's back. "You mind?"

Remy retreated behind him. "Sorry. All yours."

Tal climbed several steps, putting himself in range of the woman's next sweep of the broom.

"You the housekeeper?"

She cocked the broom over her shoulder. "I run this place."

Tal halted. This was the girl's jailer? A Filipina, her own countrywoman? Tal rose another step. He'd never before thought of striking a woman and prepared himself to do it.

At the top of the stairwell, a small Asian girl appeared. She wore a green robe, belted tight above tanned bare legs. Before the old woman could react, the little girl descended in a nimble leap. She grasped the broom from behind the old woman, yanking it away from her. The woman barely turned in time to fend off a swat of the broom at her own head. The little girl tossed the broom over the railing down to the first floor. She pointed behind her up the stairs.

"Boy," she said, smiling at Tal. "Boy Tuck. Go."

Tal strode past the old woman's nasty stare. Remy stayed beside him only to the third-floor landing, where he took a seat, blocking the woman's way up. The satisfied little Asian girl sat beside him, arms crossed.

In a corner of the landing lay a shabby mattress. A desk stood in front of a peg board. One wooden tag bearing a Japanese ideograph hung from it. Tal walked past, into the hallway. An old Filipino stood in the center of the hall. Tal approached. The man bowed his head, and with a gesture, ushered him beyond the curtain.

Chapter Thirteen

L EFT ALONE tonight, Carmen lay dressed in an army
T-shirt and khaki slacks. The clothes and the dark
helped her put a stop to the naked day.

She lay listening to the engines of arriving trucks at the
main gate. Voices in English and Japanese drifted up to her.
The camp seemed nervous.

Carmen lay still, searching for elusive sleep. Frustrated,
she pushed off the tatami to stand in her window.

In the camp, every electric light around the perimeter
had been turned on. Internees in singles and teams moved
from barracks to barracks, collecting digging tools. What
looked like the entire Japanese garrison milled around a
dozen trucks. Small fires burned outside the commandant's
office. No guards patrolled the fence. What was happening?

Carmen left her room to tiptoe down the gray hall. At
the landing, Mama snored in the corner, Papa was nowhere
to be seen. Carmen snuck into the other hall. She eased
aside the drape covering Yumi's room.

Unlike Carmen, the girl slept soundly, in the nude. She
lay on her side, a pale miniature. Gently, Carmen sat on the
tatami, poking a fingertip into her tiny waist.

"Shhh," she hushed when Yumi stirred. Even in the
dim light Carmen noted discolorations on the Korean girl's
buttocks and upper arms. Did she fight every soldier who
stepped under her curtain?

"Come," Carmen whispered, motioning. Yumi slipped
into her green *haori*. Together, they crept toward Carmen's

room. On the landing, Yumi made a jagged gesture at Mama's sleeping backside. She whispered to Carmen, "*Han.*" Grudge.

Carmen's perch had the better view of the camp. Side by side, the girls leaned out to survey the activity of the Japanese and the handful of awake internees. Carmen answered Yumi's querying looks with shrugs.

Yumi yawned and waved both hands into the open air. She'd seen enough. She left the sill and curled on the mattress. Carmen stayed at the window, gathering what she could to tell Benito and the guerrillas. Yumi lay at Carmen's brown feet.

The energy in the camp faded. The internees returned to their own barracks. The Japanese concentrated around the commandant's office and the waiting trucks. Dawn remained hours away. Carmen could guess at little and found even less she could do. She eased herself to the mattress, nestling to Yumi's shape. She lapped an arm across the girl's hip. Carmen brought her nose to Yumi's black hair. The girl's silk robe cooled Carmen's cheek.

In the hall, boot steps came her way. Carmen tightened her hold on Yumi.

The black drape across her door was shoved aside. Kenji stepped in.

He asked, "What are you doing?"

Yumi woke with a grumble. Carmen sat up.

"What do you want, Kenji-sama?"

"Why is she here?"

"Yumi is frightened, like I am. Why are you here?"

The Korean drew up her knees to sit against the wall below the window. Kenji removed his cap. Carmen rose from the mattress to switch on the one lamp in the room. Kenji shifted to a military manner, sticking the cap back on his head. He seemed finished, as if he'd had sex.

"We're leaving," he said.

"Who?"

"The guards. All of us. The internees will be on their own. So will you."

Kenji reported this as if it were bad news. Perhaps it was for him.

Carmen said, "Tell Yumi."

Kenji switched to Japanese. Yumi clapped and hugged Carmen.

"Have the Americans come back?" Carmen asked.

"They are close."

"Where are you going?"

"Our unit's been ordered to move south, to dig trenches. An invasion is expected soon. I know you'll tell the guerrillas this. It doesn't matter."

"Will you fight?"

"If we have to, of course."

Carmen envisioned Kenji firing a rifle. She believed it would knock him on the seat of his pants.

Yumi cast a question at Kenji. He replied, shaking his head. Yumi tightened her arms around Carmen before letting go.

"She asks if you can go home now. I told her you cannot. The war isn't done, Carmen. Do not leave. If the *makipilis* report you missing to the Kempeitai, nothing will change for your family. They'll be held accountable. You know this. Stay here, safe. And keep this wild one here, too. Wait."

"For what?"

"For me to come back."

Kenji slid one shoulder through the drape.

"I will come back." He said this like a hero, and was gone.

Carmen switched off the lamp. She lay down. Now Yumi could not rest. The girl put her elbows on the windowsill and chattered. Carmen understood nothing, couldn't tell Japanese from Korean, but supposed Yumi spoke curses.

The boy would come to her today. To look rested when he did, Carmen fell asleep.

"Songu! Songu!"

Carmen drew a deep breath, blinking herself awake. She opened her eyes into Yumi's bare legs; the girl slept curled beneath the window.

Papa stood at the edge of the tatami, wiggling Carmen's toes.

"Stop it," she said. "What."

"The guards."

"They're gone, I know." Carmen sat up. Yumi did not flinch.

"Wake the *chosenjin*."

Yumi snorted at Papa's voice, an instant distaste at the old man.

"Someone comes," Papa said.

"Who?"

"Two of the internees. They're not supposed to be outside the camp."

"Who?" Carmen repeated.

"A young man and an older one."

Carmen sat up, alarmed. Yumi did the same. She looked ready to pounce on Papa. Carmen spread an arm across the girl to keep her in check.

"Where are they?"

"Coming over the grass. Songu, please."

"Please what?"

"I've done my best to keep you comfortable. Away from harm. My wife. She . . . I'm afraid for the end of the war."

The *makipili* wrung his hands.

"I'll do for you what you've done for me, old man. No less."

Papa nodded, thinking Carmen had given him an assurance.

From the stairwell at the end of the hall, voices were raised. Mama spoke harshly with two Americans. Yumi jumped to her feet. She put her hand over her heart, beaming at Carmen. Before Papa could resist, Yumi flew past him, sweeping aside the curtain.

Papa nodded again, this time as though a servant to his mistress. He ducked under the drape. Carmen stood. The boy would see her as he always had, on her feet.

Papa pulled back the curtain. The boy hesitated. Papa said, "Go ahead."

The Tuck boy entered. Papa dropped the curtain and walked off.

The first thing Carmen noticed was not something about the boy, but that no obstacles stood between them. She ran her eyes along the floor; it lay open and flat, subject to mere steps. She took one.

He lifted a hand, stopping her.

"I'm . . . my name is Talbot. Tal. My father calls me Talbot but I . . . I like Tal."

"Hello, Tal Tuck."

"You know my last name. That other girl, out in the hall."

"Yumi."

"Yeah. She's a wildcat. She knew it, too."

Carmen pointed behind her out the open window. "I watch. I listen."

"I know."

"Yes, you do, boy." She called him by her heart's name. She let it stand. "I'm Carmen."

Amazing, she thought. To have accepted for months that this boy would die in the camp and she would die in the *shuho*, that they would never be close, never speak or be moments from touching. Here they stood.

She stepped forward again. He'd lived long enough in her head and in distance. She raised a hand to lay it on him, make him real and here and alone with her.

But they were not alone. With Tal Tuck finally before her, a thousand Japanese reared between them, standing, kneeling. Remarkably, through the crowd, she could see this boy. A path opened. She did not know how long it would remain. She feared it could close, and she would lose sight of the Tuck boy.

He did not reach back.

"You should go," he said.

"What?"

"The guards have taken off. You're Filipina. You ought to leave. Go home."

Carmen did not lower her arm. "I can't. They'll hurt my family."

"That's cruddy." He put out his hand. She took it.

"I guess you're stuck here, then. With me."

She focused on their joined hands, separate colors, mingled lives. With a light tug he pulled her to his chest. She released his hand to embrace him.

Carmen laid her head to his chest. She probed along his shoulders where the beating had healed, ran fingers down his spine, the furrows of his ribs. Tal Tuck seemed to be the boy she'd hoped he would be, steady and strong. He was more handsome and thin than she could have known.

He pulled out of her arms. He patted swollen pockets.

"I brought you some rice."

Carmen found a bowl. He filled it with grains. She laughed to see him burrow into his clothes for every last bit.

When he was done, he stepped onto the tatami. She wanted him off it. He stood in the center of the thousand. She bit her lip that he might sense them, too. Tal Tuck paused, silent, then moved to the window. He set his hands on the sill, leaned into the open air. She joined him.

"You got a good view," he said. "You can see pretty much everything from up here."

Carmen laid an open hand on his cheek. She pulled him down to her lips. In the window, she kissed him once, lightly.

She said, "Take Yumi and me into the camp."

Chapter Fourteen

THE GIRL said, "I'm Carmen."

She held out her hand. Remy shook it. He made himself banish the image of Nagata behind her, to give her a chance.

She was pretty in the Filipina blend of Asian and Latin, almond eyes on coffee skin. Tal, dark as his mother, stood beside her. They looked good together, like two young trees that might bend in a storm and not break. Remy wished that for them. They linked hands and headed down the stairs.

Yumi, the tiny Korean girl, enclosed Remy's hand in hers. She'd dressed in the same outfit as Carmen, baggy T-shirt and soldier's khakis. With Yumi in tow, Remy followed Tal and Carmen. The *makipili* woman shouted obscenities after them.

Leaving the building, they traced the wire back to the main gate. Remy didn't look through the fence. He had enough on his plate at the moment than to deal with the shock or bigotry of others. He'd never seen his son with a girl, hadn't even thought about it. In their three years of imprisonment, Tal had grown in so many other ways, in courage, spirit, even size, that the notion of women hadn't crossed Remy's mind. In the past year, especially, the boy hadn't wanted much to do with Remy, getting himself tossed into No. 11 just to move away. Now they were roommates again and conspirators. His boy walked in the sunshine with a girl on his arm. Remy was proud that Tal could overlook what she was, whatever that turned out to be. He prepared to stare down anyone in the camp who might give the boy a cross word or a sideways glance. Remy would have to find a place to lock away his own discomfort.

The guards at the gate took no notice. Little Yumi barked at them in Japanese, making Remy nervous. The soldiers seemed nettled.

"Can you tell her not to do that?" Remy asked Carmen.

The Filipina cast a disarming grin over her shoulder. "No."

Inside the wire, the excited mood continued. Everywhere, internees wandered in ecstatic stupors, wrapping their arms around any adult or child in reach. Committee members explored the Japanese barracks for papers. Lucas set up shop in Toshiwara's office. Young Donnelly and some of his yahoos poked their heads out of one of the guards' pillboxes. A team of women happily chased three squealing sows through the mud of the commandant's private livestock pen.

Tal squired Carmen around the camp, with Remy and Yumi in their wake. They ambled past the kitchen to the infirmary and the Protestant chapel, to the cemetery and Mac's grave. They walked south through the rows of barracks, in and out of Vatican City, over to No. 11, then to No. 12, where he lived now with Remy. The two never relinquished hands, nor did Yumi let go of Remy. They passed many internees who offered smiles. Some ladies, especially among the missionaries, gave Carmen and Yumi pecks and whispers of "Dear child." Others, mostly men, leered. A few muttered tasteless comments. Tal bristled. The Filipina's grip firmed around the boy's hand. She strolled unburdened and dignified as any young woman. Remy sped Yumi along to walk in front of the two. Along the way he told more than a few acid-faced men to keep walking and look elsewhere.

The four crossed the field to sit under the shade of the dao tree. No one else joined them on the cool patch of grass. The rest of the camp seemed incapable of being still; the thought of liberation, of Camp Freedom, drove them in every direction inside the fence like pinballs. Four hours after the departure of the Japanese, local Filipinos entered the camp to visit separated friends or sell food. They came through the gates past the handfuls of soldiers who seemed unsure of their own duties. The vendors gave them fruit and the soldiers stood aside. The loudspeaker announced that Toshiwara's guards had left behind a radio receiver which they attempted to break before vacating. This radio was under repair. As soon as it worked, the Internee Committee would broadcast the *Voice of Freedom* to the whole camp.

Carmen and Tal sat cross-legged, touching knees. Yumi lounged on the grass with ankles crossed, finally letting go of Remy. For a firebrand, she seemed patient and pleased with everything. The little Korean's experience was likely just as horrific as Carmen's. That would surely make a shady morning on the grass extra pleasant.

The four sat smiling but with little conversation. Remy stuck a weed between his teeth. He could not calculate the chasm that loomed between his son and the girl. Their worlds could scarcely be more different. Holding hands seemed a fragile bridge. They'd both been victims of the Japanese, but they'd need more. Shared words, open hearts, time. Remy considered walking away, letting them get to it. Yumi couldn't understand anything in English, she'd be fine to leave behind with them. But he didn't trust his son's temper in the event of some interlopers, drunk on their new liberty, putting their asses on their shoulders and saying the wrong thing. Tal hadn't given him a high sign yet to take off.

"Carmen?"

"Yes, sir?"

He waved this away. "You can call me Remy. He does."

The girl addressed Tal. "Why do you call your father by his first name?"

Remy added, "He used to call me Dad, when he was a kid."

Remy guessed this was a bad move, referring to his son as a kid in front of the girl. Before he could cover it up, Tal spoke.

"Mom died when I was young. In Australia. Then we moved to Manila. And Remy wasn't Dad anymore."

Remy pulled the weed from his teeth to toss it into their small circle. That stung, and he questioned that it should have been said out loud like that. But his son rushed to be known by this girl. That meant opening every vault that held secrets and scars. Decades had passed since Remy had his own young love. He'd forgotten the hurry it was in.

"Sorry, boy."

"I know."

"Just so you know. It took me a while to get over your mother's passing. Before I could fix it with you, the Japs rounded us up."

Remy reached across to pat Tal's knee.

Tal said, "You're still Remy."

"That's fine. Long as you're okay with being 'boy.'"

The girl beamed. Remy returned to the question he'd meant to ask.

"Carmen, where're you from in the Philippines?"

"Manila."

"I love that town."

"I was kidnapped."

She said this simply, not to shock but to share the way Tal had.

Tal reached for her hand. The girl took it. She addressed herself to Remy, as if she needed words to tell him, but not the boy. Tal seemed to know already.

She laid it all out. Her brutalizing, her rape, the Kempeitai.

She spoke about Hua, the Chinese girl's fight with despondency, her quiet and inevitable suicide. Carmen told Yumi's story, too, how the child was tricked into believing she was bound for factory work in Japan, her rape, the betrayal by her own father, her year in the Round Pearl in Manila. How they were called by the Japanese "comfort women" and *"pii."*

"There are tens of thousands like us," Carmen said. "I'm sure of it. The Japanese would not treat their own women this way."

Remy sat stunned. The extent of the Japanese cruelty, the organized fashion of it, made it even more atrocious. The gambler in him watched for deadness in Carmen's eyes, in her tone, to gauge the pain's depth. He felt terrible for her but he had to protect his son. Was she a girl too hurt to ever recover, ever love? Listening, Remy grew as saddened by her as he was impressed. Carmen had indeed been through hell. Here she sat describing it.

The mood of the camp settled while they talked. An early lunch was announced, serving up the first of the Japanese foodstuffs left behind. This chilled the last bits of looting, once the internees were made aware that all would benefit.

Remy clapped. "I got an idea." He pointed at Yumi. "She speaks Japanese, right? And Carmen speaks Tagalog."

Tal answered. "Yeah."

"Let's walk into town. Buy these gals some clothes of their own. Let 'em get out of these Jap togs."

"That's nuts."

"A little. You done nuttier, I recall. We get in a tight spot with soldiers, Yumi here'll talk our way out of it. Carmen can handle the locals. Carmen, you up for it?"

The girl sat up sharply, tickled. "Yes."

"Okay. I'm gonna reckon little Perils of Pauline here is up for anything." He stood. "I'll be gone less than an hour. Talbot, keep your head on your shoulders. Stay here, get to know each other better."

"Where you going?"

"We got to have spendin' money, boy."

Remy left the shade. Lazlo was easy to find. The chubby bandit sat in his cubicle alone, grumbling at the devaluation of his stores now that the Japanese had gone and left their supplies behind. Remy had little trouble talking him into a game of poker to distract his blues. Remy agreed to borrow a hundred Philippine pesos as his stake, at 20 percent interest, the first time in months he'd played for money. Lazlo summoned a few others in the building. Remy tripled his stake. He tossed Lazlo 102 pesos, explaining that ought to be enough for the forty minutes he'd had Lazlo's cash.

Under the dao tree, his son and the girls had been joined by young Donnelly and the Irishman, Bascom. Remy arrived to hear Donnelly describe the menu for lunch.

"Pork and beans, pork and greens, pork and I don't give a damn."

"We're headin' into the village," Remy told him. "There's safety in numbers. Feel like a stroll?"

"Tuck, old boy. I have waited three years to put one foot in front of the other as far as I please. We will gladly come along. But lunch first."

All joined Remy on his feet. Tal reached down to help Carmen stand. Bascom did the same for Yumi. The tiny Korean girl twinkled, flirtatious, and did not let Bascom go.

The six of them ate in No. 11. The boys recognized Carmen, the girl in the window. The presence of Tal and Donnelly kept everyone's manners in check. When Yumi flashed her smile and Carmen conducted herself with winning grace, a few admiring glances sprang up among the boys. Remy endured a few friendly jibes, but that was all the troublemakers came up with. They got in line for their first meal without the Japanese, a full plate of mango beans and hulled rice covered with gravy, beside a white slice of pork rump glistening with fat.

At the table, Remy chewed through the first mouthful. He almost wept to see so much on his plate. His felt the food drop into his stomach. All the boys and the two girls stuffed themselves.

"Easy," Remy warned. "Your guts aren't accustomed. Take it slow." They ignored him with packed cheeks. Remy considered repeating his advice to Tal, but up to this point experience had been a better parent than he. Remy gave the boy half his own lunch to speed the process along.

With the meal done, Donnelly and Bascom, Tal, the girls, and Remy headed for the main gate. "Keep a muzzle on her," Remy said to Bascom, passing the guards. "No need to poke these fellas." The Irishman brought his free hand to his lips to shush Yumi.

The path ran northwest through uncut grass and an orchard. Fruit trees and high bamboo shaded the walking party. They crossed into the deep ravine, then emerged onto a paved surface. Isolated huts stood along the road. In small fields, children at play chased chickens, lean horses swatted flies with their tails. Elderly folk shied into the shadows of their homes, afraid of Westerners walking freely past, even with no Japanese nearby. Donnelly waved at the frightened Filipinos. The others tossed pebbles into the woods and wet paddies. The boys tugged at each other to start tussles and horseplay. The hike continued in high spirits.

Ten minutes out of camp, lunch struck. Bascom's face twisted, and he laid a hand on his belly. Yumi hung on gamely while the boy sprinted for the cover of a large bush off the road. When the girl realized what he was doing she ran back to Carmen's open arms, chattering and indignant. Tal was hit next. He disappeared into the shrubs to catcalls from the rest, including Remy.

Another half mile along the road, they entered Anos, a village on the bay, one mile east of the town of Los Baños. A fleet of tricycle rickshaws pedaled out to greet them. Remy paid for rides to a Sunday bazaar at the heart of the hamlet. Donnelly kept up his regal waving. Despite their arrival in a noisy fleet, which Carmen especially enjoyed, the vendors of the bazaar received them reluctantly. No one would show their wares. An aged man approached, a battered bowler on his brown noggin. In Tagalog he explained to Carmen that the whites should return to the camp. Anos was just a small village. *Makipilis* were everywhere and would cause trouble so long as the Japanese were on Luzon. Remy said they would go, but first they wanted to buy clothes for the girls. Could they please do this?

The old man passed his arms across the many merchants waiting for his word. He called out, *"Siggy, siggy!"* Carmen translated, "Hurry, hurry."

Villagers ringed Remy and his charges, brandishing scarves, silk blouses, woven slacks, straw sandals. Remy dug out twenty pesos. He handed the bills above the shorter Filipino heads to Tal.

"Get a chicken and some eggs!"

Remy pulled Yumi and Carmen close. "Pick anything you want." Carmen waded into the crowd, holding Yumi's hand. She ordered the pressing men and women to line up and show their goods in an organized fashion. Remy stood aside. He put ten pesos in Donnelly's palm.

He said. "How 'bout another batch?"

The Aussie and Bascom faded into the bazaar to buy the makings for another few gallons of bomber lotion.

The order Carmen imposed on the villagers fell apart after Yumi made a choice, a sky blue top with pearl buttons. The other sellers saw their chances dwindle and squeezed tighter on all sides, lifting their wares high in a swirl of pastels and pleas. More villagers held aloft caged birds, dried fruits and peppers, carved icons of Mary and Jesus, any item they might sell. They drove forward, packing the girls inside the throng. Carmen selected a pair of black slacks and a pink top. The merchants turned on Yumi. The little girl vanished in a whirlpool of pants and shoes and the dark mop heads of the villagers. Carmen, holding her own purchases, got separated from Yumi's side. She waved at Remy in concern. He waded in too late.

The little girl's scream parted the crowd. Yumi, hands clutched to her face, bolted through the rift, away from the bazaar. Remy chased her down behind a bamboo hut. Carefully, he took a knee, soothing her with shushes and whispers of "It's all right." He reached to wrap her in his arms. The girl recoiled.

Carmen hurried around the corner of the hut. Yumi jabbered and took her hand.

"Leave her with me, Remy. Please."

"What happened?"

Carmen sat in the shade of the hut. She took tiny Yumi into her lap. "I can't explain."

Remy extended a hand to Yumi. The girl, soothed by Carmen, allowed his stroke under her chin.

"Try me."

Carmen laid her cheek on the crown of Yumi's head. "The crowd was too much for Yumi. Almost for me."

"Why?"

"It's . . ." Carmen searched for words. "Being touched. It's . . . difficult."

"But Yumi held my hand. She put a death grip on Bascom. You and Tal hold hands."

"We make ourselves do it. We practice, Yumi and me. To try and remember what affection feels like. It's hard. And I'm afraid it will always be hard."

Remy, heart-struck, rested his hand behind Carmen's neck. The girl closed her eyes, as if to study the feel of it. Yumi, wrapped by Carmen, shut her eyes, too.

Remy stood. "We'll have to go soon. I'll pay for the clothes, then come get you."

"Please," Carmen said, "one more thing. Could you buy some white cotton socks."

"Sure. What for?"

"Yumi has begun to bleed. We have no napkins."

Remy returned to the bazaar to pay for the selected clothes. He added emerald slacks for Yumi, barely larger than a child's size, and three pairs of white socks. The cost came to forty pesos. He found Tal and the rest, explaining only that Yumi had gotten scared of the pressing crowd, she was fine. Donnelly carried a mesh net of guavas, bananas, and mangoes, Bascom a basket of eggs. Tal held a live, squawking chicken by the neck.

Remy said, "Kill that thing."

"You kill it."

"Why me? You're the one who used to steal Toshiwara's chickens."

"Someone else always killed them."

Remy asked if anyone would wring the bird's neck. No one stepped up. The chicken made a flapping ruckus in Tal's grip. Carmen approached, towing a pacified Yumi. Remy handed the little Korean girl her bright new clothes and the socks, winking. Remy offered Carmen her new outfit. She tossed the clothes over her shoulder.

She gestured to the chicken. "Is that a pet?"

Unsure, Tal said, "No."

Carmen took the screeching bird. With three flips of

her wrist, she swung the chicken by the neck, then snapped away its head. This she threw to a mangy dog skulking nearby. Carmen held the chicken's body until it stilled, then inverted it to let the blood drain out. She returned the inert feathers to Tal.

The boy stood stunned. The others moved first, heading away from Anos. Passing him, they patted Tal on the shoulders.

"Okay," they said, "she's all yours. Great gal. Good luck."

For the trip back to camp, they ignored the rickshaws, enjoying the free, sunny stroll. The girls walked together, far in front. Tal clutched the headless bird. He and Donnelly prattled about the chicken dinner they would devour tonight, stomachs be damned. Bascom opined on what flavor bomber lotion Donnelly should brew up. The sun had dropped off past its noon apex; the road lay in the shade of the chirping jungle, then the bamboo and the orchard.

Inside the wire, two thousand internees sat outside their barracks in homemade chairs and on blankets, as if for a festival. Older folks shaded themselves under straw hats, youngsters cavorted with native children, couples reclined beside picnics of canned vegetables and fresh fruit. Filipinos wandered the grounds selling tobacco, coffee, bread, and greens.

The radio the Japanese had abandoned had been repaired. A broadcast of MacArthur's *Radio Freedom* from his command post in the Philippines was scheduled over the loudspeaker in thirty minutes. The whole camp gathered for its first shot of unfettered news.

Donnelly took the chicken, saying he'd get it cooked for dinner. Remy unhitched himself from Yumi, handing her off again to Carmen. The girls snuck away to put on their new clothes.

Tal and Remy spread blankets under the dao for the four of them to wait for the broadcast. Lazlo came by and, in front of the girls, demanded the chance to win back his money. Remy, with liberation closer and less need to appease everyone in the camp, told Lazlo to go away. The fat man slouched off.

At 3:00 p.m., the loudspeakers crackled with the voice of Douglas MacArthur. The internees applauded wildly. The old man sounded good and resolved, like he was holding a full house and eager to lay it down. Remy swore to lose his shirt to him next time they played if MacArthur would come get them out of here. The general offered his welcome to those struggling and surviving around the Pacific rim. He told them to do their best to sustain hope and the fight for freedom, then turned the broadcast over to the news.

Most of what Remy heard, he already knew from the crystal set. MacArthur had been placed in command of all U.S. ground forces in the Pacific and Nimitz was in charge of all naval forces. Preparations were being made for assaults on Iwo Jima, Okinawa, and the main islands of Japan. The British were making headway on Burma. No American forces had yet landed on Luzon, but air operations against Formosa were paving the way.

The internees cheered, until a sobering report quieted them. The battles in Europe's winter were not going so well. Germany was mounting a stubborn and bloody defense, particularly in the Ardennes. The high spirits of the camp dampened, especially among the five hundred Europeans. The mood soared again when the announcer returned to the Pacific War. Three American task forces were closing in on Luzon. A landing appeared imminent; the reporter cited the New Year's Eve bombing of Los Baños's rail yards. The internees roared themselves hoarse. Under the dao tree, Remy, Tal, and the girls joined hands and danced in a circle.

Before dinner, Donnelly and Bascom arrived with the chicken browned and aromatic. The bird was divvied up among the six of them. An hour later, they ate again in No. 12, a hearty camp stew featuring the commandant's prized Brahman bull. This was a short-sighted butchery; the committee now needed to find another beast to haul firewood. The bull had fallen victim to the euphoria of the day. Hauling wood was for tomorrow.

After the meal, all the internees returned to their outdoor seats for another transmission, a KGEX broadcast of Roosevelt's State of the Union speech recorded yesterday, January 6.

The violet gloaming behind Mount Makiling settled over a more composed camp than during the sunlit hours. The internees' precarious situation seemed to be sinking in. No children gallivanted, no couples laughed and lounged, even the missionaries seemed restrained in their thanks to the Almighty. The Japanese were gone from the camp, but not from the island. The war still had to be brought to them on Luzon. Judging from radio reports describing the ferocious marine landings of the past year on Kwajalein, Truk, New Guinea, Saipan, and Leyte, the invasion of Luzon promised to be hard fought and grisly. The Japanese around Los Baños would not lay down their arms, not alive anyway, and no one supposed they would simply surrender the advantage of two thousand Western hostages. The camp couldn't expect to be spared from the coming crossfire; even the bombs fell hazardously close. The internees' hunger may have eased, but not their danger.

In the spreading dusk, when Roosevelt's voice boomed through the loudspeakers, Remy applauded with the rest. Even though Remy had left the States well before FDR took office, he'd never liked the man. Four terms in office set Remy's teeth on edge, and he'd never bought into the paternal lectures and patrician cigarette holder.

The camp listened rapt to the opening phrases of FDR's speech. The president first summed up the condition of the war in Europe, explaining that the most critical phase was at hand: taking the battle into the German heartland. He praised the Italian campaign, the British, Russians, and French as allies.

Remy whispered to Tal, "Does the old man even know we're here?" Carmen shushed them both. Yumi lay on her back, dozing.

At last, the speech turned to the war in the Pacific. Roosevelt used grand terms to depict island landings, naval and air battles. American forces had slashed their way close enough to Japan that superfortress bombers were blasting Tokyo itself.

The internees whooped. While the camp sent up hurrahs, Remy grew concerned. Destroying the Japanese capital might sound like a good idea, but Roosevelt wasn't the one sitting defenseless in the middle of fifty thousand Japanese who might take a mind toward vengeance.

FDR called for sacrifice, for more production, raw materials, weapons research, ammunition, nurses, and "the total mobilization of all our human resources" to win the war. He closed his oration with mention of several domestic initiatives for the U.S. economy. These items lost the attention of the internees, few of whom were thinking about an investment or a job back home.

To Remy's ear, Roosevelt sounded weary, the speech of a man tallying his winnings and losses before leaving the table. MacArthur called to mind a man raring to go, a power to be reckoned with. Roosevelt sounded like a fellow who wanted to be remembered well.

Remy swatted at a mosquito. The internees gathered their furniture and bed coverings off the ground to make their way indoors. The loudspeakers announced curfew.

Yumi awoke with a snort, nudged by Carmen's toe. The girl hopped up refreshed and helped Remy gather the blankets off the grass. Tal and Carmen stood aside, aloof and unsure how to let the other go.

Remy handed the balled blankets to Yumi with a soft cuff behind her ear. He raised a finger in her face, meaning "Wait here." The girl nodded.

"Okay, you two," he said, approaching Tal and Carmen. "Time to say good night. Talbot, we'll walk the girls back to their building." Remy put hands to his hips, anticipating resistance. "Carmen, the Japs might be gone from the camp but they're not off Luzon. They're still all around us, and they're still in Manila. As long as they are, your parents are at risk. I don't know what that *makipili* woman is capable of, but I'm betting she can be nasty. She starts talkin' about you, who knows what the Japs'll do? So we're not gonna make her any madder'n she is by you sleepin' anywhere but your own bed for now. We'll sort that out soon as we can."

The boy and girl faced each other quickly, as if trying to decide which of them would mount their defense.

Remy addressed his son. "We broke enough rules today, son. I think we might've got a pass because of the new circumstances, but there's no guarantee that's gonna continue. Like it or not, we still live in the camp and the committee's in charge. You break curfew and get caught, missy here will have to visit you in the brig, where Lucas is bound to put you and I can't stop him. We'll find a few more rules to break tomorrow, I reckon, but for now, let's escort these two lovelies back."

Remy turned on his heel. He took the blankets from Yumi and reached for the girl's little hand. He strode off at a pace that made her skip beside him. Tal and Carmen followed.

At the main gate, lackadaisical guards in lawn chairs

waved the four of them past. Remy halted on the grass beside the animal husbandry building, to let the lagging couple catch up. When they did, Remy set a hand on each girl's shoulder.

"Ladies, you look stunning in your new outfits." He acted out this sentiment for Yumi, pointing to her silk blouse, and gave the okay signal. Yumi bounced. "Good night, and it's a pleasure to know you." He tipped his fedora, then leaned down to her, pausing to let the girl come to him or not. She shied, like a hummingbird hovering close, before planting a peck on his gray cheek. She hurtled off into the dark.

"Talbot, I'll wait for you here."

Carmen pressed lips to her fingertips. She lifted them to Remy's other cheek. The boy led her away from the gate, to the building. Remy thought to turn his back and let his son kiss her in private, but strained his eyes to see. From what he could tell, Tal did a good job.

On their way back to the barracks, they did not speak. Remy gave the boy a quick hug and walked alongside his glowing son.

Chapter Fifteen

◆

A N HOUR after sunup, a guard stopped Tal at the main gate. The soldier's uniform was ripped and smoky. He'd seen combat.

The other four guards formed behind him as though Tal, carrying two plates of breakfast, might make trouble.

"No go out," said the stern-faced guard.

The lawn chairs had been removed. These Japanese were not yesterday's guards.

"I'm only going there." Tal pointed to the animal husbandry building, hard by the fence, fifty yards from the gate. "Just taking food to friends. That's all. Here." Tal offered the man a plate of greens, rice mush, and beef strips. "You take one."

A soldier in the rear stepped up, until the one facing Tal barked him back into formation.

He pushed away the offered meal. "No go."

Tal said, "Please." He felt dishonored for begging, and pivoted away before the guard could refuse him a third time.

Tal traced the fence to the façade of the building. A soldier patrolled the road beneath Carmen's window. Tal presented him with one of the breakfasts. The little man surveyed left and right to see if anyone might catch him, then snatched the food. He walked away, gobbling the food.

Tal shouted up to Carmen. She did not appear. He jogged to the building's south wing to call beneath Yumi's window. Both girls leaned over the sill, green and red robes side by side.

Yumi hollered down something unintelligible, waving. Carmen elbowed the tiny girl out of the opening.

"Good morning, Tal!"

"I tried to bring you both some breakfast. I got stopped at the gate. Something's changed. They're walking the wire again."

Carmen paused to look over the camp. "What happened?"

"I'm gonna find out. I'll set the food over here on your side of the fence. Come down and get it."

Tal reached the plate far under the barbs to leave it on a clump of weeds. With a wave to Carmen—and Yumi beside her again—he hurried to his barracks.

The word buzzing in the dining hall was of a new troop of soldiers that had arrived in the night from Mindoro. They were the ragged remains of a company hit hard by fighting, sent to Los Baños to recover. While they wouldn't interfere with the camp's self-management, they'd been ordered to put a stop to Filipinos visiting inside the wire except for food and supplies and to clamp down on anyone leaving the camp. Apparently the first round of replacement guards had been too few and too lax.

Donnelly ambled up to Tal. "You heard?"

"Yeah. I don't like it."

"Can't go see your sally, eh?"

"No."

"I don't think these new Japs are going to fancy us strolling into town, either." The Australian lapped an arm across Tal's shoulder. He said clandestinely, "Not in the middle of the day, at least, eh?"

Tal returned to beneath Carmen's window. Through the wire, behind the weeds, the plate was still there. From thirty yards off, the guard he'd fed earlier held up one finger. Tal was to be given one minute. Carmen waited above.

"I couldn't come down," she said. "Mama stopped me."

"Why?"

"She said Yumi and I have to stay in our rooms now that there's guards back in the camp."

"She can't do that."

"Yes, she can."

The guard came his way, tapping his wristwatch to signal time running out. Tal took no steps back from the wire.

"Go," Carmen said.

Tal held his ground, craning his neck back to gaze up at her. The guard grunted a warning.

Carmen leaned far over her sill. Her robe parted enough to see the divide of her breasts. The guard, only strides from Tal, looked up as well. When the man brought down his eyes, he lacked malice, wanting no fight. He, too, was marked by other battles, he'd likely had enough. The soldier needed Tal to walk off.

Carmen shouted, "Go to the tree. Wait for me!"

How could she get out? Before Tal could speak, Carmen vanished from the window. The guard stopped at arm's length away. He tugged the rifle off his shoulder, rotating it butt first.

Tal flattened a palm to stop him. He indicated the full plate of food hidden in the bushes. The guard bowed his head at Tal retreating.

He sat in the shade with others. He knew them all. A young couple with a two-year-old born in Santo Tomas had both gone bony over the past months trading food to get powdered milk for the child. The widow of a man who'd had a heart attack ten months ago wrestled with depression. A preacher, a salesman with a sunny disposition, a lawyer. The dog killer, Dr. Lockett, and an army nurse; gossip in the camp linked the two of them.

High above in the morning, formations of American bombers and fighters shuttled back and forth, pounding Manila and targets just miles west of Los Baños. The internees were not forced indoors by these guards; they relished every detonation and rumble.

The talk under the tree was about the fifty new guards, how the camp was in charge of feeding them, too. That was surely why the soldiers allowed food to flow in from the locals, and did nothing to prevent the continued slaughter of the livestock. These latest Japanese looked like a pretty beat-up bunch. They could still be dangerous.

After an hour, Carmen showed. She emerged from the jungle on the opposite side of the barbed wire wearing the sky blue blouse Remy had bought. To Tal she seemed like an opal against the lush green, containing her own light. They could not touch; the fence ran doubled here. Across rusty barbs, they stood five strides apart.

"How'd you get out?"

"Yumi."

Up close, the girl seemed frantic. She'd walked a mile around the fence, much of it along the dense bank of the creek.

"Sit down. Tell me."

She composed herself, cross-legged on the grass. Tal did the same.

"I was so afraid you were going to get into a fight with that guard. You can't do that."

"I know. I just get ticked off."

"You have to hide it."

"Toshiwara told me the same thing. I'll do better. So what happened after I left?"

"I got dressed and walked right past Mama. She screamed for me to get back in my room. I told her I wouldn't go. When the new soldiers come for the *shuho* she'll tell them where I've gone. 'They'll find you,' she said. 'I won't have to.' Then Yumi came out on the landing. She did this."

Carmen imitated the tiny girl's gesture, thumping her own breast.

"Yumi was saying to Mama, 'I'll take all the soldiers. Let her go.' I ran down the steps. I don't know if I did the right thing."

Tal wrapped fists around the barbed wire. The fence remained more powerful than him, but he could hate it. He could adore what was on the other side.

"There's no right thing. There's just bad and worse. That's gonna change. And soon."

She dug into a pocket of her slacks. "This is for you."

Carmen held up a wooden tag. She sailed it through the strands of wire into Tal's hands. The tag bore a symbol, 歌.

"It means Songu," she said. "It's what the Japanese call me. You keep it, until you can give it back to me in person. Yes?"

Tal ran his thumb over the symbol. He wanted to snap it, throw the pieces into the creek behind her. He tucked the tag into his shirt.

The two sat across from each other, talking through the wires. They spoke about the past in their lives, and the futures they hoped for, but nothing of the camp or today. This was how they made the barrier between them vanish. They talked of where they would live together, imagined having children, argued over names. Tal had never seen America and wasn't sure he'd fit there. Carmen wanted to go. She described her father, brothers, and uncles in Manila, how hard they worked as street vendors, her mother's stoic heart, as if she would see them tonight at sundown when they wheeled in from the city. Tal told of his own mother. He colored his recollections to match Carmen's, making Sarah more vivid than she was in his memory, and let himself believe he knew her as well as he claimed. He spoke more fondly of Remy than he'd expected.

In the afternoon, Tal left to fetch food. He hurried back with bowls of rice and beans mixed with bacon. He'd tied one up in cloth. "Catch." He tossed the covered bowl through the two fences so it would not spill.

The meal slowed their conversation. When they had eaten, Carmen lay on her side, folding one arm as a pillow. The other arm she stretched beneath the bottom strand of wire, to Tal. Inside the camp, he took the same posture, extending his open hand into the dead space between them. They slept, Tal in the shade of the dao tree, she in the cool rising from the creek, reaching to each other.

When he awoke, Carmen was gone. The bowl had been lobbed back through the fence. The sun shone behind the jungle. Tal, creaky from the long nap, turned his back to the fence. He looked across the tops of the many barracks of his prison to her empty window. He took from his pocket the wooden tag with the symbol for "Songu."

He plotted to return it.

After dinner, Tal walked the fence. He counted the Japanese, noting the spaces between them, their level of attention. These tired boys, fresh off the front line, made sloppy guards. They bunched up to chat and smoke, they leaned or sat. The camp posed no threat, and these soldiers presented little in return.

The internees possessed a renewed vigor after years of being wary, starved, and scared. With two days of full rations in their bellies, they found themselves with unaccustomed energy and nothing to expend it on. Most were convinced liberation would arrive any day; much of the routine work in the camp slowed, or was not done. The committee had not replaced Toshiwara's bull, the firewood supply dwindled. Folks milled, restless even after dark. When the loudspeaker announced that the Japanese radio needed more repair and there would be no broadcast tonight, a cry went across the grounds. No one knew what to do with themselves now that they were no longer weak. To replace the news and placate the camp, the committee played music over the loudspeakers. Curfew would be pushed back ninety minutes.

With everyone outdoors and no current events coming from the camp radio, Tal found Remy lying alone on a blanket in front of No. 12, listening to the music. Tal asked if they might go inside, break out their radio, and dial up KROJ, get the latest news, spread the word. Remy said sure.

Inside, the two uncovered Mac's crystal set and listened for an hour. Outside, Count Basie and Chick Webb tunes occupied the camp. On the crystal set, Tal heard that Radio Tokyo had reported a large American convoy near Lingayen, another off Mindoro, a third approaching from Saipan. American forces would soon land on Luzon and intensive bombings were taking place against all coastal gun emplacements and airfields. Once the news cycled back on itself, Remy put the radio back into its hole. They shoved the bunk into place.

"Why do we have to keep hiding it?" Tal asked. "What's the big deal? The Japs're gone."

Remy sat on the bunk, pondering his own answer. "Maybe it's three years of habit, knowing the Japs'd string me and Mac up if we got caught with it. Maybe it's just a gambler's instinct. That little radio is something you and I know about that no one else does. It's an ace in the hole, and I don't feel like showin' it off just yet. I figure let's rely on the camp radio for now, and wait a little longer to see how the cards are fallin'. Besides, I ain't in a hurry to be anybody's hero."

Tal rested hands on his hips, alert to an insult. "Meaning what? That I am?"

"You're in a hurry for somethin'. That I do know. Sit down, Talbot."

"I'll stand."

Remy pointed. "You'll sit."

Tal plopped onto the mattress of the lower bunk across from Remy. He met his father's gaze. Remy looked away. He pulled off his fedora.

"I'm sorry the gals can't join us. But it's gonna be soon, boy. You understand?"

"Sounds like it."

"I don't know what it's gonna look like when the shit hits the fan. You heard the same stuff I did. Three big convoys. MacArthur's comin'. That's great news, but it scares me at the same time. All I can figure is it's gonna get crazy. When it does, we're gonna have to stick close to each other."

"I'll be there."

"Not if you get reckless. You won't be there for me, or for her. I'll say again: it's gonna be soon. You can wait, can't you?"

"You want me to lie?"

Remy rapped his fedora against his leg. "Goddamit." He turned the hat in circles by the brim, prickly and uncomfortable. "Why you gotta go now?"

Tal paused to consider. "Mostly because the Japs say I can't."

"I wish that didn't make sense. Damn it."

Tal said, "I'll be fine. I've done this before."

The fedora stopped.

"With a girl?"

"No, I mean . . . I mean sneaking out of the camp."

Remy spoke to his anxious fingers and the spinning hat. "All right. Look, this puts me in a hell of a position. Being your old man."

"I know."

"Do you? I could forbid it, but that'll get me nowhere."

"Pretty much."

"So, now I gotta ask."

Tal watched the hat spin faster. "Okay."

"What do you know?"

"Not much."

Remy blew out a long exhale. "Oh, man."

Tal added, "I figure she does."

Remy shifted the fedora to one hand, to wave it about the small room. "This ain't the way it was supposed to be, Talbot. I'm sorry."

"Sorry for what? I love her. I don't know what else you could've wished for me."

Remy lifted his face. The etches beside his eyes crinkled. "Me neither, I guess."

Remy gazed for moments, as though he saw more than just Tal there.

"All right. Don't run and don't sneak. Just walk. You can duck these new guards, they're half dead by the looks of 'em. They don't care what you do, and don't make 'em care. I'll cover for you at roll call. Be in your bunk before midnight or I come looking for you. Understood?"

"Got it."

"Okay. Anything you want to ask me?"

"Not really."

"Well, I'm sorry Mac's not here. He could've stood in for me. Now listen. I got only one bit of advice for you."

"Do you have to?"

"Yes. You're right about the girl."

Remy stood from the bunk. Tal followed.

"How so?" he asked.

His father clapped him hard in the middle of the back.

"Let her run the show."

Tal donned a black T-shirt.

He strolled through the camp. People ignored him, busy

visiting or listening to big bands over the loudspeakers from chairs and blankets. They burned smudge pots to keep the bugs at bay, children kicked empty tins. A festive atmosphere hovered. Above it all, Carmen stood in silhouette.

At the woodpile behind the kitchen, Tal grabbed a stick the proper length. Casually, he made his way to the infirmary. With no guards in sight, he slipped along the wall to the rear of the building and the double fence there.

"I wasn't gonna wait much longer, mate."

Tal jumped.

Donnelly stepped out of a shadow. "Don't piss yourself."

Tal moved alongside him. "What're you doing here?"

"I figured this was as good a time as any for a walk-about."

"How'd you know I was coming?"

Donnelly chuckled. "Because I'm not a stupid git. Everyone in camp can see your gal up in her window and you making your clever little way here in your black T-shirt. I got here first. Thought we'd go out together, more fun that way. After you."

The Australian lifted the bottom strand. Tal put aside his amazement to lie on his back. He shimmied under, then held the wire for Donnelly. In moments, they stood outside both fences. Tal stashed the stick in the weeds.

The two pushed through high grass and the bamboo grove, careful not to cause the tall stalks to waver.

"Where you going?" Tal asked. "Town?"

"Just taking the air. It smells better outside the wire. You know, down under, we got seven million people and room for ten times more. You get used to open spaces. This Los Baños has been a bit of hell."

Tal said, "I was born in Australia. Near Coffs Harbour."

"What a constant surprise you are, Tuck."

The boys reached the edge of the ravine. Both scrambled

down the dark bank, shaking hands at the bottom. Donnelly disappeared on the stones of the trickling creek. Tal crossed to the other side.

He pushed through the underbrush, making his way to the university's orchard. The Japanese had ignored these trees. Three hundred yards from the camp gate, mangoes, papayas, and lemons fell overripe and wasted.

At the far edge of the orchard, the main road into the camp lay unlit and without traffic. Tal squatted in the weeds, watching the guards at the gate until he had his best chance to cross unseen. He walked across the tarmac like a boy doing nothing wrong. In another hundred yards, he stood at the back door of the animal husbandry building.

From his pocket he took the tag that bore the name "Songu." He carried it up the steps, taking no effort to mask his footsteps.

Again, he was met on the stairs by the *makipili* Filipina. This time she had with her a bony old man. The woman crossed arms over her scrawny chest, holding the high ground of the landing. The old man stood behind her.

The woman said, "Turn around."

Tal did not stop ascending. "Get out of my way."

He stepped onto the landing. The *makipili* moved in his path to Carmen's room. She spotted the wooden tag in his hand.

"Give me that."

"Take it from me."

"You," she snapped. "You're not in New York or wherever you think you are. She's not yours. She belongs to the Japanese. I can have you shot."

"You know where to find me. Now move."

Tal advanced on the woman, with no plan except to go to Carmen. The *makipili* unfolded her arms, ready to scrap.

Behind her, the old man spoke. "Take Songu."

The woman spun on him. "Shut up."

"I've done too much of that. Step aside."

"No."

Tal had waited long enough. He moved into range of the old woman. She whipped a knobby fist at his head. He raised an arm to block it, she swung the other hand. Tal rushed her, clinching her blouse in both hands. He swept the woman onto her heels, driving her backward against the wall. She struck with a thud and hung from his fists.

He brought his face close. "You ever speak to me again, or if anything bad happens to either of those girls, I'll throw you down the stairs. You understand?"

She dropped none of her contempt. "Yes, American."

Tal put her on her feet. He moved toward the hall. She stayed pressed against the wall, seething.

Carmen waited outside her room. She pointed, shouting, "Tal!"

He mistook her purpose, thinking this a greeting. When the mop handle cracked the back of his skull, Tal whirled. Leaping faster than the old woman could retreat, he shoved with enough force to cast her into the air. She landed on her rump, skidding to the landing. The woman scrambled up. Her old Filipino moved to intercept her.

"Please, American. Leave her to me."

"I don't think you can handle her."

"I can't. I can only try to protect her."

"Then keep her away from me."

Carmen walked him to her room. He held up the drape for her to enter. Jazz from the camp loudspeakers drifted in her window.

Tal handed her the wooden tag.

"I brought it, like you said."

Carmen took it, then gave it back. "Bring it to me again."

"All right."

"How is your head?"

He fingered the spot where the woman had thumped him. He'd have a lump.

"I want to kiss you."

He kicked himself for this clumsiness. But the thought of saying that had been the only beacon he'd followed under the wire, through the brush, across the road, and past the combative old woman. He could have said a million other things, and every syllable would have been just one more obstacle to speaking those words.

Carmen blinked away her surprise. "All right."

They came together slowly. Tal kept his eyes open. When their mouths met, he expected Carmen to delve deeply into the kiss, carry him away on it. She remained shy, careful. Tal was not sure how to propel matters, so he hesitated. They lingered on each other's lips. Tal shut his eyes. Every sense in his body crowded to feel and explore the girl through this first true touch, until Carmen set her hand gently on his chest to push him away.

Tal almost lost his balance. She seemed unsteady, too. He put a hand against the wall. She left hers against his chest.

She said, "Not here."

Chapter Sixteen

T HEY CROSSED the road together into the cogon grass. In khakis and T-shirt, Carmen looked like any Filipino boy out scavenging after dark. The Japanese at the gate took no notice.

They moved into the orchard. Carmen trailed her hand through the low branches as if through a waterfall, reveling in the dark greenery and the freedom to pass here unseen with the boy. She'd traded her lamp for the moon, her mattress for wild weeds and these trees. He'd come for her as promised. She'd have to return, but before that happened she would inhale and feel as much of this open night as she could.

"Come on," he chided when she lingered too long in the orchard.

"Tell me where we're going."

"It's safe and quiet. And it's special, you'll see. Take my hand."

He led Carmen into a thicket of high grasses and bamboo. Blades swished at her legs tramping in Tal's wake, until they emerged at the bank of a ravine. Above the rocky creek bed, a canopy of trees and vines blocked all but scraps of stars.

She asked, "Down there?"

Tal clambered down the steep slope. He supported her, following close behind. Halfway along the incline, a rock broke loose beneath her slipper, clattering to the bottom. A sudden quiet cropped up on all sides, a cessation of sounds she'd not been aware had been there.

Tal smiled up at her. "You see?"

Reaching the creek bed, the boy moved carefully, guiding Carmen in his footsteps. In the faint light through the trees, he picked their way. The noises of the ravine resurged. An owl piped up, something screeched far ahead, echoing across the jungle. A monkey scurried off a branch, shaking leaves that fluttered around Carmen and Tal.

He led her to a boulder resting near the bank. Both went barefoot. They sat against the great rock, dangling feet into a shallow pool.

Carmen took Tal's hand, tracing around his knuckles. "Listen to them," she whispered. The voices of the ravine were new to her, croaks and caterwauls, the whoosh of wings like witches at night, creaking branches, scampering in the trees. Man was absent in this place. In Manila, before Los Baños, Carmen heard nothing but machines, her family hawking wares, the bells of taxis, churches and horses; in the *shuho*, only the worst sounds of men and her own growling stomach, hymns from the camp, bombers above. Tonight, Tal had brought her here to show her nothing of man but him.

A mosquito buzzed her ear. Tal waved it away from her. She kissed him.

This kiss burst out of her. The boy raised both hands to her shoulders. She stood into the kiss, as if unbound from the *shuho* she did not fall but was drawn upward. He rose with her.

The boy's lips pulled away. He stepped back, removing his hands. They stood in water to their calves.

"What?" she asked.

He hesitated.

She asked again, "What?"

"I've never done this before."

She wrapped herself with one arm across her breasts, the other at her waist, the way she would stand naked.

"Do you care about me, Tal?"

"More than I can say."

"Then I haven't done this before either."

Carmen closed the distance between them. She gripped the hem of his T-shirt, Tal raised his arms. She swept the shirt up and away and tossed it onto a rock. She tugged off her own T-shirt. Tal reached to pull her brown breast against his pink skin but Carmen held him off. She unbuttoned his shorts and made him sit on the rock for her to take them off. She did the same beside him with her khaki pants.

Carmen stood in the pool. She drew him to his feet. In the dim light, every bit of his frame was angular, from big kneecaps above the water to sharp collarbones. The Tuck boy seemed whittled from hard ivory. One day he would fill out to be a breathtaking man.

She put a hand to his chest, whiter than any she had touched. She circled behind him, trailing fingertips over his skin. His flesh lacked the fat of an officer, the stink of a soldier. The boy fidgeted, like any boy. He had violence in him. She'd seen it flash tonight in the *shuho*. Nagata had not drubbed it out of him but pounded it in deeper. She'd seen this in the Japanese, their absorption of anger and the release of it on her body. Running a hand across the lean muscles of his back, Tal frightened her more than any of them because he was not a thousand, he was one.

He turned, not waiting for Carmen to finish her orbit around him. Carmen stepped back. She ran her eyes down her own bare length, matching herself to him. She was darker and just as poorly fed. She knew how they would fit together, and nothing else.

"What's the matter?" he asked.

Another mosquito flew between them. Tal folded to sit.
The water rose to his ribs.

"Come on," he said, "take a seat. We'll get eaten up if we
don't."

Carmen lowered herself. The pool chilled for a moment.
Her buttocks found sand and small pebbles. With cupped
hands, Tal poured water across her shoulders to ward off the
insects. She wet him, too, dribbling over his head until they
both glistened. Around them the jungle stirred, accustomed
to them now.

The boy quieted. He faced the stars. Droplets channeled
down his neck, his Adam's apple bobbed when he spoke.

"I want to say something."

"Don't," she said.

"It's important."

"To you."

She slid to him until their knees bumped. She set a hand
on his leg. "You want to tell me you don't care what I've been
through."

"That's right. I don't."

"Tal, you can't say that to me."

"Why? It doesn't matter to me, is all."

"How would you feel if I said the same to you? I don't
care that you've been a prisoner for three years. I've watched
you starve. I've seen you beaten." Curling a hand behind his
neck, Carmen drew closer. She traced his shoulders, the
flesh mended soft. "What if I said I don't care what you've
been through? Then I'd be saying I don't care about you.
Because the whip will always be across your back and these
years will always be stolen. You'll never have a day that isn't
changed by Los Baños. If we live, and I want to love you, I'll
have to care. The same goes for you."

Carmen floated across his body. She had no idea what
her damage would be from Los Baños, probably greater

than his. She would need help to carry it. She feared her shoulders would never heal soft.

She framed his face in her hands to kiss him and lay him back against the rock. Under the water, she spread her legs. In the kiss, against his lips, she said, "Gently."

Carmen reached into the pool to guide him. Tal gasped against her cheek when she slid him inside. She sat tall, to take all of him. Tal's jaw slackened. The pool rippled outward from them, pushed by her movements.

"Oh my God," he said.

She bridged his lips with a finger. Words could do nothing in her life.

Chapter Seventeen

THE BOY returned before midnight. Remy stayed quiet while he climbed into the upper bunk.

In the morning, Tal slept while Remy and the others rose. Remy did not go with them for breakfast but lagged behind to stand beside the bunk gazing at his son. He looked for a grin, even sniffed the boy's clothes, but found no secrets, just a wooden tag in his hand bearing a Japanese symbol. Curious, for it surely had something to do with the girl, Remy considered slipping it from Tal's fingers but did not. He patted the bed and headed out for the morning meal.

Remy carried his food under the dao tree and ate by himself in the rising sun. He glanced over the barracks to Carmen's empty window. He missed talking to Mac, then thought of Sarah, as he often did when alone. He had no one to share his sense of remoteness. Tal would be different when he woke. He'd be on a path all sons take that leads them finally away from their fathers, as they ought. Remy thought of his own dad, long dead in France. He couldn't conceive of any advice from the old ghost, nor from his mother, whom he'd kissed goodbye twenty years ago and never seen again. Remy sipped his first mug of real coffee in six months. He wanted company.

Not far off, at the western gate, a dozen internees visited and traded with locals. The new guards prohibited Filipinos in the camp, but the rule had become relaxed everywhere but the eastern, main gate. Food and news continued to flow in behind the guards' turned backs. Remy ambled over from the dao.

No Japanese manned the dirt pillboxes outside the closed gate. Meat, bananas, greens, coconuts, and money passed through the unguarded wire. The locals over-flowed with gossip and news, claiming landings, fleets sighted offshore, bombardments and fighting every-where. With the last pesos in his pocket, Remy chose a quiet boy who had six dead chickens dangling from his belt. Remy bought a half dozen eggs.

Handing over the money, he asked, "Tell me straight. What's going on out there?"

The boy hitched his sagging belt. He had a different bearing than the others, restrained, observant. He was the only one carrying a weapon, a long *pinuti* bolo attached at his backside.

The boy stashed the pesos. He measured Remy with a slow nod. He backed away, saying only, "Today." He walked off from the gate. The bolo hung behind him like a lion's tail.

Remy headed for the barracks, to wake Tal with the promise of scrambled eggs since the boy had missed break-fast. Before he'd gone halfway across the field, forty bombers emerged above the western jungle. Remy stopped to admire them. The drone of an even larger flight of planes spun him east. The chicken boy seemed prophetic when the bombers on all sides released their whistling loads, the ground shiv-ered, and the rumbles of rolling detonations rattled the camp.

Tal came outside, rubbing his eyes.

"Mornin'," Remy said. "I got you some eggs."

"Man," Tal said, squinting into the morning sky at the waves of bombers. "That's some alarm clock. Almost knocked me outta bed."

"Big doin's, all right," Remy agreed. "So, look. Don't tell me nothin' you don't want to. But how was your evening?"

The earth shook under their feet. His son beamed and clapped him on the back.

The boy said, "Feel that?" and no more.

Air raids intensified throughout the day. In mid-afternoon, the loudspeakers at their highest volume announced that a special broadcast was coming and all should pay attention. Even then, some missed the word and did not come outdoors, tired of the constant barrages and the trembling ground.

Remy sat on the back steps of his barracks. A hundred yards off, Tal and Carmen chatted on opposite sides of the barbed wire, where they'd been all day. Yumi lay with her head on Carmen's lap.

The loudspeakers sizzled to life, Lucas's voice boomed across the camp. In moments, they would hear important news.

All heads in the camp perked up at the first tones of the broadcast. At the fence, Tal raised a hand for Carmen to listen. Yumi showed no interest.

"This is KGEX, in San Francisco. This morning, January ninth, General Douglas MacArthur led a force of sixty-eight thousand men from the U.S. Sixth Army in an invasion landing one hundred miles northwest of Manila, at Lingayen Gulf in the Philippines. Japanese defenders offered only token resistance. The battle to liberate Luzon has begun."

No celebration Remy had heard from the camp rivaled the noise that went up. The announcement, even the bombardments, were drowned beneath the internees' reaction. Tal and Carmen reached for each other vainly through the wire fences. Folks danced and threw their hats, Remy again tossed up his fedora. Little Yumi sat up applauding, likely without knowing why. The handful of guards kept plodding their slipshod patrols.

The rest of the broadcast was short on details, promising more updates as events developed. The loudspeakers went quiet. Remy stood from the steps, tempted to dig out Mac's radio and scan for more info. But the boy was entranced at the fence with his girl, tossing her old *Vogue* magazines through the wire, and Remy couldn't do it without his lookout and help sliding the big bunk aside. He fingered the pair of dice in his pocket, and went in search of a game of craps.

Remy found five men in a gambling mood. All were dizzy with cheer from MacArthur's long-promised return to Luzon. Redheaded Clem half expected to see the U.S. Army roll through camp before nightfall.

Remy set his plank in the shade of the dao. Journalist Owen fanned out a wad of pesos, claiming he'd been saving them for a rainy day. "Hell," he said, "it don't look like it's gonna rain."

The men played like wastrels, careless for their future, certain it was good. Remy read their luck easily and found it running not so high as they believed. He fleeced them all. At sunset, he wagered heavily on a few rolls of the dice. He lost most of his winnings, but this was the reason for the game, to plumb the omens of his own luck. Remy found it indeterminate. He put away the dice. Clem, the biggest loser, walked off mad. The others thanked Remy, aware that he could have kept their money. They did not ask why he gave so much of it back.

After dinner, KGEX played on. The station rebroadcast several programs from the past year that the internees had missed. For the third night in a row, the entire camp assembled outdoors, hungry for news and entertainment.

They learned about the desperate Battle of the Bulge in Europe, Roosevelt's contentious reelection, and MacArthur's refusal of a movement to make him a candidate against FDR, claiming his first priority was to liberate the Philippines. The invasion force the general led was the second largest of the war, behind only the D-day landings in Normandy. The camp heard the details of massive naval engagements with the Japanese throughout the Pacific, and the grim butchery of the Marine Corps island-hopping campaign.

Remy sat with Tal on a blanket to keep the boy company, and to watch the ongoing, imprudent carnival in the camp. Boys from No. 11 strolled by wearing abandoned Japanese items, peaked caps or high-laced boots. One older fellow stopped by to show Remy the commandant's ashtray. Lights glowed in Toshiwara's offices and Nagata's barracks. The internees had already eaten half the livestock the guards had left behind and broken into every deserted locker and storeroom.

Beside him, Tal fingered the inscribed wooden tag.

"I been meaning to ask," Remy said. "What is that? What's it say?"

Tal handed it over, tapping the symbol.

"It means Songu. That's what they call her."

Remy handled the tag, disgusted. The Japanese had even tried to steal the girl's name.

Tal continued. "Yumi's got one, too. That old *makipili* woman, it's how she kept track. Turned the tags over when the girls were busy."

Remy gave the tag back, noting the past tense in Tal's description. The boy believed he was the difference in the girl's life now. And the word he used, *busy*. So scrubbed a way to describe what those two girls' lives had been for the past year. Did Tal really understand what they'd been through? Hell was a waiting room for what they'd endured. Remy kept his skepticism to himself. This wasn't a poker table; he wasn't sure.

The boy rose from the blanket. "I'll be back by midnight."

"Talbot, sit down."

"She's expecting me."

"Sit down, boy."

Tal lowered himself with plain reluctance. Remy tapped fingertips under his chin, studying the best way to speak to this new son. Tal had grown into a bold young man under the Japanese, and now he had a woman to love and to rescue. Remy knew how hard people were to save.

"I want you to wait."

"We been through this."

"Things are different today. The Americans are on Luzon. That means there's fighting. You saw those planes today, they're hitting targets on every side of us. It can't go on much longer. But you can bet it's a lot more dangerous out there tonight than it was yesterday. The war's finally come to Luzon. Everybody's gonna be edgy, soldiers and locals alike. That makes it no time to be an American wandering around alone. I want you to hold off. A couple of days, maybe. Let's see what develops."

"No."

The boy stiffened his legs to rise. With a firm hand, Remy blocked him.

"You heard what the old man in the village said. *Makipilis* are everywhere. Even if the Jap guards don't catch you, how can you be sure one of those sumbitches won't? That old woman, you think she's not gonna be pissed about you carrying off one of her gals every night? I'm gonna assume you didn't handle her diplomatically."

"No."

"I figured. Listen, one word from her and they're out looking for you. Those Filipino boys will slit your throat and be home for supper. Stay in the camp, son. A few more days.

Let MacArthur get us out of here. Then, I swear, I'll stand by you and that girl 'til kingdom come if that's what you want."

Tal studied the wooden tag.

"You're asking a lot."

"We said we'd survive. We said we'd save her. You're risking both your lives if you go outside the camp now. You got years ahead of you. Wait. In the meantime, the two of you can still sit there at the fence and jaw all day long."

Tal looked to her blank window. "I want to see Carmen."

Seeing her, Remy thought, wasn't what the boy was itching so bad to do. Fair enough.

"I gotta advise against it. There's somethin' goin' on I can't explain. But I don't like it. Call it a gambler's instinct."

"She'll be disappointed."

"That may be. But trust me, you got time. The two of you have no idea how young you are. You heard the reports. MacArthur's a hundred miles from Manila. A couple more days, at the most. Wait. Please."

Tal stuck his tongue in his lower lip and nodded. "Kingdom come, huh?"

"Right up to the mornin' of. You got my word."

"That's a gambler's word, Remy."

"None better." Remy extended a hand to clasp his son's. The boy shook, then pocketed the tag.

Chapter Eighteen

A TANK STOPPED at the main gate. Carmen leaned out from her window to see it. The big steel vehicle cut off its lights and idled. One soldier jumped from the turret to speak with the guards at the gate. He climbed back onboard. The tank swung off the road into the grass beside the animal husbandry building.

On her tatami, Carmen drew in her knees. Minutes later, many pairs of boots tramped up the stairs.

The first soldier slapped his money on Mama's table so hard it drew Carmen into the hall to see what was happening. Across the foyer, in the opposite wing, Yumi in her emerald *haori* came out of her room, too.

Mama explained to the tanker in simple English that they had come too late. Sundown meant only officers in the *shuho*. He was a sergeant, and the four with him were below that. The soldiers would not leave. The leader pointed at Yumi's wooden tag. Mama gathered the pesos off the table and offered them back.

The tanker struck at Mama's hand, scattering the bills to the foyer floor.

From her hall, the little girl yelled at the soldier and showed her nails like they were claws. The tanker stamped toward her. Yumi hurled more shouts, cursing in Japanese.

Another soldier spotted Carmen. He came at her. Mama bent to gather up the pesos and made no more objections.

The soldier entered Carmen's hall. She wore the blue silk blouse Remy had bought; Tal liked to see her in it for their afternoon talks at the fence. The soldier advanced, reeking of sake and diesel. He was no taller than she. This was the first soldier to approach her in the *shuho* since the guards left.

Carmen held her place to look in the tanker's small black eyes. Though she'd not been raped in five days, she hadn't lost the ability to read fear. These drunken boys were headed to Manila. A woman was what they wanted, to act like men tonight so they might do the same facing death tomorrow. Carmen did not care to console this Japanese or reject him, she simply did not want him to rip Remy's blouse. She retreated into her room.

He did not appear behind her.

Carmen stepped back through the curtain, returning to the hall.

Benito, the house mop boy, the guerrilla, stood in front of the soldier. At Benito's back hung a long *pinuti*.

The tanker wore no weapon. Benito jerked up his chin for the Japanese to walk away. The young soldier stomped back to his comrades.

Benito drew the bolo from his belt. Carmen got behind him.

They entered the landing. Benito wielded the knife in one hard hand, showing it to the four startled soldiers. Mama stood on the stairs, out of the way. The Filipino boy waved the sharp blade to make the point that he could handle it. The soldiers shuffled aside. Carmen followed Benito into the hall leading to Yumi's room. Behind the drape, the little Korean mewled like a caged cat.

Benito said to Carmen, "Stay back." She put herself against the wall. The Filipino ducked under the curtain. Inside the room, Yumi quieted. In moments the soldier backed under the curtain on the sharp end of Benito's bolo, all his bluster gone. Yumi came out grinning crazily, mimicking Benito with her arm raised, holding a phantom sword.

Benito said, "Go." The Japanese stepped away from the bolo. His tunic hung on the point before releasing. The young soldier kept his face to Benito for several steps down the hall, then stopped. He seemed quickly sober and not in the mood for a fight or trouble, just a woman. He inclined his head in a short bow. The Filipino did the same. Benito slid the bolo into his belt at the small of his back. The tanker collected his men and left the *shuho*.

Carmen waited for the echoes of their boots to depart the stairwell. She hurried Yumi and Benito to her room to watch the soldiers, breathing easier after the tank revved its motor, flicked on headlights, and rolled away from the camp.

Mama pushed aside the curtain. She made fists, glowering at Benito.

"You, mop boy. You're fired. Get out."

"No," Carmen said.

Yumi caught Mama's meaning. She brushed the backs of her hands at the old woman, dismissing her. "No, *you* ge' ow! *You* go!"

Carmen reined Yumi in, tugging her back. The little girl muttered more curses.

"We trust him," Carmen said. "He stays."

"And do you run this *shuho*?"

"No."

"You don't seem to work here anymore either. Not in five days. This little one does your share." The woman stroked her chin. "But tonight, you looked like you were ready to take off that pretty blue blouse. Have you tired of your young American, Songu?"

"No."

The *makipili* considered. Carmen needed to tread carefully with the old crone. Even with the Americans fighting on the island now, Mama still spoke with the power of the

Japanese behind her. Carmen's family would pay for any mistake made here.

"Please. Let Benito stay."

Mama pointed at the bolo dangling at the Filipino's back. "That doesn't come into the building. If this little shit wants to be brave, let him do it with his fists so the Japanese can teach him manners." She aimed a crooked digit at Benito. "The only thing I want to see in your hands, boy, is a mop."

Benito nodded agreement. Mama chewed on some suspicion for a moment longer, then exited the room.

"Thank you," Carmen said to him. Yumi offered a showy bow.

Benito looked behind the curtain, to check that Mama had left the hall. He shook his head. In a lowered voice, he said, "I shouldn't have done that."

"Why?" Carmen also dropped her tone, not sure why Benito wanted this kept private. "They weren't supposed to be here. Mama told them to go away. They were just boys like you."

"And if they hadn't gone? If you and Yumi had kept the five of them here for two hours? I could have arranged an ambush for that tank. It would be on fire before it got to Manila."

Carmen hadn't thought of that.

"Thank you anyway, Benito. Mama was right, you were very brave."

The boy accepted this with a shrug. "And was she right about you? Were you going to . . . take the soldier? Were you?"

"Why does it matter?"

"Because the battle is on. We need all the information we can get. I can't talk to Yumi, and you sit by the fence all day."

Carmen touched a button of the blue silk blouse. "Yes. I would have."

"Good. I'm sorry. We all fight, Songu."

Benito left the room, trailing his long bolo. Carmen cut off the lamp and moved to the tatami. In the dark, Yumi cuddled beside her.

She would have had sex with the soldier. It would have been automatic and cold. She thought of its opposite, the joy of giving herself to Tal. One night was all they'd shared, in the jungle, surrounded by so much life. It was not enough to insulate her from Songu. Benito had called her that name, so had Mama.

Carmen prayed for the Americans to come quickly. They would chase off the Japanese and the *makipili*. Then she would be free. Songu was a slave, so wouldn't Songu go away then?

Carmen closed her eyes and leaned against Yumi. As sleep descended, she entered her own heart. She begged it to hold on until the Americans arrived. Her heart must cling to Tal and believe in love. Her heart must stay with her and not let Songu steal it away.

When Carmen awoke, Yumi had gone to her room. Carmen sat up. The single set of boots that had roused her strode down her hall.

She switched on the lamp, shielding her eyes from the glare. The footsteps halted outside the drape.

"Who's there?"

Pushing aside the curtain, Kenji stepped in.

He said, "We're back."

Baby birds cry for their food, but a samurai holds a toothpick in his teeth.

—SAMURAI MAXIM OF STOICISM, TO
ACT AS IF HE HAS JUST EATEN
WHEN HE IS STARVING

the rice bowl, murder,
and the pit

Chapter Nineteen

A T THE rumble of trucks, Remy rolled from his bed. He thrust his feet into his sandals, dashed from the barracks to catch a view of the main gate. The wash of many headlights lit the camp an eerie white.

His drowsiness gone, Remy grew excited that this might be an American convoy. A handful of other men wakened by the noise had this same thought. Together they jogged past the garage, the last building in their path. A fleet of eight trucks idled at the gate.

The first soldiers dismounted.

"I don't believe it," one internee said. "Son of a bitch," added another.

The two hundred Japanese who'd left the camp climbed down from the tailgates.

The returning guards lurched their way into the camp, slumped and shabby. Rifles hung heavy in their hands. They tossed into a pile the shovels and picks they'd taken six days ago. The internees with Remy slouched back to bed muttering disgust. Remy stayed behind.

In a minute, Pell, a bartender at the old University Club, emerged from the light surrounding the trucks, ashen-faced.

"Pelly?" Remy called. "What happened?"

"I just got woke up by Nagata with a pistol in my face."

"How'd you manage that?"

Pell snickered at his own close call. "I was in his bed. My luck."

Pell trundled off. The souring of the camp's luck was

what Remy had been divining the past few days. Now, like a foul card or cold dice, it was here.

Over his head, in her third-story window, Carmen's light flicked on. The window stayed empty.

Remy didn't head back to his bunk. Too much was going on—he stood no chance of sleep. Through dawn, he watched internees stumble out of bed, each shocked and dismayed. With the sun, the guards filtered back to their old stations, manning the fence, gates, towers, and pillboxes. Remy intercepted Lucas on his way back from the commandant's office.

"Where the hell they been?" Remy asked.

"Toshiwara wouldn't say. But he looks like crap, and he's teed off."

"Over what?"

"Three things in particular."

Toshiwara was angry that the internees had eaten through all their own stores and half of the guards'. His cherished Brahman bull was gone and most of his pigs.

"What did he expect after starvin' us?" Remy asked. "We had six days to make up for three years. What else?"

"You remember the day we had no radio reports? Well, some jackass took the radio into town to trade for food."

"Then what've we been listening to?"

"You know Berry, the math teacher?"

"Yeah."

"He's kept a radio in his mattress for two years. He brought it out. I had to explain to Toshiwara why the radio he left behind wasn't the one he found when he came back."

"Holy smokes. What'd you tell him?"

"I lied, of course. Said I had no idea where his radio was. Told him a bunch of guerrillas passed by the camp and left us the one we got now."

"Did he buy it?"

"Doesn't matter. He was most pissed about something else. His personal rice bowl is missing. Seems it was hand painted with the emperor's flag. I told him I'd look for it. And if I find it, Remy, I'm gonna crap in it before I hand it back over. I swear to God. You want this job?"

"No, Lucas. I don't. Nobody with any sense does."

"Well, that explains it. But Camp Freedom was nice for a few days, wasn't it? I'll see you."

Lucas hurried on. Before he could get indoors he was encircled by others pressing to hear the latest.

Across the camp, people awoke in a surly mood to their prison restored. The guards spread across the grounds. They were met with scowls and rough language, even in Vatican City.

At breakfast, the portion of corn mush had already been cut in half. No meat or eggs stiffened the yellow glop on Remy's plate. The coffee again tasted like scorched weeds.

Remy caught up with Tal at the table. The boy leaned over his plate, circling it with one arm. He looked annoyed.

"Back to the same ol' same ol'," Remy said, indicating his skimpy plate.

"I don't want to talk to you," said Tal.

"What'd I do?"

The boy scooped up a spoonful of mush. He chewed sullenly.

"You said I should wait. A few days, then the Americans would be here. That's what you said. Well, last time I looked, those weren't Americans with the guns out there."

"I'm sorry. It was my best guess."

"Well, your best guess kept me from seeing Carmen. And now I got no idea how long it'll be. Thanks."

Remy lifted his plate to eat elsewhere, to let his son cool off. He didn't regret the advice. Tal was alive to be mad at him.

Over the next several hours, Remy walked the camp, curious for the internees' reaction and the guards' condition. Toshiwara issued a camp-wide statement, insisting on the return of all Japanese foodstuffs and personal items taken during their absence. The internees volunteered nothing. No one knew where the Japanese had gone or what they'd been through, but from the look of them they'd been worked like field mules. The ones on patrol sleepwalked along the fence, the guards at the gate slumped and snoozed. All were grimy with streaked faces and dark quarter-moon fingernails. And whatever adventures the guards had endured outside the camp, they'd pushed Nagata over the edge.

The vile little guard was bad enough before he left. His loathing of the white race was well known. Immediately upon his homecoming, it became clear he was in a tyrant's rage. Part insane, part homicidal, Nagata was fired up beyond anything the internees had seen from him before.

His first act was to cut the camp's rations down to two thirds of the food that had been available *before* the Japanese had left. He put an immediate stop to Filipinos bringing food to the gates for sale or trade. He dispatched guards across the camp to rummage for sacks of grain and corn the internees had taken. Nagata stormed through the camp, shouting and berating the internees, all of whom were forced to bow when he passed.

He arrested the commandant's chicken.

The frail bird sat in a makeshift cage on Toshiwara's steps. A poster, signed by Nagata, explained in Japanese and English that the chicken had eaten its own eggs; the offense was that the eggs belonged to the emperor. The poor chicken was just doing what all starving creatures would do, surviving by any source of nutrition.

Through the morning, the camp settled into nervous agitation. American warplanes continued racing past, some of them at treetop level. The internees refused to go inside, the flights were so frequent. Two boys climbed into the dao tree. Nagata threatened to have them whipped for signaling the pilots. The boys' parents appealed to Toshiwara that they were simply exuberant, and that a pair of ten-year-olds had nothing to pass on to American fighter pilots. The boys were released, making Nagata stomping mad.

The commandant thwarted Nagata again at noon. Two teenagers appeared outside the main gate. They'd been in the village when the Japanese trucks pulled into the camp. They decided the safest way back inside the wire would be in broad daylight. Remy and a hundred anxious others watched them marched into Toshiwara's office. The boys came out ten minutes later, after only a tongue-lashing from the commandant. Nagata emerged, beet-red and ready to pop. With a sudden, strange, and malevolent calm, he approached Remy and the internees. Beside him walked the tall interpreter.

"I have changed my mind," the interpreter announced to the crowd, deadpan. The tall Japanese seemed no fan of Nagata's, but tried to give the little hothead no reason to turn on him, as well. Nagata grunted more of his statement, sneering the whole time. "You may keep the sacks of grain and corn you took. They are in our storehouse. Pick ten men to collect them. You may put the food in your own warehouse."

Remy, as one of the more fit members of the crowd, was selected for this task, as were the two teenagers who'd just returned. Nagata stomped away from the commandant's office, to the northern reaches of the camp, where a circular sawali hut held all the supplies the guards had found.

Nagata unlocked the door. Inside were stacked six dozen burlap sacks of rice and corn, each weighing fifty pounds. Remy boosted the first one across his shoulder and set out across the camp to the internees' warehouse, at the southern end behind the garage.

Burdened with sacks, the ten made their way through the camp, collecting cheers along the way. Nagata and his interpreter escorted them on their circuits. Nagata waved to the folks surprised by his benevolence. The interpreter looked miffed.

By the time Remy hauled the sixth sack, he was done in. He asked Clem, straining under the bag beside him, how he was holding up.

"Half bloody dead," the sailor replied. "You look about three quarters, chum."

"I haven't got the muscles for this sort of work anymore." Remy glanced at the others. Even the two boys dragged their feet. "None of us do."

Clem shot Nagata an evil glare. "You don't think the little prick knows this, do you?"

"Just one more round to go," Remy said. "Suck it up, Clem."

The Scotsman sped his steps to pull in front of Remy. "*You* suck it up, Yank."

The two men made a race of the last hundred and fifty yards to the storeroom. The others in line saw this, and with waning stamina all the men jogged the final distance under their loads. Remy staggered to the warehouse first by two strides. Nagata arrived to find the men panting, sitting on the sacks.

The guard crossed his arms, sweat stains blotting his armpits. He nodded, making a show of some thought. He tapped a finger to his temple.

"Change mind," he said.

Remy, still gasping for air, said, "What? What'd you say?"

Nagata walked close. Remy, breathing hard, took in the full scent of the little guard, reeking from perspiration and forgotten hygiene.

Nagata kicked the bag between Remy's legs. He rammed

a finger at the sack, then indicated it be carried back to the Japanese storeroom.

"No," Remy said, standing. The others joined him on their feet, ignoring their fatigue. Nagata motioned for the interpreter to come near. The tall Japanese kept his reluctance muted but visible.

Nagata spoke. His manner remained friendly, as if he'd made an honest mistake.

"Lieutenant Nagata regrets," the interpreter said, "but he has decided the grain and corn must be returned to the guards' storeroom. Now."

The men mumbled, "I knew it," mingled with curses.

"We can't do it," Remy said. "We're beat. Get someone else."

Nagata listened to the translation. He rattled his head.

"You men must move it. If you do not, Lieutenant Nagata will send guards to do it for you, and they may carry off more than just these sacks from your storehouse. It cannot be helped. Gentlemen, if you please."

Behind Remy, Clem crabbed, "Aye, I'll kill the bugger."

The interpreter spoke on his own to Clem. "Should I tell Lieutenant Nagata this?"

The Scot bit his lip. "No."

"Then please do as you're told."

Remy was the last to bend for his sack.

Nagata approached, puffing up. "Tuck papa-san." The little lieutenant hooked his thumbs in his belt and tugged many times, to be certain Remy recognized this as the strap that had flogged his son.

Remy leaned closer. He'd looked in Nagata's eyes before, but now, more than ever, he saw madness. Remy wanted to throttle him.

Clem, burlap bag sagging across his shoulder, stepped between them. "That's for another day, laddie," he muttered. "Pick up the bloody sack and let's get this over with."

The sailor held his spot, blocking the two until Remy yoked the bag over his back. Clem led him away from Nagata.

Remy fumed under the first load. With the second bag, he let go of his rancor, again reminding himself never to tip his hand.

Chapter Twenty

THE FIGHTER plane's speed was incredible, the roar bone-rattling. All five Japanese at the main gate ducked for cover.

Tal watched from the shade of an eave, on guard duty at the kitchen storehouse. He hid his enjoyment.

The P-38 zipped in so low it flew past the wire before anyone saw it coming. This same routine had been going on all day, planes buzzing near the camp, sometimes directly over it. Their targets lay close by. At every explosion in the near distance or earsplitting howl just above the peaks of the huts, the guards leaped behind trees or into weedy patches. The Yank pilots made a game of seeing how many guards they could spook, how many nipa branches they could lift in their wake.

Once the plane raced away, the guards dusted themselves off. They glowered at Tal for their loss of face.

He stayed in place for another hour, to the end of his three-hour shift. Ever since the guards' surprise inspection last week, the committee had volunteers around the camp to keep an eye on the Japanese. Their assignment was to give advance notice of the guards' increasingly unpredictable behavior. Tal had been among the first to sign up.

The light changed with the sinking sun. The sun cooled, dinner would be served soon. The sounds of preparation rang from the kitchen. Tal stepped away from the bamboo wall to get a better whiff of the evening stew. No scent of meat reached him, just more boiling greens and steaming rice. Remy's chimneys smoked. Tal rued the return of the Japanese most when he thought of Carmen, and at meal-times.

He did not see the rifle shot but jumped at the noise, though all day long there had been shooting in the sky. This sound was different, at ground level. It was personal and frightening.

At the gate, all five guards had their rifles up, pointed at the road ahead. Tal sprinted the short distance to the fence. Another volley almost tripped his running steps; the soldiers all fired at once. Then, quickly, one more shot. Tal reached the wire before the haze of cordite had drifted into the afternoon.

Outside the fence, on the edge of the road ten yards away, redheaded Mr. Clemmons lay on his back. His arms were spread, his left leg bent as if he'd tried to stand. Blood speckled the bottom of his white chin. Behind him where he'd dropped them, a dead chicken and a mesh bag of coconuts lay in the road.

The guards lowered their guns.

"What did you do?" Tal asked at their backs, horror turning him cold. He gripped the barbed wire, not feeling the spikes. Mr. Clemmons's left leg flopped over, lifeless. Tal bellowed, *"What did you do?"*

Two guards walked toward Mr. Clemmons. Soldiers laid hands on Tal to pull him from the wire, but he did not let go. The barbs dug into his palms. A bayonet pricked his ribs, sharp enough to step him back.

Tal lost sight of Mr. Clemmons behind a crowd of sol-diers and internees swarming to the gate. Someone took him by the elbows, leading him away. Finally, Tal closed his mouth. He focused on Mr. Lucas in front of him.

With urgency, the man asked, "What did you see?"

"Where's Remy?"

"I don't know, son. Your father's never far. He'll be here right smart, I expect. Now tell me what you saw."

Tal described the guards' jittery reaction to the last low-flying fighter. Moments later he heard one round. While he ran to the fence, more guns fired. Then one last shot. Mr. Clemmons lay faceup on the road. The dropped coconuts and the unplucked chicken. His left leg. Blood under his chin.

"Come with me," Lucas said. "I want to confront the commandant. Right now."

Lucas walked him to Toshiwara's office. The man kept his arm on Tal's elbow, as if he might faint or bolt. Tal had no intention of doing either.

Remy's fedora knifed through the internees massing to investigate. He showed up flushed. Before coming to a stop, he asked Tal, "What happened? You all right?"

"Mr. Clemmons was shot at the main gate."

Remy yanked his head around to the gate as if he, too, had heard the rifles.

Lucas said, "He was murdered, Remy."

"What was he doin' out there?"

"Your boy and I are on our way to take this up with Toshiwara. When I get answers, you will."

Remy extended a hand to Tal, the boy reached back. His father's mitt came away red.

"What happened to your hand?" Remy turned over Tal's wrist.

"I think I grabbed the wire."

"Lucas, hang on a second." Remy bounded away to accost an older woman, Mrs. Gretsch, a missionary's wife, for her handkerchief. Tal couldn't hear what Remy told her but he snatched the white cloth. He hustled back and knotted the handkerchief around Tal's palm.

"All right, go ahead," Remy said. "Thanks, Lucas. Boy?"

"Yeah."

"Tell 'em to go to hell. They shot Clem."

Questions and shouts were flung at Lucas and Tal making their way to Toshiwara's office door. Lucas knocked, and a guard escorted them in front of the commandant's empty desk. The undersized soldier took a position beside the desk, barely taller than the tip of his bayonet.

Tal's shoulders tingled from the last time he'd stood here. The commandant's office had changed. The fan and the little bonsai were missing, his desk and walls were blank. Tal unwound the handkerchief from his hand. He would not let Toshiwara see him hurt.

Tal watched out the windows. Men carried Mr. Clemmons's body to the infirmary. All the guards had rifles off their shoulders. The gathering internees berated them. The commandant's office vibrated with the passing of another low-flying fighter headed south.

Toshiwara left them waiting. Lucas kept a stony resolve, moving only to push his glasses up his nose. Tal dabbed the kerchief at blood seeping from two punctures in his palm.

The commandant, his interpreter, and sweaty Nagata arrived. Tal crammed the cloth into his pocket.

Toshiwara took his seat. Nagata stood at his elbow. The commandant set his cap in the middle of the bare desk. The interpreter listened, then spoke for him.

"I apologize. I have been finding facts."

Lucas hardly masked his temper. "And what did you find?"

"The man was caught trying to escape. The guards prevented it."

"*Escape?* Commandant, I have with me . . ."

"Yes, I recall Mr. Tuck."

Lucas turned to Tal. "Tell him what you saw."

Tal related everything, how Mr. Clemmons was shot in the chest, returning with food, just outside the wire. Six bullets. "He wasn't escaping," Tal concluded. "That's not true. He was coming back into the camp."

Lucas jumped back in. "The guards had absolutely no right to shoot Mr. Clemmons. The Geneva Convention specifies that an escape attempt is only a breach of discipline. The punishment cannot exceed thirty days confinement. Mr. Clemmons was *not* escaping. For him to be murdered for returning to camp with food is in flagrant disregard of any rule of humanity. I remind you, commandant, we are not soldiers but civilians under your care and protection. This was neither."

The translator waited for Toshiwara's response. He said, "Geneva is a long way from here, Mr. Lucas. Thank you. Please go outside."

Lucas was jolted. "That's it? That's all you've got to say?"

"For now."

The short guard stepped up to usher Lucas out of the office. Lucas did not move.

"For the record, commandant. On whose authority did this happen?"

"I did not issue the order. But I approved it. This is regrettable, but the responsibility lies with your people to obey the rules."

"You had no right."

"I have no need of right, Mr. Lucas."

The guard put his bayonet against Lucas's ribs. Lucas slapped the point away.

"We'll be registering a complaint, commandant. In the harshest terms."

"I expect no less than your condemnation."

Lucas drew a long, noisy breath, containing his anger.

"It may seem trivial to you, commandant. But the war is ending. And when it does we'll be very, very clear about the record. Trust that."

Lucas headed for the door. Tal moved behind him.

"Mr. Tuck. You will stay."

Lucas whirled. "You've got no business with him."

The interpreter spoke without waiting for Toshiwara. "I strongly suggest that you have said enough."

Lucas stared, livid. "Talbot, I'll be right outside. With two thousand others."

The guard walked Lucas out. Tal was left alone with Toshiwara, Nagata, and the translator.

"Mr. Tuck," the commandant said, "your hand is bleeding."

Tal opened his palm to look. He did not pull out the cloth to stanch the cuts but dropped his hand, letting it drip on Toshiwara's floor.

"I'm all right. I'm better than Mr. Clemmons."

"Yes, of course. The stalwart troublemaker. I am pleased Mr. Lucas brought you to my office. I have been meaning to come find you."

"What do you want with me?"

"I have a few issues to take up. I asked Mr. Lucas to leave so you could answer without worry of punishment from your own people. I will not punish you. You may tell me honestly. Do you know where my rice bowl is?"

"No."

"Are you no longer a thief?"

"I don't know where it is."

"But, are you a thief?"

Tal did not reply. Toshiwara aimed a finger at Tal's tattered shorts.

"Let us see. Empty your pockets."

Tal hesitated.

Again the interpreter prodded without the commandant. "Do as he asks. You do not have the luxury of refusing."

Tal dug out the bloody handkerchief and set it on the

desk next to Toshiwara's officer's cap. Beside it he laid the wooden Songu tag.

Nagata picked up the tag. He ran his thumb over the Japanese symbol. He set down the tag and raised a malevolent glare at Tal. Behind Nagata, the tall interpreter looked stricken. He continued translating.

"So you are still a thief," the commandant said. "She does not belong to you, Mr. Tuck. She is the property of the emperor. So is the old woman you threatened to throw down the stairs. For that matter, so are you."

"No, I'm not."

"It does not depend on your choice. Just as the facts do not decide if the man who was killed was escaping or returning. It depends on the emperor. And I am the emperor's voice in this camp. You may take your handkerchief. Leave the tag."

Tal lifted the stained cloth.

"Commandant?"

"Nan desu ka?"

"You had Mr. Clemmons shot. You can go to hell."

Nagata grunted. The interpreter scowled. "Mr. Tuck. I will not tell the major or Lieutenant Nagata of these words."

"Don't do me any favors."

"That favor was not done for you."

"Then let the commandant know if I find his rice bowl, I'll give it back."

The interpreter informed Toshiwara. The commandant replied.

"Thank you. Tell me why."

"Because it's worthless."

Toshiwara listened, then laughed. "Good, young man. Good. That is a samurai's insult. Now go. Continue your suffering. It agrees with you."

"One last thing."

Tal didn't stop for a response. He leaned toward Toshiwara's desk, to lay a bloodied finger on Carmen's wooden tag. He pressed a scarlet dot in the center.

"That's all I'm giving back. Understand?"

Tal spun away, shutting Toshiwara's door on the translation.

Chapter Twenty-one

◆

COMING UP the stairs at dawn, Carmen dropped her armful of laundry when she saw her tag on the board.

How long had it been there? She hadn't left her room in two days. So many soldiers.

She scooped the linens off the steps and ran down her hall. Mama yelled from the landing for her to do her washing. Carmen ignored the old woman. Mama shouted there would be no breakfast. In her room, Carmen stood in the window for an hour, wishing the light to rise faster to see the boy.

At last he appeared under the dao tree, eating from a plate. She did not need him to look up and wave. He seemed unhurt.

The *makipili* woman. She must have told the Japanese. They took the tag away from the boy, and the old hag returned it to the board. But they did not beat him for it.

Tal had promised he would bring the tag to Carmen himself. Now he could not. She guessed at his anger over this, and, watching him under the great tree, believed he was brooding over how to make it right.

Papa arrived with a bowl of rice, a slice of bread, and a boiled egg.

"You did not make your mattress."

"No."

"Well, do it after you eat. We have soldiers waiting."

Papa left under the black drape. Carmen ate, standing back from the window so the boy would not see her in the unlit room. She pretended to be an angel, sharing a meal with him from above invisibly, his protector.

The first of the day's soldiers stepped under the curtain. Within the hour, the second and the third arrived, with more on the landing. Most were young, raw recruits who'd seen no combat, who only months ago were villagers. She squeezed the muscles around her vagina to make them peak quickly; none could last more than minutes. When they were done and she was gentle with them, she peeled away the bravery they pretended to standing in line waiting for her. Many were petrified, especially the bellicose ones, the chest thumpers, heavy boys with fat still on them from their mothers' cooking or skinny peasants pared down by nerves. They believed that fear came when their scrotums shrank, so plucked at their sacks to stretch them and remain brave in appearance. The few who spoke some English, educated boys, were the most vulnerable. Alone with a Filipina after climax, they said what they could not to their comrades, that they questioned their oaths for death in the name of the emperor.

Using their fears like a penknife, Carmen whittled these boys down to their secrets. She memorized missions, unit names and numbers, dates, weapons, locations, routes. When each soldier stood from her legs, he stood a fuller man, regardless of how he'd performed; he'd had a woman, and for his while with her pictured himself grand and sacrificial. The instant each one departed, Carmen washed herself and imagined his bones picked clean. Between soldiers, she had five, sometimes ten minutes to herself, to contract and retake her own shape and mind, before she had to lie down again and become Songu for another.

Kenji arrived late, when he was not supposed to, the time for officers.

He had not paid and held no ticket. He removed his boots to sit on her tatami, his back against her wall, his crown above her windowsill. She sat opposite him. Carmen did not want him to stay. His stockings were worn at the toes. Were she a whore she might rub his feet.

Kenji shut his eyes. He seemed tired and careworn. Carmen resented this, that he should come to her looking for solace, bearing such need and worry.

She reached for the crimson knot at her waist. He sensed her movement and sat upright.

"What are you doing?"

She stilled her hands. "You do not want me, Kenji-sama?"

"No. I mean, yes, but not right now. Put on clothes, please."

With no regard for her nakedness, Carmen slipped out of the robe into T-shirt and fatigues. She dumped the wash water out the window behind Kenji and set the bowl upside down in the hall for Benito to see and come later for her report.

"Is that the signal?" Kenji asked.

"For what?"

"For your contact with the guerrillas. The mop boy?"

Carmen stood stock-still. Kenji continued.

"You don't leave the *shuho,* so your contact must come to you. The new Filipino boy carries a bolo when he's not mopping. It's him."

"You swore you wouldn't tell."

"I won't. I have something for you to tell him."

Carmen lifted the curtain to be sure the hall remained empty. She sat across from Kenji on the mattress.

"Yes?"

"I'm afraid for the camp."

"What do you mean?"

"Do you know about the shooting today?"

Carmen had heard the shots while beneath the last soldier at sundown, but did not know what they'd meant. Kenji described the death of the American returning to the main gate.

"That's not all," he said. "Toshiwara's furious. The camp ate his bull, stole his personal belongings, took half the food we left behind. When we came back, they were sleeping in our beds."

"What did you expect?"

"They left the camp against orders."

"Yumi and I went with them, to the village."

Kenji paused, then pressed on. "Nagata's cutting rations back to less than what they were before."

"The American army will come."

"They may not come soon enough."

"What do you mean?"

"Palawan."

A long, narrow island southwest of Luzon.

"What happened?"

Kenji rested his head against the wall once more. He explained.

One hundred and fifty American POWs were held on the island to build an airfield. In mid-December, an American convoy neared the shore, a fighter plane flew overhead. The guards forced their prisoners into several small air raid shelters. The bunkers were made of log roofs over shallow slits in the earth. The guards poured gasoline on the logs and into the pits, and set them afire. When the panicked prisoners emerged, clothes and hair burning, they were gunned down, clubbed, or bayoneted. A few dozen fought their way under the camp's barbed-wire fence to scramble down a cliff to the beach. The guards hunted these escapees and killed all but a few who dived into the ocean to swim five miles to another island. Some of these Americans survived.

Carmen asked, "You think that could happen here?"

"Such a thing could happen everywhere. It wasn't random. This was the result of a policy issued by the Imperial War Ministry. Prisoners of war are not to fall into the hands of the enemy. We're to annihilate them and leave no trace. That's what has been ordered."

"That's insane."

"Insane? *You* say this? You've been kidnapped and raped."

Kenji had never acknowledged these things, always glossing over them. It stunned Carmen to hear him, any Japanese, say it.

"These men," he said, aiming a thumb at the camp behind him, "all of us, were raised to worship the emperor. The guards at Palawan and in all the camps, none are frontline soldiers anymore. We're too old, damaged, or ignorant. Camp guards don't have the chance to die in combat for the emperor. Japan's losing the war. The Americans are getting closer, and these men have only got one chance for honor. That means killing the emperor's enemies before they die themselves. *Any* enemy. Unarmed men, women, and children. It's not insanity. It's not even brutal. It's a lifetime of believing."

Kenji aimed a finger beyond the curtain, to the upturned bowl. "Tell this to the guerrillas. It could happen here. Nagata wants it to happen, even if he does it by starving them. Toshiwara's too weak-willed to do anything about it. The rest of the guards just follow orders. Palawan was the first in the Philippines. It won't be the last."

Carmen set a hand on his stockinged foot. "What will you do, Kenji-sama?"

"I won't be able to stop it. All I can do is tell you what I find out and protect you the best I can."

"And Yumi?"

"Whatever I can do, yes."

"Thank you."

"Hand me my boots."

Kenji slid his feet into the boots and worked the high laces. He stood. Carmen kept her seat, cross-legged.

"One more thing."

"Yes?"

"The Tuck boy. The American thief."

Carmen caught her breath. How did Kenji know of Tal? Had he done something to the boy? Carmen rocked to her knees.

"What about him?"

"I saved him today from another beating, maybe worse."

Kenji told her about the aftermath of the shooting. The boy Tuck had been taken to the commandant's office as a witness. The Songu tag had been in his pocket. He described the boy's flash of anger, and his own refusal to translate Tuck's curse to Toshiwara and Nagata.

Kenji asked, "How did he get the tag? Is he a friend?"

"He was one of the boys I walked to Anos with. I gave him the tag as a gift."

"He threatened to throw the old *shuho* woman down the stairs?"

"Yes."

"He's one of the troublemakers."

"I know."

"It was a dangerous gift, Carmen. For you both. Nagata is uncontrollable. You need to be more careful, especially now after what I've told you. I can't protect Tuck otherwise. Or you."

"Of course, Kenji-sama. I understand."

She eased off her haunches to watch him leave under the curtain. She would wait for Benito to see the upside-down bowl, then whisper to the guerrilla what she'd wrung from this long day, especially from Kenji.

She would ask Benito to get the Tuck boy a message from her. "Be ready to leave the camp. I will warn you."

Before Palawan could come here.

Chapter Twenty-two

R EMY SAT in the garage among the tools.
        He'd need to shape this coffin longer than the others. He had enough bamboo and hemp. What he lacked was the heart to begin.

Five caskets in ten days. First Clem. Four days later, a woman died of heart failure. Two days ago, a pair of older fellows succumbed to beriberi.

Clem bore six bullet holes in his chest. Doc Lockett had cleaned him up as best he could, but a good swabbing and a fresh shirt did little to wipe away murder. It took the Japanese all six rounds to put the redheaded Scot down. The beriberi corpses had been oddly disturbing, bloated faces above caved chests and exaggerated joints. They looked like melted dolls. The old woman's body had simply aged and faded to gray when her unnourished heart shut down. Doc Lockett made it clear that the cause of death was malnutrition. They'd be alive if they'd had sufficient bread, meat, green vegetables, milk. The camp's diet of mainly white rice, containing little thiamine, would kill all the internees given enough time.

A thousand attended the first funeral, even though the woman, Mrs. Bemmel, had been unpopular in the camp. She'd been one of the mahjong set in Manila, harsh to her servants, dishonest and gossipy. The crowd didn't mourn her demise so much as the anticipation of their own. Every day, the reaper seemed to cut a little deeper into Los Baños.

The funerals for the pair of men, Utley, a road engineer,

and Cairn, a Canadian trainer of polo ponies, were held yesterday, January 27. The crowd for their back-to-back services surpassed that for Mrs. Bemmel. When Remy was done with the men's caskets, he had enough leftover bamboo to fashion one more coffin. After the burials and supper, he walked to the infirmary to see if anyone was feeling sufficiently poorly. At the moment, no one lay at death's door, according to Lockett. "Build it anyway," the doctor said.

Remy saw Nagata's hand in all this as surely as he saw his own in the making of the caskets. Two weeks ago, when the two teen boys returned to camp in broad daylight, Toshiwara let them off with a slap on the wrist. Then the youngsters in the tree cheering for the American planes; the commandant didn't punish them, either. After that, poor Clem. The guards wouldn't have gunned him down just yards from the gate without instructions. Even Toshiwara told Tal he hadn't issued the order, but had okayed it.

Now Donnelly.

Remy stood from the crate where he sat. He needed to get started. He grabbed a long bamboo shoot, green and strong because it was young. Donnelly was as tall as Talbot. Remy sawed the first rod to a length that would fit his own son.

At quarter to seven this morning, Donnelly stumbled out of the brush along the southern fence. He'd been in the village that night. Some in the camp heard him tramping around Boot Creek. They whispered for him to stay away, to come in after dark. Donnelly didn't hear, or didn't heed. When he answered them, he sounded drunk.

At the western gate, carrying a burlap bag of fruit, he walked into the sights of a sentry. Without warning, the guard fired, striking Donnelly in the left shoulder. The Aussie boy dropped the sack and lurched forward to collapse against the fence. Guards ran to the spot. Doc Lockett and the boy Santana were nearby at the dao tree and hurried over. Lockett said later that Donnelly's wound was just a graze. Donnelly clutched his shoulder; he laughed off the blood drizzling between his fingers. Through the wire Lockett told the boy he'd fix him up for his stay in the brig. Then Toshiwara arrived.

A half dozen guards forced the doctor and Santana back from the fence. Out in the yard where the camp gardens had once been, the rest of the garrison in loincloths began their morning calisthenics. To counts of *"ichi . . . ni . . . san . . . shi,"* Toshiwara and the guards conferred around Donnelly. The crowd of internees grew by the hundreds. When Remy heard the shot, he left his breakfast plate on the table and hurried outside.

In minutes Nagata arrived at the fence, changed out of his loincloth. He stormed loudly at the collected internees, blaming them. Toshiwara moved the deliberations into his office. A picket of guards kept Donnelly from the internees behind leveled bayonets. The Aussie lay calling through the fence for help.

Remy gathered with Tal and the boys of No. 11. Donnelly quieted down, weakening. Doc Lockett, Lucas, and many committee members made strong protests to Toshiwara. An hour and a half after the shooting, four guards showed up with a door. They rolled Donnelly onto it and carted him into the jungle behind Boot Creek.

From the trees, out of sight, cracked a single pistol shot.

Shock rippled through the internees. Men put hands to their heads, many spat on the ground. Women covered their mouths. Every face dammed back anger.

Remy left the fence for the garage, where he sat for an hour, unable to start.

Now he cut through another bamboo rod. Sawdust snowed on his sandaled feet. The body would be here soon.

Remy put his heart into his working hands, soothing himself the way he'd done with every death in his life. The green casket took form, tailored long and narrow. When Lucas, Doc Lockett, and four boys from No. 11 carried the body in on the door, the coffin was ready.

Donnelly lay faceup, a neat exit wound under his chin from a single bullet fired straight down into the back of the head. The doctor had mopped much of the blood off the door, but a russet stain recalled how it had spread and dribbled off an edge.

Lucas explained that he and the committee had gotten more of the same claptrap from Toshiwara. The Japanese claimed Donnelly had been escaping and was subject to the death penalty. Just like Clem. The internees could assume the same for anybody caught by the guards outside the wire, even a few steps.

Donnelly was lifted into the casket. The body seemed light without its soul. The four boys stood aside until Remy, Lucas, and the doctor had secured the bamboo top to the casket. By the hemp handles, the boys carried Donnelly to the cemetery.

Remy asked Lucas, "Where's this gonna stop?"

The committeeman ran a hand over his thinning hair. "We're all going to be dead or we're all going to be freed. Can't see any other way out."

Lucas headed for the cemetery. Doc Lockett gazed around the garage before leaving. He scuffed a toe through the white sawdust on the floor.

"I know," said Remy. "More bamboo."

Remy took the cigarette from his son's lips. He set a hand under the boy's dropped chin.

"Hey," he said, "lift this up. You owe him to be standing by that hole with your head high. That ain't who he was. You understand?"

"Yeah."

"All right. You go let people see you. You tell the Japs to kiss our asses. You get right up front. Show 'em."

"Where you going to be?"

"The whole camp's headed to the cemetery. I'm getting on the radio. I want to know what Carmen meant."

Five days ago, a message had been smuggled into the camp to Tal. The girl warned him and Remy to be ready to leave the camp. She'd try to tell them when the time was right. Plainly, Carmen was dealing with the guerrillas. But what did she know? What was happening outside the fence that made her send that message? Or was the danger she referred to *inside* the wire?

Remy took a drag on the boy's cigarette. He coughed the smoke back out.

"Th' hell are you smokin'?"

"Catnip and papaya leaves."

Remy handed the butt back, unable to comment on how sad that was. Another time it might have been funny.

Tal walked with Remy to No. 12. The camp headed toward the Protestant chapel. Remy was struck by how gaunt the population was becoming, how listless their shuffle to the cemetery. All the gains made during the six days of Camp Freedom had been erased over the past two weeks. Remy looked at his own hands, thankful they could still deal cards. He and his boy remained among the stronger ones in Los Baños, but bullets and disease were like luck, making no promises.

In their room, Remy and Tal hauled aside the bunk bed and dug up the crystal radio. Tal helped him put the bed back in place, then left for the funeral.

Clear morning weather aided the signal. In short order, Remy snared a *Voice of Freedom* broadcast out of San Francisco. The reporter cast around the world at war. He de-

scribed the German defeat at the Battle of the Bulge, the
occupation of Warsaw by Soviet forces after the Nazis had
devastated the old city. On the Russian front, the German
army was in full retreat and Lithuania was poised to fall.
Hungary had signed an armistice with the Allies.

In the Pacific, the news focused on the Philippines.
MacArthur fought his way closer to Manila. Unconfirmed
reports had the main American force at Calumpit, thirty
miles northwest of the city. The Yanks were preparing for
a fierce Japanese defense with block-to-block fighting. The
first accounts were coming in of civilian massacres inside
Manila. The Japanese had begun executing supposed underground members, smugglers, every character suspicious
to them. The claims of dead numbered in the thousands.
MacArthur demanded the Japanese government protect
and treat all Allied prisoners of war and civilian internees under the terms of the Geneva Convention, though the
Japanese had not signed it.

Doug MacArthur was not a man to tip his hand. Clearly,
the general was worried. When the cool MacArthur worried, it was time to consider putting one foot out the door.

Remy shut down the radio and hid it under his mattress
until the boy could help him lift the bunk again.

He stepped outside. For the last hour, Remy had kept the
radio whispering in his ear. He hadn't heard the shovels at
work just beyond the shade of the dao tree. The first internees returned from Donnelly's funeral. They, too, stopped
to gape at the dozen guards digging an unannounced and
unexplained pit.

sanko seisaku—"three-all policy" of the Japanese army, meaning "kill all, burn all, destroy all," dating from 1941 to the end of the Pacific War

the radioman, many massacres,
and the tenth game

Chapter Twenty-three

BOLICK LAID his portable radio, hand generator, pack, and carbine into the false bottom of the *banca*. The reek of fish, long sunk into the wood of the boat, curled his nostrils. He knelt beside his equipment. The guerrilla Gusto waited for him to lie down so he could replace the deck panel and cover all evidence of the American soldier.

Bolick asked, "There's no chance I'm going to like this, is there?"

By lantern light, Gusto pursed his lips. "Even the fish don't like it."

Bolick peered into the dark, shallow well around him. The old *banca* creaked against the rickety pier. Two hours after sunset, a fine wind had risen for the sail east across the big bay. Out on the water, Japanese patrol boats motored the coast with their lights off.

"Okay," Bolick said. "Lemme show you something, Gusto." Bolick dug into his pack for a pair of grenades. He held them up so the Filipino fighter and his unnamed sailing mate could get a gander.

"You don't trust me, Sergeant?" Gusto asked.

"I do, I do." Bolick waggled the grenades. "These are just in case I'm wrong."

Bolick sucked a last clean breath of moist air off the bay. He held it and folded his long frame into the cramped hold between his rifle and the radio, resting his head on his pack, knobby with extra grenades, ammo clips, and food. Gusto secured the deck panel, locking out the last fresh air and slim light. Water slapped the hull under Bolick's ear. He released the breath, spending it slowly. The boat pushed away from the pilings, gliding smoothly on both outriggers. Bolick took his first closeted breath. "Ah, geez," he muttered.

Gusto and his mate hoisted the sail. The *banca* surged ahead, the black and stinking hold heeled Bolick onto his shoulder. The slap of water thickened with the slicing, speeding prow.

Bolick tucked the grenades under his knees to keep them from rolling about, and to find them fast.

He searched for cracks in the flooring over his head. Maybe some good air might vent in. A century of fish had died where he lay. He imagined the flying splinters of the reeking old boat if a Japanese patrol boarded them during their crossing and he pulled the pins.

Knuckles rapped on the deck. "So, Sergeant."

"What?"

"You volunteered?"

"Yep."

"All the American soldiers say no one volunteers."

"First thing they teach us."

"Why did you do it?"

Bolick shrugged. "I like to camp out."

"Good one. Myself, I haven't slept in a bed in three years. I hate camping."

Bolick winced. Gusto deserved a better answer.

Five days ago, on January 31, the 26th Ranger Battalion, Filipino guerrillas, and Alamo scouts freed five hundred American soldiers from a POW camp north of Manila, in Cabanatuan. After two and a half years in captivity, many of these survivors of Bataan could hardly walk. Dozens of their rank were not alive to be rescued at the end.

MacArthur worried that the Japanese might take revenge on the four thousand civilians held at the University of Santo Tomas in the heart of Manila. Yesterday, two flying columns of First Cavalry knifed into the capital. The first American troops inside the city, they crashed through the main gate of the university, liberating all the captives. Again, a number of those rescued were starved and diseased.

Bolick, like every soldier in the 11th, cheered when the Rangers pulled off the first rescue, then applauded the cavalry after the second. This next operation figured to be the toughest one yet. Twenty-one hundred civilians imprisoned thirty-five miles behind enemy lines, the Japanese Tiger Division a few miles south. Surrounded by jungle and water, no open road in or out.

MacArthur gave this job to Airborne.

Bolick called through the deck. "Hey, Gusto."

"Yes?"

"The truth?"

"If you wish."

"I volunteered 'cause this time we get to save folks. Not a lot of that goes on in war."

"Sadly, no. It does not."

Bolick saw little chance for sleep.

"Gusto. What did you do before?"

"Professor of religion."

"No kidding."

"Do you mind if I ask your faith, Sergeant?"

"I'm classic Philadelphia. Father's Jewish, mother Catholic."

"What does that make you?"

"Dunno. A guy who likes cheap whiskey."

Gusto patted the deck above Bolick's head. "I think you've used that one before. I was raised Protestant."

"Well." Bolick took the pair of grenades in hand, deciding to try for some rest. "If I have to blow us up before dawn, we got our bases covered, you and me."

*

The only way to get through to these guys, Bolick decided, was to be quiet.

He slouched in a chair. His M1 leaned against the wall alongside an assortment of tommy guns, old Enfields, birding shotguns, more Garands. The twenty guerrillas in the room with Bolick were unevenly armed. That's what they argued about.

The commander of one group pointed across the table at Gusto of Terry's Hunters.

"Why can't you share? You're the only one who gets carbines from the Americans."

Gusto drummed a finger lightly on the table. Blood had purpled all his nails. Every fighter here bore some mark from three years of hit-and-run combat against the Japanese, whether scars, scabs, bruises, missing digits, a limp, or some sign of torture like Gusto's bloody nails.

Gusto's tone was patient. "The Americans give us the most weapons because we're the best organized. Sergeant," he addressed Bolick, "tell them."

Bolick shook his head. "I don't know anything about that."

He did, but saw no purpose in commenting. Before the guerrillas would even consider settling down to listen to him, they had to first thrash out their several rivalries. Bolick let them bicker.

The discussion zigzagged across a wide catalog of complaints and suspicions. Geographic boundaries, recruiting, timing, the scope of missions; Bolick crossed his arms and ankles.

All five groups had answered his call for a meeting: Terry's Hunters, President Quezon's Own Guerrillas, the Hukbalahaps, the Chinese Squadron, and Marking's Fil-Americans. The guerrillas operated independently from one another. All were positioning themselves for political gain after the war. They were small or large; two levied taxes in their areas to support operations, two did not, one stole what it needed. Every one had what Bolick called "big eyes," appetites larger than their abilities. To a man they were patriotic and courageous.

After an hour of fruitless accusations and hashing, Bolick prodded the man beside him.

Gusto rose. "That's enough."

A member of the Fil-Americans, slight and intense, who called himself "General," rose to answer for the gathering.

"Who says?"

"MacArthur says."

General took in the others around the table with a bemused manner.

"You speak for the Americans now?"

"No." Gusto indicated Bolick. "He does. I speak for him."

Bolick nodded his agreement. He didn't leave his seat, because he would tower over Gusto. That would have cemented his own influence but undermined Gusto's. Bolick needed a Filipino in charge.

In concert, the guerrillas grumbled. Gusto stayed on his feet. General sat.

Bolick didn't figure how Gusto's authority, or anyone's, would last long with this bunch.

"Get to it," Bolick said.

Quickly, Gusto outlined the mission: the rescue of the internees at Los Baños. The U.S. Army had reason to believe the Japanese were going to eliminate them. The operation was urgent.

This wasn't news. Everyone in the room knew abut Palawan, the rescue of the internees at Santo Tomas, atrocities inside Manila. The Japanese could execute the internees at Los Baños any day, without warning. According to reports, they'd already dug a great pit inside the camp.

U.S. forces were tied down fighting around Manila. MacArthur wanted to explore the possibility that the guerrillas in the area—the five groups present—could conduct the operation on their own.

"We need a plan," Gusto told them. "We've got to have arms, transport, a safe evacuation route, and the cooperation of the internees. If Sergeant Bolick and I can get all these, can we work together?"

The pock-faced chief of the Hukbalahaps, the oldest of the guerrilla groups, laced with Communists, spoke first.

"You promise enough guns and ammunition?"

Bolick replied. "Done."

The Huks would keep those weapons after the war. This couldn't be helped.

The guerrilla pouted his bottom lip. "The Hukbalahaps pledge support."

This turned the tide in the meeting. The other commanders followed suit, backing Gusto until they found an opportunity to supplant him.

Bolick produced a message he'd received from his superiors at General Guerrilla Command in Parañaque. The two-page memo, addressed to Gusto, spelled out how to proceed once the resistance groups gave their consent. The guerrillas were ordered to determine and report on Japanese strength and positions around the internee camp, the number and capabilities of guerrilla forces available, road conditions, and the extent of the internees' health. In the final paragraph, Gusto was given permission to wait for reinforcements from the Americans, or attack with the guerrilla force at hand.

The assembled commanders and fighters listened to the instructions without comment. When Gusto finished reading, one youngster, Romeo, chief of the PQOG Red Lions unit, raised his hand like the student he'd been before Japan invaded.

"What if the rescue fails?"

Bolick answered. "The Japanese'll take revenge on the internees. That's why we don't fail, boys."

"What if it succeeds?"

"Then we get everybody out."

"Everybody?"

Bolick lacked the patience to decipher what this young commander was getting at.

"Why don't you just say what you're sayin'."

"What I want to know, Sergeant, is what happens after all the internees are saved? Who's going to protect the people left behind in the villages? If the Japanese blame the locals for collaborating, who's going to stop them?"

"We will."

"I don't believe you." With a sweeping hand, Romeo encompassed the many guerrillas around the table. "All of you, say right now you'll come from your own territories to fight for my villages. Swear it. I want every man here to swear. And you, Sergeant. I want to hear it from you, too."

The little Huk commander shot to his feet. "I don't need to swear to you, Romeo. Not to nobody."

General, from the Fil-Americans, repeated the same harsh refusal. It sounded to him like the PQOG had just insulted his fighters.

Bolick edged back his chair. Under the table, many itchy hands inched toward holsters and triggers.

Bolick stood for the first time. He lifted both large white hands, brushing the plaster ceiling.

"*Tumahimik ka!*" He'd asked Gusto to teach him this phrase.

The guerrilla chieftains shut up, as Bolick directed. The ones standing sat. Gusto remained on his feet. Bolick returned to his chair. He gestured for Gusto to address the question.

With no taint of pride, Gusto said, "Romeo, you have reason to trust my word. I give it to you now. After the internees are safe, we'll stage raids on the Japanese to protect the towns. No one here is a coward. No one hates the Japanese more than the next. We all agree?"

Every guerrilla nodded. Romeo held his head high, unapologetic. Those were his people, his villages. He looked like he'd go toe-to-toe with every man in this room for them.

An unbalanced silence settled on the room, anticipating another tilt into argument. Bolick spoke, to conclude the business and get out of here with the guerrillas' shaky compact intact.

"Last thing. We need a reliable contact inside the camp."

Romeo answered. "PQOG is taking care of that as we speak."

Chapter Twenty-four

THE DOCTOR pushed a finger deep into Carmen's vagina.

"*Itai desu ka?*"

From outside the curtain, Kenji interpreted. "Does that hurt?"

"No."

The old physician removed his finger, then cleaned his hand on a towel. He probed in the creases of both legs on either side of her pubis.

"*Itai desu ka?*"

"No."

The doctor wore his hair longer than a regular soldier's. His glasses were wire-rimmed. His breath carried a hint of mint and sanitation.

Because the doctor's biweekly visits were not sexual, Carmen despised his presence. His delving made her aware of her body, its use and damage. She could not ignore him, eat a rice ball or fly in her mind away out the window, over the camp. She must lie here and listen, answer, submit. He'd come to help, he conducted himself as an innocent. This humiliated Carmen more.

The doctor collected his steel spreader from the tatami and stood. He wiped the tool on the towel before tossing the cloth to the floor. Quickly he pushed aside the curtain. Carmen lowered her legs and sat up, closing her robe before Kenji could look into the room. The doctor motioned him in.

Kenji listened to short bursts from the doctor, then translated for Carmen. "You are not diseased but you are swollen. You should rest. The doctor knows you will not be allowed to. The same goes for the Korean girl."

The doctor made one long statement that Kenji did not relate to Carmen. The man pointed at her, she had not risen to her feet. She'd been made sore by the exam. The doctor was never gentle and in his own way also treated her like a *pii*.

The doctor swept out of the room carrying his small black bag. Kenji stepped into the hall after him but the doctor did not pause. Kenji looked to have swallowed something he meant to say. The doctor's footfalls tapped down the stairs.

Carmen set her back to the wall beneath the window.

"What did the doctor say to you?"

Kenji was slow to turn from the doctor's departure. "That I'm a coward."

"Why would he say this?"

Kenji looked again down the hall as if the doctor had left a trail of condemnation.

"He understands that I am . . . fond of you. He said that you are Filipina. I should take you away from here, into the villages. He knows that can't be done for Yumi. But you would not be found."

Carmen gestured to the edge of the mattress for Kenji to sit. When he'd arranged his long legs, she spoke.

"The Kempeitai would go for my family. You know this."

"You have contacts in the underground. It would be a simple thing for the mop boy to get word to your parents in Manila. They could go into hiding outside the city. The Americans are on Luzon. This will only be for a few months. They'd be safe until the war is over."

"You're no coward, Kenji-sama."

"Am I not?"

Carmen folded her legs under her to wait. Kenji stared out the open window.

"Do you know," he said, "what recruits are called in the Japanese army? *Issen gorin*. This used to be the price of a postcard. That's what a soldier is worth, the paper it costs to send the draft notice. We are beaten and abused in training. We're the last stop in a long journey of cruelty. Every rank above treats us worse than animals. Then we're sent into battle and told to die in victory. We cannot live in defeat. The emperor, you see, would be ashamed."

Kenji pinched the bridge of his nose. Through the open window, in the far distance, another round of bombardments started. The high drone of aircraft covered Kenji's long sigh.

"I was assigned to the Eighteenth Division in Burma. It was autumn and pleasant, even with so much jungle. I was stationed near the coast. Then the Americans moved into the hills. We were sent to chase them. I lasted as long as I could, but the Americans are very efficient fighters."

A detonation rattled Carmen's room. Kenji smiled ruefully, raising a finger to imply: There, see?

"My nerves shattered after a while. I began to weep, frankly, and could not move forward. My captain handed me a knife and told me to clean my honor. He told me, *'Tenno heika banzai.'* Long live His Majesty the Emperor. I handed the knife back. Oddly, my nerve restored itself. I did not want to die for the emperor, and became rather brave about it. I accepted a reduction in rank, my portion of disgrace, and was transferred to Los Baños with the rest of these broken soldiers. So it would seem the doctor saw right through me."

Carmen waited to respond, letting Kenji order his thoughts. He didn't want to die without purpose, for an emperor he did not worship. For Carmen, that didn't make him a coward. She would have told him this, but he spoke first.

"I'll do it. Tonight. I'll take you to Anos. I'll tell Toshiwara I took you to the doctor. You tricked me, you faked being sick and escaped. You tell the mop boy to alert your family in Manila. Make your way to the guerrillas, they'll protect you."

Kenji glared, suddenly fervent. Carmen envisioned an end put to this room and everything that had happened here. She saw herself clothed all day long, fed, left alone in her body without the constant invasion. Her pain would ease, her shame fade. With the guerrillas she could live in the forest, drink from the rivers. And sleep.

Carmen rose from the mattress to place herself in the window above the camp, a red beacon for the boy. Where was he? Every day she tracked him however she could in those hours when she could stand. He stationed himself where she might see him, under the great tree, strolling the fence and daring the guards. This morning she could not find him. Was he in the barracks eating breakfast? Was he watching the main gate? She needed him right now. Appear, boy!

At her back, Kenji asked, "What are you looking for?"

Carmen scanned the camp. She needed to answer Kenji. The boy was nowhere.

She closed her eyes and located him there; he had not strayed or hidden at all. But he was not safe.

"I can't go."

Kenji stood from the tatami. They faced each other. In minutes, Kenji would walk away, she would stay. In the foyer, with the doctor's exam over, Mama would turn outward the Songu tag.

"Why not?"

"I have to save the camp."

Kenji held out empty hands. "And you?" He indicated the thin mattress under his boots. "Can you stand more of this?"

Carmen laid a soft touch on his sleeve. Fooling and using Kenji had meant little to her. She regretted it now, wishing he were not kind.

"Neither of us wants to die for no reason, Kenji-sama. But what would we do if we had a reason, hmm? We do, you and me."

She backed away.

"Go. Thank you. But go."

In the afternoon, Yumi fought another soldier. The young one on top of Carmen could not perform for all the upset in the halls and on the landing. Mama and Papa rushed to calm the angry soldier outside Yumi's curtain. The Japanese shouted threats, Yumi answered him in screeches. In Carmen's room, her bucktoothed boy withdrew from her, throwing up his arms. He pushed back her curtain, pants around his ankles, to shout down the hall at the noisemakers. He needed to concentrate. When the boy knelt again on the tatami, he was flustered, his penis wilted. He peeled off the *saku* with a snap that she wondered did not hurt him. He did not speak English, or Carmen would have finished him with her hand. She let him rail. He did not strike her but snatched his ticket off the table, clearly intending a refund from Mama.

None of the soldiers that day spoke English. They were the *issen gorin* of Kenji's description, poor-quality recruits, the bottom of Japan's barrel. None had been in battle yet, all were likely headed to the defense of Manila. From her elbows, between her brown knees, she studied them. With their pants down she saw the marks of discipline, bruised buttocks and thighs from bamboo rods. Sometimes the bridges of their noses or cheeks were cut. Who could it surprise when these boys raped or murdered? They followed their training, to treat those beneath them without mercy. In the Japanese mind, all races were beneath them.

That evening, after she'd bathed and done her laundry, Benito arrived. Carmen had not set the basin upside down in the hall. He surprised her at sunset when he knocked on the doorframe. Carmen stood in the window wearing her blue blouse. Inside the wire, electricity had been out for a week. The internees among the barracks and along the fence walked with lanterns, like fireflies. Carmen, with her power still on, had cut off her lamp to be with them in the lowering dark.

"Yes?" she called without leaving the window. She had not seen Tal once today. It was her heart's habit to look for him.

"May I come in?" the Filipino boy asked in Tagalog. He peeked around the drape. She motioned him into the room. His *pinuti* bolo was missing and he carried a mop, as Mama had ordered.

"I have nothing for you," she said without leaving the window.

"That's not why I came."

Carmen turned. "What's wrong?"

"I have something to tell you. And a question."

"Go ahead."

"The guerrillas are getting impatient."

"What do you mean?"

"Do you know the town of Bai?"

"North of Manila, yes."

"Three days ago a Japanese finance officer was killed by the Hukbalahaps. This morning the Japanese answered. They murdered three hundred people in the town. They burned the people in their homes and bayoneted the ones who ran out the doors."

Carmen covered her mouth. Benito remained emotionless.

"The Americans want us to stay patient, but that's getting harder to do. All over Luzon, the guerrillas are planning actions on their own. Around Los Baños, there are four different guerrilla groups. If we don't all stay in line, it's not going to be good for the people in the camp. It won't be long before the Japanese take some revenge on the internees."

Carmen steadied herself under visions of the charred village of Bai.

Benito continued. "We're worried about that pit the Japanese dug. It's big and we don't know what it's for. Do you?"

"I'll try to find out. Is that what you came to ask?"

"Yes. And something else. I want to know about the Tuck boy."

Carmen held herself in check. What could Benito want with Tal?

"Why?"

"I have to know if he's reliable."

Carmen froze. The guerrillas meant danger. She had to hide Tal from them just like the guerrillas had to hide from the Japanese.

She plotted a lie. Benito smiled for the first time since entering.

"It's no secret. All right?"

Carmen nodded.

"We're in contact with the American army. They sent us a radioman to get all the guerrillas to coordinate. The Americans want us to meet with one of the internees. You know Tuck better than any of the contacts we've got inside the camp. I need to know we can trust him. That he can make it out of the wire and back, and do what we need."

This morning, Carmen told Kenji she would not leave. She'd stay in this hateful *shuho,* pay with her body for secrets to safeguard the Tuck boy. Could she send him now under the fence, into the jungle to meet with the guerrillas? Two men had already been shot for leaving the camp. What if Tal became the third? What if she were to blame? She'd trusted Benito with her own life. The mop boy added to this, asking that he be trusted with Tal's, too.

"Carmen." Benito wrung the mop handle, impatient. "The meeting's in four days. We'll smuggle in a message and let him know it came from you. He'll do it then. Right?"

She approached the window. Full night had fallen. Even at a distance, she spotted Remy under the dao. By lantern light he dealt himself cards. Tal lay beside him, smoking.

Chapter Twenty-five

REMY LAID another card in the grass, not the one he needed.

In the lantern's glow, he flipped a few more cards until the solitaire game petered out on him. "Nine in a row," he muttered.

Next to him, the boy lit another hand-rolled cigarette from the ember of the one before it, to save matches.

"And really," Remy snapped, "how can you chain-smoke that crap? It smells like you're smokin' a cat's ass."

Tal tossed away the spent butt. He lay back with one arm under his head, bringing the new cigarette to his lips.

"What're you so grouchy about?"

"Ahh, these damn cards." Remy swept them off the grass. He shuffled the deck and dealt the first rows of another hand. He stopped, tossing the deck to the grass.

"Not winning?" Tal asked. "That's not like you."

Remy reached for the cigarette on Tal's lips, knowing in advance he could not stand the taste. His hands wanted something to master. He took a drag and spat afterward, handing it back.

"I keep thinking about Clem."

"What about him?"

"A couple days before he got shot. He lost a lot at dice."

Tal emitted a cloud of acrid smoke. "That don't mean anything."

"Maybe, maybe not. But I haven't lost ten games of solitaire in a row since I can remember."

"You've only lost nine, you said."

Remy tucked the deck into his vest pocket. "Forget it, I ain't playin' one more."

He doused the lantern. Fuel was another vanishing commodity in the camp. With the electricity off, the guards kept the kerosene for their own lamps.

Remy lay next to his son, copying the boy's posture, resting a hand beneath his head. He figured they had less than thirty minutes to curfew, maybe less before the bugs drove them inside. The leaves of the dao blocked the night sky. To the north, tall clouds shimmered scarlet, lit by fires and artillery from the assault on Manila.

"I'm hungry," said Tal, in answer to nothing.

"Me, too. Did you hear what Nagata did today?"

"What now?"

"Cut back the milk ration for babies. Instead of one pint every other day, it's one a week. What a sumbitch. Starving babies."

Tal finished his ersatz cigarette. He tossed it without lighting another. "Bascom traded his fifteen-jewel Elgin to a guard. His grandfather gave him that watch. Killed him to lose it."

"What'd he get for it?"

"Three kilos of sugar, two of rice. The sugar was short two-thirds of a kilo."

"You know what the guards are doin', don't you?"

"Trading us rations out of our own stores."

"That explains why Nagata's got a stranglehold on our food. We can't buy from the locals, can't grow our own, so we wind up making trades with the guards for our own supplies. And he's gettin' a cut out of every trade in the camp, you know damn well he is."

"Nagata," Tal said with distaste. "I reckon he'll get what's coming to him."

"I just hope it's me that delivers it." Remy knocked knuckles against the boy's hip. "Or you."

The two reclined quietly. Beyond the unlit fence, Boot Creek burbled with runoff from the day's shower. The voices of animals and birds in the ravine reminded Remy how close wildness lay. The unwilling deck of cards, squawks from the jungle, the darkened camp, bloodred clouds on the horizon, the stench of burnt catnip on his boy's skin, these made Remy restive. For a decade he'd earned his live-lihood reading signs as small as a flinch or a blink, parsing mysteries, betting on what would come next. Tonight, he was stymied.

In the morning, in the rain, a guard's throat was slit.

The assault happened at the western gate before sunup. Remy hadn't seen the body but the word at breakfast was that the cut almost decapitated the Japanese. The wound had come from a bolo.

Nagata canceled the morning calisthenics to lead a squad of two dozen armed guards into the bush. They hauled with them a pair of heavy machine guns. Through the morning meal, the camp listened to the shush of rain on the nipa roofs and the clap of potshots outside the wire.

In the dining hall of No. 12, Remy pushed at his steamed greens and portion of white rice. The slimy greens were the worst-tasting of the month, a mash of steamed tomato leaves, pigweed, and morning glory. Nagata had them eat-ing grass.

Across the table, Herring, a land lawyer, flattened a palm over his stomach. The man had a worsening case of bacillary dysentery. Over the past two weeks, he'd withered. He was not going to be cured; with the electricity off, serums in the hospital refrigerator that might have helped were spoiled. Herring's only chance, like the hundreds growing sicker by the day, was rescue. If Mac were alive, he'd have found the man an egg.

Remy asked, "How you holdin' up?"

"I'm holdin' up. Just not holdin' anything in. You hear about that guard gettin' his head near cut off?"

"Yeah. At the west gate this mornin'."

"Someone's gotta tell the guerrillas to calm down. I understand them wantin' revenge and all, but so long as we're the ones inside the wire, I wish they'd sit on their hands a little longer."

Remy made no mention of what he'd heard on the radio over the last several days: more civilian killings in Manila, a slaughter at Palawan, the rescue by Army Rangers of five hundred half-dead survivors of the Bataan March from a POW camp in Cabanatuan. Every one of these actions was another spark to fire up the guerrillas. No sense enflaming passions and fears in the camp. That ugly pit by the dao tree had given the internees enough cause to worry. Add to it the murdered guard this morning. Remy was careful lately to spark rumors with only good news, to keep hopes buoyed. The bad he kept to himself. For now.

Poor Herring looked cadaverous. He was as good as dead in a few more weeks. Remy would build another bamboo casket. He caught himself measuring the lawyer, thinking like an undertaker. He pushed his half-eaten plate over to Herring and left the table.

The rain and the guards' search for guerrillas around the camp delayed that day's firewood detail. Remy lay in his bunk until the sky cleared and the Japanese returned. The soldiers trudged in the west gate scratched up and tired. They were a disorderly lot, out of step, drenched, and frustrated. Nagata was the only one with a martial air left to him, swinging his arms with a pistol at his belt.

Remy assembled along with the hundred others whose

names appeared on today's labor list for the firewood detail, doubled for the past three months. The work in the forest went tediously. The men of the detail eyed the great ever-greens reaching to the top of the forest canopy. They walked past fig trees lush with fruit, coconuts on the ground, and snagged what they could without being caught. On the path, they pushed through lady slipper orchids and gossamer ferns dripping with morning rain. Remy and the rest of the internees imagined a guerrilla behind each broad trunk, every green fan in this paradise, some angry hornet of a Fili-pino ready to scrap with the dozen guards and get everyone killed in the crossfire. The guards, too, kept a wary eye out and rifles in their hands. Even with twice the manpower, the carabao sled held only three quarters of a load when time came to return to camp.

Remy plodded near the end of the line, exhausted and soaked from sweat and humidity. He fanned himself with his fedora. A mile from the main gate, the column encoun-tered a procession of local merchants and their mule-drawn *carrettas*. The vendors pulled off the downhill path to set up shop for the passing internees. The guards, weary and seeing no threat, let the internees purchase fruits, vegetables, and plucked poultry. The guards themselves bought a few items.

Remy carried no money. He stood on the path, thirsty. He walked to the water cart for a drink. Far ahead, the water buffalo bellowed against the halt in progress. This beast was new to the traces.

A small woman, old with parchment skin, beckoned Remy to her cart. He waved her off, pointing at his empty pocket. She dipped a wooden ladle into a bucket, and it came up dripping a milky liquid. She motioned him over with fervor. Remy accepted a free drink of coconut milk.

The old Filipina did not reach for the drained ladle. A lean boy appeared beside her to take the ladle from Remy's hand. He left behind a scrolled bit of paper, slipped into Remy's palm. The boy dropped the ladle into the coconut-milk bucket, then faded into the jungle. This was the boy from a month ago at the west gate, the one with dead chickens hanging from his belt.

The long bolo dangling at his rear, like a tail.

Remy lowered the earpiece of the crystal radio. He lifted his head above the windowsill, to look over the roofs of the dark camp, northwest to Manila. The sky continued to flicker there, as if the two forces battled with lightning.

"Boy."

Tal stood with one foot in the hall, on guard while Remy worked the radio.

"Yeah?"

"C'mere. I want you to hear this."

Tal entered the room to kneel beside the radio. Remy moved to stand watch in his place.

Remy waited, letting the *Voice of Freedom* news cycle in the boy's ear. Roosevelt, Stalin, and Churchill had just concluded a secret meeting somewhere in the Soviet Union. The Allies had launched an offensive to reach the Rhine in Germany. The Red Army had liberated a Nazi extermination camp for Jews at Auschwitz, Poland. In the Pacific, American troops made tough progress in the fight for Manila.

Tal looked up, excited and pleased.

That ain't it, Remy thought. He motioned for Tal to keep listening. The boy returned his attention to the earpiece.

After quiet minutes, Tal raised a hand to the top of his head. Remy watched and waited for his son's stunned reaction. He fingered the scrolled message in his vest pocket.

When Tal lowered the earpiece, Remy indicated the hole in the floorboards, for him to hide the radio. After that was done, the two slid the bunk into place.

Remy said, "Let's walk."

He led Tal out of the barracks to the open field. Curfew remained a half hour off. Some internees strolled with lanterns fueled by coconut oil, others sat on blankets to watch the jittering northwest sky. Deep, rumbling detonations accompanied the flashes. Remy stopped on the grass far from others' hearing.

"Two thousand," he muttered. The same number of people in this camp. The words felt so inadequate for the stack of dead.

"How far is that from here?"

"Calamba? Seven miles." Remy aimed his chin the direction of Manila. He wondered if some of the fiery glow of last night had come from the slaughter there.

The *Voice of Freedom* report had been graphic. Yesterday, in reprisal for the killing of an officer and five soldiers, Japanese troops herded the population of Calamba's barrio into the town's Catholic church. Soldiers gutted them with bayonets, choked them with hemp ropes. Women and children were among those massacred.

Tal gazed where Remy indicated.

Remy dug into his vest pocket. The little scroll was no bigger than a cigarette.

"Here."

"What's that?"

"I got handed this a couple days ago on the trail, when I was on firewood detail. It's for you."

Tal took the message. He rolled it in his fingers.

"Who's it from?"

"Carmen."

"Is this it? Is this the message telling us to get out of the camp?"

"No, it ain't that message. This is somethin' else. Just for you."

"What do you mean?"

"The guerrillas want an internee to go to a meeting. They've got an American radio operator working with 'em. Carmen said you'd be the one to do it. To be honest, I wasn't gonna give this to you."

"Why not?"

Remy shrugged. "Afraid of lettin' you go. People gettin' shot outside the wire, the guerrillas goin' crazy. I figured, screw it, let 'em get someone else. Then I heard that report about Calamba."

Tal unfurled the message. "You didn't have any right to do that."

The boy tried to read the small page in the dark. Remy pushed his son's hands down.

"Boy, you're all I got. I don't regret doin' anything I can to protect you. But you know what?"

Tal stuffed the scroll in his pocket to read it later by a lantern. "What."

"I came to the same conclusion Carmen did. There ain't anyone else. You're fast and you're smart. You got guts. You gotta go."

Remy imagined again the two thousand bodies in Calamba, the fires in the sky a pyre for them, another warning for the internees of Los Baños.

He said, "You remember how we agreed we'd survive, and we'd save the girl? Looks like she's saving us instead."

"When's the meeting?"

"Midnight. Tonight."

Chapter Twenty-six

THE CURFEW and shut-off electricity aided Tal's exit from the camp. The patrolling guards relaxed their vigilance and the lanterns they carried marked their locations. Tal slipped behind the infirmary, under the wire, and into the ravine.

He followed the stones and trickling waters curving around the northern bounds of the camp. He stepped lightly, sticking to the larger rocks in the creek bed. The night creatures ignored him, pleased to see the boy move past quickly, sensing no menace. Thirty minutes after slipping under the fence, Tal scrambled up the shallow cliff beneath Faculty Hill.

The mission excited him. In every step he took he felt the joint venture with Carmen, both of them working with the guerrillas. Again, just as they had for months gazing at each other in the camp, she in her high window, him inside the wire, they did not speak but were linked. He didn't know what was at stake with the meeting ahead but supposed it was all their lives.

He found the house quickly, a dimly lit bungalow behind a great willow. Tal circled through hedges to the backyard. He felt out of place sneaking across the grass to the rear door, not because he was an American escapee and it would be fatal to be caught in his company; he'd not entered a real home in over three years.

Tal tapped on a glass pane. He gazed into a crowded kitchen, beyond that to a room stuffed with books and pillowed chairs. A pretty Filipina rounded a corner to let him in.

She smiled through the glass, raven hair gathered in a ponytail. She worked a deadbolt, then pulled the door open.

"Hello," she said. "Hungry?"

"Yes, ma'am."

"Come in. I'll bring you something."

She shut the door behind him with a glance into the night.

"Go inside. I'll bring food."

Tal wanted to pause in the kitchen to touch everything, pots and pans and soft fabrics, kitchen chairs. The woman urged him into the next room. In the den, all the curtains had been pulled and a hard-looking Filipino stood.

The man looked as much of a misfit indoors as Tal. At his belt hung twin pistols, the sleeves of his shirt had been ripped away, his khakis and boots were equally dirty. He needed a shave and a week of rest.

Tal extended a hand. "Talbot Tuck."

"Gusto." The guerrilla reached back.

Tal shook firmly to give the older fighter confidence in him. Gusto winced. Tal let go quickly.

"You all right?"

Gingerly, Gusto turned over his hand to show Tal the nails, all of them blue.

"I had a chat with the Japanese last week."

The guerrilla indicated a chair for Tal, took one for himself.

"Thanks for coming. I know you're taking a big risk. We heard about the shootings in the camp."

The Filipina came from the kitchen with a platter of cheeses and bread.

"I'm boiling some eggs, they'll be ready in a minute. I'm Magdalena." She indicated Gusto. "He's with Terry's Hunters." Magdalena set the platter between them. She returned to the kitchen, where steam curled from a pot on the stove.

Tal expected the guerrilla to speak first. When the man did not, his attention wandered to the room, cozy and book-lined, a teacher's den. Unbidden, tears welled in Tal's eyes to be in this space of safety and comfort, food at his fingertips, a cushion under him, though he would be killed if found here. Magdalena returned with a bowl of unpeeled boiled eggs. She set them in Tal's reach. She rested a hand on his shoulder and waited.

Tal wiped his nose on the back of his wrist. He handed the bowl of eggs to Gusto. The guerrilla waved it off. "After you. Please."

Tal dug into the warm shell of an egg. Magdalena arranged herself on a settee. She lifted the cheese plate to Gusto, taking none for herself. The guerrilla ate without greed. Tal noticed and slowed his own gulping, putting down a second egg.

Gusto said, "The Americans are here."

"We see them flying over the camp."

"I'm not talking about planes. I mean the army is actually meeting with the guerrillas. We have a radio operator with us. We're making a plan to get the internees out. We know you're in danger."

Gusto paused, as if expecting Tal to ask for an explanation. Tal said only, "I know." The guerrilla glanced at Magdalena, then continued.

He detailed a meeting from the day before, at the town hall in Santa Cruz, a nearby village controlled by the resistance. Commanders and fighters from all five guerrilla groups had attended, plus the American radioman. The purpose of the gathering was to consider instructions sent by the 11th Airborne, tasked with the rescue of the internees at Los Baños.

Gusto unfolded two pages, handed them to Tal.

"Here's a copy of the order."

Tal scanned the document while Gusto explained it. The guerrillas were commanded to collect info on everything about the camp, the guards, and the internees. The final paragraph allowed the guerrillas to mount a rescue on their own, without the Americans.

Tal asked, "So what am I doing here?"

"We've got to coordinate with the people inside the camp. Preferably an official, someone the internees will listen to and who can negotiate for them. That's not you, I assume. But we figure you know who it is and can bring him here. Two nights from now."

Tal decided quickly on Mr. Lucas. Remy was in better condition, but he lacked the authority Gusto wanted. Not only was Lucas respected, he was the youngest of the Internee Committee, the one member of that group most likely to make it under the wire and back.

"What else?"

"That's it for now." Gusto rose, Tal with him. The guerrilla didn't reach for another handshake.

Magdalena kept her seat. "Sit, both of you." She motioned to the food left on the plates. She'd touched none of it, and Tal had controlled his hunger so Gusto would not see him desperate. At the woman's insistence, both took their chairs. She ate first, picking from the cheese. Tal and Gusto tucked in.

To let the two gorge, Magdalena made conversation.

"Gusto was my husband's religion teacher here at the college. I was too poor a student to understand his classes. I switched to history."

Gusto inclined his head in appreciation. "You had more important things to study. History is mankind's legacy. God is mankind's dream."

Magdalena said, "My husband is a commander of the PQOG. He was Gusto's best pupil."

"Romeo was my most bullheaded, at any rate."

Tal, in his three years inside the wire, had studied nothing but what and how to steal from the guards and ways to outlive them. With another boiled egg puffing his cheeks, he turned the talk to a more pragmatic topic.

He asked Gusto, "Can you really do it without the army?"

The guerrilla, with better manners, waited until Tal had swallowed before answering.

"That is the right question."

"And?"

Gusto peeled one more egg. He pushed it past his lips, leaving his answer hanging until he'd finished.

"Not without getting a lot of your people killed. No."

Gusto stood first. Tal joined him on his feet.

"So, Mr. Tuck, we will do it with the army."

Gusto extended his left hand for a less-painful parting shake. Tal took it.

Magdalena moved to a cabinet. From a drawer she pulled two packs of Lucky Strikes, not the same olive drab packaging the fighter pilot had dropped into the camp two months ago. Tal held real American-issue Luckies, a red ball on a white field, L.S./M.F.T. across the bottom.

She said, "Take these. Show them to whoever you need to convince. Tell them the Americans are close by."

Tal pocketed the smokes. With a glance around the den, the empty plate and bowl, Tal headed for the kitchen, resisting the urge to linger.

Behind him, Gusto spoke to Magdalena, "*Salamat. Paalam.*" Tal turned to say the same. Thank you. Goodbye.

She ushered both outside with kisses to their cheeks. Magdalena closed the door. The kitchen light extinguished. Gusto led the way into the darkened yard. The guerrilla stopped, to set a hand against Tal's arm.

"Bring your man here in two nights."

With that, Gusto crouched and slid away into the night. Tal left Faculty Hill for the slope leading into the ravine. He tried to move the way Gusto had, focused and blended into the rocks and arching branches. Tal advanced through the ravine with a single-mindedness he'd not had before. He imagined Japanese soldiers at every bend, along the rugged bank, listening for one careless step. He paused with every sound, figuring the animals would reveal a presence to him. Tal did not grow fatigued and his alertness did not wane.

Never had he been trusted with something the measure of this. Not just his own life but the welfare of thousands, every one an intimate to him from years of imprisonment together, hinged on his choice of where to plant his boot, when to hold his breath, whether to swat a bug from his face. Carmen had picked him for this, Remy had faith in him, Gusto relied on him. He had Lucky Strikes and a letter from the U.S. Army in his pocket.

At 1:30 a.m., Tal reached the wire behind the infirmary. He slid into the camp without noise. The lanterns of the guards swayed along the perimeter, taking no notice of him creeping to his own barracks.

Remy waited on the back steps. Tal arrived nearly beside him in the dark before revealing himself. Remy started, a hand over his heart.

"Jeez, boy," he whispered. "Like to scare me to death."

"Slide over."

Remy made room on the step. "If I kick off, who's gonna build my casket?"

"Don't worry. We're all gonna kick off together." Tal handed over one of the packs of Luckies. "Or we're all getting out."

"Well, would you looky here." Pleased, Remy split the foil to shake out a pair of smokes. The two lit up from the same match, hiding the flame. Tal dragged deeply, savoring the Virginia tobacco.

Tal said, "Smells like Uncle Sam."

Remy blew a fat smoke ring. "To hell with that. It smells like MacArthur."

He admired the hovering gray circle. Tal produced like a magician one more boiled egg and gave it to Remy.

Lucas lay faceup under the fence, snagged on a barb, cursing under his breath.

Tal wagged a finger in the dark to quiet the man. Plucking the wire out of his shirt, Tal dragged him under the armpits until his boots came clear.

Tal led the way through the high grass, orchard, and bamboo toward the ravine. He moved in a way that caused no stir in the brush around him. He looked back many times to instruct Lucas and keep him hushed.

Lucas grew winded and asked to pause at the rim of the creek bed. The creatures of the ravine did not like men to be still, they were most tolerant when they knew where intruders were. He let Lucas rest only a minute before guiding him down the slope. Unsure and awkward, Lucas reached the bottom without rolling any stones underfoot.

Moving through the ravine, Tal shortened his strides so Lucas could shadow him. This was the man's first time outside the camp without an armed guard watching him cut firewood. Lucas's attention careened from slick rocks under his feet into the trees, where monkeys dashed between branches and owls perched in vigil. He jerked at sounds Tal knew as the night concert of free creatures and flowing water. Likely, Lucas was thinking of Clem and Donnelly, that they'd followed this path, too, and died returning from it. Tal worked to keep Lucas's attention fixed on him.

Lucas still considered him a thief. The committeeman

had shown surprise when it was the Tuck boy who'd brought him the letter from Gusto and the American army, plus the pack of Luckies. Lucas had asked: How'd you get these? Remy had advised Tal not to say, to protect Carmen and the boy with the bolo at his back. Lucas sniffed, reluctant to tie his fate to one of the camp's troublemakers, the boy linked to the silk-robed girl above the camp. Lucas called a committee meeting to show them Gusto's letter and the cigarettes. He emerged from that meeting agreeing to come tonight, but had not dropped his mistrust.

Tal guided Lucas to Faculty Hill, arriving on time. He rapped on Magdalena's back door. Gusto answered.

"I asked her to stay away, just for tonight," the guerrilla explained, opening the door. "She left more eggs."

Tal introduced Gusto to Lucas. The two men shared a leanness born of different circumstances, one from starvation, the other out of constant peril. Gusto endured another handshake with his bloodied nails.

They arranged themselves in the den around a bowl of peeled boiled eggs. Tal plucked the first egg. The men showed restraint and watched him eat alone. Chewing, Tal gauged the contrasts between them, both of similar age, one a lithe brown fighter, the other stringy and pale, hesitant, a diplomat. Tal reached for another egg. Gusto slid the bowl from his reach to offer it instead to Lucas. The committeeman inclined his head and accepted. Then Gusto helped himself.

Food in his mouth helped Lucas relax his stiff hold on himself. Gusto winked at Tal, then set the bowl of eggs again where he could reach them. Tal gulped another.

"Thank you," Lucas said with a satisfied exhalation, "thank you."

"Of course," Gusto answered.

"Listen, we appreciate the risk you and your people are taking for us."

"We're all taking risks, Mr. Lucas."

Tal nodded, cheeks full.

Gusto continued, "I assume you're a responsible person in the camp. You have authority to speak for the internees."

"I'm on the committee. And yes, I have the authority. There's just one problem."

Gusto grabbed another egg and mulled it. "A problem?"

Lucas cleared his throat. "At the moment, I haven't got permission."

Gusto set down the egg. He laced his fingers, leaning back to tap his blackened nails against his knuckles. "Continue."

"The minute young Tuck came to me, I called a committee meeting. I'll be honest, the others have a skeptical view of the guerrillas. They're not happy with your activities so close to the camp. By that I mean cutting guards' throats. They don't believe we should have direct dealings with you. They want contact only with the American army."

"Did you show them the letter from the army?"

"Of course. They weren't happy about that, either. You gave a copy to Talbot to bring back into the camp. What if he'd been caught or shot, and they'd found that on him? The entire camp might've been executed ten minutes later. It wasn't a clever thing to do."

Tal flared. "You didn't tell me the committee was against you coming."

"I had good reason not to. I was afraid you'd react like you are now."

"Well, I'm not going to *get* caught."

Lucas held up a hand. "That's not the point, son. The committee doesn't trust the guerrillas or you. But I do."

"Why?" asked Gusto.

"Because we don't have a choice."

"Thanks." Tal flung himself against the sofa cushions.

Gusto said, "Then you disagree with your committee."

"I don't think we should sit around and do nothing. I've got my reservations, but yes, I disagree."

"If I can convince you, can you convince them?"

"Can't say. I'll give it my best shot."

"Does your committee even know you're here."

"Actually, no."

Gusto kneaded the furrows of his dark brow. "I like you, Mr. Lucas." He selected one of the last eggs to hand to the committeeman. "I hope we can save you." To Tal, the guerrilla said, "Stop pouting, boy. Eat."

The three crammed eggs in their mouths whole. The collective pause exposed their common hunger. This formed a pact to move forward.

When he'd wiped the last bits from his lip, Gusto said, "Since the boy and I met two nights ago, there's been progress on the rescue plan. The army has decided to take the lead, with the guerrillas in support. Does that ease your mind, Mr. Lucas?"

"Yes."

Gusto outlined the attack scenario. Sometime in the next week to ten days, a reinforced battalion of the 11th Airborne was going to launch an infantry assault southeast of Manila along National Highway 1. This force would strike at Japanese units along the San Juan River near Calamba. The action was intended to do two things: block the enemy from moving troops up from the Lecheria Hills west of the camp, and distract the massive Tiger Division away from Los Baños, the real objective of the mission.

Before the attack, a small recon force would take positions with the guerrillas around the camp, concealed in the creek, ravine, and jungle. An airborne company would drop from low altitude just outside the wire. The signal for the recon platoon and guerrillas was the pop of the first chute. The plan called for the group on the ground to charge the camp and neutralize the guards, with assistance from the paratroopers as they landed and reached the gates. Once resistance was eliminated, the soldiers would organize the internees to escort them out of the camp while the guerrillas set up a perimeter against a Japanese counterattack.

Lucas nodded through the presentation, until Gusto finished.

"Can I ask a few questions?"

"I hope I have answers."

"Me, too. Are you aware that half the camp is weak from malnutrition and disease? Plus, there's a couple hundred that are bedridden. We've got women and small children. How on earth are you going to get twenty-one hundred people in this condition through forty miles of enemy lines? We're certainly not going to walk out. You didn't mention trucks, but even if you did, I don't think the guerrillas can protect that much highway."

"We don't know yet. That part of the plan is still taking shape."

"Uh-huh." Lucas fingered his chin. "Uh-huh. Well, that doesn't fill me with confidence."

"Can't be helped."

"I see. Moving on. You mentioned a week to ten days. Honestly, what if the Japs decide to kill us before that?"

Tal, who'd be among the bodies if this happened, listened to Gusto's reply with keen interest.

"We've got someone on the inside keeping an eye on the guards. We get regular reports. We think . . . we hope we'll get a warning before something like that happens."

Carmen. Tal thought of what she had to do to collect this information. He wondered if Gusto knew or cared, or what Lucas would say with his disapproving way if he knew the Filipina in the window might be his salvation.

"One last question," Lucas said. "How do you figure the

internees will survive an all-out gun battle at the camp? We're civilians, not soldiers."

Gusto leaned forward on his padded chair. "I don't expect you to just survive, Mr. Lucas. I expect you to take part."

Lucas lowered his jaw, appearing unsure of what he'd just heard. "Beg pardon?"

"Terry's Hunters can smuggle weapons into the camp. When the attack starts, the internees can defend themselves and help with the raid."

Lucas flung up both hands as though warding off something rushing at him.

"Absolutely not. We're not arming the internees."

"Explain, Mr. Lucas."

"We're a civilian camp. Noncombatants. That's the only protection we've got. The moment any of us touches a gun, we turn into legitimate targets for the Japanese. No, sir. No."

Gusto hoisted a finger topped by a blackened nail to underscore his distaste for Lucas's refusal.

"Do the Japanese observe international law by starving you? Did they check with attorneys before they shot your two friends? Would you like to know what's happening right now inside Manila to noncombatants?"

Lucas remained motionless.

Gusto increased his volume. "We've just heard about more massacres, at Muntinlupa and New Bilibid Prison. Mr. Lucas, it's only a matter of time until the Japanese murder every civilian in Los Baños. No one knows when that's coming, but it will come. If we don't have our rescue forces ready in time, you'll have to defend yourselves. That's the simple truth. And if it happens, are you ready for that much blood on your hands?"

Lucas would not be swayed. "I'll do what I can to get you cooperation from the internees. But we won't be taking your guns. Keep them. You'll use them better than we would."

Gusto did not keep frustration off his face. Tal saw the wisdom of both positions. When the fighting started, the internees would be sitting ducks should the Japanese pick that moment for a final grand gesture in the emperor's name. If the guards turned their guns on the internees—and they'd already proven they would do it—a slaughter could arise in seconds that would exceed anything Tal had heard on the radio. On the other hand, if just one of the guerrillas' guns were found inside the camp during a search, it might kick off the killing anyway.

The guerrilla said, "We want one more meeting. Four nights from now, on the eighteenth. We'll need someone who knows the camp inside and out, to give us everything you've got on Japanese gun placements, maps, up-to-date numbers, and the health of internees."

"That's me," Tal said. "I'll come."

"We can't make that promise," Lucas answered, cutting him off.

Gusto bypassed Lucas, speaking straight to Tal.

"I'll have a guerrilla team waiting in the ravine. They'll take you to talk directly to the Americans."

The Americans? Tal was going to help the soldiers plan the raid on Los Baños!

"Here?"

"No. At their headquarters outside Manila."

"Through Jap lines?"

"The Eleventh Airborne is in Parañaque. There's something you need to understand, boy."

Lucas said nothing, making it clear he had no control over Tal.

Gusto continued. "This is twenty miles through Japanese territory. You'll be in an open *banca* on the bay for six hours, with enemy patrols on the lookout the whole way. Then through five miles of enemy jungle. I make no guarantee you'll arrive. All I can do is give you the promise that my guerrilla team will be dead with you if anything happens."

Men would die to protect him. Tal nodded, solemn at the responsibility, eager to embrace it.

"Will I be able to get back for the rescue?"

"That's up to the army."

Tal's excitement waned. Could he leave the camp and not return? What about Carmen and Remy, and Yumi? They'd promised to save each other. If Tal disappeared, Remy could fend for himself. But could he protect himself *and* the girls the day of the raid? Who'd make sure Carmen and Yumi weren't left behind? After all this time, could Tal miss the big moment?

Gusto fixed his attention again on Lucas. "Pick three of your people. All of them have to be fit enough to make the trip to Parañaque. They have to know the camp inside and out. All three will go to Barrio Tranca first. Romeo will send one west to the Americans. The other two will be taken east to Nanhaya. Romeo will keep them safe there until word comes that the first one reached the American lines. If not, Romeo will send another, then another."

Gusto rose. On his feet, commanding, he continued to address Lucas.

"Pick your people. This boy will do, but if he can't come, find another. The army gave me this order. I'm giving it to you. Three internees. Four nights from now."

Lucas stood, Tal beside him. The committeeman, far taller than Gusto, lacked the guerrilla's resoluteness. Poorly shaven, pistol at his hip, Gusto glared and did not relent.

They followed him to the rear door. Gusto told Tal, "I believe I will see you again."

Tal led Lucas back to the ravine, to the camp, and under the wire.

Chapter Twenty-seven

T HE POINT man waved his arms, hissing at Bolick and the five guerrillas. "Off the trail. Japs coming. Go, go!"

The guerrillas ducked into the brush and fanning ferns on both sides of the path. Bolick doffed the big radio from his back, dashing into the jungle. He drove his chest and knees into the mossy ground, the radio clumped beside him. He held his breath. On the dark trail, a Japanese patrol came their way

A motion beside Bolick made him jerk. Young Romeo landed without a rustle. He held a brown palm up for stillness. Romeo laid aside his carbine. With a sound that blended with the night noises of breezes and beasts, he slid from his belt the long bolo. He raised his chin at the knife on Bolick's belt.

The first boots and khaki leggings stole past on the trail. Beneath the metal brim of his helmet, Bolick saw only the legs of the passing Japanese. Romeo coiled, drawing up his knees. Bolick couldn't do much damage with a blade in hand-to-hand combat; he was a large man, the kind needed to heft a military radio, slow compared to the guerrillas or the Japanese. He pulled away the leather holster strap from the grip of his Colt .45.

Boots paraded by on the moist earth. Leaves and roots at Bolick's eye level blocked him from seeing more than the soldiers passing in front of him. Three had gone by so far. Four more stepped along the trail. The Japanese were bunched tightly. Likely, they were scared.

The jungle quieted. Bolick and the guerrillas were not the only ones watching.

The last soldier's heel rose and fell on the trail, disappearing behind the veil of plant life. A night bird cawed, a piercing imitated tweet from Romeo to signal his guerrillas.

Romeo leaped to his feet. Bolick heard nothing of the man, saw only a starlit flash of his bolo.

Bolick yanked the pistol from its holster. Still flat on his belly, he didn't know what to do. Stand or lie flat? Charge? Wait?

He made the decision of an airborne soldier. He scrambled to his feet, Colt leveled and ready.

Three Japanese were already down, the other four were set upon by long knifes. No one loosed a shot. Bolick advanced up the trail, sidearm poised. With no more than a whisk of sound, seven enemy soldiers lay dead or dying on the trail. Before any of the Japanese could moan or beg, each was dispatched where he lay by the machetes. The guerrillas teamed up to dump the bodies far from the trail. Each Filipino shouldered an abandoned rifle. Romeo lifted two off the ground. Bolick found his radio, slipped into the straps, and joined the guerrillas on the trail.

The point man vanished forward again. Bolick walked in the middle of the guerrilla pack, three in front, three behind. The young leader Romeo had not a drop of blood on him, not even his knife.

Bolick whispered, "Why'd you do that?"

"What do you mean?"

"You could have just let 'em go. They were already past us."

"A month ago, maybe. Not anymore, Sergeant."

The path twisted with the terrain until it moved into the open, alongside Laguna de Bay. The town of Nanhaya was two miles ahead on the shore. A low half moon laid a white finger on the water, always pointing at Bolick.

"Hey, Romeo."

"Sergeant."

"Where you from? I never got around to asking you."

"Los Baños. My father was on the faculty at the college there. I was a biology student."

"I'm from a big city. Philadelphia. You hear of it?"

"Yes."

"Great town. Got everything and everybody. And food. You ever have a Philly cheesesteak?"

"No, Sergeant."

"You come to Philly, I'll take you. It's the bread, that's what makes a real cheesesteak. You can get one in New York, Boston, but you don't want 'em. You like baseball?"

"I've heard of the Yankees."

"Okay, forget baseball. You married?"

"Yes. Magdalena."

"That's great. Where is she?"

"At our house, in Los Baños."

The pinprick lights of Barrio Nanhaya glimmered across the water, another ten minutes ahead. Bolick wanted to chat. The pretty path and dappled bay drew him out, but Romeo and his guerrillas moved silently, ruling out banter. Bolick missed his airborne buddies, men he could talk with.

He wanted to go home, where dying and killing were not asked of you. He didn't like Philly much anymore. He wanted to live in open spaces like this, maybe in a small town beside a lake. The war made Bolick want more quiet than a city could offer.

On the outskirts of Barrio Nanhaya, Romeo's men were met by a team from Terry's Hunters who led them to camp. Bolick set up his radio in a ragged tent close to the fire pit; the cloth stank of smoke. At midnight, he sat to a meal of rice and bananas.

No one in Terry's Hunters felt like talking, either.

Chapter Twenty-eight

REMY SLID shut the garage door. In the midday sun, he propped his hands on his knees and spat in the dirt. He shouldn't be displaying his exhaustion and disgust like this where anyone could see him. He hadn't realized how tired he was until he'd set down the tools and walked away.

Remy couldn't build any more caskets. The dead had outpaced him. Two more died today, one from malaria, the lawyer Herring, the other malnutrition, tall Janeway; four more yesterday, three the day before, one of whom, a deranged fellow, tried to eat his own mattress. Nagata had put a stop to more bamboo rods coming into the camp. He'd issued an order that anyone caught dealing with locals would be shot, along with the offending Filipinos. None of the internees had the energy to scour the camp to find materials for caskets. The gravediggers had grown so worn down they'd been tripled in manpower, needing a dozen sets of hands to shovel out each hole.

The increasing rate of deaths wore on the camp as it did Remy. Everyone was weary of bloated bodies, men and women known to all and barely recognizable in their final forms. Remy secured their green coffin tops, then joined another round of pallbearers to carry the corpses through camp to the cemetery. The loudspeaker announced the deaths, the times of their funerals. After each service, Remy trudged to the garage to begin another casket alone.

The bamboo was depleted, Remy was finished. The dead

were not. Remy wanted to crumple into his bunk. He eyed his nearby barracks; he'd get no privacy there. He set his back against the garage door and slid down, tugging the brim of his fedora to cover his eyes and announce he was not welcoming company. The camp, huddled in its hunger, left him alone.

Remy stayed through the sun's peak. He knew too much from listening to the radio and to Tal, from the caskets before he closed them. He wanted a few hours where he learned nothing more of deaths in the camp, slaughters and battles outside it.

The gray shadow from the garage crept down his legs. When his sandals were in shade, Lucas rounded the corner.

"Tuck. What are you doing?"

"Not much. Thinkin'."

"About what?"

"Same as everybody. Tired of this."

"Mind if I sit?"

"It's a free country." Lucas didn't chuckle with Remy. The committeeman arranged himself in the dirt. Remy asked, "How'd the meeting go?"

"We just wrapped it up. Not so good."

"The committee didn't believe you?"

"Oh, they believed me, all right. Problem is, they absolutely don't want anything more to do with the guerrillas. Just the army. They pretty much ordered me to stay in the camp."

"They did that before. You ignored 'em."

"Can't do it this time. I barely made it the mile and a half around Boot Creek. This mission calls for someone to go twenty miles through Jap lines."

"So you're callin' it off?"

"No."

Remy's stomach sank. "You're still sendin' Tal."

"Yeah." Lucas drew a circle in the dirt, hesitant. "I'll be honest with you. I never thought much of your boy before. I've changed my mind. You can be proud of him."

"Always was. But thank you."

"All right. I suppose you know we need to send three men total."

Remy puffed his cheeks. The boy had been tight-lipped when he returned from the meeting with Lucas. That was all right, he was supposed to be.

"No. First I heard of this. Why you need so many?"

"It's twenty miles through Jap territory. If the first man doesn't make it, the next in line has to go. Then the last one. This is too important."

Clearly, Lucas assumed the first man would be Tal.

"Who else you talkin' to?"

The committeeman picked his words carefully. "Look, you know I can't go around recruiting people to slip under the wire and run off with the guerrillas. If the committee found out, they'd slap me in the brig. Next thing they'd do is tighten the watch on the whole camp. Your boy'll be the first one they'll bird-dog. Worse, everybody's already worried about that pit. If word spread that I'm working with the guerrillas because I think the Japs are about to shoot us any day, it could cause a panic. That just might be the spark they need to start pulling triggers. So."

Remy lifted his fedora to rub a hand across his pate.

"How are the Japs gonna react to three of us missin' roll call?"

"Nagata'll probably holler a lot and send some men out to look for them. More cutbacks on rice; we're already getting no meat. Threats. Nothing the camp can't stand for a few more days until the army gets us out of here."

Remy gazed around the late-afternoon camp, vexed that this was his world, cordoned off and dying in dribs and drabs, likely scheduled to die all at once on some fast-coming morning. He beat the felt fedora across his thigh, as though to spur a horse. Scissoring his legs under him, he shoved off the ground. Remy dusted grit off his sore but-tocks and the backs of his legs.

"Where you going?" Lucas asked.

"You can't talk me into this. I'm gonna go find my kid. See if he can."

In the kitchen, Tal sat in a circle with thirty men and women. In front of each stood a twenty-five-kilo sack of *palay*.

The boy ground a rounded bit of wood into the bowl in his lap. Others pressed hard on rolling pins over metal cooking pans. From the doorway, Remy watched them labor to polish the unhusked rice. The Japanese had announced they would provide no more clean rice. Now, two thousand pounds of *palay* had to be prepared by hand, every day, to remove the razor-sharp husks. The call had gone out for volunteers. Remy kept busy building coffins. He figured Tal would be here.

The muscles in his boy's arms flexed and relaxed, stringy, veined, fading along with everyone else. The camp would live or die on this rice. The last three pigs went into the stew two nights ago. Nagata announced there would be no more meat, though a dozen cattle grazed in a field outside the camp. Even greens had become scarce, with many local farmers taking to the hills. The Filipinos sensed the same evil coming as Remy had and lit out for safety before the ill wind blew their way.

With the exception of the boy, none of the people grind-ing at the *palay* were aware of how numbered were the days of Los Baños. Each had the task of husking fifty pounds of rice, so the camp could ensure another meal. If they knew what Remy or Tal had in their heads, if slaughter was on their minds, would they work so hard to save one another? Lucas was right, he couldn't tell anyone.

One woman, then another, rose from the group, massaging their bony knuckles. They caught Remy's eye and smiled. This raised Tal's head.

Remy aimed a thumb over his shoulder for the boy to follow him outside.

He sat on the kitchen steps.

Tal arrived beside him. "What's up?"

"Lucas came to see me. The committee meeting didn't go his way."

Tal checked behind him to be sure they had privacy. "What's he going to do?"

"It's still on. He said he needs to send three, one at a time to be sure someone gets through. I'm guessin' you knew about this."

"I couldn't tell you."

"I understand. I reckon that Lucas has got you figured to be the first in line."

"He does."

"Boy."

"You're not going to talk me out of it."

"I'm not tryin' to. I just want to hear you tell me why you gotta do this."

Tal licked his lips, steeling himself. "Okay. Don't take this wrong."

"I'll do my best."

"I thought about it a lot, leaving you and Carmen behind. Then I figured you'll be okay, and you'll look out for her if I can't for some reason. But this is the first time in my life I feel like I'm in the right place at the right time. I can do this. Gusto knows it, so does Lucas. Carmen picked me for it."

"That she did."

"It'd be a help if you said you believe in me, too."

Remy recalled holding the newborn Talbot, standing beside his dog-tired and proud mother. This wasn't the first time in the boy's life he was in the right place.

"I do, boy."

Remy totted up the dangers for Tal of going, the cost to the camp of not going. He asked his luck what he had done to be chosen like this, to send his son.

"Thanks," Tal said. "Did Lucas mention who else he's thinking of?"

"No, he didn't. You got a say in this. Who do you trust?"

"Bascom. He'll do it. He can make it."

"He's a good one. I'll tell Lucas."

"You got any idea for the third?"

Remy exhaled, resolved. From his vest pocket, he pulled the deck of cards he'd carried for a week. He shuffled and laid out a game of solitaire.

The cards told him quickly he would lose. With a practiced dexterity Tal could not catch, Remy cheated so the boy would see him win.

Through the night and into the morning, the western sky rumbled. During breakfast, a pair of U.S. Navy pursuit planes circled the camp before racing south. The loudspeaker announced the names of two more men who'd died before sunup. They would be buried in their bedsheets, no caskets for them. Remy spooned in the last of his thin *lugao*, finished the dregs of his ersatz coffee, and began to cough.

From across the dining hall, Tal hurried to his side. He patted Remy's spine, asking, "You all right?"

Remy hacked. He pushed aside the plate of rice mush to lower his face to the table, covering his mouth with a balled hand. He coughed until his throat strained and his temples pulsed. Tal turned him off the bench.

"Come on, let's get you to bed."

The rest of the day, Tal and Remy stayed hidden in their room. One watched the hall while the other listened to the crystal radio. The *Voice of Freedom* reported on the Allies in Europe crossing the Rhine and the firebombing of a German city, Dresden. In the Pacific War, the attack on Manila continued with ferocity; the Japanese would not be pried out without a bloodletting. The marines readied to invade the island of Iwo Jima. Once the news cycled, Remy and Tal napped. On occasion, Remy coughed loudly. In the afternoon, Tal fetched their meal of green, meatless gruel. They played crazy eights for matchsticks and waited for sundown.

Two hours after the light died, the barracks filled. The Japanese had imposed a 7:00 p.m. absolute curfew. No one was allowed outside, including on the paths between barracks. Anyone violating the rule would be shot.

In his bunk, Remy resumed his racking cough. By nine o'clock, the others in the cubicle and around him in the barracks were relieved when Tal took him to the infirmary.

Tal lit a lantern to head with Remy down the barracks steps. Aware of the curfew, several internees watched out their windows. Remy coughed for them, leaning on Tal. He doubled over, stumbled, adding a bad leg to the performance. Tal, holding the lamp, could only catch him with one arm.

He called to the boy standing in the doorway of No. 11. "Hey, Bascom. Come give me a hand."

A watching guard waved the Irish boy over.

The two helped Remy along the paved road beside the wire. The lantern kept them visible for the Japanese. Remy's loud hacks and limp got them past more guards without challenge on their way to the infirmary.

Inside the medical building, Remy sat on a cot, Bascom and Tal flanking him. Without electricity, white beds and walls were made yellow by lamplight; the infirmary smelled of kerosene. One of the navy nurses came to check on Remy. She was thin, like everyone. As she approached, Remy gave her a cough. The young woman looked him over and smiled.

"You look fine."

"So do you."

"You should moan a little. Sell it."

She turned to leave him and the boys alone. Later, she'd need to be able to say she thought Remy Tuck was sick.

When she had gone, Tal said, "Okay."

Remy drummed fingers on the mattress. He chewed his bottom lip and did not rise.

Tal, who considered himself the leader of this mission, cocked his head at Remy's stalling. Bascom flipped his gaze back and forth between the two, not certain what was going on.

Remy took stock. He had a gambler's nerve, a straight face and a steady hand with cards and dice. But the play tonight was not for cash, eggs, or tinned fruit, it was for life and death—not just for themselves, maybe the whole camp. Remy had to follow his son, something he'd never done before. To do it for the first time tonight, under the wire and into the dark, with the stakes so high, was hard. Remy had grown up without a father, and didn't know when the time was right to switch places.

In the last month, Tal had left the camp three times. Remy never. The boy had Remy's blank eyes, and a better nerve.

"Okay," Remy said.

The nurse stood in the hall. Passing her, Remy slipped a hand around her waist. He kissed her on the lips. She stood still for it. He took only a moment for the kiss, not to embarrass her, but to carry it with him for luck. He grinned close, she returned a stare. Remy backed off. When Tal and

Bascom followed, the nurse pulled each by the hand and gave the boys kisses, too.

Outside, they left the lantern behind, to creep around the corner of the infirmary. Crickets and croaking frogs throbbed in the bamboo grove and cogon grasses on the other side of the fence.

Tal put all his weight on the lower strand, slacking it. Bascom lay on his back while Tal and Remy lifted. Headfirst, the Irish boy shimmied under without problem. He moved to the second fence and copied Tal, standing on the lower wire to stretch it.

"You next," Tal whispered. "Face up."

Remy lay on his back. With his nose under the wire, he snaked his hips and shoulder blades to skid over the earth. A barb snagged his vest. Tal picked it loose.

Once they stood outside both fences, Tal strode away toward the high grasses. Remy paused, Bascom beside him. Remy gazed into the camp, like a soul outside its body, seeing how dingy, grim, and sick it appeared. Bascom dealt with his own silent revelations from this first taste of liberty in three years.

Tal marched into the weeds and grass rising around him, free night shrouding him. Watching, Remy wondered how, even with the girl and himself left behind, the boy could ever have come back inside the wire.

"Come on." Remy poked Bascom to break his reverie. They hustled to catch up with Tal, who'd discovered their absence and waited in the middle of the field.

Tal led them to the rim of a gully, down a steep slope. He stayed in front, showing Remy and Bascom how to step carefully. As soon as they reached the stony bottom of the ravine, Bascom kicked an unseen can. The tin struck like a gong. Tal flung himself on the wet rocks, Remy and Bascom did the same. They lay under the flapping of wakened wings and swishing branches. Water trickled under Remy's chin, his shirt soaked. When Tal rose and walked on, they followed. Bascom shrugged a moon-gray apology.

More times than he could remember, Remy had sat up on sleepless nights listening to the sounds of this ravine, hoots and monkey chatter, screeching birds, sometimes a roar. The voices had soothed him, sent him skipping past his Manila years to the outback again, where he'd been younger, happier, reliant not on luck but on his hands, family, and friends. In the city he'd had to gamble; in the bush he could build. Then came Los Baños, where he needed both to survive. Moving through this ravine, the shifting creatures and damp air seemed to welcome him back to the bush, to that better man he was.

Five minutes from camp, Tal halted. Remy and Bascom were surprised to find another had joined them.

"This is Emilio," Tal said. Remy had no idea where the stocky, armed guerrilla had come from.

"We're heading south," the Filipino said, "three miles to Barrio Tranca. Stay quiet."

Emilio set his feet on the slope of the ravine to climb out. Tal said, "Let's go," and fell in behind the guerrilla.

Bascom, older than Tal by a few years, muttered to Remy, "He's quite the one for giving orders. Is this your doing?"

"You raise a kid someday. Then talk to me."

Remy turned uphill. Another young guerrilla with a rifle and machete appeared out of the black with no trace of where he'd come from.

The five slipped across a dirt road onto a deserted coconut estate. In the vast grove, coconuts littered the ground under a dense ceiling of fronds. Emilio chopped several in half with powerful swipes of his bolo, handing pieces to the three internees.

The path Emilio chose avoided roads, keeping to plantations and overgrown fields. By midnight, under clouds tufting the high moon, they arrived on the poor outskirts of Tranca. Approaching a dark copse of trees, to the smell of wood smoke, Emilio clasped another Filipino out of nowhere. Before Remy knew it, they'd strolled into a guerrilla camp.

Along with Bascom and Tal, he was abandoned in the middle of black tents and fat tree trunks. Two campfires burned in the middle of a hundred or more Filipinos sleeping on bedrolls, rifles cuddled between their dark knees, many of them barefoot. Every guerrilla had a bolo at his waist.

Out of the dimness, a white man walked up. He towered over the Filipino beside him. Remy gasped at the first American soldier he'd seen up close since 1941.

The guerrilla spoke first, extending his hand to the internees.

"I'm Colonel Romeo. You made good time, gentlemen. This is Sergeant Bolick."

The soldier shook hands all around, explaining he was with the 511th Airborne Signal Company.

"Thank you, fellas. I know this isn't easy. And there's more to do. Just wanted to tell you don't worry, we're doing everything we can."

Tal said, "Thank you."

Bascom whispered to Remy, "Christ, he's big."

"Romeo here'll take care of you," Bolick said. "I'll be seeing you soon. Good luck."

The sergeant tossed them a Yank grin and receded into the camp. He took a while to disappear, large against the trees and silent guerrillas.

"Romeo," Remy said, "how 'bout somethin' to eat."

The young guerrilla sent another to fetch food. He led them to folding stools beside one of the fire pits.

"How are you holding up?"

Tal answered for all three. "Fine."

"Good. In an hour, I'm sending you with an escort to the bay. Which one is going to Parañaque?"

Tal spoke quickly. "Me."

"It's fifteen miles by *banca,* all on open water patrolled by the Japanese. Then five more miles by foot through enemy lines. You know this?"

"Yes."

Romeo addressed Bascom and Remy. "You'll leave for Nanhaya and wait for word that he's arrived. If he hasn't made it in twelve hours, the next one will go. Whichever of you is left with the guerrillas will serve as a guide for the attack. Now tell me about the camp."

All three described the layout of Los Baños. Bascom, a surprisingly able draftsman, crafted a map with pen and paper of the fences, guard outposts, gates, barracks, and paths, the surrounding ravine and Boot Creek. The last thing added was the pit that in afternoons lay in the shadow of the dao tree.

Next they detailed the guards and their routines. Morning exercises, the routes of their patrols, lanterns after curfew, gun placements. Bascom estimated the garrison at two hundred, never more than fifty on duty at a time. Remy contributed his low opinion of the guards as fighting men.

Romeo asked for the health of the internees. Remy described the climbing number of deaths from malnutrition and disease. Tal guessed that half the camp was made up of women and children, the ones in the best physical condition. The elderly suffered the worst.

Lastly, Remy spoke to Bascom. He figured the Irishman ought to know what was at stake. He described the massacres closing in on Los Baños, of Palawan, Calamba, and Bai, the atrocities in Manila, the rescue of Cabanatuan, of Mac's crystal radio beneath his and Tal's bunk, all of it leading to the belief that the Japanese were planning on annihilating everyone in the camp, soon. No one else could know these things while inside the wire. But this was the reason they had come. Bascom nodded soberly and shook hands all around, initiated now.

Three guerrillas arrived with fried duck eggs, rice, and filets of pork on banana leaves. Romeo passed around a bowl of fruit. Bascom needed no reminder to eat lightly, recalling his stomach distress six weeks ago during the short-lived Camp Freedom.

When they were done eating, eight more armed guerrillas approached. Each was a teenage boy, barefoot, with resolute face in the fires' glow.

Romeo handed one the map Bascom had drawn of the camp. The young Filipinos surrounded Remy and the boys. The guerrilla in the lead looked them over. He said only, *"Tumulin."*

Romeo translated. "He says, keep up."

Chapter Twenty-nine

$\diamond$

A T THE edge of a dark stream, Tal kicked off his sneakers. The barefoot Filipinos, plus Remy and Bascom in sandals, continued into the shallow water.

Tal sloshed across, then sat on the bank to dry his feet. Before he could slip on his shoes, the guerrillas, with Remy and Bascom, had vanished up the inky jungle path. Tal cursed and leaped to his bare feet to catch them. The leader of the guerrillas came back for him, sour-faced.

The guerrillas didn't slow. Tal tied the laces together to loop the shoes around his neck. He withstood stones and thorns under his soles without complaint, comparing himself to the guerrilla boys. He imagined they respected him for sharing their journey shoeless like them. Remy and Bascom raised eyebrows without remark. The Filipinos made no comment. After two miles, Tal regretted his bare feet. When the guerrillas halted at the shoulder of the national highway, Tal took the sneakers from around his neck. His feet were swollen. He plucked a nettle from his heel.

Remy whispered, "You done showin' off?"

Tal bit his tongue and put on the shoes.

On the other side of the highway, the terrain changed. Jungle gave way to wetlands and endless rice paddies. Clouds blocked the moon, the watery land had little light to reflect. The guerrillas tightrope-walked across long, narrow dikes rimming the paddies. Tal strode in the slick footsteps of the Filipino in front of him. They all seemed to walk in midair above the vast black pools.

Bascom slipped first. He came up sputtering out of the waist-deep mud. The guerrilla leader hissed in Tagalog for his boys to haul the Irishman out. Bascom stood on the dike dripping mud and plant life. Tal fell in ten minutes later. When the others hoisted him out of the cool muck, all but the chief boy laughed quietly. Filthy and drenched, Tal pulled off his sneakers again. The barefoot Filipinos were not sliding off the dikes. Remy held up his sandals to show he'd already made that observation.

With dawn breaking, the party reached the shore of Laguna de Bay. Though Remy had not tumbled into the paddies, he wound up as dirty as Tal and Bascom from the constant murk and damp air. Fully dressed, Tal splashed into the bay, trailing silt. Bascom and the guerrillas followed. Remy set his fedora on the ground, then waded in.

The coast lay deserted in both directions. The sun promised to rise warm and clear. Tal came out of the lake to sit on the stony beach. Remy joined him. Bascom stayed in the water with the guerrillas, all of them stripping naked to wash their clothes thoroughly.

"I'm hungry," Remy said. "You?"

"Always."

"I reckon we'll get somethin' soon. Defeats the purpose to drag us out here, then starve us to death. Coulda' stayed inside the wire if that was the plan."

"Remy."

"Yeah?"

"I'm glad you came. It's pretty brave."

"That fella there." Remy indicated bare Bascom scrubbing his underwear. "That's your hero. He didn't have to come. You and me, we knew."

Tal lay back on the rough beach, out of sorts. He'd only

been trying to compliment Remy. Why couldn't the man have just said "Thank you" and let it go, instead of claiming the two of them had no choice, because they knew? And that comment earlier about "showing off" continued to rankle.

Tal thought about Carmen and what she knew. She stayed in the animal husbandry building, made the Japanese talk, did things, for information to save the camp. She was a hero, maybe more than Tal, Remy, Bascom, any of the guerrillas. They only risked death. She endured that life.

The party waited on the beach. Bascom remained naked, hanging his clothes over a driftwood log to dry. The guerrillas hunkered to themselves, passing cigarettes. Remy propped his fedora over his face to rest under the climbing sun. A breeze rose off the bay. Tal gazed northwest, over the horizon to Parañaque, his destination.

A pair of *bancas* under full sail appeared a mile to the east. They cut through the water well and in ten minutes bottomed out and dropped sails in the shallows in front of Tal. One Filipino skipper leaped over the gunwales of his boat to stride onto the beach. Bascom scrambled into his clothes. The six guerrillas in the sand stubbed out their cigarettes, gathering weapons.

Tal waited on his feet, as he thought proper. Beside him Remy stayed seated. The skipper spoke to the guerrilla boys first. They split into two groups, three and three, heading for the *bancas* to clamber over the sides.

The hard-faced sailor pointed at Tal, then to the boat he piloted. "*Ito.*" He indicated Remy and Bascom, to signal they should board the second vessel. "*Iyan.*"

Remy stood. Tal offered him a handshake. "Good luck."

Remy took the hand. "Boy."

"I'll make it. Piece of cake. Don't worry about me."

"I'm not."

"Good."

"I want you to go with Bascom."

Tal jerked his hand free. "What?"

"I don't want any argument about this. I'm going to Parañaque."

Tal stepped back, stunned. "No, you're not. I am. We agreed."

Remy rattled his head. "You agreed, I didn't. Bascom."

The young Irishman moved up. "Yeah?"

"Go with Tal to Nanhaya. If you get word I didn't make it, you're next. The boy goes last."

Tal couldn't believe his ears.

Bascom said, "Sure, Remy."

"You promise me that."

Bascom said, "I do."

Tal struggled to find his voice. He ignored Bascom's rap against his arm to go to the second *banca*. Remy had already taken steps away when Tal spoke.

"You can't do this."

Remy walked back to him.

"Listen to me. Go with Bascom and those boys. When the raid comes, you look out for Carmen and Yumi. Make sure they get out of there. Keep your head down. You understand?"

Why was Remy thwarting him? He was the youngest, the strongest of the three. He was the one chosen, by Carmen, Lucas, the guerrillas. Remy was here because he'd played a game of solitaire. Tal had readied himself, he expected and wanted the mission to Parañaque. It belonged to him.

With both hands, he shoved Remy.

He'd never before touched his father in anger, had never imagined it. Now that he'd done it, Tal was surprised and saddened at the feel of Remy's ribs, how light and easy he was to heave backward. He'd hoped his father would have been harder, heavier.

Remy caught his balance. He lifted his fedora, gave it

to Bascom. Bareheaded and gray, he covered the distance between them on the sand. Remy was scrawny, spotted from too much sun. He had the hands of a laborer and a gambler's vacant gaze. Remy had to incline his head to bring his nose close; Tal stood taller by an inch.

"I'm gonna say this once. I'm your father. It's been a long while since I paddled your ass, but if you're needin' one right now, I got time."

Tal wanted to reel it all back in, the shove, his barefoot imitation of the guerrillas, his tumble into the paddy. These had put him on a wrong path and now he did not recognize where he'd ended up, where Remy had lost faith. He'd wanted to save the camp, and Remy and Carmen, like they'd sworn to each other they would. He wanted to be admired, face hazards, be heroic. Wasn't that manhood, what Remy wanted for him? Tal couldn't fathom what to say, could find no way out, so he lashed at the barriers walling him in.

"I don't give a shit if you're my father."

Remy didn't back off.

"You know what the beauty of bein' a parent is? It don't rely on what your kid says about it. I hope you get the chance to see that for yourself one day. Now do what you got to do, Talbot. Or step aside."

Tal could do neither. Bascom, cherry-cheeked and embarrassed, bailed Tal out when he separated the two. The guerrilla sailor stepped between them next.

Remy snatched his hat from Bascom. Backpedaling into the water, he screwed the fedora in place. The Filipino, as young as Tal, clucked his tongue. He joined Remy in the water before climbing into the *banca* headed for Parañaque.

The boat turned to deeper water, off the sand bottom. The guerrillas on board hoisted the sail. Bascom had not released Tal's wrist. With the violence left in him, Tal jerked his arm free.

Chapter Thirty

◆

THE JAPANESE seemed distracted in their sunup exercises. Nagata stamped among the lines of soldiers in loincloths, shouting, waving madly. He slapped one balky soldier so hard Carmen heard the smack from her window.

Along the barbed-wire fence, the guards on duty did not patrol with the normal distance between them but congregated in the camp's corners, out of sight of the commandant's office and Nagata. The soldiers spoke with animated gestures. At the gates and pillboxes, in the several gun towers, they eyed the camp instead of the outside world. Some even trained their guns inside the wire, as if the threat might come from there. A patrol of a dozen armed guards assembled in front of the commandant's office, then jogged past the main gate toward the village of Anos. Like a mist, edginess rose from the camp to Carmen's high window.

The internees themselves seemed not to notice. Carmen saw no change in their dawn routines, the lines outside latrines and showers, morning mass for the Catholics, steam boiling from kitchen chimneys, the shamble in the people's steps, the gradual weakening of their vigor.

Carmen did not spot Tal. Maybe he slept late. Where was the boy? She'd search for him again at the afternoon roll call.

Someone tapped outside Carmen's door. Papa pushed aside the curtain. He moved gingerly, as though he ached. The old man set a pallid green soup and platter of rice balls on the table. Carmen inspected the meal. Bits of meat settled in the bottom of the bowl.

"*Salamat.*"

Papa withdrew. Carmen stopped him.

"You don't look well."

"I'm fine."

"No, you're not. You're too thin. Your face is swollen."

Papa shrugged. "I'll be all right."

"Are you eating?"

Papa smiled ruefully. "I should be asked this by you?"

Carmen lifted the bowl from the table. "Is this pork in the soup?"

"Yes."

"Where did it come from? The Japanese?"

"Yes, of course."

"They would not give you meat for me, Papa. They have none for the prisoners, and they think even less of me. Where did this come from? And four rice balls?"

The old man would not answer.

"How long have you been giving me your food?"

"I'm not hungry lately."

"How long?"

"It doesn't matter."

The soup bowl warmed her palms. Papa was in his sixties; he could not afford to grow so thin, hunger made him sick. The meat and the extra rice were more of his fear. Papa still sought favor with Carmen so she'd speak well of him when liberation came.

The old man coughed into a knotty fist.

She thought of nothing she could say or do to rescue him. His enemies would not be the Americans. He'd need to save himself from his countrymen, the neighbors who suffered under the Japanese and did not collaborate. From the guerrillas who left their homes for years to fight in the jungles. From the villages destroyed, the loved ones murdered. From Benito and his long knife.

Look in the skies, at the constant planes, the fires flaring every night on the horizon. She could not tell Papa that the guerrillas had an American radioman with them now. The war would end soon one way or another, either in freedom or in that ugly pit dug inside the camp. She saw no need for Papa to starve to death in the meantime. He was weak and bullied, not evil. Perhaps his own fate would forgive him. Let him live to it and see.

She reached the bowl to him. "Eat this. It's yours."

Papa pushed the soup back at her. "I have no claim on it."

"Do you want to die?"

"Perhaps. Right now, I live. And that brings its own burden. Eat, Songu."

Carmen set the bowl on the table. She tightened the belt of her crimson *haori*. "Does Mama know?"

"There's been no reason to tell her."

"I will. She has to work harder to find food for all of us."

Before Papa could react, she slid an arm under the curtain to head into the hallway. Papa followed.

Carmen walked quickly to stay ahead of the old man. Mama would be furious when she found out. Carmen intended to start the spat between them, then retreat.

Reaching the landing, she halted immediately. She thrust her arms to her sides and bowed from the waist to Commandant Toshiwara. In the corner beside her mattress, Mama took the same pose. Papa did not come onto the landing, but stayed back in the hall out of sight.

Behind Toshiwara, in her green robe and barefoot, little Yumi combed her black hair. The brush had been a gift from the commandant.

Toshiwara breezed past, stiff and martial. Yumi shined his boots when he stayed nights. He brought her food, presents, sometimes sake.

When the commandant's footfalls left the stairwell two

flights below, Papa poked his head out of the hall. Mama turned on Carmen.

"What are you doing out of your room? Get back." She glowered at Yumi. "You, too."

"You need to find more food."

"For who?"

"All of us."

"Why? Look at you. You're fat, both of you."

Yumi stopped brushing her hair. She waved at Carmen so that Mama did not see.

Carmen said, "Look at your husband."

"He's not your worry." Mama beckoned Papa onto the landing. "Come out here."

The old man shuffled forward. Mama barked at him, "What's wrong with you?"

The two *makipilis* glared at each other. Yumi motioned again, pointing to herself, then at Carmen. She opened and closed her thumb and forefinger, like a mouth. She wanted to talk.

Papa looked pitiful and small. Carmen changed her mind about telling Mama what he'd been doing. She figured the old man's chances were poor. If starvation didn't claim him, or if the Americans or Filipinos didn't kill him, his wife would. Carmen couldn't stop any of them. She signaled Yumi that she understood.

"Mama?"

The woman snapped, "What?"

"Please send a message to Kenji-sama to come today. He'll help find food."

"Who'll pay for it?"

"Take the money from what you've kept for me."

Mama sneered at the suggestion. They both knew no money had been saved.

"Kenji will pay, too. Please send for him."

"Go back to your room."

Papa said to Carmen, "I'll go get him." When he put his foot on the first step, Mama demanded him to stay where he was. Carmen and Yumi faded from the landing. Papa's old head disappeared down the stairwell below the blasts of the old woman's voice.

The sixth soldier of the morning entered her room. Carmen's thighs had hardly dried from the washing she gave herself after the fifth. She had not belted her *haori* in two hours.

According to his ticket, this was one of the camp guards. She had not served him before. He was older than most of the boys who came to her. A scar marred his chin.

The soldier unbuttoned his fly, pushed down his pantaloons. Healed bullet holes had left white buttons on his legs. He did not untie his loincloth but tugged it around to expose himself.

A breeze in the window cooled her spread legs. From her elbows, Carmen said, *"Saku."*

The soldier shook his head.

She pointed at the washed condom she kept in a bowl beside the tatami. The man chopped the air, waving it off.

He pointed at her. "Songu," he said, meaning, "you are a *pii,* that's all you are."

Carmen considered him. His penis was clean and small. He would not tolerate embarrassment with his pants around his boots. Carmen gestured him forward. The same way she did not want Papa's life on her hands, she cared little for Songu's. The Americans were coming soon, and Songu would be put to a stop.

Carmen spat on her fingers to lubricate herself. The soldier entered without clumsiness; this was not his first time with a woman. Planting his arms on either side of her head, he pumped while Carmen gazed into his scarred chin. She wondered, How does a bullet come so close to leave only that ugly pink gash? Is this man lucky or unlucky? Carmen considered herself and wondered the same. Should her damage be worse? Should she be dead? Was she fortunate?

Carmen lost patience with the soldier's scars, they made her pay attention to him. She dispensed with him quickly. He wore no sheath, so could be climaxed with little effort. She tightened in the right way and did not wait long until he finished.

The soldier bent his arms and lowered toward her, to lie on her. She reclined to wrap him in her arms.

She stroked his back.

Gently, she asked, *"Daijobu desu ka?"* Yumi had asked this of Carmen many times. Are you all right?

The soldier pulled his face from her neck. Under Carmen's gliding hand, his breathing quickened until it became a shiver. She patted him and held him.

The soldier pushed off the mattress, out of her arms, red-eyed. Carmen sat up quickly and pivoted to the wall, averting her own eyes from his loss of control. Behind her, the soldier pulled up his pants, tucking his uniform together.

When he grew motionless, she turned. He'd wiped away any emotion. He stepped on the tatami to the window, a small limp in his movement. Carmen got to her feet, closing her robe. Men when they were through did not want to see her naked, they wanted her quiet and obedient, a different sort of object.

She would not stand next to him in the window, didn't want Tal or Remy to see her again with a soldier. The man gazed over the camp, as though he'd never seen it before. The thrum of American planes filtered past. Carmen focused on his back, where she had run her hands. She waited longer behind him than she had lain under him.

From this vantage, the soldier sought something in the camp. He did not seem to find it. He turned, bolt upright.

"Songu."

The word left his tongue differently. It sounded now like a name, not a thing.

He laid a hand along her arm. "You." He removed his touch. "Go?"

Carmen said, "No."

The soldier dropped his head in a short bow. With one hand past the curtain, he stopped himself.

"Go," he said, then left her.

In the afternoon, two more soldiers did not wear *saku*. Carmen washed hard after their visits and her vagina grew dry.

Papa ushered the day's last soldier past her curtain, into the rising square of light from the sun dropping behind Mount Makiling. Papa told her Kenji waited in the foyer, then slipped out.

The young guard spoke a smattering of English. She lay back and suffered his awkward sawing at her. She squeezed him to completion, then lay with him on the tatami, stroking him. He, too, said she should disappear from the camp soon, and would not say why.

When the soldier left, she squatted over the bowl to scrub herself gingerly. She changed into pants and a drab T-shirt. Her walls flushed orange in the sunset light. Carmen's legs felt rubbery. Kenji pushed past the curtain, ducking his height under it. He curled his nostrils; the manganic acid lingered in the room. He took down his cap.

"You sent for me."

"What's going on?" she asked. "Something's wrong."

"Yes. Something is."

"What."

"I'm not certain."

"How can you not be certain?"

"I'm an interpreter. No one talks to me, just through me."

Carmen pointed at her tatami. "Some soldiers told me . . ."

Kenji cut her off. "Yes, I can imagine." His tone was stony but this did not bother Carmen.

"Please. I need you to bring Yumi to my room. Or take me to hers. I want to talk to her."

"Is that why you called me here?"

"What did you expect?"

"I'd hoped you changed your mind about leaving."

"I won't leave the camp until they're safe."

Kenji nodded. "Are the Americans coming for them?"

"Yes, Kenji-sama."

He moved to the window. "Do you know when?"

"No."

Hymns from the two churches at opposite ends of the grounds struck up while Kenji leaned on the sill. The final daylight made his face sanguine. He seemed peaceful under the songs, as if already dead.

He said, "They're not safe."

"Take me to Yumi. Toshiwara stayed with her last night. We'll see what she knows."

Kenji left the window. He held the curtain aside for Carmen to step into the hall. She slowed, letting him walk in front.

They passed the landing. Papa sat at the desk, marking in a ledger. On the board behind him, the wooden tags for Yumi and Songu had been turned to their blank sides. The old man kept his eyes down.

Kenji rapped on Yumi's doorframe before leading Carmen under the curtain. The Korean girl's room was stuffed with pillows, a cane rocking chair, a silk lampshade, drapes for her window, even books. Yumi sat cross-legged on a cushion against the wall. She wore her emerald *haori*. Carmen smelled the musk from between the tiny girl's legs. Yumi had not yet cleaned herself.

A plum bruise discolored one cheek.

"Who did this?" Carmen asked, rushing to the girl. She motioned Kenji closer. Yumi blinked and brought her gaze to Carmen, as if in that moment she noticed the two in the room with her.

Kenji asked in Japanese. Yumi replied, her manner flat, distant. Kenji translated.

"Someone. All of them. She doesn't recall."

Yumi smiled. The ruined cheek hurt, she dabbed it with fingertips. She spoke more. Kenji folded to the floor beside her. Carmen kept to her feet, uncomfortable and growing frightened. Kenji interpreted.

"This morning, Toshiwara said he's going to take her away, now that the Americans are on Luzon. He said he will send for her soon, in a matter of days." Kenji paused for the girl to continue. "She knows you won't leave the camp, so she didn't ask if you could come. She hopes you're not angry."

"No."

The girl spoke more.

"She told many soldiers today that she would live. They hit her for saying this. She was glad to be struck, it meant she was right. She will live, they will die fighting the Americans, and they knew it."

Carmen backed a short step away from Yumi. "Is this what you wanted to tell me?"

Yumi rattled her head, a strand of dark hair caught on her lip. She addressed Kenji. The tall boy interpreted.

"She says she's afraid to talk about it in front of me. I'm a Japanese soldier."

"Tell her you're a friend."

Kenji spoke to Yumi. When he was done, the girl considered him for a long moment before reaching for his hand. She pressed the back of it to her purpled cheek.

Carmen asked, "What did you say?"

Kenji waited until Yumi released him. The tiny girl beamed at Carmen.

"I told her I know you work with the guerrillas. And that I love you."

Truth was prohibited to Carmen. All day long, with the short minutes between soldiers, she'd searched for Tal. She did not see him or Remy, not even at the afternoon roll call. They were gone, they'd left her. Yumi had Toshiwara to protect her. Carmen and Tal had each other, they'd dreamed of that even before they'd spoken. But until she saw Tal again, Kenji would have to be her guardian. She had no choice.

With quiet shame for the deceit, she laid a hand on Kenji's shoulder.

She asked Yumi, "What is going to happen? Why is Toshiwara taking you away?"

Kenji stood when she was done with her reply. The dying light darkened Yumi's other cheek and her bare legs.

"Toshiwara has received orders," Kenji said.

"For what?"

"To kill every internee in the camp."

Massacre, Carmen thought. Finally it comes to Los Baños.

She did not shudder, because death, too, would be an end to this.

"Kenji-sama, go. Find out whatever you can. Then come tell me."

"I'd like to stay a little longer. Can I sit with you in your room?"

"I have to get in touch with the guerrillas. Please."

Carmen smoothed a hand over Yumi's head, wishing away the demons there. She followed Kenji out of her room.

On the landing, Papa did not acknowledge either of them. Kenji turned for the stairs. She headed down her hall.

In her room, Carmen dumped the crimson water out the window. She set the basin upside down in the hall. Returning to her window, she sought Tal in the last streaks of dusk. One by one, lanterns lit the somber camp, in the guard towers, at the gates, along the fence. In the boy's barracks, she imagined his empty bunk. She looked far to the west, past Makiling, into the black jungle. He was with the guerrillas, he had to be. He'd taken Remy with him, out of the path of the killing.

She could go, too. Kenji would take her out of the camp. Why stay?

Because the boy would come back.

Chapter Thirty-one

REMY JERKED awake at the crack of a rifle shot. The side of his neck sizzled. He clapped a hand over the burning spot and thrust himself off the floor of the *banca*.

Eduardo, the smallest of the guerrillas, stood in the bow, rifle raised. Remy cast about madly for sight of a Japanese patrol on the vast bay. His heart pounded. Had they been spotted?

The morning horizon rippled in the wind. The bay lay empty of enemies. A hot, spent cartridge tumbled off his chest, ringing when it bounced on the wooden deck floor. This had landed on his neck, scalding him.

Remy's gut eased, prickles of adrenaline faded in his limbs. The boy in the bow lowered the rifle. Remy threw the warm brass at his back.

"Eduardo, what the hell!"

The boy ignored him, pointing ahead. Young Bayani, the leader, shoved the tiller to steer the boat where Eduardo indicated. The boy leaned out to scoop up a dead duck.

In thirty minutes, the bird was plucked and grilled on a charcoal brazier in the stern. Bayani smeared melted fat on Remy's throat to treat the burn. The four guerrillas and Remy tore the meat with their hands and ate well. The sails billowed ahead of a steady stern breeze while the *banca* plowed northwest. Miles off, a Japanese patrol boat appeared but kept its distance and Remy did not have to slink into the stinking fish hold. Far behind, another *banca* plied the same winds.

They made landfall at noon. Bayani guided the boat into the rocky shallows of a vacant shore. They tied a bow line to a tree and abandoned the *banca*. The guerrillas scrambled up a bank wooded with wild banyans and palms, using their bolos to chop through the scrub. The boys were tough, as hard in purpose as they were in the soles of their feet.

Remy traveled in the middle of the four. The pair in front traded places with the two in back as they wore down from blazing the trail. Remy made more of a stir walking than the Filipino did hacking at branches and leaves. Bayani put fingers beside his black eyes and pulled to slant his sockets, an impression of a Japanese face. They were not out of enemy territory yet.

The jungle did not relent. Remy hardly caught sight of the sky behind the dense green canopy. Entering a thick copse, a jade snake fell on him, startled by their passing or in an ambush attempt. Remy jumped, shouting, and shook it off. He suffered muted laughter from the boys when Eduardo let the snake wrap itself around his own skinny arm.

They continued into the bush. Remy, padding more vigilantly now, thought about the tenth game of solitaire he played, the one he would have lost had he not interfered. The rifle shot in the boat, the snake dropped on his shoulder—these were just his lousy luck taunting him. He wondered when it would assert itself fully.

After another hour of carving through the forest, Remy sweat through his clothes. The Filipinos cut into cane stalks to sip the liquid inside. Remy's strength began to wane, he considered asking for a rest. Tal, he thought, would still be going strong right now. But he'd be here, in the enemy's jungle instead of safe with the guerrillas at Nanhaya. Even though Bayani had done a good job dodging danger, they weren't out of it. Tal had made it clear in many ways, he was eager to swap with Remy, become the master and the man. That was fine, but no father sends his son into peril when he can go himself.

At the rear, the two Filipinos whistled. Remy froze. The pair of guerrillas in front stopped swinging their long knives.

Behind them on the trail, the rustle of footsteps, of someone following, instantly quit.

Before Remy could take a stride into the bush, the four guerrillas disappeared. He moved as silently as he could off the path, found a fat trunk, and crouched. He tried to hold his breath to hear better what was coming, to sense where Bayani and the others were, but could not. He had no weapon. Stupid, he thought. Maybe fatal. The path and the jungle kept silent. Here it comes, Remy thought, the tenth game.

"Hi ya, pal."

Remy erupted at the voice beside his ear, flailing blindly in a crazed effort to fight it off. He collapsed to his backside, kicking, scrambling backward until he saw a rumpled U.S. Army uniform and a steel pot helmet on a hulking soldier squatting in the weeds.

"Don't have a heart attack," the soldier said.

Remy clapped a hand over his breast as if he might do exactly that. His heart hammered at his rib cage.

"Son of a bitch," he wheezed. "Where the hell'd you come from?"

"I started out a couple hours behind you. Bayani and his boys are good." The soldier, a lieutenant, shrugged to imply he was better.

The man stood to his full height. He was short and barrel-chested, with powerful wrists and heavy black brows, in need of a shave. His skin bore a carroty color. He reached to give Remy a lift off the ground.

Remy let the hand hover, still angry from the fright.

"What's your name?"

"Kraft."

"Why're you orange, Kraft?"

"Atabrine. They give it to us to keep malaria off. Turns your skin. C'mon, get up."

Remy was hoisted to his feet. He had the lieutenant beaten by two inches but figured he weighed just over half.

Kraft led him back to the trail. Bayani and the others waited there, bolos sheathed. Kraft shook hands, clapping the Filipinos on the shoulder. He dug into his pack for Hershey bars.

"American chocolate," said Bayani. "Thank you."

"Whoa," said Remy. "You speak English?"

"Of course."

"This whole time. Why didn't you?"

"It kept you quiet."

Kraft cocked his head. Bayani, candy in hand, turned his bolo again to the uncut bush, pushing onward.

"We're not far from our lines," said Kraft. "Half a mile."

"I'm not sure I could make it much farther. What's your unit, Lieutenant?"

"Eleventh Airborne Recon Platoon."

"Sneak."

"Absolutely. Can I ask you a question?"

"Go easy. My heart's still in my throat."

"Sorry about that."

"No, you're not."

"Okay. I'm not. Let a guy have some fun. Anyway, I'm surprised to see you here. I was told your boy would be on this trip."

"He knows the camp, but I made a father's decision and took his place."

"I bet the kid's pissed."

"You'd win that bet. Where you comin' from?"

"Los Baños. Checking out the area around the camp, getting the lay of the land."

Remy marveled at the thought of this bulky soldier creeping around the fence invisibly, skulking in the ravine and creek.

"What do you think?"

"I think getting everybody out is going to be tough. A lot has to go right. I got a question to ask you."

"All right."

"You have any idea how long the camp's got?"

"No way to tell. Hours, days. You saw the pit?"

"Yeah. I don't like it."

"You gotta figure the guards are gonna use it at some point. The Japs haven't released one prisoner in the Philippines. Los Baños isn't gonna be the first."

"Then let's get 'em out."

Soon, Bayani quit hewing at the green veil in his way. He lowered the bolo to step into the clear. Remy, Kraft, and the guerrillas emerged onto the shoulder of a paved road. For the first time since entering the jungle, Remy noticed the drumbeat of bursts from Manila, miles north.

They walked along the roadway. The tarmac surface had been badly chewed by tracked vehicles. Craters of charred dirt pocked the road and surrounding fields. Every structure had suffered damage, even farm buildings and sawali huts lay in ruin. The fighting here had been intense and blackening. The sorry landscape was deserted.

A jeep with a white star on its hood proved they were beyond Japanese lines. The vehicle weaved over the poor roadway. Kraft moved to the center of the road to commandeer it.

"Climb on, fellas."

Remy and the four guerrillas crowded into the back of

the jeep. Remy removed his fedora to wipe his brow. The driver gaped.

"You an American?"

Remy nodded, exhausted.

"Damn, buddy," the driver said. "How'd you get so skinny?"

Kraft sauntered around to the driver's side. "Move over," he told the private, "and shut up."

The jeep stopped in front of the villa. Bayani and his guerrillas piled out of the back. Remy drew his first full breath after the bouncy three-mile ride. Bayani wished Remy luck and handed over Bascom's map. He got refused by Kraft for more chocolate, then led his boys away to ferret out a meal from the hundreds of American soldiers going every direction.

Remy had forgotten what well-fed men looked like. Bronzed from the atabrine, every one of the Americans touted a full face, flush chest, and solid legs that carried them under backpacks, weapons, furniture, even sheaves of paper that were hurried up or down the steps of the Spanish mansion.

He climbed out of the jeep feeling shrimpy and old. The soldiers were in their teens and twenties; even the burly Kraft couldn't have been past thirty. Remy couldn't match the energy around him, couldn't begin to remember what it felt like to move with such muscle and verve. He felt the urge to explain himself to Kraft or any of the soldiers eyeing him, that he'd been cooped up in a camp for three years, and that's why he wasn't in uniform. Remy had given his young father to the first war, and he'd watched his son beaten, so he'd paid something, he'd anted up in this game.

Kraft put a hand in the middle of Remy's back.

"You okay, Tuck?"

"Yeah, yeah. Just tired."

"Sure you are. C'mon, a little farther to go."

Kraft led the way into the villa. The interior was as opulent as MacArthur's suite at the Hotel Manila. Marble floors, wrought-iron rails, wood paneling, ornate chandeliers—this house had probably remained intact because the Japanese had done what the U.S. Army was doing now, installed a headquarters here. Remy followed the lieutenant down a tiled hall, past men working radios, rooms where young officers at desks received and sent messengers, and men smoking, poring over maps pinned to walls.

"Kraft."

"Yeah."

"Get me a cigarette."

The lieutenant stopped a captain in the hallway. He got a smoke for Remy. The captain lit it from his Zippo.

"Gimme a minute." Remy moved to the wall, out of the way.

He leaned as soldiers bustled past. He was safe, fifteen miles from Los Baños, surrounded by an army. Remy had to absorb this, had to let go of his hunger and fear. The cigarette on his tongue was delicious. He let it make him happy for a few seconds until he ground it under his sandal. Like Kraft said, there was farther to go.

"Hey, Kraft. You know Romeo, the guerrilla?"

"He's PQOG. We got a signalman with him."

"My son's there. Get a message to him that I made it. Can you do that?"

"First thing."

"Now."

"Sure. C'mon, let's get you in front of Major Willcox."

Remy followed Kraft to what was once the formal dining room of the villa. Ceiling fans rotated over a wide, polished table covered with papers and maps. French doors opened onto a veranda and the neglected remnants of a garden overgrown by pigweed, sawali, and volunteer trees. A lithe young officer with thinning hair leaned over the table, palms flat on a large map. Like Kraft, his skin held the baked hue from the atabrine.

Kraft announced their presence. "Sir."

The major glanced up. From his balding pate, Remy had guessed him to be a man in his forties. The young face beaming behind glasses, approaching with hand extended, couldn't have been older than mid-twenties. Remy held tight to his confidence, even though all the men who would save the camp were hardly older than his impetuous and petulant son.

Kraft did the introduction. "Major Willcox, CO of First Battalion, 511th Parachute Infantry, Eleventh Airborne. This is Mr. Tuck, fresh out of Los Baños."

Remy accepted the eager handshake. "Remy," he said, removing his fedora.

"Thank you so much for coming. I can't guess what you've been through."

Kraft said, "Excuse me, Major. I've got to let the guerrillas know Mr. Tuck made it safe."

"Come back when you're done, Lieutenant." With Kraft gone, Willcox offered Remy a cigarette. He declined.

"I could use something to eat. Maybe a chair."

Willcox sat Remy beside the broad map table. He strode to the hall, gave some orders, and returned to sit on the other side of the map.

"Chow's on the way. Can I jump right into some questions? Time seems to be of the essence."

Remy dug into his vest pocket for the map Bascom had drawn. The journey to bring it here from the barbed wire to this chair seemed a decade ago.

He spread the map. Willcox stood above it, planting

hands on either side of the wrinkled paper in the same stance he'd been in when Remy entered.

"Very detailed." Willcox adjusted his glasses. "What do you know about the defenses around the camp?"

"Everything."

Remy pointed out the locations and firing angles of all the emplaced guns at Los Baños. Because of his regular stints outside the camp on the logging detail, time spent in every corner of the camp playing poker or rolling dice, and his two years of internment in a space no bigger than ten acres, Remy knew Los Baños like a long-borne malady.

Willcox whistled at his familiarity with the camp.

"Hell," Remy drawled, "me and my son built the damn place."

Willcox brought Remy around the table to stand over the large map he'd been working with.

"We put this together from aerial photos and guerrilla info." Willcox handed Remy a blue pencil. "Correct it."

Remy set to making notations on Willcox's map. He indicated the locations and heights of every guard tower around the fence, plus his guesses about the field of vision from each platform. Of the six dirt pillboxes built on the east and south perimeter of the camp, all but one faced inward, to mow down escaping internees instead of defend the grounds from outside assault. The large bunkers at the main gate had firing slits so narrow they could likely cover only the road and nothing of the fields on either side.

Remy identified every building, first by residents: bachelors, married, nuns, priests; then by purpose: chapels, butcher shop, ice plant, garage, kitchen. He marked Toshiwara's office, the guards' quarters, the infirmary. He made no mention of the animal husbandry building just outside the wire.

Kraft returned with a tray of food. He set in front of

Remy a steaming bowl of soup stuffed with chicken, slick with yellow fat bubbles, and a loaf of brown Philippine bread. Remy sat, tore into the bread, and dunked. He ate without haste, not wanting the soldiers to see his hunger, to have none of their sympathy. Remy pulled off a bit of the loaf and offered it to Kraft, who accepted.

Willcox continued his questions, not dropping his urgency. "What can you tell me about the guards?"

Remy answered around the wad of bread in his cheek. "Maybe two hundred of 'em. Never more than eighty at a time on duty."

Taking the chair beside Remy, Willcox asked, "What's their attitude, as best you can tell?"

"I don't think the commandant's very strong, and his second in command is a first-class tyrannical son of a bitch. The way the guards cheat and trade all day long, my guess is they're all out for themselves. Most of them boys have served somewhere else, got the crap shot out of 'em, and got assigned to Los Baños 'cause the Japs couldn't use 'em anywhere else. To be honest, I don't see a lot of fightin' spirit."

Kraft answered, "In my experience, Mr. Tuck, there aren't any Japanese soldiers without fighting spirit. Not alive ones, anyway."

Remy paused. Kraft looked like he knew what he was talking about. For his own part, Remy thought of the dead in Los Baños over the past two months: Donnelly, Clem, Mac, the body count rising daily from disease and starvation.

"Well, Lieutenant, you might be right. Certainly where we're concerned, the Japs are in a murderous mood."

Remy finished his soup and the bread. The two soldiers let moments pass without queries, as though out of respect for the camp's dead and dying.

When he slid aside the tray, Willcox said, "I'm sorry."

"Me, too. What else you got?"

The intel officer patted Remy's shoulder. "What about the camp routine? Anything there?"

Remy related the roll calls, morning and afternoon, and mealtimes. He described the likely reaction to him, Tal, and Bascom going missing, patrols in the villages, cutbacks on rice. At night the Japanese carried lanterns to walk the fence since the electricity failed. The 7:00 p.m. curfew for the internees; violators used to get a *binta,* now they would be shot. The ban on Filipinos inside the wire. Again, Remy chose to say nothing of Carmen, Yumi, and what role they played in the Japanese soldiers' day. He mentioned the guards' daily calisthenics.

Willcox slid forward in his chair.

"They exercise?"

"Yeah. Never made sense to me."

"How many?"

"All the ones not on duty. A hundred and twenty or so."

"When?"

"They get going around six thirty in the morning. Finish up by seven fifteen." Remy described the lines of guards leaping around in nothing but loincloths, Nagata screaming.

Willcox asked, "Where are they when they exercise?"

Remy circled the spot on Bascom's map. "Right here, what used to be the garden."

"Where are their guns while they're doing this?"

Remy stabbed a finger onto Willcox's big map, over the narrow breezeway connecting the guards' quarters with the commandant's office, near the main gate.

"Right here."

Kraft seemed amazed. "You're saying two thirds of the camp's guards are basically buck naked every morning?"

"Yep. And trust me, bare-ass jumpin' jacks ain't pretty when you're trying to eat weeds for breakfast."

"And their weapons are seventy yards away?"

"Thereabouts."

The two soldiers exchanged looks. The big lieutenant folded arms across his bearish chest. Willcox rapped knuckles on the map table.

"Remy," the intel officer said, "you just could be our good-luck charm. You know that?"

"I'm tickled to be somebody's."

Willcox stood to conclude the meeting. Kraft reached a hand to Remy. "Mr. Tuck, it's been a pleasure, sir."

The lieutenant headed for the door. Remy asked, "Where you going?"

"Back to Los Baños. I've got to find a drop zone close to the camp."

Remy grabbed his hat. "I'm comin' with you."

Willcox held up a hand. "Stay put."

Remy tugged on the dirty old fedora. "Boys, I got two-thousand-odd friends in that camp, though there's a few I like more'n others. I know that place with my eyes closed. If Kraft here is going to Los Baños, I'm goin' with him. I can be right handy. That's why I came here in the first place. And that's why I'm goin'.'"

Willcox pointed at the chair behind Remy. "Sit. Please."

"No, sir."

"Remy, you're on your last legs. Stay, eat some more, rest up."

"I'm fine."

"All right." Willcox took his own seat. "Fact is, I can't let you go right now. Lieutenant Kraft has to move fast and I don't believe you can keep up with him. I can't have you slowing him down, and I won't risk you being caught by the Japs. Not with what you know. So take a load off, Remy. I'm sure there's more you can tell me."

Kraft moved behind Remy's chair to pull it backward like a maître d'.

Remy said, "One condition."

Willcox answered, "All due respect, but you know I don't have to listen to conditions."

"When you attack the camp, I want to be there. Please."

Willcox looked at his recon officer. Kraft bobbed his stubbled chin.

Willcox said, "Deal."

Remy removed his fedora.

The big lieutenant came to a quick attention, said "Sir" to Willcox, and headed out of the room. At the door, he almost bumped into a messenger. He took from the soldier a yellow sheet, then walked it to Willcox without reading it.

The major scanned the page quickly. "It's from Bolick." He handed the page to Kraft. The recon man read, also without reaction.

Willcox pointed to Remy, for Kraft to give him the message. Remy took the flimsy paper. He read:

ROMEO TO KRAFT. HAVE RECEIVED RELIABLE
INFORMATION THAT JAPS HAVE LOS BANOS
SCHEDULED FOR MASSACRE PD SUGGEST
THAT ENEMY POSITIONS IN LOS BANOS
PROPER BE BOMBED AS SOON AS POSSIBLE PD

                    W.C. ROMEO
                    Col. GSC (Guer)
                    Chief of Staff

Remy, Tal, Lucas—they'd all believed this could happen. But the execution of the camp had been supposition, a spectral possibility like death itself. This message made the massacre real, "scheduled."

The warning was the work of Carmen. He handed the

page back to Kraft. Remy considered telling the officers he knew the source, and that she was reliable.

He held his tongue. He didn't expect Willcox or Kraft to put much stock in intelligence from what they would likely consider a Filipina whore, even if Remy could explain what she was, what the girl had undergone to get this information.

It wasn't vital that the army knew about Carmen. Let them imagine where the guerrillas got their intel; they'd concoct someone more convincing than her, anyway. She'd be safer if Remy stayed mum. The fewer who knew she was an informant, the better, until they were all out of Los Baños for good.

"Clock's running," Willcox said to Kraft. Without ceremony, the lieutenant took his leave.

The major spun the yellow message onto the map table. He asked Remy, "You still want to go back?"

Remy pushed aside the sheet to clear the map. He stood the way Willcox had, with hands buttressed on the table, gazing at the blue lines depicting Los Baños.

"Yeah, I do. With a fuckin' army."

ichioku gyokusai—one hundred million broken jewels

In early 1945, this slogan appeared throughout Japan, expressing that the nation's entire population was prepared to be "shattered," or exterminated, together in a final, absolute commitment to the war and the emperor

the ravine, a race, and
a choice

Chapter Thirty-two

B OLICK PLANTED his boots in the dirt. The boy bull rushed him, face flushed in the campfire light. Bolick couldn't tell if the kid was angry, but he'd knocked him down twice already. The Tuck boy didn't sound mad, he didn't make a noise at all. He just came.

Bolick had side-stepped Tal's first charge and tripped him, sending him flying out of the ring with a shove in the back. After that, they'd grappled. Bolick let Tal test his strength until he flipped him with a hip toss. The boy landed hard with no training in how to fall, to rotate to his side and slap the ground, exhale to keep from having his wind knocked out. Tal jumped up quickly. If he was hurt he hid it. In the circle around them, twenty guerrillas and the Irishman, Bascom, egged the boy on. Bolick doubted if any of them would get in the ring with him bare-handed like Tuck did. Five chickens roasted on spits across the flames, sizzling beneath the cheers. Tal barreled in, shoulder lowered. Bolick took him head-on.

Tal rammed him in the abdomen, driving his legs to topple Bolick over. He came in too low, Bolick's center of gravity held. Bolick wrapped the boy's rib cage, leaving Tuck to heave as hard as he could. The boy was so emaciated, Bolick could have lifted him like a sack, held him upside down and pile-driven his head into the earth. But the boy was no Jap. Bolick held his ground and waited for Tal to tire.

The boy did not weaken. Instead he made his first sound, a growl. Bolick's heels skidded backwards, the force of Tuck's attack grew. Impressed, Bolick figured he'd best end it before the boy lost his temper and got hurt.

Bolick relaxed his legs, giving way for Tal to shove with all his power. Bolick kept his balance, riding backward, still latched around the boy's chest. With a sudden collapse, he fell to his right shoulder, using the boy's momentum to yank him sideways and down. Bolick landed on his back with Tal on top, wrapped in his arms. On the ground, Bolick spun to put the boy under him, facedown. Bolick opened his knees around the kid's head to snare him in a vise grip. Like a boa constrictor, Bolick crushed.

"Say uncle."

The boy struggled but had no chance. The guerrillas and the Irishman booed.

"Uncle."

Bolick released his squeeze. He rolled off the boy to accept a hand up from the man who'd spoken, Lieutenant Kraft.

"Lieutenant." Bolick worked to catch his breath.

"Sergeant." Kraft surveyed the boy in the dirt. "Is that the Tuck kid?"

"Yes, sir, it is."

Tal dragged his hands beside his shoulders to push himself up. He muttered something angry. Kraft set a big boot in the middle of Tal's back, shoving him down again.

Ignoring the boy's wriggling and curses, the lieutenant asked, "What were you doing, Sergeant?"

"Hand-to-hand training. The boy asked if I'd show him a few things."

"Can he fight?"

"He's tough, but not a lick."

"Tough's enough."

Kraft spoke to the boy squirming under his foot.

"Tuck. Calm down."

The kid finally gave out.

"I met your old man in Parañaque. He says you know the camp like the back of your hand. This true?"

"I know it better. Get off me."

Kraft pulled his foot from the boy's spine.

"Get him up, Sergeant."

Kraft walked to the fire pit. The guerrillas stood to greet him. The Filipinos admired the recon officer, who knew the jungle as well as any of them. Kraft could appear anywhere like a spirit, the way he had tonight.

"You okay?" Bolick checked the boy's temper before hauling him off the ground.

Tal reached up a hand. Bolick put the kid on his feet. The Tuck boy dusted off his front and the dirt bits on his cheek. He didn't appear ready to go again, but did not look defeated. Facing Bolick, he bent at the waist and lowered his head, bowing. Bolick returned the gesture, feeling foreign imitating a Japanese. The boy did it naturally.

Chapter Thirty-three

   ◆

TAL LAY beside Kraft in the middle of a dried-up rice paddy. The small square of land was bounded on the west by the barbed wire of the camp; a thick stand of trees held the opposite side. Across the northern edge ran railroad tracks that had been a target of American bombers for the past month. A high-voltage line marked the southern limit of the open ground.

Kraft grumbled. "Is this the best you got?"

"It is if you want to land close to the camp."

The soldier made marks in a battered notebook.

"Jesus. Some drop zone. It's a bandbox." He put the booklet away. In the northwest, the night sky continued to jump from the bombardment of Manila. "All right, let's check out the camp."

Tal led the way out of the field, down into Boot Creek. On the rocky bed, he moved in front, stepping stone to stone, never ruffling the pools or trickling waters. Many times he glanced over his shoulder to see if Kraft was still behind him, the soldier walked so silently. Kraft was always there in the pitch black, a broad, scribbling silhouette.

The two disturbed nothing. The jungle sang in full voice, croaking and chattering, scuttling in the branches. On the other side of the wire, the Japanese stirred with their lanterns. The occasional dot of a cigarette glowed in the towers; the aroma of tobacco drifted over Tal and Kraft creeping past.

Tal guided the soldier in a circuit around the camp.

From Boot Creek in the south and west, flat on their bellies in the open fields north of the wire, ranging into the deep ravine along the east, the recon man scratched in his notebook. In whispers, he asked for descriptions and details. Kraft charted every footpath inside the camp, the dao tree and ominous pit, the dwindling pile of firewood near the kitchen, the barbs of gun barrels sticking out of pillboxes, each guard post and bunker, no detail escaped his sketches. Tal stole him close enough to hear praying nuns who could not sleep, a guard humming in a watchtower, a cough inside the infirmary.

Lying on the damp banks of the creek and on dewy grass, Tal caught only distant glimpses of Carmen's high window. He wished he could rise from hiding and walk through the air, treading only on the dark tops of the sawali barracks like the creek stones. He would not wake her but visit like a dream, murmur he was near, kiss her, and return. He didn't know what Carmen's fate would be if the Japanese began killing everyone in the camp. He saw no reason why they should harm her, and no reason why they should not. He whispered nothing of Carmen but watched Kraft make note of her building and the tarmac road running below its face. Kraft hadn't been sent by MacArthur to save Filipinas. Only the internees were his mission. Carmen was Tal's to protect.

After two hours, Tal and Kraft had completed one loop. The big lieutenant found a boulder in the ravine to lean against. With little light, to the soft beat of hunting bats, he worked in his notebook. Tal settled beside him.

Quietly, he asked, "How'd Remy look?"

The lieutenant didn't raise his eyes. "Bushed." The soldier jotted more items. "Your father said you were mad at him. That true?"

"Yeah."

"What'd he do that was so bad?"

"He took my mission. I was supposed to go to Parañaque, not him."

"There's a war on, kid. Your old man made it, that's what matters. Quit your bitching."

Soundless, Tal rose. The recon man blocked him with a burly arm.

"Sit down."

The arm was immovable.

"What's up with you? You got something to prove? To who? Your old man? Yourself?"

"None of your business."

"I agree. But let me give you one piece of advice. That ain't how a man operates. A man does the right thing. He does it for the greater good. If that proves something or not, what the hell, he does it anyway. War's not a place to show what you're made of. I've seen what men are made of. Mostly guts."

Kraft pocketed the notebook. He rose and dropped a hand to give Tal a lift.

"I'll tell you something else, about your pop. He delivered a map and some valuable intel through some pretty treacherous territory. When he was done, he put on that piece-of-shit hat of his and said he was heading back to Los Baños with me. Dead tired and finally out of danger, and all he could think about was stepping up again to help the folks inside the camp." Kraft prodded a finger into Tal's chest. "That's not proving something, kiddo. That's just being a stand-up guy. If you want a role model, you don't have far to look. You get me?"

"Yeah."

"And don't worry. The colonel's keeping him in Parañaque. Said your old man'll have to wait for the assault. Same as you."

Tal swelled. "You're gonna take me on the rescue mission?"

"You're the best guide I got. Just watch your step."

"I will, I promise."

"Okay." Kraft checked his watch. "It's two fifteen. You got it in you for another lap?"

"Do you?"

"You're lucky you're not wearing a uniform, sonny. Move."

The camp drowsed. The last coconut-oil lamps in the barracks were doused, the prayers and the worriers all went to bed. Lanterns floated along the fence, ghostly in the hands of sleepy guards. Old man Kolko in the kitchen snored loud enough for Tal and Kraft to hear him where they lay behind the infirmary, in the cogon grass.

On this second course around the camp, Tal brought Kraft closer to the wire. He began to see Los Baños through Kraft's eyes, as an objective to be attacked. The place was clearly meant to keep prisoners inside the wire, not fight off an invasion from outside it. A hundred soldiers, stealthy and dangerous, could slink through the ravine into the bamboo grove, then lie here in the high grass. Cut the barbed wire, rush in and take the camp.

Kraft crawled away while Tal imagined himself in that gun-blazing rescue. He followed the recon man closer to the main gate.

They stopped at the edge of the weeds, beside the road. Thirty yards away, six guards sat near the pair of bunkers.

"Built out of dirt." Kraft winked. "Ready-made graves."

They lay drawing shallow breaths. Tal knew nothing of the battle plan. He supposed Kraft had said nothing in case they were captured by the Japanese. Would Tal talk under pressure? Never.

Kraft elbowed him, pointing with his chin across the pavement. He whispered, "What's the name of that building?"

"Animal Husbandry."

"Any Japs inside?"

"No."

Kraft took a note, then slithered backward. With a hand on the soldier's back, Tal stopped him. Something in the scant light, almost imperceptible in the open ground between him and Carmen's building, had caught his attention. Neither he nor Kraft saw it on their first orbit of the camp. A long slash, darker than the earth, surfaced out of the night. The harder Tal stared, the clearer and blacker it became.

A trench.

Tal whispered, "That wasn't there when I left."

Kraft made marks in his notebook. The ditch could not be for defense. The camp was not defensible.

"I've seen enough," Kraft murmured. "Let's go, kid."

Tal led the soldier back to the ravine. Leaving Los Baños, they moved at a faster clip returning south through the paddies and plantations to Nanhaya. Around them, in the chirps of crickets and water frogs, the splashes of fish, and the last twinkling stars above a pale horizon, a clock seemed to tick in the world, ticking down.

Chapter Thirty-four

◆

CARMEN SERVICED only three soldiers in the morning. Each was a camp guard who had taken sex from her before. They wore *saku* and pierced her sadly. They were lean and an unhealthy yellow. When they were finished, they were mild mannered. None struck her, all thanked her, one left a piece of candy.

At noon, the camp loudspeaker announced the funerals of two more internees. In her red *haori,* Carmen listened to the names and causes. She received no food from the *makipilis* and was left alone to watch the gravedigger detail at the north end of the camp. The dozen internees stabbed at the ground with painful slowness, handing the picks and shovels off as their strength waned.

Yesterday, the Japanese had dug also, an odd trench beside her building. Carmen had leaned far out to see them. The thirty guards and dozen Filipino laborers worked with the same listless energy, as sapped as the prisoners. Carmen did not question the purpose of either set of holes; they were obviously the same, both graves.

In the early afternoon, the pair of internees' bodies was carried from the infirmary to the cemetery. Wrapped in sheets, they garnered no procession and the burial crowd was light. Throughout the camp, people hunkered around bowls and wooden planks, grinding at *palay* rice, a grain at a time, to perhaps save their lives.

For eleven months, the camp had been Carmen's only reality beyond this room. She'd watched every moment she could, nude beneath her red robe with the sun glinting off the silk, or in her drab T-shirt at night when the camp could not see her in return. She'd stood above it, apart, until she fell in love with a boy inside the wire, then like a tumbled angel risked everything to share his world.

Though the boy was gone now, she stayed behind to protect the camp. She could not save it. It was being starved and bled white. Tomorrow it would be gunned down.

She knew this because she watched Toshiwara leave his office. The man strode past the main gate and along the wire to her building. His boots, even with his small feet, filled the stairwell. Carmen moved into the hall to watch him in secret, to witness the arrival of the camp's other angel, death.

On the landing, the commandant called for Yumi-chan. The tiny girl came to him, bowed, and received instructions. Toshiwara left after a kiss.

Chapter Thirty-five

M R. TUCK?"

"Just a second."

Remy rattled the dice beside his ear, listening to the bones. He spilled them on the bare patch of dirt, rolling a pair of threes. In the circle around him, four soldiers groaned. Two others clapped, the ones who'd bet on Remy making his point. The pile of buttons and pebbles in the pot was split among them.

Remy looked up. "What can I do for you, Lieutenant?"

The young officer hooked a thumb over his shoulder in the direction he'd come through the trees.

"I'm about to brief my platoon. I wondered if you'd give me a hand."

"Son, can I take a break?"

"The men'll appreciate a few words from you, sir. Honest."

Remy sighed. "Okay. Be right there."

He thanked the soldiers kneeling with him, all copper-skinned and crew cut. He pushed his winnings into the middle. "Divvy it up, boys, and say nice things about me."

Remy followed the lieutenant through the bivouac. Camouflaged tents sprawled under the jungle roof, hiding four hundred paratroopers. Three hours before, Major Willcox's 1st Battalion of the 511th had trucked here from Parañaque, Remy with them. Hasty defenses had been dug, outposts manned, headquarters and communications set up. A hundred yards beyond the trees, the waters of the bay lapped the shore of Mamatid, the battalion's launch point at dawn. Eight miles across the water waited Los Baños.

Remy emerged with the lieutenant out of the tangle of trees and brush. At the young officer's order, four dozen soldiers knelt in front of a folding table. The lieutenant spread out a map based on the one Bascom had drawn.

This was Remy's fifth briefing since the battalion set up camp in these woods. Major Willcox, the commanding officer, had filled in his company commanders first. In turn, they briefed the platoon leaders, who—including this lieutenant—brought the individual troops up to speed on the raid.

"Men, this is Mr. Tuck, one of the internees from Los Baños."

Remy doffed his fedora, aware of his reedy arms.

The lieutenant continued to point at him. "There's more'n two thousand civilians just like him still inside the barbed wire. We're gonna go get 'em out."

Remy replaced his hat. He stood aside, scrawny and a bit ragged. One more time, he was being trotted out to display the Japanese brutality these boys were assigned to put a stop to. Remy was gaunt, he knew it, and let himself be gaped at. He had no weapon, so for now this was how he could best serve, fidgeting and pitiable.

The lieutenant stepped before the table. "This is going to be a multipronged, simultaneous assault. Sea, air, and land. It's going to require perfect timing. That's why we were handpicked for the job. Gather 'round, gentlemen."

The soldiers formed a semicircle around the table. When all had a view of the map, the lieutenant continued.

"Here's the setup. Right now, a task force under Colonel Shorty Soule is making its way down Highway One. In this task force are a battalion from the 188th Glider Infantry, the 675th and 472nd field artilleries, and a platoon of engineers from 127th Airborne. Before dark, these units will arrive at the north bank of the San Juan River, in range of the Japanese on the south bank and the Lecheria Hills."

With a fingertip, the officer highlighted the names and terrain as they became part of the plan. His platoon nodded. Some removed their helmets or rubbed the backs of their necks.

"H-hour tomorrow morning for the raid on the camp is 0700. When the assault begins, the Soule task force will attack across the river toward Los Baños. They'll take and hold this territory while a guerrilla force captures the *makipili* town of Calamba. This will be our overland withdrawal route after we secure the internee camp. The Soule force will arrive at the camp with trucks to transport the raiders and the internees out. That's the first purpose of the task force. The second is to act as a diversion, pulling the Japs' attention away from the camp. This is mighty damned important because the whole Jap Tiger Division is positioned eight miles south of the camp around San Pablo. If the Tigers don't bite on Soule's fake, if they get wind that our target is really Los Baños, we're gonna be in for a long day. The Soule force will engage the Tigers to slow them down if they move our way, but Shorty can only buy us a few hours. That's why we're going to hit the camp fast and get the hell out of there. Finally, the Soule force will provide assistance to us at the camp, as needed."

One soldier said, "Ain't gonna be needed, Lieutenant."

"Good to hear. Next is the jump component. Tonight, B Company is sleeping under the wings of nine C-47s at Nichols Field. Tomorrow morning, at 0640, they'll take off. At precisely 0700, the first of a hundred and twenty chutes is going to open at five hundred feet altitude just east of the camp. The drop zone will be smoke-marked and defended by guerrillas. Once B Company's on the ground, they'll regroup and take part in the raid."

"Sir?" A soldier raised a hand. "How big is the Jap garrison?"

The lieutenant motioned for Remy to stand beside him. Remy felt tired and stunted. A day and a half of moving, talking, and worrying was gaining on him.

He told the soldiers all he knew of the camp's guards, their number, condition, plus how the assault was timed to interrupt their morning calisthenics. Remy skipped the locations of the gun towers and pillboxes, leaving those for the lieutenant. He drifted back to the perimeter of the briefing. One soldier offered Remy his canteen. Another mumbled a quiet "Don't worry, sir."

The lieutenant continued, addressing the details of the camp's defenses, plus the ditches and arroyos where the platoon could find cover approaching the Japanese machine guns.

The young officer ordered his soldiers to kneel again on the forest floor. Remy sat, struggling to keep his eyelids up. He sipped from the soldier's canteen to keep himself awake.

The lieutenant continued: "Early tomorrow morning, Lieutenant Kraft's recon platoon and a guerrilla force will move into concealed positions around the camp. They'll remain hidden until the first chute from B Company pops. That'll be the signal to start the raid. Recon and the guerrillas will breach the wire and engage the Japs' outer defenses. If all goes right, we should be arriving at our debarkation point at the same time. Our job is to dismount along with two howitzers from D Battery, 457th Artillery, and defend the beachhead."

Another hand went up. "Lieutenant?"

"Yes, Corporal?"

"Dismount from what?"

The officer checked his watch. "Come with me, boys."

The platoon rose as one. Remy, so tired he could have slept where he sat, tagged along.

The lieutenant led them out of the Mamatid woods to the water's edge. During the short walk, a grumble of many engines swelled out of the north. The platoon looked up and around, confused at the growing motor roar that was neither airplane nor tank.

"What the hell?" the men muttered. "It's comin' from the bay." These were airborne soldiers, accustomed to dropping into battle vertically, silently. Many of them had taken off in airplanes but had never landed in one. Whatever bore down on them raised enough ruckus to alert every enemy for miles in all directions.

The platoon reached the bay in time to catch the first amphibious tractor waddling onto the beach. The dripping leviathan churned sand under spinning metal tracks, spat a vile exhaust, and made an earsplitting clank, louder on land than in the water. It featured armored flanks, two mounted machine guns, and a loading ramp in the stern.

Three abreast, a long rank of more than fifty amtracs rumbled ashore off the shimmering water. The paratroopers complained about their deafening clatter and slothlike pace. Remy gazed in awe at the ingenuity to construct a machine that was part tank, part boat, two vehicles seemingly impossible to combine. He wondered what other marvels the world had ginned up while he was in prison.

The lieutenant led the platoon off the beach before the last amtrac powered onto the point. Remy veered off the path to find a soft place to lie down. He found it at the fat base of a banyan tree. He plucked an armful of ferns, gathered it over him, and slept into the dusk.

Chapter Thirty-six

A N HOUR before midnight, a lovely and grim young woman arrived at the guerrilla camp. Three Filipino fighters accompanied her to Colonel Romeo, who embraced her.

"Magdalena," he said beside the fire, "this is Sergeant Bolick."

Bolick stood to shake her hand. "Ma'am."

All three sat. One of the guerrilla boys disappeared to bring her food. The other two faded back to their posts in the dark.

"I came alone."

Romeo asked, "How can that be?"

"I tried. No one listened."

During the day, Romeo had spoken to Bolick of his wife. He called her as brave as any guerrilla. In the steady light of the campfire, she appeared shaken. She folded her arms in her lap, believing she had failed somehow. Romeo took her hand. This did not lift her gaze.

"Tell me."

Magdalena patted her husband's hand before releasing it. She addressed Bolick.

"Sergeant. Thank you for being here."

"My pleasure, ma'am."

"Tomorrow, during the raid. If there is a battle with the Japanese, the people of our village may be in the way. I know you're here to free your own, but please."

"I understand. All I can guarantee is that we'll do everything we can to get in and out as clean as possible.

If things fall our way, the fight'll stay just in the camp."

"I will pray for that, Sergeant."

"I'll join you, ma'am."

Food arrived. Magdalena set the bowl at her feet.

"I knocked on fifty, sixty doors," she said to Romeo. "I told them the Americans are coming. You should leave. Go into the jungle where Romeo is. He will keep you safe."

She paused to swipe a fingertip beneath her eyes. The fire leaped and a gust of smoke crossed Bolick.

"They all said the same thing. The Americans are coming, we'll be safe then. No, I said. The Americans are coming only to rescue their own countrymen at the camp. The village could be caught in the middle. If that happens it'll be a battlefield. You have to leave."

Magdalena pleaded with her husband as though he were one of the people in the village. Futility glistened down her cheeks.

"What about reprisals? The Japanese have convinced themselves every Filipino is a guerrilla. They'll believe the villagers helped the Americans rescue the camp. What will you do if the Japanese come here for revenge? Will you run then when it's too late? Run now. Run with me."

Romeo took down his wife's hands to hold them in his own lap. She halted her plea.

"I came alone."

Escorted by Gusto of Terry's Hunters and General of the Fil-Americans, the thirty-man recon platoon arrived out of the night.

Bolick rose to greet Lieutenant Kraft and his men. The lieutenant was one of the few men in the 511th who came close to Bolick's size.

"Good work, Sergeant," Kraft told him. "It's almost game time."

"Ready when you say, Lieutenant."

Bolick shook hands with the six sergeants in the platoon. He knew none of these men and was struck by the ruggedness of each. Every recon man hefted at least fifty pounds of weaponry: M1 rifle or carbine, bayonet, pistol, phosphorus, incendiary and fragmentation grenades, knives, and ammunition. Bolick carried a radio of similar weight, but none of Kraft's men looked like they'd blink if he added his burden to theirs. Three of the recon men, Kraft included, lugged bazookas.

Quickly, Romeo ceded his authority in the camp to Kraft. He sat with Gusto, one on either side of Magdalena. Romeo's guerrillas, as many as a hundred, filtered into the glittering circle of firelight. With them came the internees Tuck and Bascom. Both appeared rested. Along with the guerrillas, they took seats on the earth. Kraft waited for all to settle before speaking.

He thanked the guerrilla commanders for coming to Nanhaya. He made mention of Gusto and the help his Hunters had given ferrying the recon platoon across the bay, and Romeo's PQOG for the valuable intel they'd been gathering and sending to 11th Airborne through Sergeant Bolick.

"This is your last briefing, gentlemen. After this, we'll get into position by dawn and wait for H-hour."

Kraft reviewed the assignments for the several guerrilla units. The Hukbalahaps and the Chinese Squadron were already moving into place around the drop zone east of the camp, to defend the perimeter at H-hour while the hundred-plus paratroopers would land and regroup. Marking's Fil-Americans had responsibility for securing San Antonio beach from the twenty Japanese troops stationed there, then set up roadblocks to hold the beachhead until a battalion of the 511th arrived in a fleet of amtracs.

General, the peacock commander of the Fil-Americans, stood and took a bow. Kraft continued.

Romeo's PQOG would provide guides for the recon platoon to the camp, then take up positions between the barbed wire and the drop zone. Gusto's Hunters would form the main guerrilla force assisting the recon platoon in the assault on the camp itself.

Next, the lieutenant addressed his own men. He broke his platoon into six teams, each led by one of his sergeants. The first team would mark the drop zone at 0658 hours with green smoke canisters. Once the paratroopers were on the ground and organized, they'd lead them into the camp. A second team had the task of marking the landing beach at San Antonio for the amtracs. The remaining four teams were given specific points of attack for the raid on the camp. Every guard tower and pill box was targeted. For himself and his squad, Kraft took the job of knocking out the pair of pillboxes and six guards at the main gate.

Romeo was to assign eight to twelve guerrillas to each team, and another dozen to the squad tasked with holding the beach for the amtracs.

Kraft raised both hands, encompassing every soldier and guerrilla present. "Now listen close. On your approach to your positions, under no circumstances will you return enemy fire. This is an absolute order. Do not give away your positions. Let the Japs think they've heard animals in the bushes and the ravine. If any of your men get hit, carry them out of there. Leave no evidence that you're in the area. If the Japs catch our scent, they'll start mowing down internees before we can stop them. Understood?"

A hundred and thirty men answered, "Yes." Bolick did not respond because he did not have an assignment. His job as signalman was pivotal to communications, but he wanted a role in the fighting itself.

Before he could speak, Bascom got to his feet.

"What about me and Tuck?"

In the firelight, Kraft strode to the thin boy. He clapped a hand on Bascom's shoulder to walk him to the recon squad assigned to the southern approach to the camp.

"He's yours," Kraft said to the sergeant.

Bascom sat with the recon soldiers. The team greeted him with hard pats on the back and head.

Kraft pointed, curling a finger. "Tuck?"

The boy stood. Kraft guided him by the shirtsleeve to sit at the fire beside Bolick.

"Tuck here," Kraft said to Bolick, "knows the camp better'n anybody. He's yours, Sergeant. I'll give you four more from my platoon. Commander Gusto will assign you ten of his guerrillas. When that first chute pops, Tuck will lead your squad to the spot where the guards keep their guns while they're exercising. You run like hell. Don't stop to shoot anybody, just get your asses there first. Then shoot 'em. Got it?"

"Roger that."

Tuck beamed. Gusto, Magdalena, and Romeo all reached for the boy in congratulations.

Gusto said to Bolick, "I'll give you ten of my fastest runners."

"Thanks."

The boy grinned at Romeo. "Tell them I said 'Tumulin.'"

Magdalena translated for Bolick. He asked Tuck, "And what do you plan to do when you get there first, hotshot? Say boo?"

Bolick unbuckled the shoulder holster for his Colt .45 automatic pistol. He handed the big sidearm and harness to the kid.

"Here. Say boo with this."

Chapter Thirty-seven

T HE TWO dozen *bancas* made no sound sailing in the dark unless they bumped hulls or outriggers. The Filipino captains snapped at one another to keep their distance.

Tal rode in the bow of a reeking fishing boat, in the middle of the fleet. An hour ago, Bolick had said only "pee-yew" when he climbed aboard. The big sergeant and four recon men pinched their noses in disgust, then settled in stoically. Tal tried to sit beside Bolick for whispered conversation, to calm his own nerves. The stench drove him forward, where the breeze hit him before it swept over the century of dead fish stained in the *banca*'s beams.

He fiddled with the shoulder harness for the pistol Bolick had given him. Tal drew the Colt, practicing with the weight and balance. The gun needed both hands to hold steady. He dropped the magazine the way Bolick showed him and thumbed the cartridges of the seven rounds. Tal imagined Nagata on the other end of the barrel.

For an hour the boats traced the black shoreline. The vessels dodged fishing traps and great clusters of water hyacinths. The four recon men in the boat with him had barely spoken to him at the guerrilla camp. They slouched in the belly of the *banca* with their helmets hiding their eyes. Tal leaned over the side to watch the prow split the bay.

One at a time, the fleet turned into the narrow mouth of a river and dropped sail. The lanterns of a small village glowed through the trees.

"San Antonio," the skipper said. "Out."

The recon men and Bolick slipped into the knee-deep water. Tal removed his sneakers so he wouldn't lose them in the mucky bottom.

On the beach, the recon soldiers split into squads with the hundred guerrillas. A dozen of Romeo's PQOG guerrillas emerged from the nearby village to guide the raiders. Tal and Bascom found each other on the beach.

"This is it," Tal said. "Long time coming."

"See you in the camp, lad. I wish Donnelly were here for this."

"That goes for a lot of folks, I reckon."

"Well, keep your head down."

"I'll be glad to keep it on."

Bascom asked, "You goin' for the girls?"

"Yeah, as best I can."

"Good luck, Tuck."

Bascom linked up with his sergeant. Bolick collected Tal.

The big radioman gathered his squad around him. Gusto's ten guerrillas were a mix of older, hardened men and boys Tal's age. Half wore shoes. All were armed with a rifle and bolo. These were the men Romeo said were his swiftest. Mingled with them, Kraft's heavily armed Americans looked like titans.

Bolick said, "We've got four miles to Los Baños." He addressed Romeo's two PQOG guides waiting nearby. "You know the way, right?"

"We all do."

"Good. You two go in front. Tuck and me will follow." Bolick assigned a pair of guerrillas to walk between each of the four recon men. This way, if the staggered column were interrupted for any reason, each soldier would have a two-man team to guide him to the camp.

"Remember what the lieutenant said. No noise, no response to the Japs. We'll regroup in Boot Creek at 0600."

The small beach began to empty. Merged squads of soldiers and guerrillas dispersed into the scrub. Bolick's two guides set out. Tal strode beside the big sergeant.

Bolick pointed at the .45 strapped to Tal's chest. "You gettin' used to that gat?"

"No."

"Wait'll a Jap aims his at you. You'll get the feel pretty quick. Just hold tight, she's got a kick."

In the shallow water, the *bancas* hoisted sail and glided away. Romeo's guides led Bolick's team off the sand. Within a hundred yards, the waters of the bay and the village lights disappeared behind dense jungle. Tal caught no hint of any of the other raiding teams. Each was being led by a separate path to Los Baños.

The first two miles of the journey went quickly. Above the bay, the sky cleared, and the squad traipsed by the pinlight of stars through plantations and open fields. When the ground became sodden and the dark earth glistened ahead, Tal told Bolick to take off his boots.

Bolick balked. "I'm not taking off my boots."

"Then give me the radio. I've been through these paddies already and, trust me, you're going in."

Tal kicked off his sneakers and held out his arms. Bolick had a choice to make, radio or boots.

Bolick cursed, then squatted to untie his laces. The four recon men and Gusto's ten guerrillas arrived from behind, waiting at the edge of the dike for the sergeant to go barefoot. Bolick told the soldiers to shed their jump boots. All four resisted; Bolick did not insist. The Filipinos held their tongues. Apparently the locals enjoyed watching Americans take a dunking.

Tal and Bolick trailed their guides into the dark paddies. The berms were slick and narrow as before. Tal walked behind Bolick. The large man pulled the radio off his back to carry it by hand. If he slipped, he planned to toss it to Tal at the last moment. Tal worried that the big sidearm strapped to his shoulder would throw off his own balance.

Crossing the paddies took another hour. Tal and Bolick stayed dry, though spattered in mud. Behind them in the dark, the recon men tumbled one at a time into the flooded paddies. The splashes grew more distant as Tal and Bolick progressed through the canals in advance of the rest of their squad. Faint sloshes and curses cut across the black vista of canals and dikes from the other six teams slogging their way elsewhere through the paddies, also in their jump boots.

Reaching dry land, Bolick's two guides were plainly disappointed. Bolick and Tal washed themselves from a trickling drainpipe. The big sergeant put on his boots. Dawn lay thirty minutes off. Only a mile and a half was left to the camp, and ninety minutes to H-hour.

Bolick and Tal waited for their squad to catch up. After five minutes, another pair of Romeo's guides arrived, leading a soldier sopping from the waist down.

"Son of a bitch," the recon man said.

"Where's the others?"

"Dunno, Sarge. I lost track."

"But they're behind you, right?"

"I reckon. That was like walking on a greased pig."

The wet recon man filled his canteen from the pipe. Bolick and Tal aimed their senses across the paddies. Not a sound floated out of the darkness beyond the buzz of mosquitoes.

After ten minutes, Bolick told the recon soldier, named Cubby, to make his way to the camp with Tal.

"Take the boy. Get in position. You know the job."

Cubby shook off the suggestion. "I'll stay back. I know these guys. I'll find 'em and get 'em there on time. Don't worry, Sarge. You take the kid and go."

Bolick considered his watch and the pinking sky.

"Yeah," Tal said. He wanted Bolick beside him, no one else. "Let's go."

Bolick tapped the face of his watch at Cubby. "0700."

The recon man glanced at his two Filipino escorts. The guerrillas fingered the hilts of their bolos. They didn't want to miss the start of the attack either. They nodded.

"We'll be there," Cubby said. "Go on."

Bolick shrugged into the straps of the radio. He pointed the way forward to Romeo's two guides and trod off behind them. Tal moved beside the big sergeant.

"You think they'll make it?"

"No idea. We'll be okay, you and me." Bolick reached across Tal's chest to tap the big Colt handgun. "And this ol' hand cannon. Let me ask you something. You said you're fast."

"Yeah. I am."

"Good." Bolick grinned in the rising light. "'Cause I ain't."

Chapter Thirty-eight

R EMY GRIPPED the steel gunwale to leap overboard in case the machine sank. Around him, all ten armed paratroopers did the same.

The amtrac lurched across Mamatid beach toward the shallows. Just one of these behemoths raised enough noise to wake the dead, Remy thought. Fifty-four of them surely ought to rouse the Japanese.

The first three amtracs in the long procession wallowed into the dark water. The dozens of soldiers on board rimmed the open bays, poised like Remy to go swimming. The machines, true amphibians, bobbed on the surface before the water could swallow them. A great, burbling howl coughed out of the wake boiling at their rears. The amtracs surged forward. The amazed soldiers did not take their seats.

Remy's amtrac plowed into the bay, bracketed between two others. Every paratrooper ogled the rising water until the things proved themselves buoyant. Not until the full column had chugged several hundred yards offshore and the coast vanished in the inky night did Remy and the wary soldiers sit.

Remy accompanied a headquarters squad of the 511th's C Company. He made no conversation, the din of the amtracs would not have allowed it. The paratroopers settled in for the 7.2-mile voyage across the bay to San Antonio. The amtracs' top speed on land was 15 miles per hour, but on water they could cruise at only a third of that. The sluggish, thunderous procession would be in enemy waters for seventy-five minutes. With a .50 caliber machine gun in the bow of each and a .30 caliber beside it, the transports could marshal a lot of firepower, but a shootout with a Japanese patrol boat would be among the worst things that could happen. Surprise would be the first thing lost, thousands of lives would be second.

The soldiers checked their weapons and sat bolt upright on the benches. Remy imagined these boys in the fuselage of a drop plane, chutes packed, battle faces on. They looked fearless. The best Remy could muster was a poker face. He didn't know what to do with his own fears. He'd listened to and spoken at a dozen briefings about the raid, and still had no idea what was coming. He was not a soldier. These bronzed boys were. Remy was a good enough gambler to know when to bet on someone else's hand. This calmed him enough to think about Tal.

He worried that the boy was not surrounded by as war-like a force as he was, by so much steel, even afloat. He'd left Tal with the lightly armed guerrillas. Was the boy with Kraft's small recon team right now, crouched in the ravine? Of course he was. Tal wouldn't miss the raid any more than Remy would. He wouldn't desert the girl, break his word, wouldn't consider it. Remy looked into the predawn sky, the one thing he and his son could both see at the moment. Be safe, he thought, I'm coming. And again, Be safe.

Remy turned his mind to Sarah, the one the boy was most like. Because Remy was afraid, he considered that he might be killed today and he would see her. He'd tell his wife they'd made a good and brave son. A lucky boy. He would ask Sarah to ask God if they could watch him together.

Forty minutes into the journey, the first light seeped out of the eastern horizon. With no landmarks on the bay, guided only by watches and compasses, the whole column cut a hard right turn. Every soldier in Remy's amtrac scanned for patrol boats. The fleet clamored like a column of tanks on land; maybe that's what the Japanese in earshot thought they were. Remy hoped his own luck would hold a while longer; he didn't want to pass it on to Tal just yet.

Miles away, bonfires dotted the coastline. The villagers knew the rumble out on the black bay was the American army. They lit the way to Los Baños. The breach of secrecy was alarming, but the paratroopers were pleased to see land. Over the many engines, the boys shouted that nothing could stop them now.

At dawn, the long column made one more course adjustment, a smaller turn to the right. An early mist obscured the peak of Makiling. The slender outline of San Antonio's point lay dead ahead.

The amtracs slowed their pace to realign their formation into rows of nine. The fifty-four tractors would hit the beach in six waves. Remy's took up position on the far right flank of the first echelon.

The fleet churned toward shore. The paratroopers tightened their grips on the stocks of their rifles. A few laid foreheads against the gun barrels as if praying into their weapons. To ready himself, Remy tugged down the bill of his fedora.

Ashore, a few hundred yards off the bow, a green burst of smoke billowed. The front rank of amtracs gunned straight for it.

In the northern sky, a dark sliver headed their way. Remy pounded on the knee of the soldier beside him, pointing into the dim distance. The squad pivoted to catch the V formation of nine C-47s charging across the bay.

The jump planes could not be heard above the amtracs, but every soldier on the water balled a fist at B Company swooping in, on time and on target. In the slow-going, wet amtracs, the soldiers all wished to be in the air.

The C-47s zoomed so low that the jumpmasters in every door waved to the troopers below. Five hundred feet of altitude didn't look like much.

Remy's amtrac vibrated. The giant tracks on either side whirled. The first echelon was about to strike the shallows. The troopers with Remy were fired up. They knocked fists on their helmets to screw them down tighter. They got to their feet. Remy yanked down on his brim one more time.

An emerald haze blew over the water to greet them. Remy's machine thumped the sand shelf and powered out of the bay. On the beach, guerrillas raised high their rifles and long knives to welcome 1st Battalion. The amtracs belched and scattered to offload their soldiers and artillery. The second wave arrived close behind, dripping and roaring.

Two miles south, the first silk canopy opened above Los Baños. Instantly, all nine jump planes sowed parachutes like white confetti.

Remy heard no gunfire. But across the San Juan River, in the tiny drop zone beside the camp, in Boot Creek and the jungle outside the wire, and on San Antonio beach, the attack was on.

Chapter Thirty-nine

CARMEN WOKE with a start. Her room remained dark and still, just as it had been when she'd drifted off. She rubbed her face to wipe away sleep.

She stood in her window, anxious, like a guard on duty who'd dozed through his watch. Artillery fire continued to quake in the northern sky. Below, the camp had not changed. Dawn remained hours away. The Japanese carried sallow lanterns in their slow circuits around the fence. Cigarettes burned in the gun towers and a few barracks windows. The camp slept to its final dawn.

Carmen felt rested and regretted it. She'd lost the numbness of fatigue. She was keener now than before, and her helplessness deepened.

Outside the wire, the creek and jungle cawed, louder than they had before she'd fallen asleep. Were the creatures sensing the coming massacre? Could an approaching event be so horrible that animals might read it in the air like scent? Were they calling a warning? Carmen imagined adding her own voice to the beasts and birds in Boot Creek, the ravine, the forest. She'd shout from her high window, waking the internees, alerting them that today they would all be murdered. But this would only rob them of their last hours, they would die on the end of her voice, and her warnings would become a lament until the Japanese came to kill her, too.

She left the window to creep down the dark hall. At the landing, Papa snored on his mattress. The old man looked pitiful, splayed crazily on the tatami as if he'd fallen there.

Even his rest appeared a struggle. Carefully, Carmen lifted her tag off the board. She left Yumi's hanging on its peg—no need to bring trouble to the little girl on the morning of her escape. Carmen returned to her room. She slid the tag into a pocket of her fatigue pants. She would keep it on her like an American dog tag, to identify her.

The sun came very slowly this morning, as if it, too, were reluctant. Carmen gazed at the nipa roof of the Tuck boy's barracks. Tal had been gone with his father for four days.

Where was he? He swore he'd return. Had she waited for him too long? Should she have let Kenji steal her away? Was her trust in Tal her death?

"If you're coming, boy," she said aloud, to conjure him, "now is a good time."

The first internees shuffled out of the barracks to their latrines and showers, cooks to the kitchen. Carmen could not stop herself envisioning how easily they would die, the women and children in doomed shock, the men with little meat on them, no strength to fight. She saw it all play out. The guards machine-gunned most, bayoneted the rest. A thousand bodies were dumped in the great hole near the dao, another thousand in the trench beside her building. Dirt pushed over the mass graves. The barracks blank and silent, the guards purposeless. Kenji stood powerless and innocent, Nagata staring up at her from the bloody ground.

Dawn broke before Carmen knew it. The butchery in her head stopped when the real guards in their loincloths marched into the old garden for their exercises. Nagata formed his men into lines beneath a morning haze. She feared that Nagata and not the Tuck boy was her fate.

The roll-call gong rang. On the landing, Papa would rise and see the Songu tag missing from the board. She expected him soon, to ask about it. She would send him away. If Mama came instead, Carmen would ignore her.

The guards chanted in their ugly, naked calisthenics, *"Ichi, ni, san, shi!"* eclipsing the banter of the jungle. Among the men, Kenji flung himself about, gangly and out of step.

A large civilian car entered the main gate to stop at the commandant's office. Soldiers loaded boxes into the open trunk. Toshiwara stood aside, supervising.

A knock sounded on her doorframe. Papa stepped under the curtain. Carmen did not leave the window.

"Why did you take down your tag?"

Below, the internees formed up for roll call. Every day they grew more listless. The guards' exercises were a shambles. They, too, were fading.

She faced Papa. "You asked me to protect you when the time comes."

"Yes," he said, eager. "Yes."

"I do it now. Turn your back. Walk away from the camp. Far away."

"I can't do that, Songu. She'd never go with me."

"Leave her."

"She's my wife."

"Then stay with the rest of us."

Carmen pivoted to the window.

Behind her, Papa said, "The Korean girl is singing."

"Is she?"

"Yes. Why? If things are so terrible."

"She's a bird. It's a warning."

"I don't understand. What's going on? A warning about what?"

"If you're going to stay, old man, bring me food."

"Are the Americans coming? Is that it? Why should I leave the camp? You said you'd speak up for us."

Carmen measured her own hunger. Papa would report to his wife the cryptic things Carmen had said. The rotten old woman would come back with threats, without food. Carmen preferred to eat.

"Yes, that's what's happening. Today the Americans arrive. Keep this to yourself."

"Today. You know this for certain?"

"Yes. Now will you find me something to eat?"

"Yes, of course. I won't ask how you know. Keep the wooden tag. There's no need anymore, right?"

The old *makipili* bustled out under the curtain. Yumi was in her room, chirping, brushing her hair, waiting for Toshiwara to fetch her and put her in the big car with his luggage and papers. The commandant would drive away and the slaughter he ordered would start. Where could a man go to outdistance such a thing?

The guards' calisthenics fell apart. Nagata bellowed in frustration. The men would not focus. Their exertion quit. Their heads turned to the sky. Toshiwara beside his sedan bent his gaze skyward. Beyond the wire, from the deep creek and the jungle behind it, birds twittered out of the trees in a startled swarm.

All the Japanese and internees peered up. The rumble of many engines swelled over the camp. Under Carmen's hands, her windowsill vibrated. Was this another bombing raid on the train tracks, the national highway? The internees pointed into the air behind the animal husbandry building, where Carmen could not see.

In every stretch of the barbed wire, explosions erupted. Concussions rattled Carmen's walls and her chest. Around the camp, light and fire flashed, swallowing guard towers and bunkers in smoke, plumes of flung dirt. In reflex, Carmen stepped back from the window. Were the Americans actually bombing Los Baños? This made no sense, it was so risky. She pressed herself back to the window. Moments after the first blasts, chaos had not yet taken hold on the ground. Every soldier and internee stood rooted, flabber-gasted.

Gunfire cracked. Carmen's heart seized.

The start of the massacre! The Japanese would commit murder even under American bombs!

Internees scattered. Some fell to their faces. Most stampeded toward their barracks while gunfire snapped on all sides.

At the west gate, a watchtower blew up.

The guards in loincloths came to life. Nagata's screams cut above the thumping din. More than a hundred mostly nude Japanese dashed out of the field, flapping and barefoot, to reach their quarters.

Cutting across the same open ground, racing them full bore, ran the Tuck boy.

Chapter Forty

T AL BRACED his feet on the rocks and moss of Boot
Creek. He held the grenade the way Bolick showed
him, how Bolick and the two guerrillas held theirs, arm
extended with elbow locked, like a catapult. His thumb held
down the release lever. The pin lay somewhere at his feet in
the trickling water.

Nine planes zoomed in low, east of the camp, on time.
The first parachute opened, followed by dozens more.

"What do we do?" Tal asked.

Bolick sent one look down the shaded length of the
creek bed. The rest of their assault team was still missing.
They'd passed only one other squad while creeping to this
spot, hidden below the western gate.

The big sergeant puffed his cheeks, resigned. "Throw,
boys."

Tal heaved the heavy lump over the bank of Boot Creek,
to the unseen base of the gun tower there. Five guards typically manned this post. Bolick had crawled close and reported only three. The other two were likely on the exercise
field.

All four grenades sailed through the leaves. Tal got on
tiptoes to see the explosions. Bolick shoved him down into
the slope.

The thuds went off in quick succession, shaking the
earth under Tal's chest. With a battle cry, both barefoot
guerrillas scrambled up the bank. Bolick beat Tal to his feet
and followed the Filipinos.

At the crest of the bank, boiling gray smoke obscured the tower. The guerrillas' first shots put down two guards staggering in the fog. Bolick turned his gun on the tower, killing the Japanese up there.

Through the shifting smoke, Tal surveyed the camp. Parachutes continued to stream from the jump planes. Around the fence, other guard positions were under attack by small-arms fire and grenades. In front of every barracks, internees fell to their faces in their roll-call lines or scurried for cover. In the garden field, a large crowd of Japanese in loincloths stood gaping into the camp, as stunned as Tal.

From the creek bed behind him, a yell rose, "Go, goddamit, go, go!" and the thump of boots on stones.

Tal called to Bolick. "That's Cubby!"

In the garden, the hundred bare-skinned guards broke into a mass rush for their quarters.

Bolick shouted, "Run, boy!"

Tal took off. The guerrillas trailed him; Bolick, slowed by the radio on his back, hustled behind them. The big Colt .45 joggled at Tal's armpit. To speed his strides, he left the gun in its holster.

A cry rose from the running Japanese when they spotted Tal and realized he was racing them to their weapons. The guards tore across the open field at a diagonal to his path. Even barefoot, the nearest soldiers narrowed the gap, surging for the alley between two barracks that led to the guards' quarters. Tal pumped his legs and arms as fast as he could. He calculated quickly: he might reach the opening between the buildings first, but a hundred frightened and angry Japanese would be right behind. He fumbled for the pistol banging at his chest but found he couldn't dislodge it and keep up this clip. Tal gritted his teeth and ran for his life.

He couldn't do this. He was only halfway to the weapons

locker, another fifty yards. Even if he made it there first, he'd have no time or stamina left to defend it alone. Before Tal could get the Colt into his hands, before Bolick and the guerrillas could arrive to stop them, the guards would tear him apart.

Tal closed in on the alley. To his left, the Japanese screamed at him. On the ground in front of the barracks, internees watched him gallop ahead of a crowd of naked guards. Tal hollered, "Out of the way!" Some leaped up, the rest lay flat, bewildered.

Tal pushed himself to his limit, sprinting past the first internees in the dirt. The people added their shouts to the racket. Twenty yards later, he reached the narrow way between buildings.

He drove his heels into the earth, skidding to a stop. He clawed at the holster to yank the big pistol loose.

Tal panicked for a moment at the heft of the gun, forcing himself to firm his grip and remember Bolick's instructions. He charged the slide to put a round in the chamber. With barracks walls on either side, he whirled, bringing up the .45 with both hands. Tal breathed so hard he could hardly steady the gun or see beyond the short barrel.

Backpedaling, he aimed at the center of the throng of Japanese narrowing to fit between the buildings to get at him, then past him.

He put his finger to the trigger, convinced he had to kill or die. He stopped retreating.

Before Tal could shoot, the pack of Japanese caved in, attacked from the side. Their advance buckled. Tal eased his finger and lowered the Colt.

The two guerrilla guides running behind him had bowled into the onrushing guards, slashing their bolos. A third joined them, long knife whirling. Gusto! In the midst of swinging at the guards, he raised his chin at Tal, keeping his promise to see him again. The unarmed Japanese began to scatter; several were chopped off their feet.

Bolick, slow and great like a juggernaut, waded past the hacking Filipinos, flashing his rifle at the naked, recoiling guards. He jogged into the alley beside Tal. Both caught their breaths.

A hundred yards back, surging out of Boot Creek through the smoldering west gate, Cubby led the rest of the squad. The four recon men and ten guerrillas came at a dead run, determined to get into the fight.

In a window of one of the barracks, a head popped up. An elderly woman, a teacher, stared at Tal bug-eyed.

She turned to someone ducking beside her. "You won't believe it," she said. "It's that Tuck boy."

Chapter Forty-one

BOLICK SHOT two Japanese, both in the gut. They'd rushed at him together, as if they'd made a pact to die like this, stripped down to leather thongs and empty-handed, shouting *"Banzai."* This was suicide, a senseless death. Bolick gunned them both down without flinching, before Tuck could raise the big Colt.

One of Gusto's guerrillas ran over with his bloodstained bolo. The barefoot Filipino spent a few seconds on the downed guards. Bolick turned the Tuck boy away.

He took the Colt from the lanky kid and eased the hammer to disarm it.

"Put it in the holster," he said. Bolick wanted the boy to get through the raid and not fire the gun once. Killing would be common today. That didn't mean it would be meaningless tomorrow.

From all quarters of the camp, gunfire sparked. Every few seconds a grenade went off. Machine guns ripped back and forth between the raiders and the few remaining guard towers.

Cubby and his three recon men hustled up to the guards' quarters. Bolick allowed Cubby a moment to settle.

"You made it."

The four soldiers straightened their steel helmets after the long tear across the field and between the barracks. Mud from the paddies smirched their fatigues.

Cubby said, "Sorry, Sarge."

"What happened?"

"Their damn guides took off on 'em. By the time I rounded everybody up, it was already sunup. We ran the whole friggin' way."

"All right. Stay here and guard the Japs' barracks." Bolick clapped a hand on the Tuck boy's shoulder. "You did good, kiddo. That took stones."

"I didn't do anything. I just ran."

"We'll argue about that later. For now, I want you to stay here with Cubby's squad. Can you do that, 'til things calm down in the camp?"

The boy squirmed under Bolick's hand. "I've got to get to somebody."

"Whoever it is ain't goin' anywhere, trust me. I got to go do my job and I need to be sure you're safe and out of the way. Keep that hand cannon quiet as long as you can, okay?"

Tal looked crestfallen. Cubby put his own mitt on the kid's other shoulder and spoke for him. "He'll be fine, Sarge. We got him."

Bolick tightened the straps of the radio and headed toward the heaviest fighting, at the main gate. He hurried in a crouch alongside the building next to the guards' quarters. Peeking in a window, he noted this was not a barracks but an office.

Bolick crept up a set of steps, rifle lowered and ready. He pushed in the door. His weight creaked the bamboo floorboards, making a Japanese dash from behind a filing cabinet. The soldier, skinny with black glasses, maybe a clerk, leaped through an open window. Bolick plugged him with two rounds, once as he took flight, once in midair. Bolick stayed low and swept his rifle across the office to be sure it was empty. He moved to the window on the far side. The Japanese lay in the dirt, writhing. His glasses had come off. Bolick put another round in him, figuring this was a better end than a bolo.

Outside, he took cover behind the front steps of the building. The firing in the camp had stepped up in frenzy, now that the recon teams were inside the wire along with a hundred guerrillas hunting down the Japanese. A few dozen guards were making a stand, dying hard. Maybe half the garrison had already lit out for the jungle. The rest were hiding.

One hard-core group had hunkered around the two dirt bunkers at the main gate. Ten Japanese were taking potshots from behind the pillboxes. The machine guns in the little fortresses protected their backsides. The squad that Kraft had assigned to capture the main gate was stuck in a firefight with them. A bullet zinged past Bolick's helmet; one of the Japanese had seen him and tried his luck. Bolick figured he'd try his own.

With a piercing two-fingered whistle, Bolick caught the attention of a recon corporal. He wigwagged for the squad to stay clear of the gate. The corporal gave him a thumbs-up and spread the word.

Bolick checked his map. With the radio between his knees, he raised B Company, the drop team on the ground and assembling east of the camp. Bolick pinpointed for his counterpart the location of the bunkers on their shared map, warning him also that civilians and fellow paratroopers were close by.

One minute later, a mortar round whistled almost straight down, fired from a few hundred yards away. The 60-mm shell missed the right-hand bunker, short by twenty feet. The Japanese behind it, with dirt clogs raining on them, increased their firing, screaming at the Americans. Bolick corrected the mortar's range. The next round landed squarely between the two bunkers. Bolick said into the handset, "Fire at will." Five more rounds dropped one after another. When the haze and flying earth cleared, the pillboxes were gouged, blackened, and quiet. The ten guards around them were all dead, cast backward, smoking as if their spirits were leaving them. Two recon boys dashed past the bodies to toss grenades into the bunkers' firing slits. With a pair of muted wallops, the main gate's defenses were silenced.

Again, Bolick strapped the radio to his back. Ducking behind cover when he could, he moved among the barracks to help chase internees back inside. Hundreds had not moved from their roll-call positions, they'd just lain down. Bolick was unprepared for the awful condition of the prisoners in the camp. Tal and Bascom were stick thin, and he'd assumed that was typical of the internees. Most of the ones Bolick rousted off the ground were grossly malnourished, some children had swollen bellies, many elderly had dark sockets and legs stained the color of gentian violet. Bolick told them to get in their rooms and crawl under a mattress because their straw walls were not going to stop bullets. Most did what he ordered, some wanted to thank him first, lay a hand on him, ask why he was orange. One young lady asked him his unit.

"Eleventh Airborne, ma'am."

She kissed him full on the lips before running away. An older gent hurrying past identified the woman as a nun.

Bolick moved carefully along the perimeter of the camp, alert for ambushing guards or those trying to flee. Behind the chapel, four guerrillas had chased a Japanese into a drainage pipe. The Filipinos rolled grenades in at him from both sides. The resulting boom sounded like an artillery piece. At the south gate, Bolick came across one intrepid old American gal with wire cutters snipping the chain to let in a late-arriving recon team.

Small-arms fire burst from the trees east of the creek. The first paratroopers from B Company jogged in from the drop zone. The firing inside the camp swelled, then quickly subsided.

Paratroopers and guerrillas together began to track down the stragglers of the Japanese garrison hiding in the ravines and surrounding brush. Fewer enemy bodies than Bolick expected lay inside the wire. The majority of guards had been caught by surprise at their exercises; without weapons to stage a fight, most hotfooted it, barefoot, into the jungle. The ones who stayed behind to fight stood no chance against the firepower of the recon platoon and the anger of the guerrillas. The pillboxes, gun towers, and gates had all been neutralized in the raid's first minutes. With B Company's hundred and twenty troopers pouring into the camp, Los Baños had fallen.

The next step: hold it long enough to get everyone out.

Bolick checked his watch. 0715. Two hours was the predicted safety margin. After that, the Japanese Tiger Division to the south would get wind of the rescue. If they chose to come this way, every soldier and civilian in the camp would be doomed before the day was done.

Bolick tuned his ears west, keen for Shorty Soule's artillery attacking across the San Juan River down Highway 1. The detonations would signal that the trucks to haul the two thousand internees and six hundred soldiers to safety were on their way.

Bolick heard a different clamor.

Clacking, snorting, and spitting fumes, the first amtrac smashed through the barbed-wire fence, knocked it down, and roared into the camp.

Chapter Forty-two

THE SQUAD in Remy's amtrac wished him luck, then offloaded on San Antonio beach. With the rest of their platoon, a pair of 75-mm cannons, and the thirty guerrillas who'd greeted them ashore, the paratroopers dug in to defend the landing zone. Green marker smoke swirling around them, the amtracs put the water to their backs and powered out of the sand.

Remy rode alone with the driver in the second amtrac. The rest of 1st Battalion, three hundred soldiers, filled the column of amtracs behind him. In the transport out front, setting the snail's pace at 15 miles per hour, rode Major Willcox.

The camp lay two and a half miles south. The road wound past scattered bamboo huts, beneath leaning palms and clustered banyans. Filipinos lined the pavement, clutching babies, children by the hand, and goats on tethers. Few cheered outright the sight and fury of a mile-long column of American armored vehicles, roaring out of the bay to take back their own from the Japanese. The area remained occupied territory, and *makipili* informants had yet to be reckoned with.

The long column charged past rice paddies and the lanes of plantations where nights before Remy had walked with Tal. The land appeared quiet and unwary in the morning cool. No reports had come in from the camp's raiders; no one in the convoy had any idea how the assault was progressing. If the camp's guards were fighting back, or killing the internees in desperation, the natives and the countryside showed no evidence.

Five minutes into the convoy, still a mile from camp, Willcox's lead amtrac approached a shanty close to the road. The little house stood on its own at the edge of a small orchard. With the column bearing down, the front door swung open. A Japanese spurted out, bare-chested, pulling up his trousers and gripping a samurai saber. One of Willcox's team manned the .30-caliber and cut the running soldier down before he could disappear into the fruit trees. Remy's driver shouted over his shoulder, "For that fella not to hear us comin', he musta' been *busy*!"

The column surged down the forest road where Remy and others had chopped firewood until they ate the carabao that hauled the wagon. Through the trees, the concrete pillars of the camp appeared, the wire invisible from this distance. No smoke rose above the buildings, and if there was gunfire it could not have been heard above the din of the vehicles. No one inside the fence ran for cover. Was the fighting over already? Was Tal there, was he safe? What had he done? In another minute, Remy would find out.

The amtracs bypassed the main road into the camp, to swing around and enter at the smaller, less protected north gate. A hundred yards from the perimeter, near the overgrown baseball fields of the college, a pair of guerrillas stepped out of the scrub. They flagged down the column. Willcox's amtrac halted and the major climbed down.

Both Filipinos carried ancient Lee-Enfield rifles, holdovers from the Great War. They pointed at the north gate and its twin guard towers. They were warning Willcox about the Japanese defending the gate.

Willcox trained his binoculars on the tower. He nodded to the guerrillas and climbed into his amtrac. His driver hit the gas before the Filipinos could get out of the road.

Willcox's boys manned the two machine guns. His driver showed no hesitation barreling for the closed gate. Remy's amtrac bellowed to keep pace; behind him the whole column spun tracks and rolled.

Thirty yards from the gate, Willcox's .50-caliber loosed a burst into the tower. The wooden structure disintegrated into pinwheeling splinters. A body tumbled out; another corpse stayed behind in the shattered remains. Willcox's gunner backed off the trigger. The guerrillas were mistaken; the guards in the tower were already dead.

Remy recognized the riddled Japanese on the ground: the scarred veteran Ito, who wanted Remy to remember him when the war was over.

Willcox's amtrac rammed the gate, snapping the barbed wire, crunching the frame into shards. Bits of post and concrete were dragged into the camp by the vehicle's nose.

The column slowed. Remy, returning after four days gone, rode on the high steel back of the amtrac, searching for signs of the worst. His heart climbed his ribs for the first moments inside the wire. Internees bustled among the many barracks, gathering their belongings, soldiers walked with rifles shouldered, children skipped at the knees of the big paratroopers, who gave them candy and rations. Remy let go his held breath. There had been no massacre.

Willcox rode past the infirmary. He halted the convoy with only a half dozen amtracs inside the fence, then dismounted. The battalion followed suit, flooding the camp with soldiers. Remy patted his driver on the back and climbed down. Willcox's three hundred troops formed up quickly before heading to the camp's south gate. Their mission was to intercept the leading elements of the Tiger Division if they came to stop the rescue.

Internees approached Remy, a hundred or more. Since slipping under the wire, he'd gobbled three meals a day. He'd seen no one but bronze American soldiers, well-cared-for warriors. The people milling about him looked so badly worn. Their sudden liberation did not fatten or heal them, and did not raise the dead. Remy rebuked himself for those moments over the past few days when he'd failed to remember he was one of them. He swore he would never again forget the barbed wire, bamboo coffins, white rice, Mac, the guard Ito, and how awful Los Baños had been.

"It's Remy," the crowd said.

"He brought the cavalry."

Remy stepped into their midst. He took down his fedora, with nothing else he could do to honor them in greeting. They touched him and shouted to be recognized. Remy scanned faces, wading into their number.

Over and over, he asked, "Anyone seen my boy?"

Chapter Forty-three

S HE WAS not in her window.

Tal wondered where she might be, but without concern. So long as Carmen was safe somewhere nearby, they'd find each other.

Did she know he was back in the camp? Did she see him run? Tal was eager to hold her, but he didn't want Carmen or Yumi inside the wire until the fighting had stopped. The raid was twenty minutes old, and paratroopers and guerrillas kept ferreting Japanese out of hiding places around the camp, in the nearby jungle. None of the guards were taken prisoner, every one who didn't hightail it was killed on sight. A squadron of twin-tailed P-38s circled the treetops, scanning for more enemies.

Carmen could wait a little longer. Bolick handed Tal a smoke grenade.

"Go to that barracks across from the infirmary," the big radioman told him. "See if you can get 'em moving. If they won't, use this."

Tal jogged off with the smoke canister. The weighty Colt and black harness at his shoulder labeled him as one of the fighters come to free the camp.

Everywhere, internees packed their belongings, those meager and precious bits that had kept them alive. A setting of china plates, a Sunday blouse, books, secret diaries, a preserved pair of Keds, these went into battered suitcases and muslin sacks. The internees could not conceive of a world outside the wire where these items would not be needed.

The American soldiers ordered and pleaded with them to hurry, but the people of Los Baños were insistent about packing or eating their last cans of Spam.

The paratroopers handed out rations, crackers, cheese packets, and Hershey bars to every internee who approached. The soldiers took kisses from women young and old. They carried stretchers out of the hospital. One soldier lifted his shirt to show his own ribs so an older fellow would not feel embarrassed by his emaciated state.

Bascom, with a dozen boys from No. 11 in tow, caught up with Tal.

"We made it!" the Irishman shouted. Judging by his khaki shorts, he'd fallen into the paddies again last night. The two hugged. The others crowded around. Bascom poked Tal's Colt .45.

"Where'd you get that?"

"Bolick gave it to me."

"Damn it. I didn't get one. You shoot anybody with it?"

"No. Almost."

"Too bad." Bascom indicated the smoke grenade. "Where you going with that?"

"Barracks One. I've got to make the people in there get out."

One of the boys asked, "You gonna use it?"

"If I have to. You guys all packed?"

"The hell with this place," Santana answered. "I'm not takin' anything outta here but me."

Bascom said to Tal, "We'll come with you."

The boys walked in a gang through the camp, Tal and his Colt in the lead. Sporadic gunfire from the ravine and Boot Creek punctured the morning; the last hiding Japanese were being rooted out. The boys strutted undaunted. They saluted passing soldiers and got salutes in return.

Barracks 1 stood near the north gate. Married couples

lived here, most of them older. In the past month, many of the funerals called over the loudspeaker had come from this building.

"Wait out here," Tal told the boys. He took the bamboo steps in one bound. Sounds of chaos and elation crisscrossed in the long hall. Tal poked his head in a dozen cubicles. In each, animated folks examined their few possessions to pick which would go with them to freedom. Some husbands argued with wives, others sat resigned on cots while the women decided. Many ate out of tins they'd squirreled away.

In each room, Tal said the same: "Hey, folks, the soldiers say the Japs have a full division just ten miles south. We gotta go." In different words, he heard the same response from every couple: Welcome back, son. Hold your horses, we'll be along.

Tal lifted a bench from the common room and set it in the barracks hallway. He placed the smoke grenade on a high rafter where none of the folks could get to it. Before he could take the pin in his fingers, a woman tugged at his shorts.

"Shoot him!" she said, pulling Tal down off the bench. "Shoot him, he's getting away!"

Confused, Tal reached for the Colt. "Where? Where is he?"

A guard, hiding in the barracks? Did he have a gun? Tal yanked the big pistol out of the holster while the woman dragged him by the shirtsleeve to the back door. Could he kill a guard? Maybe he'd just tackle him, let one of Gusto's guerrillas do the rest. With his thumb, Tal dropped the hammer on the Colt. He wanted to shake loose from the woman. He hurried alongside her down the hall, not sure what he was about to do.

"There!" She pointed between barracks. Only two people were on the path, Mr. Lazlo and his wife. The old hoarder carried a hefty suitcase in each hand, his wife lugged away a trunk and their fat Siamese cat.

"Shoot him, boy," the woman insisted.

"Ma'am." Tal peeled her grip from his shirt. "Get ready to leave."

He eased the hammer and holstered the Colt. Tal left the unhinged woman staring after Lazlo. In the hall, he stood on the bench and set off the smoke canister. Tossing the bench aside, he hustled out to Bascom and the boys. They cheered Tal's exit, gray billows spilling behind him. The boys wanted to watch the old folks flee. Curses searched for Tuck through the smoke but were quickly exchanged for coughs. Tal cupped his hands and shouted into the building, "I *told* y'all to get out!" The boys found this a grand, final prank.

Tal stepped away from the gushing smoke. The first folks stumbled through the back door, clutching what they could gather. Tal went to ask Bolick for another job. The boys from No. 11 fell in step.

P-38s zoomed over the camp, so low the boys raised their hats and hands to the pilots. When the planes blared away south, another clatter replaced them, this time a grinding, metallic whine from the tarmac outside the camp.

A volley of gunfire shrieked from the roadway. Tal and the others dived to their bellies. At the north gate, a guard tower disintegrated, chewed up by a five-second burst from a machine gun as powerful as any strafing plane. A body jackknifed out of the watchtower. Tal's chin dropped to the ground when the gate burst apart. A vehicle he'd never seen the likes of broke through. The colossal thing had tracks, squealed and rolled like a tank, but was open in the middle. A dozen soldiers rode it behind a pair of mounted machine guns, one of the barrels smoking.

Following this clanking transport, with shreds of the busted gate hanging off it, more just like it rumbled into the camp. The column stretched past the weedy ball fields and Baker Hall outside the wire.

On the second machine, alone except for the driver, stood Remy.

Tal flew off the ground. The armored tractors outpaced him running full tilt. He left the others behind, dodging internees drawn to the tarmac and the new flush of soldiers flooding into the camp. Remy dismounted, folks flocked around him. He'd taken off his fedora. Remy dropped it when Tal flew into his arms.

Both laughed loudly, pounding each other's back. Remy held Tal at arm's length to look him up and down. Someone handed Remy his hat off the ground.

"You're all right, then."

"Yeah," Tal said. "You, too."

"I'll be better when we're outta this place." Remy latched an arm across Tal's shoulders. Together they turned to the crowd. No one had any idea where he and Remy had gone four days ago or why they'd returned with the raiders. Tal wanted to announce what the two of them had done, that they hadn't just escaped, they'd brought back the army. They were heroes. He forgave Remy everything.

Lucas stepped up. The committeeman embraced Tuck and Remy equally.

"Well." Lucas laughed. "I'm now a big believer in the Tuck boys. Welcome back."

Lucas turned to address the internees, shouting above the idling transports for the people to head to the ball fields and load up. Tal and Remy ducked away.

Tal whispered, "I reckon it's time to go fetch the girls."

They walked the road along the fence. Soldiers swarmed in every direction trying to herd internees to the amtracs. Tal and Remy traded quick versions of their different adventures, Tal with the guerrillas, Remy at Airborne headquar-

ters. Tal described big Bolick, the soldier who'd given him
the Colt. Remy claimed his most terrifying moments had
come this morning before dawn, expecting a Japanese patrol
to nab them on the bay, not knowing what sort of battle was
going to be waged for the camp, and fretting about Tal.

"I made my peace," he said, "just so long as you were
okay."

"I'm good, Remy."

His father indicated the .45. "You any good with that?"

"Don't know. I pulled it out twice. Haven't fired it yet."

"Let's hope you don't have to. For now, take it in hand."

Tal slid the Colt from its holster. He and Remy passed
through the main gate, where the concrete pillars had
been sundered by explosions. Both dirt pillboxes had been
breached and ruined. Japanese bodies sprawled on the
pavement and into the cratered grass, uniforms shredded.
They crossed the field along the rim of the long, freshly dug
trench.

"Let's keep it quiet," Remy said. "We don't know what's
waitin' for us."

Again, Tal pulled back the hammer on the pistol.

Chapter Forty-four

I N THE hall, Carmen waited for the footsteps to arrive. One pair of soles pounded the stairs fast, climbing with frantic hurry. On the landing, Papa waited, too, and Yumi outside her room in the opposite wing.

Furious breaths rose with the echoes of the rushing feet. Then Carmen knew the feet were bare, they slapped the treads, and she was not surprised when Kenji skidded on the landing, past Papa, running for her.

Naked save for the loincloth, Kenji bolted down the hall. Long yellow arms and legs and heaving yellow chest halted in front of her. A pistol filled one hand.

"Where did you get that?" she asked.

"The Americans." He panted and pointed through the walls to the camp as if Carmen did not know. "I ran . . ." he labored to rein in his breathing ". . . ran here. There's bodies everywhere." Kenji showed the gun to himself as though surprised to be holding it, then looked to Carmen. "I picked it up."

Behind him, Yumi returned to her room. Papa watched from the landing.

"Hide me."

"Come in."

Carmen held the curtain for Kenji, the first time she had done that for anyone entering her room. She followed him inside.

"Did anyone see you?"

"I don't know." His galloping breath slowed. "I went

through the main gate with others. They ran for the jungle. I came here."

"I mean did the Americans see you?"

"I don't think so."

"Stay back."

Carmen crept to the window, dropping to her knees to reveal only her eyes and forehead. She did not see the boy. Yes, Kenji, she thought, you ran and the boy ran faster. He will run here next.

Fighting raged around the camp. Filipinos barefoot and shod spread across the grounds, firing guns and swinging bolos at the stripped Japanese. American soldiers moved with efficient malice against the guards' defenses, as merciless in their firepower and tactics as the guerrillas were in their wrath. Many guards who'd been on duty when the attack started held their ground and died on it, others mocked their Bushido and scampered away.

Timid Papa put his head inside the curtain. Carmen pulled in her head from the window.

Papa indicated Kenji. "What is he doing here?"

"Hiding. Trying to save his life. What do you want?"

"I don't know what to do."

"Run away. I told you. Go to another island. Change your name. Never admit you were here. Leave her. She is going to die."

"Will you speak to the Americans?"

Carmen reached to her pocket. She held up the Songu tag for Papa to see.

"No."

Papa, sickened and lost, dropped his eyes from the wooden tag. His swollen head withdrew from the room. Down the long, empty corridor, which for almost a year had told Carmen of soldiers coming and going, Papa ran. To Mama, or away from the old woman, Carmen could not care.

Kenji stood unmoving. He, too, waited for instructions from her. Strange, this turnaround.

Behind her, the sounds of fighting rattled the morning sun and easy breeze. Gunsmoke and dust drifted in. She turned from Kenji to get on her knees again and watch the battle.

A great gout of flame and dirt jetted high above the main gate; the noise and concussion battered her walls, shaking the plaster. Behind her, Kenji squeaked. Another explosion rocked the main gate. Carmen took the chance to stand and lean out far, to see the Japanese killed in and around their pillboxes from American shells. She searched quickly for the boy. She wanted to call for him, see him fashioned like a genie out of the smoke of the battle.

Carmen returned herself to the room.

"Kenji."

He did not have his finger over the trigger. He held the gun like a brick.

"Yes."

"I have nowhere to hide you in this room. Go across the hall. Don't let anyone see you. Not even Yumi."

"What will you do?"

I will leave, she thought, when the boy comes.

"Go," she said. This sounded selfless and brave, as if it were not for him to know what she might do.

Kenji slipped a hand behind the drape. He halted to look back on her.

Carmen clamped her lips. For so long she had not told Kenji that he could never save her, only Songu. And Songu died today. A few more minutes of silence were all that was needed. She pushed Kenji through the black curtain.

Carmen propped her tatami against the wall beneath the window, some small protection against a stray bullet. Dropping low as before, she put her eyes above the sill to watch over the camp a last time, and to keep an eye out for the boy.

The fighting moved outside the camp, flaring up when the Americans found guards hiding in the ravine, in drainage pipes, breaking out of cover into a run. The commandant's big sedan, the one he would have whisked Yumi away in, had left without her.

In minutes, Carmen saw Tal walking with a crowd of boys. The Irish lad, Bascom, was with him. Where were they going? She followed Tal and his pack to a barracks at the north end of the camp. He disappeared alone into the bamboo building. The fighting inside the wire had eased, the gunshots became erratic, mostly outside the fence in the ravine and creek. The Americans had turned from raiders into hunters. Another long minute passed, until a gray cloud boiled from the barracks where the Tuck boy had gone. Old men and women poured from the doors and windows ahead of the smoke. Tal stood outside with the boys, waving their arms at the people evacuating.

A flight of American fighter planes swept in low over the camp. In the wake of their engines, gunfire rattled from the north gate, close to the smoking barracks. The guard tower there fell apart like a matchstick house. Carmen peered through the rising smoke, beyond the gate, to the game fields where she had never played or walked. An enormous column of odd vehicles, steely like tanks, rushed the gate, smashed into it. The vehicles charged into the camp, deafening and powerful, loaded with hundreds more American soldiers.

The first tank through the broken gate trailed wire and wood off its nose like whiskers. Remy rode erect on the second. Remy did not see Tal darting to catch him.

Remy climbed down. Father and son reunited. Carmen stayed low in her window, patient now that she would be with them. She imagined the stories they would tell her, disputing each other, competing for her approval. She would favor Remy in order to annoy Tal, then laugh with him when she admitted doing so.

The two came her way alone. She watched them exit the camp through the main gate, past the many Japanese corpses and the new trench. Like Kenji, Tal carried a gun. They walked out of sight behind her building.

She dressed quickly in the black slacks and pink top Remy had bought her six weeks ago. She carried her sandals to sneak away. Carmen said goodbye to her room, wished it to hell, and left quietly under the curtain.

Chapter Forty-five

REMY HAD not seen the new trench before, it had been dug while he was away from the camp. The gouge in the earth was deep enough to hold hundreds of bodies. The mass grave would have been shallow and temporary, an ugly contrast to the permanence of slaughter. Remy and Tal both sped away from it.

At the rear door to the animal husbandry building, Tal moved in front. The boy was nineteen and no soldier, but the gun in his hand made this the order of entrance into the building. Remy tiptoed behind the boy up the stairwell.

They reached the first landing with no sound above them. Before heading up the second flight, Tal raised the pistol in both hands. The gun was harder and more menacing than any part of the frail boy, looking wrong at the end of his reedy arms. Remy followed, peering up into the empty stairwell, listening for a boot, alert for a hand on the railing, any hint that they were not alone.

Tal kept the pistol ready while rising to the third-floor landing. The old *makipilis'* mattress lay there, abandoned in the corner. The desk stood empty of papers. Only Yumi's wooden tag hung on its peg.

The boy moved without sufficient caution for Remy, striding across the landing to the hallway that held Carmen's room. He lapped a hand over Tal's shoulder.

"Hold on, boy."

Tal shrugged from under Remy's fingers, too much trust in a gun.

Remy did not know how to stop him, or if he should. He had no sense of how this was playing out, no feel for the hand dealt him. This was Tal's game, and it would be his luck. Remy accepted this.

He hung back, not to crowd the boy. Tal jutted the pistol ahead of him. Where was Carmen, why wasn't she greeting them? Was she gone? Had the girl lost faith that they'd come back for her, had she lit out on her own? Worse, was she hurt? Had the Japanese caught her, sniffed out that she was an informant working for the guerrillas? Was she dead? In the five days Remy had been away from Los Baños, the Japanese had time to dig another massacre pit. They could have done much else.

Remy had a bad feeling, the same one he'd experienced dealing the tenth solitaire.

He spun on his heels to a noise behind him. Tal swung the weight of the pistol. In the opposite wing, down the dark hall, Yumi dashed out of the shadows wearing the emerald slacks Remy had bought her. She lifted her small arms and ran like a child. Trailing Yumi, also dressed in an outfit Remy had bought in Anos, came brown Carmen.

Yumi leaped into Remy's arms, circling his neck, crossing ankles behind his back. Remy hugged her and through her black hair watched Carmen step into his son's arms.

Yumi babbled in Korean. She shivered in Remy's grasp.

Carmen said, "We have to go."

Tal had waited a long time to hold the girl again and had risked much to do it. His embrace pleased her, but she pulled away, her mind on something else, urgent. Tal did not release her as she wished. He reeled her in for a kiss, which the girl made short. Remy reached behind his waist to unlock Yumi's clutch.

"Come on, darlin'," he said, "get down."

Carmen stepped back from Tal, holding his hand to

tow him to the stairs. In pink and black, she appeared like any teenage Filipina. Tal, haggard, dirty, and as sleepless as Remy, looked like the one being rescued, though he held a gun.

Yumi chattered in Remy's ear, gratitude or curses. With both hands behind his neck, he pried at her clasp. He bent to lower her feet to the landing.

Yumi tightened, seizing him. Remy pushed at her ribs, her little breasts, to make her let go. Against his cheek, her head raked from side to side, no.

Above his shoulder, one of her arms tensed. She pointed behind him. Remy straightened. His head turned as she screamed, *"Yamete!"*

In the hall to Carmen's room, a tall Japanese in a loin-cloth advanced, a handgun lifted. At a dozen paces, the snub barrel was aimed at Tal's back.

Remy, with Yumi hanging off him, could only leap in front of the bullet.

Chapter Forty-six

T AL WHIRLED and fired before he aimed. The big Colt jumped in his hand. He missed.

The Japanese advanced and shot again. Tal tensed for a bullet. The near-naked soldier's second round thudded into the wall. Tal ripped free of Carmen to bring his other hand up to the pistol grip. He fired two-fisted like Bolick had shown him. The .45 slug knocked the guard off his bare feet. Tal squeezed off one more shot; this bullet ran high. The naked soldier hit the floor, his gun spun away from him. Yumi tried to stop Remy's crumple.

Tal kept the Colt riveted on the soles of the downed man's feet. Was he dead? Tal didn't know what to do next, go to the Japanese and check him? Remy was shot! Both girls wailed in despair and alarm. Tal risked a quick glance at his father. Remy had fallen but not past one knee. His right arm hung limp, his left clutched against his chest. In the back of his tatty vest, above the right shoulder blade, a neat hole had been drilled. His fedora had come loose, tilted on his head. Yumi fluttered hands around Remy.

"Be quiet!" Tal barked. He threw his attention back to the Japanese, seeing him over the short barrel of the Colt, smelling gunpowder.

One of the soldier's knees bent, the leg drew in. Tal bore down behind the gun.

Carmen pulled Yumi back from Remy, wrapping the little girl tight to stop her frantic flapping. Remy held himself up on the one knee.

Tal's pulse raced in his temples, in his raised hands.

"Remy?"

"Son of a bitch." Remy sounded winded.

"You all right?"

"Damn well hurts. You get him?"

"He's down. I don't think he's dead."

The girls helped Remy to his feet. He gasped and clung to his chest, though the hole was in his back. Painfully, with one hand, Remy straightened his hat. He hawked and spat a gob of blood.

"I think he nicked a lung."

The Japanese moaned. His pistol lay far from his hand; he showed no inclination to go after it. A dark wing of blood unfurled under him. Tal lowered the Colt. Carmen stepped toward the hall. Tal snagged her elbow.

"That's Toshiwara's interpreter."

"Yes."

"What's he doing here?"

"I was hiding him."

"Why?"

"He's a friend."

Remy hunched and leaned on Yumi. His eyes hid beneath the brim of his hat. Yumi clucked her tongue that Tal and Carmen should linger while Remy suffered.

Tal fumbled for a reply. "You what? You have a Japanese friend?"

"One."

"Then why'd he shoot Remy?"

"He didn't mean to. He was trying to shoot you." She flattened a palm to Tal's chest. "Stay here."

Carmen went to kneel beside the interpreter, opposite the puddle of his blood. She inspected his gunshot. The dim hall hid her whispers and his reply. Gently she cupped his left hand to lay it across his right chest, into the armpit. She pressed on his hand, to show him how to plug himself.

The gun nudged Tal to stride forward and find out how this Japanese came to be a friend to his girl.

From below, boots pounded in the stairwell. An American soldier shouted up, "Anyone there?"

"It's okay," Tal called down. "We're all right."

The footfalls slowed. "We're comin' up."

Carmen came back to Tal. He slid the gun into its holster to quiet it. Crimson stained her fingertips.

The soldiers below reached the second staircase. They came with a deliberate clatter of rifles and laden belts.

Tal walked to his father. He examined the punch in Remy's vest. Silk threads spiraled around the hole but he wasn't losing much blood. Under the fedora, Remy gritted his teeth in a drained face.

"That was my bullet, Remy."

"Mine now."

Yumi brushed Tal aside with a stream of mutters. Her arm around Remy's waist, she guided him down the first step. Carmen took Tal's hand. Three soldiers rounded the railing below.

"Everything all right, folks?"

"Yeah," grunted Remy, easing to the second stair.

"What was the shootin' about?" The soldiers eyed the two girls, unsure. One climbed to reach Remy. "Sir, you're hit." Instantly all three crouched in the stairwell, aware of some threat that had done this. Rifles came up, hawk eyes narrowed at the landing above them.

"It's all right," said Remy, waving a pained hand. Carmen raised hers, too, the bloodied one. Yumi ignored the soldiers and continued to press Remy down the stairs, annoyed and unintelligible.

Remy set a hand on one soldier's shoulder to move past

him. The trooper slipped under Remy's good shoulder to help Yumi get him down the stairs. The remaining two eyed Tal.

"Where'd you get the Colt, buddy?"

"Sergeant Bolick. He's recon."

"That Jap dead?"

Carmen said, "Yes."

The paratrooper's bronze face stayed expressionless. He asked Tal again, "Is he dead?"

"Yeah."

Both helmets bobbed. The men pivoted, their interest here waned, no Japs to kill. They clomped down the stairs.

Carmen laid a kiss on Tal's cheek. Below, Remy wheezed, making his way out of the building. The paratroopers stayed patient behind him and Yumi.

Tal cast a last glance at the hall where the Japanese lay dying.

"Time to go." He extended his hand the way he'd imagined he would.

Carmen reached into her pocket. She held out the Songu tag.

"One last time," she said, "bring this back to me."

She did not put her hand into Tal's palm, but the piece of wood.

Chapter Forty-seven

N O, SIR," Bolick said. "Not a thing."

The three officers standing around him, and Bolick, too, tuned their ears west to see if they might hear something from Soule's task force through the morning air.

Major Willcox made a sour face. So did Lieutenant Kraft and Lieutenant Colonel Thibeaux, the officer in charge of the fifty-four amtracs.

Kraft said, "Shorty ain't comin', Major. Not in time, anyway."

High overhead, P-38s, 40s, and 51s circled. The fighter planes would be the first to react if the Tiger Division made a move against the American raiders. So far, the planes had made a few low-level dives to strafe fleeing guards, then returned to their pattern. The fighters gave the paratroopers on the ground a security blanket, but what the soldiers really wanted to hear was the thump of Shorty Soule's artillery getting closer, then the rumble of 150 trucks rolling into camp to whisk them and the internees out of here. So far, none of the 188th's big guns had been fired close enough to be heard above the engines of the sentinel planes or the occasional croak and squeak from the surrounding jungle. The radio on Bolick's back had raised no one outside the barbed wire all morning.

Willcox asked Kraft, "Casualties?"

"Between recon and the battalion, two wounded. Two guerrillas killed and four wounded, all in the first minute. Nothing after that."

"The internees?"

"A few dings, that's all. The rest are fine."

The assault had gone off better than hoped. Bolick surveyed the camp from where he stood, on the grassy spot where the guards had been surprised in their exercises thirty minutes ago. The whole Japanese garrison had been either dispersed or eliminated. A hundred and fifty airborne troops were sorting through the camp trying to organize the stunned internees. Three hundred more held positions on the perimeter, blocking the roads into Los Baños, alert for a counterattack.

The only thing missing was their ride home, Shorty Soule's trucks.

Willcox pulled off his helmet to scratch his balding pate. Big Kraft rested his arms across the tommy gun hanging to his waist. Near the main gate, the guards' barracks was in flames. Tracers from the firefight with the guards had ignited the sawali walls and nipa roof. A wind from the south blew haze and sparks at the six amtracs that had roared into camp on the paved lane. The rest of the vehicles waited on the ball fields outside the smashed north gate.

Willcox replaced his helmet. "Shorty's not coming, boys."

Kraft and Bolick answered as if the observation belonged solely to the major.

"No, sir."

"All right. I made a decision. Lieutenant."

"Yes, sir."

"You empty the infirmary. Get every stretcher case and internee who can't walk onto the amtracs first. Load every vehicle. Tell all the folks they're allowed to take one piece of luggage. One, Lieutenant. They're going to try to talk you out of that."

"No worries, sir."

Willcox addressed Lieutenant Colonel Thibeaux next. Though the man was his superior officer, Major Willcox remained the soldier on the ground in charge of the rescue.

"Colonel, I figure we can get maybe fourteen hundred on your amtracs at a time. I want you to load every one of them with internees as soon as possible. When that's done, get your vehicles out of the camp and on the water pronto. You'll ferry the first group back to Mamatid, drop them off, then come back here to evacuate the ones left behind and us. I reckon two trips ought to do it."

Willcox didn't wait for the colonel's agreement. He continued with Kraft.

"Soon as the first wave takes off, I want the rest of the internees walking to San Antonio."

"That's three miles, Major."

"It is, and if these folks want to put Los Baños behind 'em they'll run it. You'll arrange security along the route. The battalion will withdraw and head to San Antonio behind you. We'll wait on the point for the colonel here to come back for us. Questions?"

"Loud and clear, sir."

Thibeaux, a blocky sort like Kraft but without the muscle, spoke up. His voice carried a Louisiana drip of honeysuckle.

"That's two trips total."

"You have a concern, Colonel?"

"I do. We got over two thousand folks on our hands. Not a one of 'em knew we were comin'. They're not exactly packed."

"How long 'til we can load 'em up?"

"I can't figure the last one climbing on before noon. By then the Japs are bound to have mortars and artillery in place to make those rides across the bay something we'd rather not have to face."

"Recommendation?"

"Do the first part of your plan. Load up all the stretchers and the lame, as many women and children as we can carry. I'll get them the hell out of here, you can count on it. You and your men escort the rest of the internees west. Link up with the task force and roll out on their trucks. That was the original plan and I still believe it's the safest and fastest way."

Willcox pursed his lips, considering. His eye rested on the burning Japanese barracks.

"Lieutenant?"

Kraft took his arms off the tommy gun.

"Sir."

"Get to loading the stretchers. Then load up the elderly, women, and children. Leave the able-bodied men for the second round."

Willcox nodded for the order to be executed, now. Kraft lit out.

"Colonel Thibeaux?"

"Major."

"Due respect, sir, but we're gonna go with my plan. Bolick here hasn't heard word one from the task force. I got no idea where they are or how far I'll have to walk my men and the internees to find 'em. I got no intel on the Tiger Division, where they are or what they're up to. You get your vehicles ready to roll, Colonel. I'll have the internees lined up and waiting for you."

Thibeaux licked his lips, pausing at being overruled. He had one last question.

"Due respect, Major, but how d'you intend to do that, exactly?"

"Sergeant Bolick?"

Bolick snapped rigid. He thought he'd been left out of the discussions.

"Sir."

"You a smoker?"

"No, sir."

"How'd you manage to survive a war without smoking?"

"I worry a lot, sir. Keeps me just as good company."

Willcox produced a silver Zippo. He pointed to the fire consuming the guards' barracks. Smoke coiled thick on the wind, blowing north. Internees in neighboring structures, fearful the flames would spread, herded toward the six parked amtracs, luggage in hand.

Willcox said, "Those folks have the right idea. Sergeant, take my lighter and head for the south end of the camp. Soon as the stretcher cases are on board, you enter those barracks there along the fence and torch 'em. The wind'll do the rest."

The major flipped the lighter to Bolick.

"That oughtta speed things along. Don't you think, Colonel?"

Chapter Forty-eight

REMY MADE it past the fresh trench, the Japanese corpses at the bunkers, and through the main gate before collapsing.

He labored for breath, dangling from the arms of Yumi and the nameless airborne soldier. Smoke from the guards' barracks made him cough. Some of his breath escaped from the perforation in his back.

The soldier left him sitting in the dirt with Yumi beside him to fetch a stretcher. The girl laid her hand over the hole in Remy's shoulder to block it but his exhalations felt like they were collecting inside him and he asked her to let it vent. She understood and pulled away her hand, a spot of blood on her palm. Remy fingered his chest to feel the nub of the bullet under the skin. The Japanese round had lacked the caliber to go all the way through him.

He tried shallow breaths to ease the stabbing inside his ribs. He couldn't move his right arm. The shoulder blade was shattered, no question. He fought dizziness and reached for Yumi to come where he could see her.

"Where's Tal?" The girl rattled her head and shrugged. "Tal," he repeated. "Carmen? Where are they?"

Yumi lifted a small finger at the animal husbandry building. The boy and Carmen were still in there? Doing what? The sudden thought struck Remy that the dying Japanese soldier might have revived somehow, enough to grab his gun and shoot Tal, Carmen, or both. Carmen was hiding him. Had Remy and Tal walked into an ambush? Did Carmen set them up? Where was Tal?

Remy had no answers and too much pain. He couldn't think clearly, clouded by the ache in his torso, the wreckage of his right shoulder. The first tendrils of panic wrapped around his throat; his breath grew shorter. He glanced around for his boy, knowing he wasn't there. He jumbled his legs under him to stand.

Wordlessly, Yumi put her arms around Remy's rib cage, easing him back to the ground. She knelt in front of him, laying her head to his chest, putting her small ear over the bullet protruding inside him. She held him and listened to him breathe. "Okay," she whispered, "okay."

The soldier hustled back with a stretcher and another trooper. Yumi removed Remy's fedora. Once he lay back, his view fixed on the sky. Planes circled, smoke from the burning soldiers' barracks hazed the blue. Exhaustion heaped on Remy like shovels of dirt, catching up to him after days of motion, nights of the unknown, finishing with a bullet hole and a wheezing spout in his back. Two soldiers lifted the stretcher. Remy tried to sit up against being off his feet and carted away. Where was his son? He wouldn't leave without Tal. Yumi, with only the weight of one hand, held him down.

The stretcher jostled his shoulder blade. A whimper slipped through his teeth. The moan convinced Remy to surrender. No reserve was left to him, on his back was how he would leave Los Baños. He considered his luck and the ill omen of the tenth game. Was being shot his price for losing, had he paid in full? Remy closed his eyes and asked his fortune to let this be it, collect no more, and not touch Tal. The boy had his own luck, judge him by that and not mine, asked Remy.

His eyes stayed closed. He was surprised to find his left hand clutching Yumi and that he was crying. Voices along the way through the camp called "Remy" and "Tuck." He opened his eyes for none, did not let go of Yumi to acknowledge them with his good arm. She wiped the tears off his cheek, allowing Remy to leave the camp with a brave face. The last of Los Baños slid away behind his lids. He opened them only when the stretcher was rested in the baseball field outside the north gate. Remy raised his head. On all sides, amtracs blocked his view. His stretcher lay at the steel rear of one, in line with many stretchers, with more being delivered across the trampled field. Faces bloated by beriberi or emaciated grinned at him, flat on their own backs, borne out of the infirmary in time to save their lives. Maybe a hundred others milled about, all of them elderly and frail, holding suitcases or bundles tied to sticks like hobos. None of the tailgates had been dropped, though the engines cranked for departure.

"You're gonna be all right, sir," said the soldier who'd been in the stairwell and stayed with Remy until now. "Hang in there." The trooper patted Remy's good side.

"Do me a favor, son?" Remy regretted how weak he sounded.

"Sure thing."

"Check on my boy. Talbot Tuck. Make sure he got out of that building. Get him on a ride out of here."

"Will do, sir. Rest easy."

The soldier turned away. Yumi rapped knuckles on Remy's chest, drawing a wince.

"Carmen," she called to the troopers. "Carmen okay."

"The girl," Remy added, smarting, "the Filipina. Her name's Carmen. Her, too."

Both soldiers gave a thumbs-up. They waded into the sea of internees gathering around the idling amtracs.

Remy lay back. He wished for the deck of cards he'd long carried in his vest pocket. He would play another game of solitaire, and another. Maybe peel some poker with the others on stretchers waiting for deliverance, or the codgers shambling around. He'd make the right arm work, and he'd win. This would summon Tal out of the crowd, safe. He could rest.

Yumi put on Remy's fedora. The battered felt hat swallowed her head to the tip of her nose. She did this for slapstick, to lift his spirits. Remy coughed, air bubbled out his back. He said to Yumi, "Okay," so she would stop trying to amuse him.

Soldiers moved among the amtracs, shouting orders to the internees. "One piece of luggage. Only one! You throw the rest away or we'll have to do it for you!" Complaints rose but not above the engines, the squeal of tailgates lowering. The field became littered with leather bags and woven *tampipis* set aside by the internees or tossed off the amtracs by soldiers. Finally, Remy was hefted up the ramp by two able-bodied internees. Yumi walked alongside, holding Remy's hand. "Who's she?" they asked. Remy answered, "She's coming with me." They did not object more.

Seven more stretchers were loaded on before the tailgate slammed shut. Yumi joined the driver and his gunner as the only ones on board sitting upright. The amtrac's engine shuddered under them. Remy and the other stretcher cases waited.

He lay gazing up, sniffing smoke. Were the amtracs overheating from idling so long? Far overhead, gray puffs rode past on a strong wind. Not the amtracs. The camp was on fire.

At last, the column lurched forward. Branches slid by overhead as the amtracs ratcheted up speed. Remy considered sitting up to glance over the gunwales, to say goodbye to the old dao tree in the distance, the only good and protective thing in the camp. He kept himself flat. Nothing in Los Baños, not even the old dao, was worth the effort. Instead, he watched Yumi. The others on their stretchers did not sit up either, like Remy, seeing enough glee on the face of the girl to satisfy their own leave-taking.

The convoy powered onto the dirt track leading to San Antonio. Palms shaded the way, exhaust fumes and roiled dust swept over Remy from the amtracs in front. Cheers from villagers popped up beside the road. A bouquet flew in over the gunwales, landing on the chest of the old woman on the stretcher beside Remy. She held the flowers to her nose with a shrunken, happy face. Yumi waved to the villagers like a beauty queen.

The tractors rolled into a forested stretch. Remy pulled his hand from Yumi's to rub at the film of dust settling in his sockets. A different sound, sharper than the squeak of treads or the rumble of engines, made the little girl duck beside his stretcher. Another *ping* struck the armored flank of the amtrac.

The gunner heaved himself behind the big .50-caliber up front. He swung the machine gun into play but did not fire. The die-hard Japanese in the hills taking potshots at the convoy quieted down. Yumi slipped her hand back into Remy's. She sat tall under the brim of his fedora for the other internees on their stretchers to see and be assured.

At the bay, the amtracs slid into the water with little hesitation. Yumi stood amazed and pointing, chattering in Korean to the driver, probably warning him they were driving into the water. The ride changed immediately from bouncing on land to a softened glide, the engine growl became a burble. One by one, the internees on stretchers sat up; some looked as if this was their first time upright in days. Every misshapen face, swollen or drawn, grew enthralled with their floating tank. The woman clutching the bouquet said, "Oh, my." Yumi would not let Remy lie flat. She tugged him to a sitting position.

The amtracs plowed into the water three abreast, Remy's vehicle in the center of the second rank. Behind him, guerrillas and soldiers on San Antonio beach raised bolos and rifles to the rescued internees. The sight swelled Remy's hurting chest. He coughed again. When he wiped his chin, blood marred the back of his hand. He wanted to lie back. He fought for every breath against the fluid leaking into his damaged lung. He lowered to his elbows. Yumi caught him, careful of the hole in his back. She climbed on the stretcher to prop him up. Remy leaned against the girl.

The rest of the amtracs dunked themselves; the defenders of the point cheered them into the water. Three miles south, behind the trees, the burning camp belched smoke into the morning. A few hours ago, these fifteen hundred internees bobbing on the bay with Remy were slated to be annihilated. Some of them knew it, some suspected, all feared it. Now they paddled away together on a slow steel flotilla. For the sick folks in the amtrac with Remy, the whirlwind of their rescue had not faded. They beamed at one another, at Remy, and at the distancing land as though it might never fade.

The convoy churned in its long procession away from the shoreline. Another ninety minutes to Mamatid lay ahead. Remy considered himself finished. He did not know where Tal was. He could not do nor influence anything. Instead, he hoped, a sensation he'd not had in years, and felt it oddly satisfying.

He said to Yumi, "Let me lie down."

Chapter Forty-nine

FIRE ENGULFED the southern third of the camp. All of Vatican City was burning. A wind whipped up by the heat carried sparks to neighboring structures, igniting them in turn. Flames sprouted in the nipa roofs of the butcher shop, the garage, and No. 11.

The camp was being deserted ahead of the fire. Internees crowded through the main gate, hauling what belongings they could carry. Soldiers walked alongside or hurried through the last buildings calling for stragglers. Guerrillas were now nowhere to be seen; they'd vanished to their barrios soon after the initial assault on the wire.

Barracks 12 would go up in a few more minutes. Tal hurried to his room. He heaved aside the bunk where Mac had died, where he'd slept above his father. Tal dug up the floor plank and scooped the crystal radio from its hole. Ignoring his trunk and every scant possession, he left the barracks beneath smoke ghosting in the rafters.

Outside, a soldier approached, no older than Tal. He was the one who'd helped Remy down the stairwell.

"Hey. I been lookin' for you. Your old man's gonna be all right."

"Where is he?"

The trooper pointed beyond the fence, at the immense convoy of amtracs pulling away from the ball fields. "There he goes. He had that little cutie with him."

"Yumi."

"Whatever. Anyway, he said for me to make sure you're good. You good?"

"Fine."

"He mentioned another gal. Filipina."

Tal bit his lip.

"I'll leave that one to you," the soldier said. "Get out of here, pal. The sooner the better." The soldier grinned at him like an equal, for Tal wore a weapon. He hurried off to other duties.

Tal did not join the exodus from the camp, but went to stand below Carmen's window. He had no reason to be here other than this spot was close to her and he wanted the last minutes, the dregs of time with her. He considered shouting up to her, but for what? She'd made her choice to stay behind. Calling her name through the smoke would not change her mind. He'd said what he could already.

Let him die.

Behind him, the sawali of No. 11 began to crackle and lift. Embers drizzled around Tal.

"Tuck!"

Bolick approached. The sergeant raised a meaty hand in greeting, the field radio across his back.

"You still here?" Bolick called.

"Yeah."

The big sergeant ambled up. "What're you standin' around for? Everything okay?" Bolick looked in Tal's hands and distracted himself. "Hey, what you got there?"

Tal showed him the radio.

"That's a crystal set. You make that? Does it work?"

"My father made it with a friend. It works."

"All that time, you hid this from the Japs." Bolick whistled when he took the set to examine it. "How 'bout that, we're both radiomen. Hey, you said you had to get to someone when the raid started. How'd that go?"

Tal unbuckled the harness of the Colt. While he was grateful for the gun—it had saved his life—he could not hand back to Bolick the memory of shooting it.

"Here."

Bolick swapped Tal the radio. He dropped the magazine out of the pistol's grip.

"You fired two rounds."

Tal nodded.

"You hit anything?"

"With one."

"Kill him?"

"No."

Bolick slid in the magazine. He stuffed the Colt in his web belt and tossed the holster over his shoulder. "He didn't get far with a forty-five round in him. How're you feelin'?"

"I'm thinking on it. How long 'til the army comes back here?"

Bolick wiped a sleeve across his brow. "Don't know, kiddo. Could be a couple of days, maybe weeks. Depends on the Japs. Right now, we gotta go."

"Weeks?"

"I said I don't know. Come on. Say goodbye."

Tal glanced at the flaring camp. He gauged the destruction, the force of the place's emptiness. He did not look up to Carmen's window, and did not say goodbye.

Beside Bolick, he walked to the main gate. Around him, the last internees filed out. Soldiers showed off Japanese flags, guns, caps, personal items, any plunder they could nab before leaving Los Baños. Two priests carried chalices and ciboria they'd salvaged from the chapel. One large soldier lugged a bundle wrapped in a white sheet, a corpse from the infirmary.

Outside the gate, at the spot where Mr. Clemmons had been gunned down, Tal turned for a final look. He was familiar with every inch of the camp, every barb in the fence. He wished he could stand in Carmen's high window to watch the camp burn to the ground. He would hold her in the glow and heat, and later wash the smell of smoke from her hair.

The interpreter would die. Or he would not. Either way, Carmen said she'd stay with him until it was decided, then go to the jungle with the guerrillas. She'd be safe, and wait for Tal to come back. She told him, Go now.

Let him die.

No.

Why not?

Because he did not let me die.

She held Tal on the landing. Behind them in the hall, the interpreter moaned.

Finally they kissed. Carmen retreated into the hall. When she turned away from him in his memory, Tal turned on the road to go from the camp.

Chapter Fifty

T HE TUCK kid seemed a little spooked over shooting a Japanese. Bolick patted the boy's shoulder, complimented the clever crystal radio again. He slowed to let the boy walk ahead, to give him some space for his thoughts.

A quarter mile out of the camp, a pair of diced-up Japanese corpses lay beside the road. The bodies had been shot, then boloed in a grisly fashion. All the limbs on each plus the heads hung by tendons. Most of the marching internees averted their gaze. A few strode right up to take a closer look. The ones who turned away, Bolick thought, they're missing the point. The others got it. Those two Japanese were dead long before the last cut. For a while to come in the Philippines, this was what healing was going to look like.

The road ran past a railroad station bombed to bits, then hamlets of bamboo and concrete block. Locals handed out fruit and vegetables. Some provided latrines for the scrawny internees whose stomachs weren't dealing well with the surge of rations and chocolate given them by the raiders.

Many of the internees wore items of clothing that stood out against their tatters and sun-bleached outfits. Polished shoes, a white skirt or blouse, a fresh shirt, an unbattered straw hat, some bit of frippery they'd kept tucked away over the years just for this moment. They were so thin, even though these were the strongest ones, who'd let the others ride out while they legged it to San Antonio.

On the edge of a village one mile from the camp, an old man and woman were roped to a coconut tree. A crowd of

Filipinos flung tomatoes and mangoes at them. The woman's head had been shaved, the symbol for sleeping with the enemy, but she was too old for this. The man, gray and limp against his bonds, wore a sign around his neck, *"makipili."* His splattered face drooped. He was mortified, ill, or both. The old woman howled in Tagalog at the flingers and jeerers. The Tuck boy stopped to gaze before moving on. Bolick thought this a waste of food.

Soldiers pitched in to help the internees carry their parcels and luggage. The long procession drew isolated fire from high caves and headlands but no one was hit. The paratroopers trained their guns when passing these hot spots, firing once in a while to keep the Japanese heads down. When a bullet cut through the leaves over Bolick's head, a nun in front of him ditched her bags and executed a perfect drop and roll into the weeds. No one else twitched. The Tuck boy helped the sister to her feet.

By 1100 hours, the internees and soldiers reached San Antonio. The spit of land was treeless, exposed to sun and the warm bay breeze. The sandy soil had been mashed by the fifty-four amtracs. A hill of luggage and packages mounted at the water's edge; these possessions would be loaded last, after every internee was safely on board an amtrac. The people complained at being separated from their belongings. None of the soldiers took notice. They had other issues.

The two hours on San Antonio beach were going to be the most vulnerable time of the raid. Even with fighter planes circling overhead, if the Japanese counterattacked before the amtracs returned from Mamatid, the result would be a bloodbath. Four hundred soldiers couldn't hope to defend this open beachhead with their backs to the bay against an onslaught from the Tiger Division. Add to that the chaos and panic from six hundred civilian internees.

Big Lieutenant Kraft took over. He dispersed the troops

into the surrounding terrain to thicken the perimeter already guarded by Marking's Fil-American guerrillas. The internees sat on the sand in clumps, searching the lake. Jubilant and protesting, they were plainly oblivious to their peril.

Before Bolick could join the defenses around the point, Major Willcox beckoned him and his radio over.

"No word from the task force, I assume," the major said.

"Not a peep, sir."

"All right. Crank it up. I want to make contact."

Bolick slid the heavy radio off his back. "Shorty Soule's not an easy man to get hold of, Major."

"Not him." Willcox aimed a finger west over the brown shoreline. An L-4 artillery aircraft, a two-seater Cub, puttered along the coast. "Him."

Bolick set the radio in the sand to open the metal face. The battery was good, he charged it every night with the hand generator. He extended the antenna. Willcox removed his helmet to slip on the headset. The radio's tubes warmed.

"Go ahead, sir."

"Lima Four, Lima Four," Willcox intoned into the mike. "This is Jackpot One. Do you read?"

Willcox repeated this call while Bolick flipped through the frequencies the L-4 would likely be monitoring.

The major raised a finger. "Loud and clear, Lima Four. Over."

Something drastic on the other side of the conversation made Willcox almost come to attention.

"Yes, sir."

Willcox waved at the passing spotter plane. In response, the plane waggled its wings.

The major listened. The plane banked to stay in range. Then Willcox summed up the situation on the ground. The internees had all been evacuated from the camp. Three quarters of them were already on the bay, headed for Mamatid. The amtracs were expected back in San Antonio by 1300 hours. At that time, he'd bring out the rest of the internees, the remainder of his battalion, and the recon platoon. His men had suffered four minor wounded. The internees seemed in good shape, none seriously hurt.

Willcox said, "Over."

Clearly that was a superior officer in the spotter plane. Willcox watched the Cub arch around for another sluggish pass over the beachhead. The major nodded under the headset. Then, with eyes wide on Bolick, he drew a finger under his throat fast, twice more, until Bolick cut the reception.

Willcox handed the headset back to Bolick.

"Stow the radio, Sergeant."

"Yes, sir. Major?"

Willcox picked his helmet off the sand. He cleaned it before topping his bald head with it.

"You keep a secret, Sergeant?"

"I just spent two weeks behind enemy lines, sir. I reckon I can stay quiet enough."

The slow L-4 flew past, steady, as though suspicious, eyeing Bolick and the major.

"Who is that, sir?"

"General Swing. Come to check on us." Swing was the commanding officer of the 11th Airborne Division.

Bolick had not met the general but like every soldier in the 11th knew the legend: classmate of Eisenhower's at West Point, fought under Black Jack Pershing in Mexico, in France in the Great War. Many called Swing the father of Airborne. Iron-willed, hard-charging, cared just as much for results as he did for his soldiers.

"Did we just hang up on General Swing?"

"That we did."

Bolick snapped the radio's faceplate into place. He slung the big box onto his back.

"Can't wait to hear why, sir."

The major trailed a hand over his lips, considering his words. The Cub did not turn for another pass but continued north, turning its tail to the beachhead.

"This goes nowhere, until I handle it later. Understood?"

"Yes, sir."

"General Swing wants us to stay here."

"What?" Bolick forgot to say "sir."

"He figures we already took a chunk of Jap territory, so why not put the internees on the amtracs, then hang on to it. He asked if we could take the town of Los Baños, then meet up with Shorty Soule. Problem is, I have no idea where the task force is, or what the Tiger Division is up to. I got four hundred men running on no sleep and now no rations because they gave 'em all away. He wants me to lead an eight-hour forced march through enemy positions to an unknown location. I was so surprised, I didn't know what to say."

"No would've been good. Sir."

"You haven't met the general. The radio died before I could answer. You'll back me on that."

"Damn useless radio, sir. Piece of crap."

"Don't get carried away, Sergeant. As you were."

When the amtracs returned, the Japanese lobbed mortar rounds to greet them on the beach. The internees needed no urging to climb on board. None doubled back for their baggage or parcels. No soldier had to shout, "Go, go!" The folks scrambled for seats.

The enemy shells landed short, raising geysers of empty sand, snapping branches in the woods. The more the paratroopers on the perimeter pulled back to evacuate, the closer the Japanese crept. The better their aim became.

Bolick found Tuck sitting on a driftwood log with a half dozen other young men, none of them in a hurry. He told them to get moving. Bascom said they'd like to be in the last group off the point, just to say they were. All of the boys held on to something from the camp, a signpost, a Japanese bayonet, Tuck's radio. Bascom clutched a porcelain rice bowl.

"Stay low another twenty minutes," Bolick said. "We'll ride out together."

Out on the bay, the leading amtracs took a zigzag course, dodging falling artillery shells. The vehicles and explosions churned the water white in a vast swath. Bolick helped load as much of the luggage as possible into four empty tractors. The Japanese mortars were getting the range. After the second shower of sand and concussion, one of the skippers yelled, "Let the locals have it!" and raised his gate. The other three amtracs followed his example. All four squealed away, leaving half the pile behind.

The final paratroopers arrived on the beach. Kraft showed up with his recon boys covered in leaves and dirt. Willcox shouted and twirled a finger in the air. Atop six amtracs, each driver stood at his throttle, waving his hands for the boys, the soldiers, and finally Major Willcox, to move it.

The last amtracs rumbled into the shallows just after 1500 hours. On San Antonio point, fifty guerrillas raised their bolos in tribute, then vanished into the landscape. Another Japanese shell erupted on the abandoned beach, empty of all but the internees' suitcases.

The six amtracs formed the tail of the long procession on the riled-up bay. All fifty-four vehicles plowed at top speed to gain distance from the shore. Their slow pace would keep them in range of mortars and small-arms fire for long minutes. A bullet ricocheted off the water behind Bolick's amtrac with an evil *zing*. Another banged off the armored flank. Every head ducked below the gunwales. The skipper bellowed over the engine at Bolick.

"Man the fifty!"

Bolick set aside his radio. Stumbling over the boys' knees and laps, he leaped to the gun, not sure why until he noticed the amtrac changing course, chugging closer to the jungle.

The other five amtracs in formation did the same. They strung themselves out into a firing line, aiming their machine guns at the jungle to suppress those Japanese taking shots at the departing amtracs.

Bolick charged the weapon and laid open the ammo box. The six amtracs powered within a hundred yards of shore. Far behind them, on either side of the fleeing flotilla, columns of water blew. Bolick, an artilleryman, knew how hard it was to hit a moving target, and how often it happened anyway. He eyed the shoreline for movement. One of the gunners in another amtrac loosed a burst into the brush. Bolick fisted the grips, then thumbed the trigger. He swept the long barrel across the emerald face of the shoreline, slamming ten slugs per second at nothing in particular. Palm fronds snapped, branches shivered, earth spewed until Bolick let off the trigger and another gunner in line took over.

The six amtracs prowled the shoreline, blasting at random while the rest steamed farther from shore. After ten minutes, Bolick's knuckles had gone white on the big .50's handles. He stripped away his tunic and stood bare-chested and sweating. Far behind them, the escaping fleet had at last scuttled out of range. Bolick and the other amtracs close to shore had done their duty. Before he could shout this to the driver, a stitch of automatic fire zipped below the waterline. Bolick jerked in reflex, cursed, then gathered himself at the trigger. He opened up blindly on the shore, blasting foliage and saw grass. The other five gunners did the same.

Bolick's driver concluded that they'd done the brave and selfless thing; the time was ripe to retreat. He turned the amtrac sharply, pivoting its steel ramp to face shore while they forged toward open water. The boys around Bolick were pie-faced, excited at being fired on.

Bolick ducked while Japanese bullets beat on the heavy gate. What a crazy thing this was to do, he thought. Not just motoring close to the shoreline looking for Japanese, but the whole enterprise. The rescue by sea, air, land; a thousand soldiers, five hundred guerrillas, two thousand civilians. Split-second timing under the nose of ten thousand Japanese. It should not have worked so well, but it did, and no one could have predicted that. War redefined what was crazy.

The automatic fire from shore quit. Bolick took his seat on the bench. The flight of fighter planes that had been monitoring the raid swooped low over the six amtracs; their prop wash tousled the boys' hair. One P-40 executed a barrel roll fifty feet above the water.

Bolick left his shirt off to pick up some sun. The ride to Mamatid still had an hour to go on the bay.

The boys looked at him with admiration. Their fight was done. The weight they'd lost would be regained, the stolen years would turn into stories and lessons for their own children someday. Bolick's war had more left in it. The Japanese weren't close to surrendering. Bolick had this to look forward to.

The Tuck boy seemed melancholy. He dropped his head with an inward gaze. Tuck's war wasn't finished, either. Something he did in the camp, or didn't do, had yet to cut him loose.

Bolick had no idea how long the war would endure for him or the kid. That would depend first on the Japanese, then on nightmares and memory. He could think of nothing he might do to shorten his own. Maybe he could do something for Tuck.

He drew the Colt from his shoulder holster, popped out the magazine.

"Tuck."

Bolick set the pistol in the boy's lap.

"The army'll get me another one. Toss it."

The other boys reached, telling him no. They wanted the pistol. Tuck put his finger on the trigger where it had been that morning. He examined the metal, loading it up with some baggage out of his head or heart that he wanted to leave behind.

With a flick over his shoulder, not watching it go, Tal flipped the gun into the water.

Chapter Fifty-one

$\diamond$

CARMEN DRAGGED Kenji by his bare feet, through his blood, into her room. She sat beside him on the tatami, tearing with her teeth at her red silk robe. She could not start a rip to make bandages and strips. She had nothing sharp in her room and could not leave to find something to cut with. Kenji might faint, then his thumb and middle finger could slip out of the holes in his chest and armpit. Carmen yanked down the black curtain that had covered her door for a year. This she could gnaw and shred.

"How do you feel?" she asked.

"Cold."

"You've lost a lot of blood."

Carmen spread the *haori* over Kenji's legs to warm him. He groaned with every breath. Scarlet dribbled down his ribs. She stopped tearing at the curtain to stuff his thumb and fingertip in deeper. Kenji would not look at her.

He said, "I should have known. In Toshiwara's office, he had your tag in his pocket."

Carmen kept focus on her hands and teeth. She spat bits of thread off her lips.

"I gave it to him."

"You hid him from me."

"I did many things, Kenji."

When she had torn several strips, she ripped patches until the curtain was all in pieces. Carefully, she plucked his hand away from the holes and laid his arm out wide, startled at how light the limb was. Carmen wiped at the two wounds.

The bullet had burrowed a neat tunnel through Kenji's chest. A scarlet trickle pulsed out with every heartbeat. Inches away, in the meat of the armpit, the jagged exit hole wept steadily. Carmen poked with tacky fingers, looking for nothing particular beyond what the Tuck boy's gun had done. She needed to close Kenji's wounds or he would bleed to death. Carmen was neither afraid nor nauseated, but did not anticipate the copper stench. It made her lift her nose to the open window for a clear breath.

He said, "You lied to me."

"You have to sit up."

Carmen slid hands under Kenji to lift. He bit his lower lip to keep himself quiet.

"Raise your arms."

"Dizzy," he mumbled. Carmen worked fast. Holding Kenji upright, she pressed cloth squares over both punctures. Elevating his arms, she tied the silk *haori* belt around his sunken chest to hold the bandages in place. Quickly, she swathed him with the strips from the curtain, circling his torso and shoulder, pulling the black wrapping tight until Kenji gasped. He wavered, his arms grew lax. Carmen knotted the last length, holding him up by the strip because he had passed out.

She settled him on the mattress and waited, rubbing slick thumbs and fingers, to see if the bandage would halt the bleeding.

When the wrapping did not soak, she left the room to find a mop and water. She used the bowl from which she had cleaned herself daily to swab the hall and the floor of her room. Again the bowl held red water.

She went to Yumi's room to search for food. The girl had been Toshiwara's pet; the commandant would have brought her treats. Carmen found a small box of candies and a tin of yams. She didn't mind that Yumi had not shared. Yumi had earned these and it was her right to survive.

On the landing, in Mama's desk, Carmen found a claw hammer, an odd thing to find lying alone, a reminder that Papa was the old woman's husband, the man who fixed things. Carmen drove the claws into the tin of yams. She sucked down the juice first, then pried a hole big enough to pick out the potatoes. She ate all of them and threw the tin down the stairwell, pleased at the clatter and the freedom to make it.

In her room, Carmen sat against the wall, waiting for Kenji to become conscious. She stayed away from her window, did not want to see Tal in the camp. She ran a hand through Kenji's black hair, hoping this might rouse him. She wanted to talk, because even a halting talk through Kenji's pain would distract her from the boy. Smoke drifted in her window and the sound of crackling. The American soldiers had torched the camp. That would drive the Tuck boy away.

She was not afraid. She thought of her parents and brothers in Manila. They would all be alive, because Carmen had been spared. They would embrace her, forgive her, and thank her quietly for bearing the brunt of tragedy in their family. They would love Tal. As an American he would lead them to better times after the war. He was a lucky boy, like his father. He was loyal, hardheaded as any Filipino.

She gazed down on Kenji. The color that had drained from his face sitting up had returned during his faint.

For a long time, Carmen traced fingertips over his yellow forehead. She was stealing Kenji from the war. He was supposed to die, be one more of the millions war fed on. Kenji had done this for her. She was meant to be dead like Hua, or mad like Yumi. Kenji had not allowed it. She and Kenji and the Tuck boy were the same. All three tried to save themselves by saving another.

Under her hand, Kenji's brow creased.

She smiled down on him. He was her defiance, her act in the face of the war. She knew why Kenji loved her.

He drew a long breath like a man waking in his own bed.

"Are you waiting for me to die?"

"Yes. Though I think you might live."

Kenji raised his left hand to his chest. Without looking, he probed the wraps as if he did not remember Carmen putting them there.

"I know that boy. He's a troublemaker."

"Yes, he is."

"Will you go with him if I die?"

"He'll come for me and I'll go with him, either way."

"If I get the chance, I will shoot him again."

She stroked his hair. From Yumi's tin of candies, she put a sweet in his mouth.

"Of course you will, Kenji."

Carmen peeked out her window. Smoke coursed past but the wind drove little of it into her room. Flames rippled out of half the bamboo structures below. Some had already buckled into cinders. Embers sailed from blazing roof to roof and the rest would burn soon. The Tuck boy was gone with all the internees and American soldiers. The camp had been abandoned by the Japanese, too, except for the few bodies sprawled in the dirt under sprinkling ash. Crashing rafters were the loudest sound. Heat throbbed on Carmen's cheeks. The air rumpled above the fire.

She did not watch the camp vanish. The flames would rid only the earth of it. She went to Yumi's room to take down the curtain and rip it apart, too. Kenji would need more bandages.

When killing Filipinos, assemble them together in one place, as far as possible, thereby saving ammunition and labor. The disposal of dead bodies will be troublesome, so either collect them in houses scheduled to be burned or throw them into the river.

—Manila Navy Defense Force
and Southwestern Area Fleet
Operation Order, December 1944

when killing Filipinos

Chapter Fifty-two

THE BULLET came out of Remy's chest easily. An army doctor wiped alcohol over the bulge, slit the skin with a scalpel, and plucked it out with forceps. The doctor cleaned the bullet before dropping it in Yumi's hand. She pocketed it and helped Remy sit up. The doctor poured sulfa powder into both holes, dabbed more alcohol, and stitched Remy up front and back. Remy gritted his teeth at the doctor's apology for the lack of a painkiller. Bandaged and in a sling, he walked out of the prison medical room on Yumi's arm, the way he'd walked in.

Remy waited in line to register as "Released from Los Baños Internment Camp." A nurse handed him two Hershey bars and a roll of Life Savers. He insisted space be found for Yumi, explaining only that she was Korean and had been a prisoner of the Japanese, too. The nurse promised she'd find room. Remy did not go to his assigned cell but joined a chow line with a hundred lean faces he knew well. The people understood what Remy had done and showed it; they stood aside for him and the little Korean girl. He hobbled forward, still short of breath but, with his holes closed, better able to keep his feet. A soldier behind the chow counter filled two bowls of bean soup. He handed them over with fat slices of white bread.

Remy and Yumi found places at a table in the great concrete hall. The odor of antiseptic mingled badly with the body odors of the internees and the aromas of hot food. New Bilibid Prison in Muntinlupa had been emptied, scoured, and lardered in preparation for the internees as their first haven from privation. The irony was not lost on them that they'd gone from a jail to a jail. After the amtracs had dropped them off in Mamatid and dashed back into the bay, a convoy of trucks and ambulances hauled the first fifteen hundred here. Banners festooned the ten miles of road to the prison, Filipinos threw petals in front of the trucks. The internees sped under bamboo arches reading "Welcome Victorious Americans and Guerrillas." Arriving at New Bilibid, the ecstatic and famished internees were nourished, examined, treated, and interviewed.

Remy gazed into the piping bowl under his nose without touching the spoon. He stared at the empty bench across from him. Yumi scooped dripping beans to his lips. Remy took the spoon from her—he was no infant—and put it down.

"You eat," he said. "I'll wait."

Remy did not eat the bean soup in the mess hall. Yumi carried the full bowl while she walked him to his scrubbed cell. The girl sat cross-legged on the stones holding the pan like an offering, silent and goaded, until he took up the spoon and finished it. The soup had gone cold and within minutes gave him gas. He lay sleepless on the hard bottom mattress of the bunk. On the upper bed Yumi snored lightly, making the sound of a sharpening knife.

There'd been no news in the mess hall and none afterward of the missing internees. Any number of bad fates could have befallen them between Los Baños and New Bilibid. Did the Japanese counterattack the camp? Were the amtracs on the bay right now fending off Japanese patrol boats? Did the amtracs even make it off San Antonio? Were there snipers, artillery, did the Tiger Division catch them on the point? Were they shelled from shore, were they sunk?

Why hadn't Tal been behind Remy in the stairwell?

Through the barred window of his cell, the sunlight reddened. Remy's shoulder and lung ached and he wanted whiskey, or some of Donnelly's bomber lotion. The Aussie boy's death and those of so many at Los Baños lifted Remy off the mattress. He put his face to the small window, where he stared like the prisoners who'd stood here before, at the fading light. Remy sucked through the pack of Life Savers, waiting.

After dark, Yumi dropped from the top bunk to her bare feet, nimble at the first rumble of transports. She grabbed Remy by his good arm to tow him out of the cellblock. The five hundred internees unloaded from fifty trucks, to queue at the registration tables and receive their first chocolate bars, candy, and cigarettes. Remy stood on tiptoes behind the crowd gathered to see the last ones rescued from Los Baños. Yumi bounced vainly. Remy lacked the strength to push through the wall of internees. Fresh aromas from the big prison kitchen swelled across the stone yard, under brick arches.

Toward the front, hugs and shouts began. Remy was bumped by internees pressing past, jolting his sling. Yumi scowled, unable to see over any of the shoulders. She held up a palm for Remy to stay put. The girl folded her arms to make herself smaller and like a weevil burrowed into the crush.

Remy removed his fedora. He held it as high as he could reach.

On all sides, the New Bilibid internees welcomed the last of their number. Remy waved his fedora despite the ache it caused him.

When he saw the tall top of Tal's head weaving through the throng, Remy froze. He left his arm in the air, unaware that he had done so.

Yumi elbowed out of the wall of people, clearing a path for the boy. The two ran across the stones to Remy who dropped his raised arm around his son's neck. Tal smelled of sweat and earth, smoke. Remy pulled him in as hard as one arm allowed. Tal embraced him also with one arm, the other cradling Mac's crystal radio.

"You're safe," Remy said. He drew a breath too deep for his wounded lung and coughed, not letting go of his son until the pain bent him and made him back away. Tal supported him until the coughing eased.

When he straightened, Remy put on the fedora. Yumi moved beside him with a worried look. She tugged on Remy's vest.

"Okay," he said to the tiny girl. "Tal?"

"Yeah?"

"Where's Carmen?"

Chapter Fifty-three

◆

THE RUINS cooled slowly. Every seared timber and bamboo rod Carmen touched held the fever of the fire that had destroyed it. Smoke ribboned from smoldering embers.

In the fast-falling dusk, she stepped over blackened floors without roofs or walls, to search for trunks and stowage where food might have gone unburned. She covered herself in soot and was glad to have changed into her fatigues before rooting through the camp.

Not everything was scorched. Carmen found clothes, handmade toys, carpentry tools, books, and china plates on tables that had withstood the fall of flaming rafters. Carmen looked up to her own small room, where she'd been stripped of everything. In a seared crate she found a box of powdered milk and a forgotten cloth doll. She took both.

She hurried to beat the setting sun. The camp was too gutted and sharpened to be tramping around after dark. She snared a lantern from the body of a guard beside the barbed wire. He lay facedown with no marks on his back. She rolled him over, curious how he'd died and to see if she recognized him. She did. He was the young, scared one from two days before who had come for Songu to soothe his conscience, then warned her to leave the camp. Three bullet holes in his tunic told Carmen what she wanted to know. She rifled his pockets for matches and found them.

In the last strains of light, she picked through the barracks where Tal lived before he bunked with Remy. She knew the boys there were thieves like Tal and were likely to have a cache of food. Carmen crunched over wood made flimsy by the flames. She scrounged up a tin of Spam lying under a burnt and stinking mattress.

She hurried along the tarmac road to the untouched infirmary. Inside, Carmen rummaged shelves and drawers for gauze wraps and antiseptics. She found no supplies, taking instead two clean white bedsheets.

Passing through the main gate, her arms nearly full, Carmen paused at the trench the Japanese had dug beside her building. A dozen corpses lay in it side by side, orderly, as if waiting for inspection. This Carmen gave them, and selected the tallest of the bodies. She dragged the stiffening soldier out of the trench. She spent no time on his face or death, just the buttons and buckles. His uniform bore only a few small rips and no bloodstains. Carmen finished pulling off his boots and socks in the fallen dark.

She did not douse the lantern. She left it burning low through the night, so every few hours she could check Kenji's bandages.

He slept bare-chested; she'd managed to slide the dead guard's pantaloons over his loincloth. Kenji wanted the boots and socks on also, an issue of pride for him, to lie wounded as a soldier. Carmen hid the pistol he'd brought.

The white sheets from the infirmary made better wrappings than the curtain. They tore more easily and betrayed blood instantly. Changing his dressing, Carmen looked into Kenji's wound. The muscles inside had tightened. The puncture did not gape, blood spilled more slowly. During the late day Kenji had begun to sit up without wooziness, though his face blanched and he could stay upright only for short periods. Conversation filled little of the long silence. Carmen stood in the window or sat beside his moaning dreams.

Past midnight, she lay beside him. Her arm stretched across his ribs, over the white swath of bandage. Her open hand nestled in his armpit above the wounds. In the months she had known Kenji, he'd never been permitted to sleep in the *shuho,* that was the right of officers alone. Of the hundreds of nights she'd spent on this tatami, this was the only night when she rested her head on a man's shoulder, the first when in the morning she would wash only her hands and face. Carmen raised her hand. None of Kenji's blood marked her palm. Settling against him, she tucked the cloth doll close to her own chest.

Her sleep was shallow so she would not lose track of Kenji's breathing. The animals of the jungle and ravine made little clamor, suspicious of the abandoned, moonlit camp. The burned grounds felt haunted below her window. The remnants of people were stored there like the heat in the blackened timbers: the moving sallow phantoms of guards along the wire, the dim glow of coconut-oil lamps in the barracks of the elderly, the Catholics always reading late into the night.

She lifted her arm from Kenji so as not to wake him. She sat up to a noise in the camp that was real.

Dimming the lantern, Carmen set aside the cloth doll and crept to her knees. She edged her eyes above the windowsill. A three-quarter moon had topped the trees. Pale figures in loincloths and bare feet moved in the ruins. They sifted through the remains of the camp police hut, the commandant's office, and the guards' barracks. They shoved aside tumbled walls and blistered frames to dig into the ashes for guns. Like Carmen, they stripped the dead for uniforms and boots. One man's voice was unmistakable, his form unforgettable. Nagata.

Carmen sneaked across the hall to retrieve Kenji's pistol from where she'd hidden it. Standing in her doorway, she pondered whether to wake him. Kenji sighed, not out of pain but like a man who in sleep senses someone missing.

Carmen entered her room. She put out the lantern.

She'd never held a gun before. She took it with her to the dark landing, to sit on the top step. The pistol required no special insight, the thing was designed to invite the hand. Carmen put her finger over the trigger and waited.

Her focus on the stairwell was so great she did not hear Kenji's dragging feet until he lowered himself beside her.

"Kenji, you should not be up."

"I heard them."

"Nagata is alive."

Kenji slipped his good hand down Carmen's arm, to the hard nub of the pistol. "Is this for him?"

"If he comes."

"I'll tell him you saved my life."

Even in the faint light of the stairwell, the whiteness of Kenji's face stood out.

"I'll protect you," he said.

Carmen tucked the pistol in the waistband of her trousers. She stood behind Kenji to help him to his feet.

"Back to bed, Kenji."

When she had lain him on the tatami, Carmen did not hide the pistol but set it near her on the floor. She struck a match and did not hold it to the lantern wick but to Kenji's cheeks. His color was slow to restore. Another match at his armpit showed a coin of scarlet staining the bandage. Carmen would wait for him to gain more strength before changing his wrap. She stood in her dark window.

To the northwest, Manila rumbled and flared, still under siege. Nearby in the west, black Makiling rose into the night. The camp had returned to its charred hush. Kenji, at Carmen's feet, asked for water she did not have.

✳

In the morning, Carmen and Kenji ate the salvaged can of Spam. Kenji was able to sit up for a longer period and his color did not wane. He did not try to stand again. Carmen helped him urinate into the empty tin.

The fire had wiped out all electricity to the building. She twisted faucets that gurgled and dried.

She left Kenji with the last of Yumi's candies. She told him to finish the sweets. He put one in his mouth as she left the room.

In the basement laundry, Carmen found a bucket. Leaving the building, she hurried through the cogon grass to the orchard. Tal had shown her this place six weeks ago on the way to the ravine. She kicked at rotten mangoes on the ground until two of them felt firm enough to take. The papaya and lemon trees had no edible fruit. In the ravine, she took off her pants and slippers to squat over the cool trickles. She urinated, washed herself free from the odor of soot, then dipped the bucket full. Returning, Carmen stayed careful to encounter no one. She passed close to the trench of dead Japanese. All the guards lay naked down to loincloths and bootless, stripped after midnight by the Japanese survivors. The bodies were no longer arranged neatly but had been tossed in a tangle to the bottom of the ditch. Carmen pinched her nose at a smell that would worsen and backed away from the buzz of flies.

In her room, Kenji dozed. She guessed he'd lost enough blood to fill half the bucket. She poured ravine water into her washbasin, then used some to mix with the powdered milk. Kenji awoke when Carmen unbuttoned his pantaloons to slide them and his loincloth below his knees. He tilted his head to watch her dip a cloth strip, then lay back while she swabbed his legs, penis, and waist. She rolled him onto his good side and did the same for the backs of his legs and buttocks.

She patted him dry and pulled up his pants.

"I have milk," she said, "and a mango."

"Help me sit up."

Kenji squirmed against the wall, showing more strength than Carmen had anticipated. She peeled one mango. He ate with spills of golden juice onto his bandaged chest, like medallions. She poured lukewarm milk into a glass she'd found near Mama's mattress. Kenji gulped and left a mustache. Carmen wiped it away for him.

He sat upright longer than Carmen believed he ought. His cheeks sapped while she peeled the second mango and sipped milk.

"Will you do this for him?" Kenji asked. "Look after him?"

Carmen ran a wrist across her milk-wet lips. She pretended the Tuck boy was where Kenji sat, wounded and helpless. She saw Tal both young and old. Herself old, too. She tried to see herself beside him.

And there were the thousands, springing up when Carmen thought of love. They hovered between her and Tal, naked like the flyblown corpses in the trench, like they had been between her legs. Carmen had to fight through them to reach him, just as the Tuck boy had done in his return to her. She did not know if she could do it forever.

"I'll try. Have you been in love, Kenji?"

"Before you, no."

Carmen covered his hand with hers. "You'll love again."

Kenji slid down the wall. When he lay flat on the tatami, he gazed at the ceiling.

"I can feel my heart pushing the blood I have left. The bullet hole hurts. I'm afraid. I'm dizzy. I feel many things, Carmen. But I don't feel that."

She scooped up the cloth doll and knelt at the window to peek over the sill. At dusk, she would forage again in the wreckage of the camp for food and lantern oil. Tomorrow, she'd sneak back to the ravine for more water and to soak the smell of smoke out of the doll.

Beyond tomorrow, the path petered out. Could she abandon Kenji and head into the jungle as she'd promised Tal? Even if Kenji were able to stagger away from this building, where could he go? The first guerrilla to spot him alone would cut his throat. Could she stay with Kenji, somehow escort him back to the Japanese? Even if the guerrillas let them pass, what about Nagata? Now that he was alive and close by, could she risk it? Nagata had seen the Tuck boy racing into the camp alongside the American soldiers. Nagata had been in Toshiwara's office with Kenji when the Songu tag came out of the boy's pocket. He knew to link Carmen and Tal, and if Nagata was watching the camp at sundown yesterday, he knew she was alive, too. How long until he sorted out that she'd been the one funneling secrets to the Americans?

Carmen could not leave Kenji, that would mean his death. He would starve, bleed out, or be murdered. If she stayed, there remained a chance. Someone would find them, the Japanese, the guerrillas, or the Americans. Who would climb the stairs first? Each walking through her door would bring a very different fate.

Kenji rested his hand on her knee.

"I want to tell you something. It should be said."

"Yes, Kenji."

"Every Japanese should say this to you. But you may never hear it again."

"What."

"I am sorry."

Carmen stood in her window, framed herself there, and beckoned whoever would come, to come.

Gunfire jolted her awake.

She scrambled to her feet. A high, bright moon shone

over Makiling. The camp remained skeletal and quiet. The ravine and jungle held its million breaths.

Another burst split the night, then single shots. The gunplay came from a little village at the foot of a hill, west of the camp.

"Help me stand," Kenji said.

He struggled up beside her. Kenji gripped the sill to steady himself.

She asked, "Is it the Americans?"

"No. Those are Japanese guns."

The firing swelled, automatic weapons brayed nonstop. The sounds didn't seem to be answered. This was not a pitched battle on the hillside, but some one-sided affair. No battle shouts of soldiers or the yelps of wounded rose from the village.

"What are they doing?" Carmen asked. "Why are they shooting?"

"I don't know."

Slowly, in fits and starts, the firing ceased. Carmen's heart thumped, dreading what would come next. She considered fetching the pistol, but it would be useless if those guns turned on her. Should she run and hide? Only Kenji stood any chance of protecting her from the Japanese. Only she could save him from the Filipinos. The two of them could not be separated, not right now.

By the wan light of the lantern, she checked the strips she'd wrapped around Kenji before midnight. The bandage was clean. Kenji wavered, but his gaze held firm.

An owl's hoot flew from the jungle, an inquisitive call.

A glimmer shivered out of the moon shadows on the hill. A firebrand had been struck. Quickly, one roof in the village became a torch. For the second time in two days, Carmen in her high window watched flames spread. The

Japanese carried the fire from door to door, until most of the homes became engulfed.

The flames grew bright enough to light the disgust on Kenji's face. Carmen draped the dead soldier's tunic around his bare shoulders. His legs wobbled but he would not turn from the fire until Carmen, to save his stamina, pulled him down to the tatami.

They leaned together against the wall. She turned down the wick to save the small store of oil. Orange flickers tinted the moonlight in her room. From the forested slopes of the hill and out of the creek below, animals and birds shrieked their fear at another blaze near their homes.

Kenji slumped to the mattress. Carmen stayed upright and sleepless, sensing that the night held more.

Before dawn, the smell of smoke drew her down the hall and stairs, outside to the open field. She stood on the grass where she and Yumi had played, where Hua was buried. Smoke fled through the orchard, across the cogon grass and ravine, blew like fog against her building. From behind the trees came the screams the Japanese had sought in the hillside village but did not find, and the gleam of a fire that burned more than wood.

Carmen's dream contained nothing of her horror. The vision was the opposite of what she'd brought back to her room. She found her family alive and well, Manila the bustling city it had been, nothing out of order. She looked for hints or symbols of the village's slaughter and found none. She felt fooled by the dream, did not trust the sense of peace and safety. Carmen woke herself.

Beside her, Kenji was warm. Morning had come. Carmen lifted her head.

She scrabbled backward, banging the wall.

The guerrilla boy Benito squatted at the foot of the

tatami. At his back, his bolo hung to the floor like the third leg of a stool. He held Kenji's pistol. She'd left it close to her hand when she lay down terrified hours ago.

Kenji awoke and did not startle. He propped himself on his good elbow.

"Hello," he said to Benito.

The boy reached behind him. With a slow hiss, he drew his bolo.

Aiming the point at Kenji, he asked in Tagalog, "What's he doing here?"

She answered in the same tongue. "Please don't hurt him."

"Are you a *makipili* now?"

"No. His name is Kenji. He's been kind to me. He gave me many of the secrets I brought to you."

"And what did you give him in return?"

Carmen was older than this boy. She didn't know what he had done with his youth besides mop her floor and wave his bolo at a few soldiers. She knew what had happened to hers.

"Do not speak to me that way."

Benito dropped his eyes, only for a moment. "When was he shot?"

"In the raid. The Tuck boy did it."

Kenji set his shoulders against the wall next to Carmen. The guerrilla boy glanced at spent tins, the water bucket, the cloth doll, and the pile of bloody bandages.

"You stayed behind to save this guard."

"He wasn't a guard. He was an interpreter."

Benito laid the knife across his knees. "It doesn't matter."

"What are you doing here?"

"You were seen in the camp. Colonel Romeo sent me to bring you out."

"I'm not leaving."

"You have to." Benito raised Kenji's pistol. "I'm going to kill him."

Though he was a boy, she believed him.

Kenji showed no sign that he knew Benito was as dangerous as the holes in his shoulder. Or was he too weak, too accepting of his own death to care how it was delivered?

"Do you know what happened last night?" Benito asked.

"I saw flames. I heard . . ." She could not describe the sounds. "Tell it in English. He should hear."

"All right," the guerrilla replied in English. "Listen to me, Japanese."

Blood had begun to blot through Kenji's wrap, a red eye widening at Benito.

"Yes."

"After midnight, eighty soldiers came down from the slope of Makiling. They went to the college gate. The barrio there is empty. We'd already moved the people to Faculty Hill to protect them. The Japanese shot up empty houses, then burned them."

"We saw that," Kenji said.

"Did you see what they did next?"

"No."

"Villagers in the town heard the shooting at the gate. A hundred of them got scared and ran to the Catholic chapel. Mostly women and children. The Japanese found them. Some ran out the back door. The others barricaded themselves inside the church."

The fire behind the orchard, the smoke gusting past Carmen.

"The soldiers bayoneted the ones who tried to get away. The rest they burned alive inside the church." Benito gazed at the pistol in his hand. He seemed to weigh it against the bolo across his lap. "We found the bodies at dawn."

Kenji's face was white. He pursed his lips against the sickening tale and the steady loss of his own blood.

"It was a reprisal raid," Kenji said. "It was Nagata."

"We know. That's why Romeo sent me to come get her."

The guerrilla lifted the long knife from across his legs. In his other hand he held the pistol, as if granting Kenji the choice from which to die.

Carmen pushed herself from the wall, folding to her knees between Kenji and Benito.

"He had no part in it."

"I told you." The guerrilla shook his head. "It doesn't matter."

From behind, Kenji touched her. "Go with him."

She pushed Kenji's arm down. "No. Benito, tell me what you want."

"What do you mean?"

"What do you want from me? To let him live."

Kenji tried to turn her again to make her face him. Carmen shirked him off.

She said to Benito, "Anything."

The guerrilla lowered both weapons. "Don't do that, Carmen. Let the war end." He stood, not a tall boy, in tattered sneakers.

"Benito," Kenji said.

"What?"

"You're young. Have you killed before?"

"No."

"I have. It's best to avoid it. But I understand."

Carmen rose from her knees. She returned to Tagalog, close to the boy's face.

"I know you're angry. I know you've seen the dead. But I . . ." She pressed a hand to her own breast. "I am among the dead. For the life I have lost, please."

Benito glanced at wounded, weary Kenji.

"If I leave, another will come for you. Maybe Romeo himself. You'll never talk him out of it if that soldier's found here. And what will you do if Nagata comes? You think this one can save you?"

"That's why you have to help."

"I won't kill him. But I will not help him."

"Then do this only for me. And tell no one."

"What."

"Go to the Americans."

"Why?"

"Bring back the Tuck boy."

Chapter Fifty-four

THE LITTLE Korean girl shuffled. The Tuck kid's father, with one arm in a sling, could only deal and play.

Remy Tuck called the game while spinning cards to Bolick and the four other soldiers around the table. "Let's go deuces wild this time. Live dangerously."

Remy was in an expansive mood. His stack of candies, cookies, Life Saver packs, and Hershey bars rose higher than anyone's in the little prison cell. Tal watched from his bunk.

A stocky corporal opened the betting with a mint.

Bolick, with mock disgust, folded his hand first. He said to Tal, "Good thing I didn't meet your old man 'til this afternoon. I'd be skinny as you. Come on, kid." Bolick pushed his few remaining sweets over to the corporal.

Tal left the bunk to move beside Remy. "You okay?" The Korean girl answered, "He okay."

"Go on," Remy told him. "Yumi'll help me carry all this."

Bolick pointed at Remy. "You take care, sir. Heal up."

"Watch yourself out there, Sergeant. Thanks for keepin' an eye on my boy."

Bolick hefted his radio and rifle off the cell floor. Tal grabbed two Hershey bars from his father's pile. The girl, Yumi, gave them both hugs; her arms did not link around Bolick's waist.

Walking out, Tal handed Bolick one of the candy bars. Bolick crammed half in his mouth at once. An internee girl walked past and grinned. Bolick couldn't return the smile without drooling milk chocolate down his tunic. The girl giggled and moved on.

When Bolick could speak, he said, "These are the first American girls I've seen in two years."

"You can have 'em."

"Yeah, I guess there'll be plenty of gals waitin' for you back in the States."

Tal unwrapped his own candy bar and nibbled.

Bolick said, "When I dropped in to say goodbye, I didn't figure on gettin' in a poker game. Your dad, he's some guy."

"That's Remy. I have no idea where that table or the cards came from. They just showed up. It's his gift. He draws people in."

The kid seemed bothered. All the other internees celebrated, ate until they got sick, grew giddy at the mention of going home. The army gave them movies and newsreels to watch, music on the loudspeakers, shelter, safety, medicine, soap, food, mail. Tal appeared cool to it all. No matter what the army provided, or what tomorrow promised, the boy was missing something. It seemed his nature, from the moment Bolick met him, to swim against the current. Small wonder the kid chafed against his more amiable father, who played poker with a bullet hole in his back and a Korean cutie watching over him.

Tal was the same age as a lot of the guys in Bolick's squad. He could've been a soldier. He and Bolick might have served together. Yesterday they'd both run into battle and had shot men. Today their paths split. Bolick was headed back into the war. A civilian's fate waited for brave, contrary Tal Tuck.

Bolick led him outside. The road running past New Bilibid Prison was choked with soldiers on foot, vehicles pulling out, towed artillery, deuce trucks, tanks, half-tracks. All this and more, Bolick himself, had been mustered to whisk Tuck out of Los Baños before the Japanese could gun him and two thousand others down. The power of America rolled past, kicking up a ton of dust and fumes. Bolick was proud even if the kid was moony.

"Well, pal. I gotta go."

Tal extended his hand. "Where to?"

Bolick jerked his chin in the direction of the convoy. His battalion was assigned to take positions along the San Juan River five miles west of Los Baños, at the spot where Shorty Soule's task force stalled yesterday when the Japanese blew a bridge. The Japanese had expected American tanks to motor down Highway 1, not sail around them on the bay.

By tonight at sundown, after one rare night in a bed, the smiles of some American girls, then a fifteen-mile hike, Bolick would be shoveling a foxhole a few thousand yards from the Tiger Division.

He took Tal's hand. Bolick gave it a firm shake, as the boy deserved.

"Stay outta trouble." He hooked a ride on a jeep.

Chapter Fifty-five

TAL COULDN'T bear more of prison, even one he could walk away from. He sat on a hillock outside New Bilibid, watching soldiers rolling or marching past. Many waved, some tossed him food as though he were a waif. When he'd collected a dozen packets of crackers and candy bars, he flagged down a chaplain's jeep to hand them over.

He turned to go back to his shady spot near the road. A Filipino boy stood there, dressed like Tal, in shorts and sneakers. A rifle strapped across his chest and the dangling bolo marked him as a guerrilla.

Beside the exhaust and grinding whine of the road, Tal held his ground. The boy stayed in the afternoon shade. They stared for long moments, keeping their distance. Compared with the modern army thundering at Tal's back, the guerrilla looked solitary, small, almost primitive. He was the barrio and jungle.

Tal shouted, "What do you want?"

The guerrilla motioned him to come away from the road. Tal did not. If this boy had a purpose with Tal, let him say so. If not, he should walk on. Tal was not an internee anymore. He didn't come, bow, eat, or sleep when told to.

The guerrilla did not step out of the shade, as if he'd traveled far enough. He cupped his hands around his mouth, and called. "The Japanese you shot . . ."

Tal bolted up the short slope. The Filipino finished his statement with Tal in his face.

"He did not die."

✳

Tal and the guerrilla boy, Benito, shoved the *banca* off the beach into the green shallows.

When the boat bobbed, Benito jumped on. Tal walked alongside. Water rose to his waist.

"Get in," the guerrilla said.

The water buoyed Tal as if it, too, wanted him to climb on.

Benito pulled on a line to hoist the old cloth sail. He was going to leave, and not ask Tal again.

A few of the soldiers guarding Mamatid point waved farewell. The boys looked to be off for an afternoon of fishing, two friends, brown and white.

Tal had not said goodbye. He'd told no one he was leaving. How could he? If the army knew he was going back to Los Baños, they'd stop him; the camp and village were still inside enemy territory. If Remy knew? He might've tried to prevent it. He might not. Carmen could not afford that coin toss.

Tal whispered goodbye now and pulled himself over the side.

He moved to the center while Benito tied off the sail for a breeze coming over the bay. The boat slid quickly into deeper water, heeling against an outrigger. The deck stank of tar and fish. At Benito's feet lay his rifle and long knife, a water skin, and half a dozen mangoes. The boat creaked easily. When Benito pushed the tiller to leave the shore, the lowering sun moved behind the sail.

"Eight miles," the guerrilla said. "It'll be dark when we get to Anos."

The shoreline receded fast. In ten minutes they covered a distance Tal could not swim to land. He closed his eyes.

"Tuck boy. Do you know how to sail?"

"Not very well."

"Then keep your eyes open and watch what I do. I won't be coming back with you tonight."

Tal sat up. Benito was no older than seventeen, but he had a swagger, and he had weapons. He would make a good ally. To not have him along for the whole undertaking was a worry.

"Why not?"

"I told you Nagata was alive. I didn't tell you what he's done."

Slowly, Benito described the midnight massacre at the Catholic chapel, the burned or bayoneted corpses of women, children, and elderly. It made sense why he'd not told Tal of Nagata's revenge on the village before they'd climbed into the *banca*. The story was fearsome, and anyone hearing it would consider not coming.

Benito said, "You should've killed that Japanese."

"I thought I had."

The guerrilla spat into the water. "I almost did this morning. She stopped me. She won't leave him."

"And you won't help him."

Benito shifted the tiller. "No, not after last night. No Filipino will. He's dead the second anyone sees him."

Carmen was protecting the guard who'd shot Remy, been part of the regime that had starved, beaten, and humiliated thousands, turned Carmen and Yumi into slaves. Suffering opened the way to honor. Was this honor? Yes, and something more. Mercy.

Tal put out a hand for the water skin and took a slug. Behind them, Mamatid grew smaller. The wind in the sail urged the *banca* on.

After an hour on the bay, a pall of smoke five miles ahead became Benito's landmark on shore. He sailed the *banca* straight for it. When the sun disappeared, he steered by the flickerings of fire.

Neither boy spoke. Tal did not want to seem afraid, and he assumed the same of Benito.

From the surging bow, he watched the barrio draw closer. The wind lessened as the boat neared shore. The water lost depth and flattened. Benito eased the sail to slow the *banca*, gliding past in silence. Nothing moved inside the barrio. The breeze pushed smoke away from them. The flames licked lower, dying and finishing their work.

Benito grounded the *banca*. Tal stepped out to drag the prow onto the narrow beach. Benito gathered his rifle and long knife. He joined Tal in the pebbly sand. The two stood gaping, shoulder to shoulder and exposed should there be any Japanese left among the ruins with a desire for more murder.

Anos was empty and absolutely dead.

Tal followed Benito under palm trees scorched of their fronds. Electricity was gone from the barrio; the only light flicked from the fading flames in the charred crevices of the village. Heat pulsed from the wreckage. The barrio was soundless save for the crackle of embers. The one paved road through the center remained clear, the same road where, six weeks ago, Remy had bought new clothes for Carmen and Yumi. Benito took his rifle in hand. Neither he nor Tal crouched in their walk down the empty tarmac.

Many of the bamboo-and-stave homes were built on stilts to protect against monsoons. Some had crashed to the ground, their legs burned away. Others, gutted, stayed supported on scarred posts. Tal stepped close to one elevated house, curious at the rumpled, swollen outlines of the blackened piers.

The smell struck him before the sight, a sweet aroma hiding the bland stench of burnt hair. Tal recoiled into Benito. The guerrilla moved past him into the shadow, under the seared floorboards of the house. Benito reached out his rifle to poke at a cooked arm, as if he needed to test his belief in what he saw. Tal's breathing quickened. He closed his throat against a rising puke and stepped beside the guerrilla under the house.

Filipinos had been tied to all four pillars. Eight bodies stood with their backs seared to the poles. They were ebony and naked, featureless as men or women. Hands were rounded nubs missing fingers, bald and rigid faces grimaced without lips, eyelids, or noses. Benito stood in their center, turning a slow circle.

Tal slid his hand inside Benito's elbow. "Let's go."

He towed the young guerrilla from beneath the house. They did not return to the road but made their way through the heart of the barrio. Under every charred dwelling they found the same, more than two hundred corpses black and bubbled as pitch. They came across dozens of bodies that had been bayoneted then tossed onto the burning shanties like pyres. Here and there, dogs sat whining by their destroyed homes and did not follow when Benito and Tal walked past.

Tal asked, "Where were the guerrillas? Why didn't they stop this?"

The Filipino jabbed a finger at him. "Where were the Americans?"

The two said no more, and moved through the carnage noiselessly. Any living sound seemed indecent. Tal wanted to leave the village. This place was like an underworld; he felt the pull of death here.

The guerrilla was hard to tug away. Benito seemed mesmerized, intent on cataloging every horror of Anos. Tal stepped in front of him.

"Look, the Japs that did this can't be too far away. We've gotta go get Carmen."

The boy's eyes fixed on the last fires in the ruins.

"Benito?"

The guerrilla held out his old rifle.

Tal took it without knowing why. "What are you doing?"

"I'm staying here."

"What for?"

"Someone might be alive."

Tal spoke gently. "They're not."

"Then like you said, the Japanese can't be far. Hurry, Tuck boy."

Benito slid the bolo from the loop at his back. The long knife reflected red until the boy vanished into the remains of the village.

Tal strapped on the rifle. He watched the dark ground to trip over nothing, and ran toward the camp.

Chapter Fifty-six

"THEY'RE BACK," Carmen said.

Kenji struggled to his feet. He stood beside her in the window.

Smoke billowed above Anos a mile and a half north. Quickly the gray pillar thickened to black as more of the village was put to the torch.

The sun retreated into its own red blaze. For the third day in a row, the world around Carmen burned. The charred bones of the camp below, the razed church behind the orchard, now the village by the bay; she gazed at Makiling and imagined the horizon on fire, set off by the sun touching the mountain like a match.

She sat before Kenji did. He held himself at the window a long time. His shadow cast on the wall behind him, boxed in burning gold. Carmen gathered to her the pistol and the doll.

Kenji remained in the window until nightfall. In the fresh darkness, he slumped beside her beneath the sill. He lowered his chin and breathed deeply, regaining the strength he'd spent.

He said, "I will die with shame."

"You're not going to die, Kenji."

"It doesn't matter. Tonight, a hundred years from now."

She checked his bandage, newly wrapped in the late afternoon. The white under his arm held. The hole in Kenji obeyed no logic, it bled or not as it saw fit. His stamina gained, only to ebb. How much longer he could survive this room, the pitiful food she scavenged, the creek water she washed his wound with, she did not know. She wondered the same for herself, not because of the food or water, but the smell of smoke again in her window, the rampage of Nagata.

"How many bullets are left?" she asked.

"Give it to me." He reached for the gun.

"No." She smiled. "I don't want you shooting the Tuck boy, like you swore."

Kenji worked his right hand to test the grip. A sad humor lit his eyes. "I may have to shoot him some other time."

He showed Carmen how to drop the magazine. Four rounds remained.

Kenji lay flat on the tatami. Carmen pulled the water bucket close. It was only a quarter full. She soaked a cloth strip to squeeze drips into Kenji's mouth. She did the same for her own thirst.

Holding the doll in one hand, gun in the other, Carmen watched the annihilation of Anos in red splashes against her walls. Kenji lay motionless.

The village burned hot and high, but not long. All the structures were of bamboo and wood and did not resist the flames. Carmen's room regained its gloom. She held the doll and the pistol in her lap. The creatures of the ravine, tricked and delayed by the fire, began their night calls. Carmen had no clock, the time ticked by on their screeches and chirrs.

She watched the doorway without its curtain, opening into the darker hall. Who would come through it next? Another guerrilla, to kill Kenji? A Japanese to kill her? The Tuck boy to rescue them both?

She believed Kenji was sleeping, but he stirred first, lifting his head off the tatami.

Carmen had to choose which to drop. She set the doll aside, to put both hands on the gun.

Kenji sat up beside her.

She whispered, "It might be Tal."

Kenji shook his head. "It's not."

Carmen bit her lip. She slid her finger over the trigger and held the pistol away from her, aimed at the heart of the doorway. Her arms prickled but the gun did not quake.

Kenji laid a hand over her wrists. "Put it down."

"No."

"They'll kill you. Let me talk to them. There's no other way."

Carmen lowered the gun but kept it at her side.

The soldiers clattered on the stairs. They reached the landing. One of them inched down the hall.

Kenji took Carmen's hand.

The long barrel of a rifle topped by a bayonet appeared in the doorway. The gun crept forward until the Japanese holding it cleared the opening. Seeing Carmen and Kenji seated side by side, the soldier ducked behind the wall. The bayonet dropped, the soldier had gone to a knee. He hissed to others on the landing. They jangled down the hall to stop outside her door.

One set of boots followed, unhurried.

A guttural voice spoke. *"Nitouhei, yakushitamae."*

Kenji said to Carmen, "He wants me to interpret."

Two soldiers flashed across the doorway. One crouched, the other stayed upright. The bayonets and barrels of three rifles protruded into the doorway, barbs for Nagata's voice.

"All right," she said.

Kenji answered. *"Hai."*

Nagata spoke. The sound of the man spilled into Carmen's room as bloody as the firelight from the village.

When he paused, Kenji translated. " 'Thank you for saving my interpreter, Songu.'"

Kenji replied, *"Sore wa kanojo no namae de wa arimasen."* To Carmen, he said, "I told him you are not Songu."

She squeezed Kenji's hand.

Nagata spoke.

"He says he wants to put his head around the corner. Please do not shoot him."

Carmen answered. *"Hai."*

When Nagata's face appeared past the doorjamb, Carmen was reminded of how short he was to be so vile.

Through Kenji, he said, "I will not hurt you. I have come to protect you."

"Tell him thank you but I am glad to stay here."

"You cannot. You must come. There is little time. My squad has already gone back to the mountain. I have come to take you there to safety. The guerrillas are everywhere. They know you have served the Japanese."

"The guerrillas will not harm me."

"They will when they learn you have saved the life of a Japanese soldier. I thank you for this. The corporal is very valuable to us."

"And to me."

Nagata bowed his head. "I understand this. You will come with us now. We will care for you both."

Carmen raised the pistol.

"Take back your head."

Nagata, without interpretation, retreated behind the wall.

She said to Kenji, "I don't know what to do."

"We have to go."

"I don't believe Nagata."

"There's no choice. There are four of them. You'll die if you fight. Give me the gun."

"The Tuck boy is coming."

"He has not come in time. But no matter where he is, he does not want you dead. Nor do I. Please. I know Nagata. Do not test him."

Carmen handed him the pistol.

"Kenji?"

"Yes?"

"Are you afraid?"

"Always."

She kissed his cheek. "It does not show."

Not taking his eyes from her, Kenji called out, "*Watashi wa juu o motte imasu. Hairinasai.*"

Two of the rifles lengthened in the doorway until the soldiers holding them appeared. They stepped inside. Both weapons were leveled, one each at Carmen and Kenji. Nagata entered between them.

His uniform was darker than the soldiers, sweated through. Composed, Nagata reached for the pistol. Carmen assumed he would be frenzied, to murder so many, so coldly. Nagata crammed the gun in his waistband. Kenji drew in his legs to stand. Carmen got to her feet to help him. The rifle's aim rose with her.

Nagata motioned to Carmen. "*Kanojo hairubeki da.*"

Kenji gathered himself, fighting lightheadedness. He answered in Japanese. The argument was fast and decided when Nagata swept out of the room with a gesture for the soldiers to bring Carmen.

Kenji said, "He refuses to leave you here. We'll go together."

He raised his left arm for Carmen to slide his tunic sleeve over it, then rest the shirt across his shoulders in a mantle. When Kenji was ready, she turned to her window and the murky ruins of the camp.

A bayonet and a grunt prodded Carmen in the back. She looked once at the ruins of Tal's barracks, then put the camp behind her.

Carmen took Kenji's arm. Bearing his weight, they left the room.

Nagata stomped down the dark stairs. Carmen and Kenji followed. The three soldiers walked close behind, rifles ready. They stank of soot.

Chapter Fifty-seven

TAL'S WIND did not give out until he reached the orchard. He set Benito's gun on the earth and propped his hands on his knees. He panted beneath a mango tree that Carmen had passed her hand through. The memory made him grab up the rifle and continue. He hurried through images of her touching these trees.

Tal burst into the field of cogon grass. Trampling the tall blades toward the road, he lost steam again. At the edge of the tarmac he stopped, dizzy with exhaustion.

He stood beside the pavement leading into the camp. The pillboxes guarding the main gate were shattered, the concrete pillar he'd been tied to lay busted in the dirt. The barbed wire was knocked down, the ground cratered. Beyond the gate, the camp dissolved into darkness, burned featureless like the bodies of Anos.

Tal entered the field that led to Carmen's building. His breathing eased, clearing his head. She waited in her room for his return. Tal would climb the stairs to her, take her hand and dash with her through the ravine and bamboo, paths and dead village, all the way to the *banca*. They'd push off onto the black water and sail north by the moon.

Only if the interpreter was dead. Benito said he was not. Tal had no clue what kind of man waited for him in Carmen's room. He and the soldier had fired at each other. The Japanese shot Remy. Tal shot him.

Tal slipped his finger over the rifle's trigger, leveled the barrel, and walked on.

He came near the long trench dug after he'd left the camp. Scattered in the bottom lay the corpses of a dozen Japanese, stripped to their loincloths. The dead guards were all thin, rib cages and joints bulging, cut up and battered by what had killed them. Tal moved along the edge of the open grave, holding his breath until he could get past the bodies, and wondered why they were naked.

Before he could exhale, a sound snagged his ears. A clomp, coming from Carmen's building fifty yards ahead. Footsteps in the stairwell! Was Carmen coming to meet him? No, she'd never make that sound, hard boots and anger on the steps.

Tal froze beside the trench. He fell to his chest. A putrid reek curled out of the ditch. Tal slid a few feet away from the edge to get a clean breath.

Someone emerged from the building.

Tal picked out only the motion of a shadowy form, coming in his direction. More shapes issued from the rear door.

Japanese soldiers!

Had they gotten to Carmen first?

Tal lay uncovered in the grass. He could run off into the night, come back after they were gone, then dash to her room. She must have hidden from them!

What if they'd found her? The Japanese had reason to kill Carmen; she was an informant for the guerrillas. Did they know? Tal's stomach wrenched in the dirt. Was the wounded interpreter behind this? Tal should have killed him.

The soldiers headed his way. Was Carmen with them? Tal had to find out. How would he save her? He had no confidence he could hit anything at a distance with this rifle. How could he fight soldiers at night? And if he started shooting, would guerrillas come, or more Japanese? He cursed Benito. The boy would've known what to do.

Tal had no choice. He slithered over the rim of the trench, down among the rotting, naked soldiers.

Chapter Fifty-eight

O VER THE dark field, the three guards walked behind Carmen and Kenji. Nagata set a pace Kenji could not keep up with. The gap between them widened.

They approached the long pit where the Japanese corpses lay. Kenji, who hadn't left Carmen's room since his wounding, had not yet seen the bodies there. She hurried him along, guiding him away from the rim of the ditch. There was no need for Kenji to see so much death while he struggled against his own.

Ahead, Nagata crossed the pavement. He stamped into the high cogon grass leading to the orchard. Kenji lengthened his strides and straightened his back so they would not fall too far behind.

Carmen said, "You are stronger than I knew."

Nagata disappeared into the grass. In the middle of the road, Carmen looked back at the animal husbandry building, knowing she would not see it again. When the Tuck boy came, where would he find her?

They followed Nagata into the orchard. The guards urged them through the fruitless trees with nudges. Kenji asked for patience. Leaving the orchard, he lost his balance and faltered. Carmen caught him before he fell. The guards complained to Kenji.

"I'll run ahead," she said to him. "I'll tell him you need to rest."

"I can go on. Stay with me."

Carmen strengthened her support under his good arm.

Kenji drew a deep and weary breath. They headed for the ravine where Carmen had bathed and gathered water the past two days. A stand of bamboo topped the rim of the gully. In the gaining moonlight, Nagata waited for them to catch up.

Nagata reached to Kenji's cheek, checking his color. Kenji's pallor was not difficult to see. Nagata tugged the unbuttoned tunic aside to look at the bandage. The night drained the small bloodstain to black.

Nagata sucked his teeth in disappointment. He dropped Kenji's shirttail. "*Hayaku.*" Hurry. He tramped off into the cogon grass.

Carmen took Kenji's arm. He faltered stepping forward. From behind, a hand pushed him along. Kenji stopped her from whirling on the guard.

Kenji struggled through the bamboo, then down the slope of the ravine. Carmen helped him pick his way across the creek bed, stepping stone to stone. Kenji and the soldiers slipped many times, soaking their boots. Nagata seemed unconcerned with quiet, only making speed.

They clambered up the opposite bank. Nagata led them out of a narrow band of jungle lining the ravine. He moved onto the road to stride down the center.

Kenji's boots scuffed on the pavement. He struggled to lift his feet. Beside the tarmac stood the charred remains of the chapel torched last night by Nagata and his raiders, with a hundred villagers inside. Around the church stood a dozen untouched sawali huts, abandoned and lightless. Their owners were likely dead.

Carmen had walked this way only once, with Tal, Remy, Yumi, and the raucous boys of Tal's barracks. They'd ridden into the village in rickshaws. Remy had bought her and Yumi clothes at the bazaar. Carmen had throttled a chicken and shocked Tal.

This was the road to Anos.

The moon let Carmen keep Nagata in sight. They walked for ten minutes on the tarmac. Kenji began to fight for every step. She bore as much of his weight as she could, afraid to look at his paling face or his bandage. Kenji pressed on, and the guards trailed like silent ripples.

The road wound through a copse of palms and tall banyans. The outlines of the first humble houses of Anos lay not far ahead. Nagata stopped in the road, lit by stars, waiting for them.

Kenji leaned more on her with every stride.

She whispered, "Why are we in Anos?"

Kenji licked his lips, mouth dry. "Maybe this is where his soldiers are."

No, she thought. In her room, Nagata said his unit had returned to Makiling.

Kenji said, "I don't know." He sounded light-headed.

Carmen tugged him to a standstill. She said, "That's enough."

She slid aside his tunic. The bandage was soaked. A dribble of blood inched down his bare stomach.

Kenji said, "Yes."

His knees buckled. Carmen reached to catch him; he sank through her hands to the pavement. He landed sitting upright, legs spread.

She faced the three guards for help. They stood back, resting their rifles.

"We need to stop," she told them. "This is killing him."

Nagata approached. Kenji mustered enough strength to lift his head. The tunic had slipped off his shoulders.

Nagata came close to Kenji. He knelt and spoke in quiet tones. Kenji nodded. He lowered his eyes and reached out, like a man begging. Nagata stood erect. He pulled the pistol from his waistband and offered it to Kenji. Changing his mind, Nagata backed off several steps to set the gun on the road. Kenji dropped his arm. He would need to crawl for it.

Carmen went to her knees. She cupped Kenji's face.

"Kenji-sama, please. What are you doing?"

His head felt heavy; it would drop if she did not hold it.

"Nagata has suggested I may have an honorable death. He is wrong."

"Tell him he needs to let you sit, until you stop bleeding."

"He will not."

Carmen touched her forehead to his. "Don't do this. Try to stand."

In her hands, against her brow, Kenji slowly shook his head.

"Not long ago, you asked me a question. What would we do if we had a reason? Do you remember?"

She fought the quavering of her voice. "Yes."

"Well." His voice was sleepy. "Let us see."

Nagata motioned to the guards. Two of them pulled Carmen away. Her last sight of Kenji was him sitting in the road, his chest black, the gun out of reach.

Chapter Fifty-nine

◆

TAL BURROWED into the jumble of bodies.

He squirmed between rigid arms and brittle chests. The Japanese were not fleshy, they'd been hungry, too, on the day they died. With seconds left, he pulled a cadaver across him. The soldier's skin was warm after a day in the sun.

Tal could not hold his breath for his nerves. The stink of feces and decay in the pit repulsed him, he fought down a gag. Around him, marble eyes gazed in all directions. Tal watched the rim of the trench. He kept the rifle close.

Footsteps passed near. Tal's hand tensed on the rifle. The jangle of weapons moved beyond the trench and no one peered in.

He waited until the sounds were faint but not gone. Tal cast the corpses off, stood among them aghast, and scrambled out.

Away from the ditch, he crouched, scanning the dark. He brushed himself off as if the bodies had left bits on him. He smelled his own arms and hands. Fifty yards ahead, the dark outline of a soldier strode across the road leading into the camp. Others trailed, among them one taller than the rest.

Tal looked to the animal husbandry building. If Carmen was still inside, he could double back. But what if she was with them? He had to pursue the figures disappearing into the high grass to find out, or he might never see her again. He bent at the waist to jog across the open field.

The shapes entered the cogon grass. They were easy to track through the trampled blades. Tal stayed at enough distance to tail them without being heard. Before he knew it, the grass thinned, giving way to the orchard. Entering the fruitless branches, he lost sight of them.

They could have taken any number of paths through the orchard. Tal couldn't break into a run, that would betray him. He stepped cautiously forward, keen for a voice, a snapping stick, something to guide him onward.

Where would Japanese soldiers take Carmen? To safety, to protect her? That didn't fit with what Tal knew of them. Why murder so many, then save Carmen, a Filipina they'd abused and degraded? It made no sense.

Would she go with the soldiers without being forced? No. She'd sent Benito to bring Tal back, expressly to keep her out of the hands of the Japanese.

They wouldn't take her into the villages, not where guerrillas might swarm them. A handful of armed Japanese would get hacked to pieces if they wandered into the wrong barrio.

Unless that barrio was empty.

Anos.

The little village was lifeless. The Japanese had killed every inch of it. Why go back? Why take Carmen there?

Maybe she wasn't with them. What if the soldiers had gone to her room to collect their wounded comrade, and left her behind?

What if they hadn't?

No time to puzzle. Tal had to choose a path through the orchard. Lacking Remy's ability to read his own luck, he trusted in the promise he'd made Carmen to always return. He sped his gait, keeping low under the dark branches, careful to stay silent. He moved north, toward the bay and the dead village.

He hurried under mango and lemon trees, over earth silvering with the rising moon. At the boundary of the orchard he paused, casting out his senses. Ahead lay a field of scrub and wild acacia. Beyond that, a bamboo grove masked the bank of the ravine.

Tal stepped out of the orchard, into the open.

Voices dropped him to the ground. He raised his head to trace the sound but could not see the source for the grass and night.

He heard her.

"I'll run ahead. I'll tell him you need to rest."

She was here!

That was all he knew for sure. Not where she was being taken or why, or how he could save her. He had no plan, no ally, and a weapon he'd never fired.

Tal didn't recognize the next voice. "I can go on. Stay with me."

Was this the interpreter Tal had shot?

If it was, whose side would he be on? He'd tried to kill Tal and needed Carmen to stay with him. He was wounded. Tal would not count on him.

Silently he sat up in the grass, straining his eyes for movement in the gray light. There they were, walking toward the ravine. Four soldiers and Carmen. Tal rose to do the one thing he could be certain of, follow.

A palisade of bamboo stood beside the ravine. Carmen and her guards stopped. Another voice cut through the night.

"*Hayaku.*"

Tal's spine chilled.

Nagata!

The man moved into the bamboo. Carmen and the soldiers disappeared into the stalks behind him, slowed by the wounded interpreter.

Nagata had burned the village church with a hundred people inside. The murder of Anos was likely his doing, too. For months in the camp, no day passed without a vicious act from him.

Now he had Carmen.

Tal tracked them into the ravine, creeping noiselessly while the soldiers clambered over the rocks and skidded into pools. The animals and birds hooted at the Japanese for their careless passage, masking Tal fifty strides back.

Nagata led the way up the opposite bank. Tal waited behind the boulder where he'd met the guerrilla Emilio. The tall interpreter had trouble getting up the rocky slope.

Tal glided behind them. Over his head the old owl swooped in a hunter's farewell. Tal squatted in the cover of trees and brush along the Anos road.

Nagata moved to the middle of the tarmac, with no risk of traffic. Every Filipino along this road had either fled for the hills or died in his home.

The interpreter, Carmen, and the soldiers walked behind Nagata. Tal stayed off the road, darting from palm tree to bush, fence post to ditch. The moon had risen enough for him to trail from farther back. Carmen and the soldiers did not speak. The one sound was the interpreter dragging his boots.

The road curved beneath a stand of trees close to the shoulder. Nagata walked into the moon shade, then Carmen and the soldiers. Tal could not see them clearly and slowed his pace. He stole through the small yards of darkened huts still unburned. The carnage of Anos began on the far side of the trees.

Carmen spoke. Tal froze behind the trunk of a palm. She implored someone, "This is killing him," and in a lower volume, "What are you doing?" Tal couldn't make out the rest of her words. He waited; her voice was not moving on the road.

He heard a brief scuffle and nothing more. The road under the blocked moon fell silent.

Tal waited no longer. He scurried forward, staying on the grass, behind cover, into the darkened patch. He closed in on someone sitting in the road, torso wrapped in white.

The interpreter. They'd left him behind.

Keeping off the road, Tal passed the downed soldier, who did not register that he was near.

Tal stepped from behind cover, onto the pavement. The soldier was swathed in white only from the rear; from the front, his whole bandage glistened black.

The interpreter raised his dull face. Carmen had stayed back in Los Baños to save him. Now he was dying, and it had all been for naught.

The soldier raised his good arm. Tal gripped the rifle, ready to club him, until he saw the interpreter's hand empty. The man pointed at a pistol steps away on the road.

What did he want? For Tal to give him the gun? To take it?

Gunshots rang.

Tal ducked in reflex. He came face to face with the wounded interpreter.

In pain, the Japanese said, "Carmen."

Tal took off running through the darkness, into Anos.

Chapter Sixty

CARMEN HAD been brought here to die. There was nothing in the village but death.

The guards let her loose not far from Kenji. She did not run back to him. For what? To watch him bleed? See him commit suicide? Or have Nagata kill her in front of him?

Every hut in the village had been torched. The moon and stars lit charred bodies standing below their homes. Other houses had crashed down, their stilts burned away, the families buried.

The numbers of the murdered all around gave Carmen an unexpected calm. She would not meet death alone. She was Filipina, and would die as they did, because they were Filipino. Though she knew the ones upright beneath their homes had been tied to the posts, they were on their feet nonetheless. Carmen took a bitter pride in this. She would not run and take a bullet in the back. She would stand, Filipina, and stare Nagata in the face.

He waited in the center of the road. Carmen led the three soldiers to him. She thought of Tal and what could have been. Of Kenji as a good man. Yumi in safety, Hua in the grave. How many comfort women were there? Carmen would never know. Her family in Manila, would they be told she died in Anos? She had nothing to identify her, not even the Songu tag. The Tuck boy had it. She was sorry that his only memento of her should be that thing.

Carmen wanted more life, but she would give the Japanese what they valued most. A good death.

Nagata swept his arm across the village, the whole black panorama.

"*Aw-rr* die."

He'd failed to kill the internees as he'd threatened, so had visited himself instead on Anos.

Nagata pointed to the pavement in front of Carmen. He wanted her on her knees.

She said, "No."

He flicked a finger at one of his soldiers. A rifle butt smashed into the back of her knee, buckling it. Carmen held herself up with one leg until it, too, was struck, harder and from the side. This knee exploded. She crumpled to the tarmac.

Nagata leaned close, stinking of sweat. She could not rise; agony made her legs inert.

He snarled, "*Mikkokusha.*" Nagata batted together his fingers and thumb in a talking, biting gesture.

He'd figured it out. She was an informant. Nagata had brought her to Anos to be killed in the road, in the heart of the murdered village, one more warning to other collaborators.

"*Hai,*" she said.

Nagata motioned for another of his guards. The short man stalked in front of Carmen. He glared down with hatred equal to Nagata's.

The soldier did not hesitate. He reared his rifle high, to drive the bayonet into Carmen's chest. She held her breath, away from the stench of Nagata and Anos. She kept her eyes open, clenched her hands to stop them shaking, bared her teeth. She thought of her father, fighting at the train station to keep her. She tried to do him honor.

The soldier stepped backward. The rifle over his head seemed suddenly too heavy and he stumbled under it, dropped it clattering on the road.

Benito, the mop boy, the guerrilla in sneakers, stood behind the soldier. He yanked the bolo out of the man's side as if out of a hewn tree. Freed from it, the soldier collapsed.

Before Nagata or the other guards could raise their weapons, the boy swung again, hacking deep into the ribs of the closest soldier. This one dropped to his knees. Benito, in continuous motion, swept the bolo above his shoulders with two fists and swung the blade into the kneeling Japanese's neck. The soldier's head lolled off kilter, attached by little. His body tumbled, spraying blood.

The remaining soldier fired from the hip. He shot once, twice, a third time. Each bullet hit Benito only steps away. The first stopped the boy's charge at the soldier, the second knocked him back, the third felled him. Benito lay in the road between the two Japanese he'd killed.

Nagata picked up the rifle from the first soldier Benito had chopped down. He stood over the boy and rammed the bayonet twice into his belly, leaving the rifle standing, the point buried in the dirt beneath.

Nagata turned on Carmen holding the boy's bolo. He examined the machete with a sound of disgust, not for the blood on the steel but the long knife's peasant design.

He did not lift the bolo. He dropped it. The blade clanged on the pavement.

The soldier raised his weapon. Nagata yanked the erect rifle out of Benito. Neither gun pointed at Carmen, but at a scream out of the darkness.

Chapter Sixty-one

T HE FIRST bullet struck Tal as he emerged from the shadows. The round grooved his hip but did not stop him. He ran at Nagata and the soldier, driven by fear, rage, now pain.

At a dead sprint, he pointed the barrel of Benito's rifle and fired. He couldn't slow to aim. Nagata and the soldier had their rifles up and feet solid, shooting back. Tal would die where he stood.

He screamed again, charging these men who'd killed Carmen and would die for it if he could reach them. He dodged once to throw off their sights, then fired another wild round. Nagata and the soldier did not shift a step in the road. Tal's bullets flew nowhere close to them. They loosed another volley. Two rounds whizzed past his head. Tal closed the distance to thirty running, moonlit strides. In seconds he'd be close enough to empty the rifle at them and not miss.

On the black tarmac around Nagata and the soldier, bodies lay scattered. Between them, someone kneeled. Someone living.

She shrieked his name.

She was not dead!

Tal hesitated, confused and desperate. He slowed, to place his shots. He could not hit Carmen.

Nagata and the soldier fired. One round zinged near Tal's shoulder. The second pierced his calf below the furrow in his hip. The bullet knocked Tal's leg from under him. He tripped, but caught himself on one knee. Focusing everything, Tal raised Benito's rifle to his cheek. He found Nagata standing at the end of the gun and squeezed the trigger.

The rifle kicked. Nagata held his ground, leveling his own gun barrel. With no time to better his aim, Tal pulled the trigger again, believing this might be his last living act. Tal sank backward, his leg no longer holding him up.

Nagata spun around, struck. The soldier beside Nagata fired. The bullet tore through the meat of Tal's left forearm and blazed across his chest. Benito's rifle fell out of his hands.

The soldier ran at Tal, rifle up, ready to finish him. Carmen screamed, "No!"

The soldier bore in. He stopped close enough to kick Tal.

Nagata shouted, *"Yamete!"* Huffing, the soldier stared down the length of his rifle and bayonet.

Twenty steps away, Nagata bent to the road. When he stood, he held a glinting *pinuti* bolo.

It was Benito's. The boy must have been one of the bodies. The shots Tal heard were the guerrilla's killing.

Nagata lurched away from Carmen.

"Tal."

Her voice passed Nagata, the crunch of his boots on the Anos road.

Tal bled from six wounds. He fingered the holes in his calf, the pair in his forearm, and traced the gouges in his ribs and hip. Nothing hurt, and this amazed him.

"I'm sorry," she said.

Nagata shuffled the last distance. The soldier backed off to give him room. Nagata turned the bolo in his hand, getting the feel of it. He laid down his rifle beside the one Tal dropped.

Tal could not see her. Nagata stood between them.

"Carmen," he called. "Can you get up and run?"

Nagata widened his stance. A bullet hole in his thigh oozed.

"No," she said.

"It's all right." Tal dragged himself sideways; he wanted one look at her in the dim light. Nagata shook his head, at the vain effort to evade him.

She sat like him in the road, twenty steps away. They were together; the Japanese had not kept them apart.

He dug his good hand into his pocket for the Songu tag. Before Nagata could raise the bolo to stop him, he pitched the wooden tag. It slid on the road against Carmen's leg.

Tal had kept his promise.

"Tuck-san." Nagata lifted his chin, for Tal to do the same. Behind Nagata, the soldier urged his rifle forward, to make Tal comply.

Nagata waited.

Tal flipped him the bird. He raised his chin.

Nagata grunted, putting both hands on the long knife. With the bolo at his waist, he halted.

Nagata's gaze snapped into the darkness behind Tal, to the border of shadow on the road.

A shot cracked. The soldier, focused on Tal down the length of his rifle, jerked backward, lifting the gun. Three more shots barked in quick succession. The soldier reeled to the thud of bullets hitting his chest. Holes broke in his tunic. The rifle slipped from his hands, he went down on his back.

Nagata let go of the bolo. On his bleeding leg, he was slow to bend for the dropped rifle. Tal scrabbled for it the same instant. The pain in his arm, quiet until now, burst open. Nagata tugged the gun away.

The wounded interpreter staggered out of the shadows, clutching his pistol high above the sopping bandages, centered on Nagata's back. Unbalanced, Nagata hoisted the rifle to swing it around.

The interpreter's gun clicked once, then twice. He stopped his approach, reaching the pistol at Nagata from ten strides away. The hammer clicked once more.

Nagata faced him with puffed cheeks, out of danger. He shook his head at the interpreter.

The two Japanese stared with weapons raised. The interpreter lowered his empty gun. As if Nagata willed it, the soldier tottered on his feet until he, too, fell to his knees.

Nagata did not shoot. He took in the black ruins he had made, and the living three he'd mastered on the Anos road that he had left to kill.

Dropping the rifle to his hip, Nagata shuffled forward, leading with the bayonet.

The interpreter raised his head, white as the moon.

Nagata stopped close. He laid the point of the bayonet against the interpreter's bandaged chest. Nagata considered the kneeling, shuddering soldier.

A gunshot made Tal cringe. The interpreter crumpled at the end of Nagata's rifle. Nagata took one broken step then toppled, not to his knees but on his face.

Tal swung to Carmen.

The girl lay flat on the road with a dead soldier's rifle steadied across Benito's body. Her cheek was pressed to the stock, her eye down the long barrel.

Carmen lifted her gaze, surfacing from the gun. Somewhere in the ruins a dying flame crackled.

She called, "Is he dead?"

Tal drew his good leg and arm under him. He pushed off to stand. Blood trickled from his left hand. On his wounded calf, Tal limped to Nagata.

Carmen's shot had ripped into the small of the guard's back. The bullet might have cut the man's spine, might have gut shot him. With pain, Tal bent to pry the rifle from Nagata's living grip.

In the guttering silence of Anos, Tal raised the weapon. The back of Nagata's head came up. His hand flexed to find the rifle gone. Tal set the three-sided bayonet tip between Nagata's shoulders, behind where he guessed the man's wicked heart would be. He pushed down, feeling nothing of the layers the bayonet passed through, surprised how little resistance a man's flesh put up. Nagata shuddered when the bayonet was all the way in; this Tal felt through the rifle. He let the gun go and stepped back. The rifle tipped over but stood. Nagata's gaze did not follow Tal's dragging foot, and Tal the thief took one last thing from the Japanese.

Gritting his teeth, Tal turned from Nagata to kneel beside the interpreter. He lifted the pistol out of the soldier's vacant grip.

In the dark, Carmen said, "His name is Kenji."

Kenji's eyes were closed. His soaked wrapping rose barely and fell. He was alive.

"Hey."

The interpreter wore his black hair long like Tal. The two had been the same height the times they'd stood near each other in the camp.

"Can you hear me?"

Kenji's lips moved but did not meet to form a word.

Tal touched a fingertip to the bloody wrap. His own bullet had done this. He'd killed this man after all.

Tal looked at the village in ashes, the bodies in the road, the raped virgin girl he and this Japanese both loved. The things, he thought, a fella will do.

"Pal, I'm sorry we met." Tal brushed a strand of hair off Kenji's brow.

The soldier's mouth widened. He did not speak but loosed a long, draining breath. Kenji sagged into the Anos road.

Tal made his way back to Carmen, pistol and bolo in

hand. She could stand on one leg; the other knee was excruciating. Benito lay on the tarmac framed between his two kills. Tal left the rifle Carmen had steadied across the guerrilla boy's mangled chest. He set the bolo beside the gun.

Together, hopping and walking, blended into one by their injuries, Tal and Carmen left the bodies and ruins of Anos. Nearing the boat, Carmen faltered. Tal lifted her in his arms.

On the starry bay, they sailed ahead of a breeze that blew away from Los Baños. Carmen ripped Tal's shirt into strips to bind his forearm and leg. When they were far from land, Tal dropped Kenji's pistol into the water.

In revenge there is something which satisfies one's sense of justice. . . . Our sense of revenge is as exact as our mathematical faculty, and until both terms of the equation are satisfied we cannot get over the sense of something left undone.

—INAZO NITOBE,
BUSHIDO: THE SOUL OF JAPAN, 1905

July, golf

Chapter Sixty-two

FOR HER size, Yumi had good length off the tee. She combined that with a light touch around the greens and was a born putter. Remy intended to get her lessons soon.

Her first drive this morning found the fairway.

Tal followed with a hard slice. Carmen's ball disappeared in the tall grass out of bounds. Remy topped his drive; it rolled straight to stop behind Yumi's.

"You still weakling," Yumi said, needling Remy with a poke.

The little girl was the only one of the four who hadn't spent weeks in a hospital: Carmen after knee surgery, Tal and Remy for bullet holes, malnutrition, and parasites. Yumi's game was ahead of theirs.

They shouldered their bags. Tal and Carmen split up to opposite sides of the fairway. Yumi and Remy walked together.

Remy brought his son and the girls here once a week, a few miles outside the city. Golf was good for Carmen's knee, Tal's calf, Remy's lung. Yumi loved the gay outfits.

A work detail of Japanese POWs in coolie hats labored alongside the fairway. Some dragged rakes to clear the grounds of shell casings. Others carried away rubble from the blown-up fuel dump and antiaircraft battery the Japanese had kept here. The rest of the prisoners laid sod to help restore Wack Wack Golf Course to its original condition.

The renovation of the course progressed slowly, from a shortage of manpower. Months ago, Remy and the internees watched the night sky shiver over Manila, cheering the bashing the Americans were giving the Japanese. When MacArthur finally liberated the capital in March, the butcher's bill of the Japanese defense of the city came due. One in seven citizens of Manila lay dead, a hundred thousand killed by bombs, crossfire, street fighting, and a surge of mean-spirited murder from the last Japanese holdouts. The surviving Manileños were busy picking up the pieces and mourning.

Few Japanese had surrendered. At Iwo Jima, Okinawa, Rangoon, across the entire Pacific War, they died in the futile defense of lost islands, in banzai and kamikaze attacks, in droves. The number of POWs the U.S. Army could put to work at Wack Wack was low.

Carmen's ball lay farthest away. She swung first, punching back into the fairway. Tal tried to hack his way out of trouble. He left his shot in the opposite rough near the prisoners. Carmen came to stand with Yumi and Remy in the fairway. They waited for Tal to reach his ball.

"Just put it in play," Carmen called while the boy crossed in front of them.

Tal grumbled and kept walking. Yumi pointed to her shot for Carmen to see how she'd outdriven Remy by ten yards. Remy thought both girls beautiful. Carmen looked like her mother, whom Remy had met for the first time in April, at the funeral of one of Carmen's uncles. No body had been found—the family buried a picture of the man. Carmen had stood in a cast, Tal with a cane, Remy in a sling, Yumi in bright yellow.

Most of the internees from Los Baños and Santo Tomas had left the Philippines, returning to their nations after losing homes, jobs, and fortunes. Many missionaries stayed behind with more work to do now than before the war. Remy and Tal chose to remain in ruined Manila. The boy and Carmen were set to marry. Remy's trade, gambling, did not go down in rubble with the city. Manila was lousy with Americans flooding in to remake the place, military to occupy it, with no other forms of entertainment.

Remy's luck was back in the pink. He'd been right, it had turned against him, the tenth game tipped him off. Tal was supposed to die when that Japanese shot at him in Carmen's hallway. When Remy stepped in front of the bullet, he beat his luck. He turned it around.

Yumi was going to stay with Remy. As soon as the American School was repaired, she would attend. Remy, like any father, feared the day she began dating.

In the weeks after Los Baños, Tal talked of joining the military before the war was finished. Then the fighting ended in Europe. The U.S. Marines in the Pacific geared up for an all-out assault on Japan's home islands. There wasn't much war left. Tal got the notion instead that he might like to work in one of the hotels being rebuilt in Manila. He'd learn the business, then start a hotel himself. He liked the idea of a hotel, a place where folks could come and go as they pleased. Carmen would handle the kitchen. Remy could gamble in the bar. Remy said this was a great idea, knowing it might not be. The boy had turned twenty last month. He would have many ideas.

Tal stood over his ball, in grass high enough to cover his shoes. He chose a long iron for a shot at the green, ignoring Carmen's advice to pitch out. The boy had four pale dots in his flesh now, the bullet scars having tanned more slowly than the rest of him. These were the only evidence of his ordeal. Tal walked fine and his left arm was strong again. It was not strong enough, Remy figured, for the shot the boy was lining up. Remy kept his counsel and let him learn, as always, after his own fashion.

Tal stood behind his ball, waiting while the POWs got out of his way. A dozen former imperial soldiers shouldered their rakes to move in a bunch. Their peaked straw hats reminded Remy of the roofs of the barracks at Los Baños. A single American guard kept watch over the prisoners. The Japanese had no intent of escaping. Where would they go? The first Filipinos to see them would beat them to death.

The boy's line was cleared. He didn't address his ball for the shot but stared at the shuffling POWs after they took up work behind him. Carrying his club, Tal walked into the fairway.

Remy called to him, "Change your mind?"

"Pitch out," Yumi said. "Crazy shot."

Tal rapped Yumi on the shoulder. The two bickered like siblings.

"Look at those Japs."

"What for?" Remy and the girls eyed the laborers.

"Look close."

Carmen saw him. "On the right. The older one."

Tal breathed the name. "Toshiwara."

Remy eased his hand over his son's shoulder. The boy had filled out. If he wanted to break away from Remy, there was nothing that could be done.

Tal tensed to step forward. Before he could move or Remy speak, Yumi bolted across the fairway.

The POWs did not notice, busy with their rakes under their wide straw brims. The big armed guard moved to intercept the girl, but too late.

With both hands she shoved the narrow, damp back of the camp commandant.

The old man stumbled but did not go to his knees. Too bad, Remy thought.

Keeping his hand on Tal, he said, "Boy, please. Stay right here. Understand?"

Carmen took Tal's hand.

Remy hurried across the fairway to free Yumi from the American guard. The soldier had put his hands on the little girl in bright colors. She'd pushed him, too. Remy would try to explain.

I doubt that any airborne unit in the world will ever be able to rival the Los Baños prison raid. It is the textbook airborne operation for all ages and all armies.

—GEN. COLIN POWELL
FORMER CHAIRMAN,
U.S JOINT CHIEFS OF STAFF

Annotations

CHAPTER ONE

- In late December of 1944, American fighter and bomber planes were a common sight above Los Baños. The planes were based on the southern island of Mindoro, which had fallen in mid-month. American pilots frequently flew low over the camp, performing aerobatics and other feats to hearten the internees and alert them that their plight was known. One flier did, in fact, loose four cannon bursts in the forests beside the camp, in the rhythm of Beethoven's Fifth Symphony, also Morse code for the letter V. Many pilots also dropped items into the camp, including cigarettes.

- The Japanese considered a slap, the *binta,* to be an act of ultimate disdain. American prisoners suffered this indignity in all Japanese wartime camps.

- Dr. Dana Nance, the medical director of Los Baños, was a known curmudgeon. He was tireless in his efforts to preserve the internees' health against the encroaching effects of intestinal parasites, edema, roundworms, skin fungi, beriberi, pellagra, malaria, bacillary dysentery, dengue fever, pernicious anemia, scurvy—all treatable but made far worse by malnutrition and the absence of medication. Nance had little patience with fools or the Japanese. The day before Thanksgiving 1944, he beat Poochie, the pet dog of Polly and Bill Yankey, to death with an iron bar. Poochie had grown fat on food sacrificed by its owners. The pet compromised Nance's ability to complain to the Japanese about decreasing rations for the internees.

Poochie's owners got into a fistfight with Dr. Nance, then retrieved the dog's carcass before the doctor could drag it to the kitchen. They smeared the corpse with poison to prevent Nance from digging it up, and buried Poochie in the camp garden.

CHAPTER TWO

- One comfort woman existed for approximately every fifty soldiers of the Imperial Japanese Army. The author has taken the liberty of placing a comfort station, or *shuho,* at the internment camp of Los Baños; the Japanese garrison at the camp numbered approximately two hundred soldiers, and the town of Los Baños was a major crossroads and rail terminal.

- Suicide was a common escape for many comfort women. Girls were also invited into double suicide pacts by depressed soldiers. As the war turned against the Japanese, a great number of comfort women were simply deserted; in extreme cases, they were driven into ditches or caves and executed by the retreating soldiers. Some estimates state that fewer than one quarter of the comfort women survived their enslavement.

- Injections of 606 (the compound salvarsan) were used not only as a treatment for venereal disease but to prevent pregnancy and to induce abortion. The drug was exceptionally strong; after the war, comfort women reported that they had become sterile due to the frequent use of 606 by Japanese medical staff.

CHAPTER THREE

- The internment camp at Los Baños was run by a series of commandants, ranging from benign to weak. Toshiwara is meant to represent an amalgam of these men. None of them were punished by the Allies at the end of the war.

- Nagata is a composite drawn from the actual Lieutenant Sadaaki Konishi. The guard has been described by several chroniclers of Los Baños; none leave out the word *sadistic*.

  He is well depicted in *Angels at Dawn*, Lieutenant General Edward M. Flanagan, Jr. (USA, ret.), Presidio Press, 1999, page 38:

  > Konishi was universally despised by the internees. He was about 5'7" tall, with a scarred face and a generally "mean" look. The internees felt that he had "an intense hatred for the white race," that he was "very cunning" . . . that he was "an arrogant, brutal type of person." He "had a vast effect over the commandant . . . not only within his own sphere, which was food and supply, but also in other matters of camp administration." . . . There is no question that he hated the Americans with a consuming passion. He vowed at one point that "they would be eating dirt before he was through with them."

CHAPTER FOUR

- A comfort woman typically serviced between fifteen and thirty soldiers per day, with officers arriving at night. The worst periods of activity came when the women were visited by soldiers passing through their locations. According to *The Comfort Women*, George Hicks, W. W. Norton & Co., 1997, page 73:

  > What the women dreaded most were visits by bodies of troops in transit. A stable attachment to one particular unit would at least tend to limit the volume of service required, and perhaps improve the chances of developing some degree of fellow-feeling. But in

the case of transients, the demand would not only increase in volume, but also in intensity. Such troops would often be headed for action, and would regard this as possibly their last chance for sex. After a quick succession of such visits, the woman's performance would become mechanical. The men would regard this as poor service or coldness. This could lead to violence.

CHAPTER FIVE

- The Japanese guards identified those internees whom they considered troublemakers and placed them in barracks 11, located near their own quarters. The residents of barracks 11 were mostly younger males with a taste for insurrection and mischief.

- Gen. Douglas MacArthur insisted that his suite at the Hotel Manila be built with seven bedrooms, the same as President Quezon's residence, Malacañan. MacArthur had his rooms ringed with an outdoor parapet where he could stroll and be seen from all sides. When the general retreated from Manila to Bataan in December 1941, his wife left two bronze Japanese vases outside their door, to appease the invading commander Yamashita and to seek protection for her home. Yamashita took MacArthur's quarters for his own. Three years later, during the battle to liberate Manila, Yamashita directed the suite be burned. He waited until MacArthur and his troops were across the street from the hotel. The general watched his beloved quarters and immense military library go up in flames. The bronze urns remained at the front door.

CHAPTER SIX

- Terry's Hunters was one of several guerrilla groups in the area of Los Baños, and was arguably the best equipped and led.

    Because the rescue of the internees was such a notable historical event, much jockeying for credit has ensued in the aftermath. The effectiveness of the guerrillas in the liberation of the Philippines, and the rescue at Los Baños in particular, remains a contested matter. The guerrillas themselves make a strong case that their role was pivotal, while the American military tends to minimize the Filipinos' combat claims. This is to be expected, as regular soldiers would have had little opportunity to see the guerrillas' hit-and-run fighting in the isolated jungles and mountains.

    To the author, this seems a debate only over matters of degree. What is not in question is that the Filipino resistance was brave and effective, independent of their discipline or tactics. Were the guerrillas not terribly bothersome to the Japanese, there would not have been so many slaughters of Filipino villages as retaliation.

    An in-depth discussion of the guerrillas' role in the Philippines can be found in Flanagan, *Angels at Dawn*, pages 72–98.

CHAPTER SEVEN

- A common use of comfort women, and a further degradation, was to put them naked at the head of tired Japanese columns to encourage the soldiers to march forward.
- The "recruitment" of comfort women took every conceivable shape, from trickery to outright kidnapping. Shady dealers roamed the countryside searching for virginal girls to snare and sweep off to China or some other battleground nation. Soldiers and police grabbed whom they pleased; families were bribed, fooled, or bullied into sending away their daughters.

The Japanese military believed that comfort women would help reduce the incidence of venereal disease among the troops, ease the incidence of rape against the women of conquered populaces, and protect military secrets from being drawn out by sex with civilians. In the end, rape continued unabated (which must include that committed against the comfort women), sexually transmitted diseases continued to spread among the troops, and many comfort women fed information to the local militias.

CHAPTER EIGHT

- In the years following their imprisonment, many Los Baños internees wrote memoirs describing their time in the camp. All referred to guards both cruel and kind. Many were ruthless in the mold of Konishi, others profited from the internees' misery by striking one-sided trades, while some tried in secretive ways to ease the starvation and sickness inside the wire. In the end, the Japanese officials and guards of the camp were as diverse as the internees themselves.

- The camp was the equivalent of a small American town, with a commensurately wide range of personalities. Among them was a man named Harry Sniffen, the basis for the character Lazlo, who reportedly lived very well in the camp while others starved, sickened, and died. Sniffen and the rest of the internee community are well described in *Deliverance at Los Baños,* Anthony Arthur, St. Martin's Press, 1985, pages 49–78.

CHAPTER NINE

- At both Santo Tomas and Los Baños, a handful of internees, including Dr. Nance, created secret radio receivers and transmitters out of spare parts. The methods of concealment were as ingenious as the designs of the apparatuses. These men kept their fellow internees supplied with news from outside the wire, an irreplaceable service to camp morale, all the while knowing that being caught with such a device was a death sentence.

CHAPTER TEN

- Comfort women were treated as prisoners in their stations. They were rarely allowed out of doors, never without escort. When not servicing soldiers, they were forced to labor for the troops, doing such menial tasks as laundry and sewing. Their pay was almost always a joke; they were either cheated out of it by their *shuho* handlers, given Japanese scrip that proved worthless at war's end, or simply not paid at all.

CHAPTER ELEVEN

- The Japanese left Los Baños in the early morning of January 5. Before departing, they gathered every digging tool in the camp. History does not record the reason; it has been speculated that the guards were ordered to dig trenches and defense works around Manila, or for the Tiger Division bivouacked ten miles south.

CHAPTER FOURTEEN

- Far more than "tens of thousands" of conquered women were enslaved by the Japanese as comfort women. Conservative estimates range from two to three hundred thousand.
- The Imperial Japanese Army did infrequently employ its own citizens as comfort women. The practice was restricted to Japanese professional prostitutes of at least twenty-one years of age at the time of their recruitment. Japanese com-

fort women, unlike their foreign counterparts, received approximately 40 percent of their pay, with 60 percent going to the military establishment that housed them. They were not kept in conditions of slavery (physical restraint) and were not abandoned or killed at war's end.

In *Comfort Women,* Yoshiaki Yoshimi, Suzanne O'Brien (trans.), Columbia University Press, 2002, page 155, the reasons for avoiding nonprostitute Japanese women are stated clearly:

> If Japanese women who were not prostitutes were sent from Japan . . . as comfort women, it would exert a grave influence on citizens, especially on families whose sons were stationed overseas. Also, if the sisters, wives or female acquaintances of soldiers stationed overseas came to the battlefields as comfort women, it would probably destroy soldiers' sense of trust in the state and the army . . . Therefore, the rounding up of comfort women from Japan was extremely limited.

CHAPTER NINETEEN

• The Japanese returned to Los Baños at three o'clock in the morning of January 13, 1945. They were worn out and short-tempered.

The commandant, Iwanaka, normally a taciturn man, was visibly upset over the return of a camp radio that was not the Philco his guards had left behind (an internee had traded the guards' radio in the villages for food), and the pilfering of his private rice bowl, hand-painted with the emperor's flag. The internees had also looted the storehouses during the guards' absence. Lieutenant Konishi responded by immediately cutting the camp's rations.

• Konishi did jail the commandant's chicken for ten days. According to *Delivery at Los Baños,* page 109, the chicken sat outside the commandant's quarters

> in its tiny cage built especially for the occasion. . . . It had eaten its own eggs . . . in dire need of calcium, like all of the internees at Los Baños, and had instinctively tried to eat the nearest source, which was its own shells.

• Konishi—out of little more than spite—instructed exhausted internees to carry heavy sacks of grain back and forth under the guise of allowing them first to keep the grain, before changing his mind.

CHAPTER TWENTY

• On January 17, the guards at the main gate shot thirty-eighty-year-old Pat Hell, a mining engineer from the Arkansas Ozarks. Hell, recalled as an intrepid and affable man, had ignored the Japanese order for internees to stay in the camp. Returning at four thirty in the afternoon after a foraging trip to the villages, Hell was shot four times in the chest. He dropped a bag of coconuts and bananas, with a dead chicken clutched in his right hand. He died on the road, in plain view of the internees. The camp commandant, Iwanaka, issued an official statement that Hell had been caught escaping.

CHAPTER TWENTY-ONE

• The massacre of American POWs on Palawan was one of several factors for General MacArthur's decision to prioritize rescue operations. In his autobiography, *Reminiscences,* the general relates:

I was deeply concerned about the thousands of prisoners who had been interned at the various camps on Luzon since the early days of the war. Shortly after the Japanese had taken over the islands, they had gathered Americans, British and other Allied Nationals, including women and children, in concentration centers without regard to whether they were actual combatants or simply civilians. I had been receiving reports from my various underground sources long before the actual landing on Luzon, but the latest information was most alarming. With every step that our soldiers took toward Santo Tomás University, Bilibid, Cabanatuan, and Los Baños, where these prisoners were held, the Japanese soldiers guarding them had become more and more sadistic. I knew that many of these half-starved and ill-treated people would die unless we rescued them promptly. (Cited in *Captured: The Japanese Internment of American Civilians in the Philippines,* Frances B. Cogan, 1941–45, University of Georgia Press, 2000, page 262.)

CHAPTER TWENTY-TWO

•   At eight o'clock on the morning of January 28, George Louis (on whom the character Donnelly is based) returned to the camp from the villages. He staggered a bit, as if he'd been drinking. Arthur, in *Deliverance at Los Baños,* page 145, calls Louis a "hard-luck guy," describing him as a former Pan Am mechanic who'd spent much of his time in Los Baños trying to scrounge enough penicillin for his "good dose of clap." Upon his return to the camp, Louis walked into the sights of a sentry, who shot him in the arm. He collapsed against the fence. Despite pleas from the internee committee and Dr. Nance, Louis was rolled onto a door, carried into the jungle on the orders of Commandant Iwanaka, and shot through the head.

Again, the committee protested vigorously. The commandant responded with the standard line that all internees caught attempting to escape would be executed.

The diarist George Mora observed, "Well, murder was done today and the Japanese will do it again if they can find the slightest excuse."

- The deep pit dug by the Japanese in the southwest portion of the camp carried no explanation. In light of the news of massacres creeping closer to the camp and the worsening war situation for the Japanese, the internees and guerrillas alike were reasonable in their fears that this trench was being prepared to conceal evidence of a coming slaughter.

CHAPTER TWENTY-THREE

- Bolick is a composite of two actual soldiers: Staff Sergeant John Fulton, age twenty-four, 511th Signal Company, 11th Airborne Division, sent into the field to relay messages back and forth to the Filipino guerrillas; and Major Jay Vanderpool, the representative of General MacArthur to the guerrillas of southern Luzon. Vanderpool established the General Guerrilla Command (GGC) to coordinate the activities of the several guerrilla bands.

- Sergeant Fulton's initial journey to join the guerrillas was in the smelly hold of a *banca,* clutching a pair of grenades in case of a Japanese patrol boat or perfidy by the guerrillas.

- Gusto is based on the Filipino guerrilla leader Lieutenant Colonel Gustavo "Tabo" Ingles. In the winter of 1941, when the war began, Ingles was a first-year student at the Philippine Military Academy, class of 1945. He, with several fellow cadets of the academy, formed the core of the Hunters ROTC (to "hunt" the Japanese). Major Vanderpool used Ingles as a go-between for the GGC and the guerrilla bands in the area of Los Baños.

- On February 12, at Vanderpool's instruction, Tabo Ingles arranged a meeting of all five guerrilla groups in the town hall of Santa Cruz, in guerrilla-held territory. The gathering discussed the feasibility of conducting an all-guerrilla assault on the camp to free the internees. The guerrilla chiefs argued their various points and interests, including access to American-supplied weapons. Though a fractious meeting, in the end it was determined they would support one another, so long as Tabo Ingles made good on a promise to requisition enough guns and ammo for all of them.

    One guerrilla leader, Colonel Romeo "Price" Espino (the basis for the character Romeo), raised a stern objection. Price, who before the war had been a biology student at Los Baños, questioned who would protect the villagers around the internment camp after such a rescue. The other guerrilla chiefs in the room viewed this as an attack on their loyalty and courage, until cooler heads prevailed. According to Flanagan, page 84, "only after Ingles assured him (Price) that raids on Japanese concentrations after the mission would be integrated in the recommended plan did the 'Colonel' agree to participate in the mission."

CHAPTER TWENTY-FIVE

- Inexplicably, the February 3 rescue of the Santo Tomas internees was not announced on the Voice of Freedom until the end of the month. The internees of Los Baños did not know that their compatriots in Manila were safe. This news would have greatly cheered—and worried—the endangered people at Los Baños.

CHAPTER TWENTY-SIX

- The night of February 12th, the internee Freddie Zervoulakos (one of the inspirations for Talbot Tuck) slipped under the barbed wire. He made his way a mile and a half to the home of Helen Espino, wife of Colonel "Price" Espino, for a meeting with Tabo Ingles of the Hunters ROTC. Freddie, half Filipino, half Greek, was answering the call to attend the meeting from his brother, a captain in the Hunters who'd gotten word to him inside the camp.

  At Helen Espino's home, Freddie received from Tabo Ingles a copy of a letter from the guerrilla coordinator Major Vanderpool, and a few packets of American cigarettes to certify that the Army was, in fact, nearby. Tabo also instructed Freddie to select a "reputable" member of the internee community and bring him back to the Espino home in two nights.

- George Gray (Lucas in the novel) was the youngest member of the internee committee. The night of February 14, Gray followed Freddie Zervoulakos under the wire and through the ravine, to the Faculty Hill home of Helen Espino and a rendezvous with the guerrilla leader Tabo Ingles. The meeting lasted almost until dawn. During their long talk, Tabo suggested the guerrillas could arm the internees in order for them to assist in their own liberation. Gray refused the offer absolutely. In departing, Tabo handed Gray several gleaming American dimes that he'd been given by American soldiers as proof that they were near. He requested Gray to return for another meeting four nights later, on the eighteenth. Gray did not agree that he would come back, saying only that he would take up the issue with the internee committee.

CHAPTER TWENTY-EIGHT

- On February 15, the internee committee instructed George Gray to have no more contact with the guerrillas. Gray did not agree, and secretly recruited Freddie Zervoulakos, Ben Edwards, and Pete Miles to keep the rendezvous requested by Tabo Ingles for the night of the eighteenth.

  Pete Miles (an inspiration for Remy Tuck) was a rough-and-tumble Texan. Arthur, in *Deliverance at Los Baños*, page 116, describes Miles:

  > Nobody knew as much about animals as Pete Miles. Though an engineer by training, he'd been sent to the Philippines before the war by the St. Louis zoo to collect animals. He remained there after his assignment was over to work as a bouncer in a Manila nightclub, though with his clean cut F. Scott Fitzgerald profile and easy manners he relied more on charm than on muscle to send boisterous customers on their way.

  Before his capture, Miles had also blown up an important bridge for the American army to stem the advance of the Japanese on Manila. He was wounded in a skirmish with the Japanese, and hid out around Manila for months until betrayed by *makipilis*.

  Ben Edwards (along with Freddie Zervoulakos, the basis for Talbot Tuck) was known in the camp as a husky fellow with a blazing fastball in the early days of the camp when the guards and internees played softball. Edwards was one of the leaders of barracks 11.

- After dark on the eighteenth, at eleven o'clock, Pete Miles faked an illness. He was assisted to the infirmary, despite the strict curfew, by Edwards and Zervoulakos. They snuck under the wire behind the infirmary and made their way to the gully. There they were met by PQOG guerrillas, then led south to the camp of Colonel Price at Barrio Tranca. They encountered Sergeant John Fulton (Bolick in the novel). The following day, the three split up: Miles was sent with guerrilla escorts to 11th Airborne headquarters in Parañaque; Edwards and Zervoulakos were taken to Nanhaya on the east shore of the bay, to await word that Pete Miles had reached the U.S. Army safely.

CHAPTER THIRTY-ONE

- At eleven a.m. on February 19, Pete Miles arrived at the 11th Airborne's headquarters in Parañaque. He brought with him a map hand-drawn by Ben Edwards and a wealth of knowledge about the layout of the camp, the routines of the Japanese—including the pivotal piece of information regarding the guards' morning exercise ritual—and the physical condition of the internees.

- Miles was debriefed in Parañaque by Lieutenant Colonel Henry "Butch" Muller, age twenty-six, G-2 (Intel) officer for the 11th Division. (Muller is one of the models for Major Willcox.)

  When the debriefing was done, Pete Miles insisted he be allowed to return to the camp. Colonel Muller forbade it, but did promise Miles he would be in on the coming raid.

- Lieutenant George Skau (the basis for Kraft), 11th Airborne recon platoon leader, was a rugged fighter and outdoorsman. He headed a unit of some of the toughest and most resourceful paratroopers in the division. Skau personally made several reconnoiters behind enemy lines in preparation for the assault on Los Baños.

- The actual radio message read as follows:

    21 February 1945
    To: Sgt. J. Fulton—please
    transmit this communication
    upon receipt

    URGENT

    ESPINO TO VANDERPOOL. HAVE RECEIVED
    RELIABLE INFORMATION THAT JAPS HAVE
    LOS BAÑOS SCHEDULED FOR MASSACRE PD
    SUGGEST THAT ENEMY POSITIONS IN LOS
    BAÑOS PROPER AS EXPLAINED MILLER *(sic—
    meaning Col. Muller)* BE BOMBED AS SOON AS
    POSSIBLE PD

    W.C. PRICE
    Col. GSC (Guer)
    Chief of Staff

CHAPTER THIRTY-TWO

- In the early hours of February 19, Lieutenant Skau of the 11th Airborne recon platoon, along with the engineer Lieutenant Haggerty, crawled through the ravine and brush surrounding the camp, guided by the internees Freddie Zervoulakos and Ben Edwards.

    One of their discoveries was a newly dug trench outside the wire, in the open field beside the animal husbandry building.

CHAPTER THIRTY-SIX

- The night before the assault, Colonel Price's wife, Helen Espino, arrived in her husband's guerrilla camp. She'd spent her day warning the residents of the villages around the camp to leave and head for the hills, where they would be safe. Few believed her warnings of danger.

- On the eve of the raid, Skau met one last time with his recon platoon and the guerrilla chiefs to go over the plan of attack. He had at his disposal thirty-one recon platoon troopers and approximately 190 guerrillas. He divided his squad and the guerrilla force into teams, each with a distinct assignment for the opening moments of the assault on the camp.

    Skau also had the two internees, Ben Edwards and Freddie Zervoulakos, to assign. He attached Ben to the team of six recon men and twenty guerrillas to hit the guard posts on the northwestern portion of the fence. Freddie was teamed with the radioman Sergeant Fulton and seven guerrillas to block any Japanese who might flee south out of the camp. One team drew the assignment of breaking through the fence in the opening moments of the raid, then racing the exercising guards to their gun lockers. Skau, armed with a bazooka, picked for his own squad the toughest assignment: knocking out the pillboxes at the main entrance to the camp.

CHAPTER THIRTY-SEVEN

- After landing by *banca,* Ben Edwards and his recon team and guerrillas made their way through two miles of flooded rice paddies. They dodged Japanese patrols until dawn. Nearing the camp, with H-hour approaching, the leader of Ben's team, Sergeant Squires, made a startling discovery: four of his six recon troopers and all but four of his guerrillas had disappeared behind him in the dark paddies.

    Squires gave Ben his Colt .45 sidearm and shoulder harness, and sent him ahead to the camp with the lone recon soldier and remaining guerrillas. This reduced squad made it into the ravine and to their assigned position on time. They were one of only two recon and guerrilla teams in position when the first parachute popped and the raid began at exactly 7:00 a.m. The rest of the recon troopers and guerrillas sprinted to join the action, only seconds behind.

CHAPTER FORTY-TWO

- The 1st Battalion of the 511th Parachute Infantry Regiment was commanded by Major Henry Burgess, age twenty-six (a source for the character of Major Willcox). While not the ranking officer on the rescue, he was in absolute command of the assault on the camp.

  Burgess, on the day of the raid, had been in command of 1st Battalion for only twenty days. Prior to that, he'd served as assistant G-3 (operations and plans) for the 11th Airborne under General Joseph Swing. Burgess led the way for his three hundred paratroopers, riding in the first amtrac to burst into Los Baños.

- On the approach to the camp, the amtracs passed a hut near the road. A Japanese officer bolted out, trousers loose, gripping a samurai sword. A machine-gun volley from the lead amtrac cut the running soldier down.

- Ben Edwards was given a smoke bomb and instructed to place it in a barracks full of elderly men and women slow to pack up and leave. While setting the canister, a woman shouted for Ben to shoot a fellow internee. The man she indicated was Harry Sniffen (the character Lazlo), making his way with his wife, Genevieve, to the waiting amtracs. They carried two stuffed suitcases and their obese cat. Sniffen was a hated man in the camp, a hoarder and a black marketeer. Just as bad, Sniffen, his wife, and their cat were all overweight while others died of malnutrition.

CHAPTER FORTY-SEVEN

- Almost an hour into the raid, Major Burgess had heard nothing from Soule's task force, either by radio contact or reports from the 188th's artillery. The original plan called for the Soule force to fight its way into Los Baños from the west, arriving with sufficient trucks to transport the sick and lame. The remainder of the internees would be escorted out on foot, while guerrillas and the task force protected the escape route against Japanese counterattack.

  With no information regarding the location or condition of the 188th, Burgess made the command decision to alter the plan.

  He informed Lieutenant Colonel Joseph Gibbs (Colonel Thibeaux in the novel), the commander of the amtrac fleet and his superior officer, that they would not wait for the arrival of the task force. Gibbs was instructed to load the infirm, children, and women onto his amtracs and evacuate them to Mamatid. When they were delivered to Mamatid, Gibbs was to turn around and come back for the rest of the internees and the remaining troops.

- At 7:45, Lieutenant John Ringler—the officer in charge of the parachute jump—and Lieutenant Skau reported to Major Burgess that the camp was secure. Ringler made the observation that the guards' barracks was aflame from tracer fire during the fight for the main gate. The internees in that area, he noted, were staying ahead of the flames and moving toward the amtracs inside the camp.

  Burgess, searching for a way to get the internees to move faster—every passing minute raised the threat of the Japanese Tiger Division getting the raiders' scent and turning in their direction—ordered Skau and Ringler to torch the barracks at the south end of the camp, and let the wind do the rest.

CHAPTER FORTY-EIGHT

• Pete Miles, the man who'd reached 11th Airborne's headquarters and returned with the paratroopers across Laguna de Bay, left Los Baños on a stretcher. He'd finally
succumbed to exhaustion.

CHAPTER FIFTY

• On San Antonio beach, while awaiting the return of Colonel Gibbs and the amtracs, Major Burgess made contact
with a Piper Cub L-4 spotter plane cruising along the
shore. Aboard the plane was General Joseph Swing, CO
of the 11th Airborne Division.

After giving the general an update of the conditions
on the ground, Swing asked Burgess if he could put the
internees on the amtracs when they returned, then stay
behind, take and hold the village of Los Baños, and link
up with the missing 188th.

Burgess did a quick assessment of the situation. Without answering the general, Burgess told his radioman to
stow the set. General Swing would have to assume they
had lost contact.

Flanagan, *Angels at Dawn,* page 209, provides an excellent analysis:

> In "losing" radio contact with the commanding
> general, Burgess violated one of the fundamen-
> tal laws of the military: a subordinate does not
> knowingly or deliberately cut off contact with his
> superior officer in any situation. It is particularly
> hazardous to one's future in a combat situation.
> But Burgess got away with it for two reasons: 1) he
> was right; 2) in this particular case, the command-
> ing general was a very understanding man.

CHAPTER FIFTY-THREE

- The raid on the empty homes of Faculty Hill, followed by the burning and bayoneting of one hundred Philippine civilians in and around the village church, occurred in the early hours of February 25.

    The leader of this raid was Lieutenant Sadaaki Konishi, of the guard garrison at Los Baños.

    Konishi survived the paratroopers' raid, along with roughly a hundred others. He hid in the jungle surrounding the camp, emerging after midnight. He found his way to the slopes of Mount Makiling, where he located the camp commandant, Major Iwanaka. The commandant ordered Konishi and his ten-man remnant to join a larger Japanese force, also on Makiling, the Saito Battalion.

    According to Flanagan, *Angels at Dawn*, page 226, this battalion, under Captain Ginsaku Saito, received orders "to kill all guerrillas, men, women and children in Los Baños," and "to prepare to kill a hundred thousand men, or seventy men for each of us. Also, each man must destroy one tank before he dies."

    Konishi obeyed these orders to the best of his ability.

CHAPTER FIFTY-FIVE

- The slaughter of the village of Anos took the lives of several hundred Philippine citizens. The massacre was one of a series of raids conducted by the Saito Battalion as reprisals for the rescue of the internees. Lieutenant Konishi was known to have taken part in many of these attacks.
- Hank Burgess and his 1st Battalion of the 511th were the first American soldiers to view the slaughter of the Philippine civilians in the villages around the camp. Burgess estimated that fifteen hundred civilians were burned, shot, or bayoneted to death by the Japanese retaliation

raids. The discovery was made while the 1st Battalion was moving east through Los Baños, on March 3, eight days after the rescue.

CHAPTER SIXTY-TWO

• In July of 1945, Lieutenant Sadaaki Konishi was spotted by a former internee, Henry Carpenter, at the partially restored Wack Wack Golf Course outside Manila. Carpenter, formerly a Colgate-Palmolive executive in Manila, picked Konishi out of a gang of Japanese POWs laboring at the course.

Konishi was tried from November 23, 1945, through January 15, 1946, by the War Crimes Commission. On June 17, 1947, he was hung for atrocities committed against Los Baños internees and Filipino citizens.

That same day, before his execution, a Maryknoll nun, Sister Theresa, baptized Konishi.

Appreciation

No work of this magnitude can be accomplished without many competent and generous people on board throughout.

Liza Greenberg of Miami Beach was indispensable with her knowledge of Japanese. Liza was diligent and always understanding of my need to know now. My old friend Dr. Jim Redington, as he has been throughout every novel I've written, proved indispensable for the design and description of every medical state, wound, and malady. He is the smartest man I know when it comes to living and dying. Sam Hageman of Seoul and Philadelphia accompanied me in Hong Kong on part of my research journey. Old reliable Tom Donnelly, of Coffs Harbour, Australia, lent me his personal history for Remy's past, his own name for the novel's brave bootlegger, and showed me the Coal Sack in the southern sky, for which I pine even now. Jon Wattis of Wattis Fine Art, in Hong Kong, gave me an invaluable map of prewar Manila. Howard Hart was rescued at Los Baños as a child and took the time to describe it to me and show me his extraordinary military collection; Lieutenant Colonel (ret.) Roger Miller, one of the paratroopers who dropped in to rescue Mr. Hart and 2,100 others, also took the time to share his remembrances with me. The staff of the Library of Virginia, again, obtained for me several hard-to-find books for my research. The esteemed author and Dutch uncle Tom Robbins was a great adviser on Japanese culture, as well as a constant friend and sounding board for all things spiritual, though he is frequently mistaken. Anthony Gilmore of Nameless Films and Alex Ferrari of the Enigma Factory generously sent me a copy of *Behind Forgotten Eyes,* their searing movie about the comfort women. Beth Sutherland, my research assistant and former student, proved anew she is uncommonly and marvelously clever. Clay McCloud Chapman and Dr. Susann Cokal, both creative geniuses, serve as dear friends, sounding boards, and muses.

Special thanks must be reserved for the two readers who helped shape this manuscript during its writing. Lindy Bumgarner, along with being among my firmest critics, is one of the smartest people I know, and knows me perhaps best. Lea Cantwell, along with impressive brain power, brought her unwavering romantic lens to the book, always reminding me that love had damn well better conquer all. Reading aloud to both these women gave me invaluable feedback, peace of mind, comradeship in the lonely world of the story, and an outlet for my occasionally manic need for feedback.

Without my old mentor and friend Tom Kennedy, I would not have known about Los Baños. Wow, do I owe you, Tom. Wait . . . you owe me. So we're even.

Throughout much of the construction of this book, I was a creative writing teacher at my alma mater, the College of William and Mary. My students there kept my editing and writing skills polished and sharpened. The kids were some of my best writing teachers ever. Thanks to Kathy O'Brien for keeping me straight, Dean Carl Strikwerda for keeping me around, Lynn Allison of the Corner Pocket for keeping me fed, writer and friend Tom DeHaven for keeping me company, and the entire W&M campus for all those wonderful Tuesdays. I'd like more, by the way.

Finally, I thank my agent, Tracy Fisher of the William